Famine

Book 2 of the Justice Cycle

J W Kiefer

JWKiefer.com

Front cover image by Joshua Recene.
Special effects makeup provided by Gibbore SFX
Cover Model: Maddy LaFave

Edited by Kimberly Huther
wordsmith-editing.com

For information contact :
Website-www.jwkiefer.com
Email-Authorjwkiefer@gmail.com

First Edition: August 2025.
10, 9, 8, 7, 6, 5, 4, 3, 2, 1

Other Works

The Justice Cycle
Death
Famine

Storming Area 51 Volume 2
Bayonet Books
Dark Matter

For Emma and Connor.
Love you always.
Daddin

The branches slapped at her pale skin, leaving red welts and deep, painful scratches. She ignored the pain and continued to blindly run through the thick foliage. She squinted her dark green eyes, trying to see in the dying light as the sun slowly slipped below the horizon, plunging the world around her into darkness.

No! It was too soon. Please, God. I am not far enough away yet.

Her eyes darted back and forth, searching the growing blackness. Every tree looked like a pursuer and every shadow a threat. The musty smell of moss and damp leaves filled her nostrils with every ragged breath she took. She stumbled blindly onward, ignoring her fatigue.

Crack. Her breath caught in her chest. Was that a branch breaking? Had they found her already? She strained to hear, but the constant thumping of her heart in her ears made it impossible.

She ignored the burning in her muscles and ran, renewed terror driving her forward. She had to escape. Had

Famine

to reach freedom. They wouldn't be far behind. She had pretended to be unconscious, and when she was sure they were asleep she had made her escape. At least, she thought they were asleep. They never came when the sun was out. She shivered, remembering those horrible nights. She had learned quickly to fear the sunset.

Her dirty t-shirt snagged on a jutting tree limb, twisting her painfully and nearly causing her to lose her footing. She grimaced at the tearing sound it made and the smoldering agony that erupted in her left bicep. Tears filled her eyes, causing them to burn from the sudden wetness, and she blinked rapidly, trying to clear her vision. She ignored the pain and blindly stumbled onward, waving her hands back and forth in front of her body, attempting to feel for obstacles.

Pain erupted in one of her bare feet as she snagged it on a raised tree root, and she lost her balance. She fell forward, landing hard on her knees, scraping them and widening the rip in her shirt, exposing one of her breasts.

They had kept her barley clothed and shoeless, allowing her only a long t-shirt and underwear. It wasn't sexual but rather done to keep the captives disoriented and feeling exposed and powerless. A vulnerable captive was less likely to attempt an escape.

Well, they had sorely underestimated her. She may be barely clothed and fatigued, but she would be damned if she were going to simply lie there and wait to die.

She was too exhausted and injured to care about her exposed chest, so she rolled over into a sitting position. Her back heaved as she gulped in the clean night air, sending her into a fit of coughing. She curled up into a fetal position as pain shot through her torso. Each desperate breath felt like knives being rammed into her chest. Her lungs felt like they were made of iron and each breath seemed to barely be taking in any oxygen. She felt like she was drowning.

Calm down, Sophie. You are hyperventilating and you need to slow your breathing down before you pass out.

Her heart still raced, and her lungs still felt like cement, but with each deliberate breath she took she could feel herself calming and her breathing slowly returning to normal. She sat back on her hands and continued to deliberately exhale until she felt sufficiently recovered enough to scan her surroundings.

All she saw were trees and shadows, so she closed her eyes and listened. The sounds of the forest came alive. Crickets chirped loudly and something moved just to her left, disturbing the dead leaves and branches, causing her to jump. She focused on the noise for a few seconds until she was sure it was nothing. An owl hooted in the distance, and she could hear the soft gurgling of a stream.

Her eyes popped open. *What was that sound*? She closed her eyes again and listened. Faintly, somewhere in the distance, she thought she heard a dog barking. Where there was a dog there had to be people, and where there were people, she could find help. Using all of the strength she had left, she slowly rose to her feet and started shuffling off in the direction of the faint barking.

As the sound of the animal grew louder, her heart began to beat faster. Waves of relief washed over her, and she began to sob softly as she hurried towards the noise. She was going to make it. She was going to find help. Thank God for upstate people who leave their dogs outside. Never again would she make fun of rednecks and good old country folk.

It was becoming harder for her to see as the faint traces of sunlight slowly lost their fight to the encroaching darkness. She squinted in the dying light and moved her hands from tree to tree, feeling her way as she inched forward. Up ahead she saw, like a lighthouse beaming faintly in a storm, a dim ray of white. It was a light. She quickened her pace, stumbling blindly through the trees towards her salvation.

Crack. Her head snapped up and her eyes went wide in terror. Something was there, just beyond her sight. *Crack*. *Crack*. *Rustle*. She bolted as fast as her emaciated body would allow in the direction of the light. Whatever had been watching her from the darkness gave up all pretense of stealth and charged after her, tearing through the foliage.

Her breath was ragged and coming out of her in wheezing gasps as she stumbled forward, heedless of any obstacles in her way. The dog became increasingly agitated as she drew closer, and its barking was intermingled with yelps—as if it were trying to break free of a restraint. Just a little farther.

Suddenly leaves and small branches began to rain down upon her, causing her to have to slow her pace. She heard the cracking and rustling of foliage and saw the branches bow and sway as something big tore through the trees above her.

She thought her heart was going to beat right out of her chest as the adrenalin and fear kicked in, full force. She watched in horror as the branches broke and bowed until whatever it was reached the clearing where the light and dog were. The dog let out a feral growl before yelping in pain and going silent.

She gathered her courage and gritted her teeth in frustration. "No!"

A growl of rage and impotent frustration burst out of her, scaring her with its intensity, and she ran as fast as she could in the direction of the light.

"No! No! No!"

As she drew close enough to finally see the large white farmhouse, her survival instincts to fight kicked in. She expected to see whatever had killed the dog appear at the edge of the clearing, but it didn't. Then something far worse happened.

Her teeth began to chatter uncontrollably, and her breath condensed in the air in front of her like tiny clouds as a wave of intense cold washed over her. Her muscles twitched and contracted in response to the cold, and she stumbled and fell to the ground, unable to move.

She lay there in the fetal position, shaking violently as her body attempted to ward off the invading cold. Her jaw muscles tightened and she bared her teeth, gritting them to stop the shivering. As she lay shaking, a pale, delicate, woman's foot appeared near her face. It was bare, and so white it was almost translucent. The nails were perfectly manicured and polished a light ice blue.

She knew those feet. Using what little strength she had left, she turned her head so she could see the thing that stood looking down at her. The eyes that looked back at her were almond-shaped and the color of the sky on a cloudless day. As beautiful as they were, they held an edge of cruelty to them like the eyes of a predator.

The woman shook her head and her long, straight, black hair fell into her face, slightly covering her delicate, angular features. She brushed it away and clicked her tongue against the roof of her mouth disapprovingly.

"Dear Sophia. You have been an awfully bad girl."

Sophia met the woman's gaze with defiance. She wanted to say something witty, but she was too tired and still shivering too much to speak.

The woman closed her lovely eyes, and her face was serene as she breathed in deeply through her nose and then exhaled. Her hair seemed to constantly sway in some unseen wind as it fell gracefully down to her waist. Her white dress, which was so low-cut that it barely covered her breasts, also swayed in the unseen breeze, making her look more like a wraith than a solid being. Her skin was so pale that it seemed to glow, making the effect more pronounced.

"I so love the smell of defiance. It makes everything taste so much more...delicious."

The pungent smell of decay and death drifted in on the wind, causing the woman to scrunch up her nose. She pulled her lips into a sneer, revealing a mouth full of sharp, elongated canine-like teeth. Sophia had to fight her gag reflex as the stench almost made her vomit.

"Is the animal dead?"

A dark silhouette stepped out of the darkness and into the light. The creature was humanoid in appearance but with limbs that were too long for its frame and clothing that was torn and filthy. Its dirty, stringy hair grew out of the bulbous scalp like patches of dry grass, and its mottled grey skin clung to its frame, making it look like the starving children they show in commercials. Its beady, black eyes looked down at Sophia, showing an unabashed malice.

"Yes, my lady."

It moved closer to them, and the smell of decay was intermingled with the distinctly sickly-sweet metallic scent of blood. It did not take its eyes off the prone girl as it spoke. It smiled, showing a mouth full of razor-sharp teeth that still had flecks of gore hanging from them. It lifted its hand, pointing one elongated clawed finger at Sophia.

"Can I eat her, Mistress?" it croaked in a dry, grating voice. "I am so hungry. Always so hungry."

The woman's face twisted into a mask of savage rage, and she turned on the creature. Before Sophia could register what was happening, the woman had the thing by the throat and was lifting it off the ground with one arm.

The woman was beautiful and terrible, and exuded the power and grace of an apex predator. The creature struggled in her grip, its feet flailing as it tried to free itself. The woman bared her teeth and hissed.

"Now, Nayati, do I need to repeat the lesson we went over the other night?"

Nayati stopped struggling and went limp. "No, Mistress," he replied softly. "No lesson is needed."

She dropped him unceremoniously and he sat on the ground, coughing and gasping for air. She dismissed him and turned to Sophia, who was still shivering uncontrollably.

Famine

"Now, where were we? Ah, yes. We were discussing your disobedience. What shall we do about that, my dear? I should just let Nayati have you and be done with you. Use you as an example for the others, but there is something in your smell that appeals to me. Any thoughts? What would you do if you were in my place?"

Before Sophia could reply, a man's shocked cry startled them. It came from the farmhouse. Apparently, the owner of the dog had discovered its mutilated corpse. Sophia's heart jumped with hope, and she mustered her strength and shouted.

All she managed was one word before a kick from the woman knocked the breath out of her lungs. She gasped and choked as tears filled her eyes.

"Be silent!" she snarled. "Or I will tear you apart myself."

Muffled angry voices and more commotion could be heard as others came out to see what the man had been shouting about. Sophia whimpered and tried to drag herself in the direction of the people.

"Help me," she wheezed softly through gritted teeth. "Please."

Another wave of intense cold struck her, and she curled up into a ball, shaking and groaning.

"I said be quiet."

The woman turned in the direction of the people, her face intense. She then looked down at Sophia and grinned, her eyes wild with malice.

"Nayati, dear. Are you still hungry?" She never took her eyes off the prostrate girl as she spoke.

Sophia's eyes went wide in horror. "No. S...s...stop. I will ga...go with you, just stop. Please."

Sophia heard the wendigo tearing through the trees before she even had time to finish her sentence. The white lady continued to look at Sophia, her face stern like that of a disapproving parent as the screaming started.

"This is what happens when you do not obey, little one. Innocent people die. And make no mistake, this tragedy is your fault. If you had simply done what you were told, these people would still be alive."

Sophia curled up into a ball and wept. It was her fault after all. She had tried to save herself and, in the process, had gotten an entire family brutally murdered.

The shouts turned to pleas of mercy, and then she heard a child's scream that turned into croaks of pain. She covered her ears, trying to block out the shrieks. It didn't work. She could still hear them. They would be burned in her mind forever.

Famine

ana awoke with a start, and immediately grimaced. She tried to move and was instantly wracked with pain. She squinted and lifted her hands to shield her eyes from the light that was streaming in from the small window across the room. Blinking in an attempt to drive away the grittiness in her eyes, she tried to sit up again. More pain shot through her, and she groaned and fell back onto the bed she was lying in.

She grimaced and shut her eyes, waiting for the pain to subside. When it did, she opened her eyes again and looked around. She was in a hospital room. If she had to guess, it was most likely Lourdes.

How had she gotten here? The last thing she could remember was...Jared. But that was impossible since he was dead. Wasn't he? Had she imagined him?

She had shot Steve—at least, the thing that had looked like Steve—and then she had passed out. Before she had lost consciousness, however, she could have sworn she had seen Jared looking down at her.

Her mouth felt like it was stuffed with cotton, and she tried to drum up some saliva to alleviate it but found she had none. A Styrofoam cup sat on the small table next to her bed and she reached for it and felt the tug from an IV line. Her hand was shaking so much that she knocked the cup off the table instead. Her energy spent, she fell back onto her bed, gasping.

"Finally awake, huh?"

She turned her head at the voice and saw a large African American man wearing a Boston Red Sox cap sitting in a chair in the corner of the room. She snorted when she saw him and scowled.

Her eyes bore into the man as he stood up and stretched. He ignored her gaze and grunted, rubbing his neck and rotating one of his arms. She noticed his corded muscles through the white cotton fabric of his wrinkled dress shirt that was half tucked into his black trousers.

Thomas Johansson, the FBI agent who had showed up unannounced; heralding murder and death. The FBI agent who knew more than he had led on. The FBI agent who had lied to her and manipulated her. The FBI agent who was inadvertently responsible for Jared's death. At least, she suspected that his tight lips had kept vital information from her that could have prevented his death. Either way, in her mind, he was partially responsible.

He sighed and then met her gaze. "I suppose you want answers."

"A little late for that, don't you think?"

Famine

He looked away and closed his eyes. "I can see why you would think that."

She gritted her teeth and clenched her fists. "Don't patronize me."

He turned towards her and his eyes showed genuine shock. "I would never do that. I told you all I knew at the time."

"Really? I find that hard to believe," she spat.

He shook his head and set his jaw. "Dana."

"Detective Campbell," she scolded. "Only my friends are allowed to call me Dana, and you are not my friend."

He glowered back at her and stiffened. "You're being unreasonable."

Unreasonable? Unreasonable! Really? Jared was dead, and she was fairly sure she was being more reasonable than he deserved.

She continued to scowl at him and crossed her arms. The motion released another wave of agony that made her stomach lurch and her head swoon.

Johansson took a step toward her and reached out to help her. She swatted his hand away, setting off a violent fit of coughing. More pain. She grimaced and shut her eyes again.

"Oh, God. This really hurts," she said through gritted teeth. "I think I just tore something vital."

He withdrew his hand and rubbed it, grumbling something under his breath. "Seriously, Dana? That was uncalled for."

She shot him a withering look and rolled her eyes.

He stepped back from her and flopped back down in the empty chair. His mammoth frame made the chair look like a toy. It creaked in protest as he adjusted his weight, trying to get comfortable.

As she watched him, she noticed that he had a few days' worth of stubble on his wide jaw. His eyes were bloodshot and ringed by dark circles; the clothes he wore were wrinkled, like he had been wearing them for days.

She sighed and her face softened a bit. "How long have you been here?"

He glanced up at her, "A while."

"How long is a while?"

"Since we brought you in," he replied wearily.

Had he been here with her the whole time? Why? The revelation caused her anger to recede a bit. Maybe she was overreacting. After all, he couldn't have known that Steve was the killer they were looking for. Could he?

He may have been hiding things from her, but she was sure Steve's true identity was not one of them.

She licked her dry lips and ran her hands across the sheet that covered her. She breathed in deeply and exhaled slowly, the anger she had been feeling slipping away.

"How long have I been out?" she asked.

"A few days," he replied. "Maybe more."

She blinked a few times and her mouth dropped open. "A few days?"

"Give or take."

A few days? Had they found Steve's body? Was the man he had been fighting still alive?

19

Famine

She was speechless. There were so many questions running through her mind, but all she could manage was stunned silence.

He continued to watch her, waiting patiently for her to speak again.

A nurse entered the room, walking between the two of them. She smiled at Dana with friendly eyes the color of emeralds. "How are we feeling today?"

Dana grimaced but smiled back, masking the pain she felt. "Like someone took a chainsaw to my insides."

The nurse laughed a hearty laugh that caused her cherub-like features to jiggle. The woman was older, with short grey hair and a round face. She moved to the side of the bed and checked the IV, her baby-blue scrubs rustling as she moved.

"Well, dear, that is to be expected. You're due for some more pain medication, so your morphine pump should kick in soon. Hopefully, that will help with the pain. If the discomfort gets too unbearable, I can ask the doctor if you can have something else to help take the edge off."

"Thank you."

"You're very welcome, dear," she replied cheerily, patting Dana's leg in a grandmotherly fashion. "My name is Helen; just let me know if you need anything else. I'll let the doctor know you are awake."

After checking a few more things and agreeing to get Dana another drink, Helen left the room. She returned a few minutes later with a Styrofoam cup of cold water and, after asking Dana one more time if she needed anything, retreated, leaving the two of them once again alone.

Dana greedily gulped down the cool water. It tasted so good. She hadn't realized just how parched she was. She drained the entire cup before gingerly setting it on the small table.

Johansson continued to watch her, his face a mask of concern. He said nothing, waiting for her to talk first.

She met his eyes and just observed him for a few minutes before speaking. "I assume you found Steve's body. Was he still alive?"

Johansson furrowed his brow. "Who?"

Dana blinked. "Steve Cadrette. Jared's younger brother. You know, the Eastside Stalker."

Johansson looked thoroughly confused. "Dana, the only people at the scene were you, Lee, and an injured woman."

"That can't be," she insisted. "I saw him standing over some guy. I emptied an entire clip into him before I collapsed."

Johansson's face grew dark. "Are you sure you hit him? What did the other person look like?"

"Of course I'm sure I hit him. I watched his body fall into the river. After that, I passed out."

She omitted the part about seeing Jared. Even if it hadn't been an hallucination, she was sure he wouldn't have believed her anyway.

Johansson sat up straighter and glared at her. "How do you know he was the Stalker? Did you find some new evidence we missed?"

She shook her head.

Famine

"Then how do you know that this man, Steve, is the Stalker?"

"I just know."

Johansson said nothing for a few minutes.

"He killed Jared. I'm sure of it," she said, breaking the silence.

"Okay, I'll let your department know that you shot a perp suspected of being the Eastside Stalker. If you truly killed him, then his body couldn't have gone far."

She considered her next words carefully before speaking again. "I'm hesitant to say this, since I know it will sound crazy, but Steve used some kind of strange shadow weapon to stab me. I don't really know what I saw, but it seemed like he lifted his hand toward me and then I was impaled by something."

This seemed to pique Johansson's interest and he narrowed his eyes, leaning forward in his chair.

"Dana, this is important. In the fight, did either man have a sword?"

"A what?"

"A sword. Did either man have a damn sword?"

She was taken aback by his sudden intensity.

"No. Well, I'm not sure," she replied awkwardly. "It was dark."

He closed his eyes, sighed deeply, and rubbed his forehead with his left hand.

She remembered him asking her a similar question the day she had arrived to find Steve and the phantom stranger fighting in the city streets. Why was he so fixated on swords?

She had just revealed the name of the Stalker, that he had killed Jared, and he had just brushed it off like it was unimportant. Moreover, she had just told him she had shot him and his body was missing, and that barely seemed to register as well.

"Tom, what is going on? What is it you're not telling me?"

He glanced up at her, still holding his forehead. He seemed to be contemplating what he should say next.

"Tom."

He sighed again. "I don't know how much I can tell you. Or rather, I'm not sure you would even understand if I did."

Dana gritted her teeth in frustration. Jared was dead, she had nearly been killed, and there were strange explosions all over her city and he was still being coy.

"You had better start talking right now, or so help me God, I am going to get up out of this bed and throttle you even if it kills me."

He chuckled and shook his head. "You really are something, aren't you, Detective."

She huffed. "You have no idea."

He smirked. "I have some."

"Then you know that I will not let this go until I have the truth."

His face grew solemn, and she was sure she saw a hint of fear in his eyes. She was certain it wasn't fear of her, but rather fear of what he was unwilling to say. He fidgeted, causing his chair to creak loudly in protest.

After a few moments he seemed to come to a decision, and he looked her in the eyes as he spoke. "I'm sorry. Sorry

23

your partner died and sorry that I have no answers for you. I wish I could tell you more, but for your own safety, I can't."

Her face grew dark. "Can't or won't?"

"Does it matter?" he replied. "I'm trying to protect you, Dana. You may not understand that now, but someday you'll thank me for keeping you out of this."

"Out of what?" she asked angrily. "I have no idea what *this* is."

"Trust me, it's better that way."

"Trust you. Ha," she spat back, looking away from him. "All you've done since you got here is lie to me."

He sighed and stood, genuine regret showing on his features. "I am sorry, Dana; but for your own good, let this go."

With that said, he turned and walked out of the room, leaving Dana to stew in her anger.

He was crazy if he thought she was going to let this go. No. She would turn over every rock in the entire Southern Tier if she had to. Jared had died, and now she was certain there was more to his death than just dumb luck and bad timing. And she would get to the truth no matter how long it took her.

Jared watched the hospital from the tree line on Kneeland Ave. It was late in the day and the sun was still in the sky, but he avoided it. Its light and warmth felt somehow wrong to him now, as if he no longer belonged to the day.

He had been standing watch over the hospital since they had brought Dana in. Tzedakah had assured him that she was okay, but he could not bring himself to leave until he knew for certain.

What would he do when she finally woke up? He wanted to rush in and hug her. To kiss her and tell her everything was going to be fine. Of course, she would probably scream and pull her duty weapon on him and shoot him in the head like some zombie horror movie. The truth was, he had no idea what he was going to do. All he did know was that he couldn't let her go.

Famine

He sighed and rubbed his forehead with his free hand. He was unsure why he still did that; his head didn't hurt. Perhaps it was simply an echo of his old life. A life that he could feel slipping farther and farther away each day. Even though everything else seemed to be growing fainter, his feelings for her were still constant and strong. Would they fade in time as well?

He reached up and adjusted the cheap dollar store sunglasses he had found in some random backyard and slunk farther back into the shadows of the tree line avoiding oncoming traffic. They weren't very stylish, but they hid the one thing that made him stand out from normal humans: his nightmare-black eyes.

"I can make something more stylish for you if you would like."

The voice was not audible, but in his head, and came from the sentient sword that he held strapped to his hip underneath his long black trench coat.

Tzedakah, the spirit of Justice. The being who had chosen him to be his next wielder. The sword was both his benefactor and his jailor. The being whose will held him bound to the mortal world.

The sword emitted a soft blue glow from underneath his jacket; he pulled it tighter around himself, stifling the light.

Jared ignored him. He didn't hate the blade, but he wasn't happy with it either. It was what it was, and it did what it did. He couldn't blame it any more than he could blame himself for breathing or eating. Well, at least if he still needed to do those things anyway. He didn't, of course, but the comparison was still valid.

"God, I miss pizza."

"I do not understand," replied the sword.

Jared grunted. "You know, pizza. Dough with sauce and cheese and cooked in a big oven. What I wouldn't give for a slice of Grande's pepperoni."

The sword was silent while Jared continued to watch the building.

"You do not require food for life. I do not understand why you still desire it."

Jared groaned. "Never mind, it's a human thing. You wouldn't understand."

Jared found his gaze drifting from the building to the surrounding area. People came and went. going about their daily lives.

A delivery man was unloading a truck, and nurses, maintenance men, and other workers moved in and out of the building from every entrance. No matter where he looked, however, all he saw was pain and death.

The deliveryman was an alcoholic but not abusive. He did, however, spend most of his money at the bar, so his family struggled. He could see his life unfold before his eyes. His past, his present. Every sin he had ever committed. All the pain he had inflicted.

His gaze moved to a woman who had been raped in college. He felt the fear, rage, and violation of it as if it had happened to him. She felt perpetually dirty, as if no amount of washing could make her clean again. It screamed in his mind, causing him to growl under his breath.

Famine

She flinched as the deliveryman passed her, her feelings of insecurity and wariness apparent in her body language. No matter how much time had passed, she could never bring herself to trust another man.

She left a line of broken hearts and relationships in her wake, dooming her to loneliness. She moved away from him quickly, avoiding his gaze.

He watched them all and saw everything. All the brokenness and pain. Everything that was hidden was laid bare to his eyes, and he detested it.

His eyes fell on two people in green scrubs: a young man with stylish dark hair and a pretty young woman with bright red hair and freckles. They were sitting on the grass underneath a tree, sharing lunch and enjoying each other's company.

His heart ached when he saw them. They laughed and smiled the way only new lovers did, and he reached up and grabbed his shirt where his heart was and squeezed.

He would never feel that again. Never look into her eyes and see her smile. Never feel her touch on his skin or taste her lips. He was doomed as surely as the women who had been raped was. At least she had a chance to heal; he could never regain what he had lost. No, what was stolen from him.

He looked away as soon as the hidden sin started to be revealed. He didn't want to taint their moment. He could feel his eyes wanting to go back. He closed them, fighting the urge. Fighting Tzedakah.

"No," he growled.

The urge subsided. At least the sword was trying to understand him now instead of simply overriding his will. He hated it when it did that.

He blew out slowly, allowing the anger and feelings of impotence to flow out with his breath. It did not do to dwell on the things he could not change. After all, he had an eternity to master feeling sorry for himself.

"Jared!" the sword shouted into his mind. "Something is wrong."

As soon as he snapped out of his melancholy he could feel it, too. An electricity in the air around him. A presence. It felt like Tzedakah but warped and twisted somehow. His stomach turned in revulsion, and he could feel the sword vibrating angrily underneath his coat.

Suddenly, powerful arms wrapped around his chest and he was wrenched backward. His feet dug deep gouges into the ground as he was dragged farther into the trees. He struggled against the unknown assailant, but he was strong and he could not break his grip.

With a growl, Jared snapped his head backward and was rewarded with a loud crack as the back of his head slammed into the center of the attacker's face. The grip loosened.

He spun around, drawing Tzedakah as he did, and used his momentum to slash horizontally at the attacker. All he hit was air.

How had the attacker been able to evade his strike? It wasn't possible for any normal human to move so fast.

Famine

Tzedakah glowed a bright, angry blue-black and the waves of hatred that were flowing from the sword pulsed up his arm, causing it to shake slightly.

Before he had time to contemplate what was happening further, he was caught once again from behind. This time, however, the attacker pulled him close so that his mouth was directly next to his right ear.

"*Bonjour, mon ami.* It is a pleasure to finally make your acquaintance."

There was a flash of blinding violet-black light, and then they were gone.

Jared felt like he was being torn apart. The world appeared twisted somehow, like he was being pulled in two different directions at once. The man who had grabbed him was still clutching him and they both seemed to be extending unnaturally.

He looked down and saw his feet and legs. They were farther away than they should have been. Was he being stretched somehow? This was new. His torso seemed longer as well, and he could feel the tension of it on his internal organs, which were screaming in protest.

Flashes of brilliant blue and violet energy sparkled around them, snaking and twisting over their bodies. Each time the energy came in contact with its counterpart it erupted violently, sending them spinning out of control.

Just when he thought his body was going to be torn apart, he felt the man let go of him. There was another blinding flash of light, then he was falling.

Famine

The wind whipped against his face and his coat beat wildly as the air rushed by. Tzedakah continued to vibrate ferociously, and he held on to the blade like a life preserver.

He looked to his left and saw the other man spinning uncontrollably. He was gripping a large, brimmed hat with one hand and holding a sword in his other. His black uniform slapped loudly as it was whipped against his body. Was he laughing?

The man's face came into view, and he winked. His long goatee fluttered violently above a wide, toothy grin. Was he insane? He certainly looked insane. Then Jared noticed his eyes. They were black, just like his.

He turned his eyes back to the earth and flinched. It was only a few yards away now. He put his hands up defensively, closed his eyes, and braced himself for the inevitable impact. Tzedakah suddenly blazed brightly, and he came to a jarring halt.

When he finally opened his eyes, the earth was about two feet away from his face. He could smell the soil and grass. It was earthy and alive with a faint musty wetness, as if it had recently rained.

A slight wash of blue light was reflecting in the green of the grass. He lifted his hands and saw that there was an aura of dark blue energy surrounding his entire body. He still gripped Tzedakah, which was emanating the same blue glow.

Without warning, the light suddenly winked out and he unceremoniously dropped the rest of the way to the ground.

Grunting, he turned himself over. The sun was slowly fading below the horizon, and he could just make out the faint twinkling of stars which were trying to peek through what remained of the closing day. He was lying in a field somewhere outside the city.

Something in his periphery caught his attention and he turned his head to get a better look. The man who had snatched him quietly floated into view. Violet-black energy surrounded him as he slowly descended. His strange musketeer uniform settled around him as he gently landed, the grinning skull on his chest seeming to glare directly at Jared.

The man chuckled and brushed his hat off before setting it on his head with a flourish. He surveyed the surroundings and tapped a finger to his lips. When he was finished, he turned and looked down at Jared, who was still lying on the ground.

"Well, that was humiliating." His voice was heavily accented and tinted with a bit of sarcasm. "I see you still need time to work on your... How do you say, débarquements? Ah yes, landings."

Jared grunted and sat up. He eyed the man warily. Tzedakah's vibrating was so intense now that he feared the sword would shake right out of his hand. Whoever this man was, the sword really didn't like him.

"Take your time, *mon ami*. I am in no hurry."

Jared gingerly got to his feet and turned to face the man. "Who are you?"

The man cocked his head slightly and furrowed his brow. He was quiet for a few seconds and when he finally spoke, his voice was distant. "No one."

"No one?" Jared asked, confused.

Famine

The sound of his voice seemed to rouse the Musketeer, and the grin returned to his face. He exhaled and his posture changed back to one of confidence and motion. He radiated an almost predatory air, as if he knew that he could strike Jared down whenever he chose.

"A better question might be: what am I?"

"Destroy him!" Tzedakah screamed into his thoughts. "Destroy him now!"

Why? he thought.

Before he could react, his arm snapped up and outward in an arcing slash at the Musketeer's midsection. With elegant grace the man deflected the blow harmlessly to the side.

Before it had time to strike again, Jared grabbed the sentient sword with both hands and held it fast. He gritted his teeth and his muscles strained against the blade as it continued to try and lash out at the man.

"Why do you fight me?" Tzedakah shouted so loudly it caused his head to hurt. "The abomination will kill you if you do not fight."

"Just wait a minute!" he shouted back audibly.

The Musketeer actually laughed. "Well, now, this is interesting."

Jared shot the Musketeer a dangerous look, continuing to strain against the sword, trying to hold it at bay. "He wants me to kill you. Do you know why?"

The Musketeer raised an eyebrow in response. "Very interesting indeed."

"What is?" Jared asked through gritted teeth.

"The fact that you are fighting him instead of simply listening to him. And that he has not yet forced you to do his bidding. Curious."

"You didn't answer my question."

"Ah, that. Well, of course I know why."

He suddenly jumped into motion. He was fast. So fast that Jared was sure if he were still normal, he would not be able to track his movements.

He released his two-handed grip on Tzedakah just in time to deflect a jab to his midsection. The Musketeer, however, followed up the jab with a punch to his face that struck him hard across the jaw. His head snapped forcefully to the side from the impact and his body soon followed. Before he knew it, he was tumbling through the air.

Tzedakah screamed another warning in his mind. Before he had time to react, however, he saw the Musketeer appear above him. Had he teleported?

Jared managed to put his hands up in front of his face just in time to absorb another wicked punch with both his forearms. The blow sent him careening towards the ground like a meteor. He struck the earth so hard that he almost dropped Tzedakah. Almost.

The Musketeer alighted gently on the ground next to the large crater Jared had left. Debris fell back to earth around him, and a slight cloud of dust hung in the air over the basin. He leaned down and peered into the depression.

Jared exploded out of the hole. The Musketeer reacted immediately by leaning backward, away from Jared's rising fist. The uppercut, however, skimmed his chin, stunning him slightly. Jared used that split second of hesitation to whirl in the air and lash out at the Musketeer with a spinning kick.

He felt bones break as his foot connected with the Musketeer's chest. A shockwave exploded outward from the point of impact and the Musketeer was launched backward.

He tumbled through the air, slamming into the soil a few times before planting his sword into the ground. It dug deeply and he used the friction to halt his backward momentum. When he finally came to a stop, he had left a twenty-yard scar in the earth.

He removed his sword from the ground and stood up, brushing small particles of stray debris from his shoulder. The two men stood staring at each other from across the expanse, their swords glowing brightly.

Jared had allowed Tzedakah partially into his consciousness, and that had saved him. He could feel the power of the sword coursing through his body. He knew he was not fighting at his full potential, but he at least could hold his own.

Why hadn't Tzedakah simply taken over his will? He certainly had before when they had faced imminent danger. He glanced at the man turning his dark gaze upon him, and blanched.

"What the heck?"

What he saw was the man himself but engulfed by a massive shadow creature. The faces of the creature were constantly changing. It rotated from face to face in rapid succession as if he didn't know which one to choose. There were women's faces and men's, and at one point even a child's. Black, white, Asian, Arabic, and Indigenous—every race of humankind was represented.

It stopped for a second on the face of what looked like an Arabic man with a thick black beard and a brand on his right cheek. His eyes were afire with hatred and murderous rage. It glared at Jared for a few seconds before being lost in the ever-continuing rotation.

The vision ended and all that remained was the Musketeer. He was cocking his head slightly in contemplation, that mischievous grin plastered across his face.

"What the hell are you?" Jared asked quietly.

"I am you."

"That makes no sense."

"It is true nonetheless."

"Do not listen to him," Tzedakah warned.

Jared frowned. He could feel waves of malice emanating from the Musketeer. Or was it coming from the sword? He couldn't tell where one ended and the other began. It was almost as if they were two separate entities, but one being.

He lifted Tzedakah and examined it. Two beings who were one. His eyes went wide, and he snapped his head up to stare at the Musketeer. Two beings who were one!

The Musketeer's grin widened. "Now you begin to understand, *mon ami*."

Before Jared could track his movements, the man was upon him again. He jabbed at Jared's midsection ten times in quick succession. The movements were so fast that he didn't register the strikes until a few seconds after they had landed.

His torso shook violently, and he doubled over. My God, he was fast. Faster than before. Had he simply been toying with him till now? He felt another blow land solidly under his chin and the force of it lifted him off of his feet.

Tzedakah screamed in his mind and he reached out for the sword, attempting to give it further control. Too slow. The Musketeer jumped and twirled in the air, mimicking the same kick he had landed earlier. Unlike his, however, the Musketeer's struck him squarely across the side of the face instead of the chest.

He spun to the side and flipped a few times before hitting the ground hard. He was stunned and confused, but he could feel Tzedakah. Their connection was growing stronger with each passing moment. If he could just hold out for a few more minutes he might be able to regroup and merge his consciousness with the sword.

A crushing weight landed on his sword arm just below his wrist, pinning his hand to the ground. He looked over and saw a black leather boot firmly planted there.

He tried to reach up with his free hand and punch out at the Musketeer, who was standing over him. He swatted the blow away like it was nothing and stomped down hard on his stomach with his other foot.

The foot rose and fell a few more times, pummeling Jared's midsection before he finally stopped struggling. As soon as he did, the blows stopped coming.

The Musketeer leaned down without taking his foot off his arm. That frustrating grin was still plastered on his face.

JW Kiefer

"Are you finished?"

Jared glared up at him, defiant, but lay still.

"Despite how much fun this is, I really do not have any desire to kill you just yet. You are still too...weak."

"He lies," Tzedakah said. "He cannot kill you yet."

Jared stayed silent, ignoring the sword. Two things were nagging at him. One, why hadn't Tzedakah simply overridden his will; and two, why couldn't the man kill him? Both questions were implications that there were rules at play he didn't yet understand, and that worried him.

He was sure Tzedakah wasn't lying about the man not being able to kill him. The sword had not lied to him yet. Bent the truth a little, sure, but not outright lied. He wasn't even sure it could.

The Musketeer sighed deeply and removed his foot from Jared's arm. He stepped backward a few paces to give Jared space to rise.

"As much fun as this was, I did not come here to destroy you but rather to simply introduce myself."

Jared sat up slightly, bracing himself with his arms. He looked up at the Musketeer and squinted his eyes warily. What madness had he landed himself in?

The Musketeer simply shook his head at Jared's silence, that damn smile never leaving his face. He chuckled and then turned to walk away. When he had gone a few paces he turned his head slightly, so he was looking at Jared in his periphery.

"Make no mistake, Detective, I am going to destroy you, just as I did the Shogun. Not today and not tomorrow, but someday."

Famine

Who was the Shogun?

"No one you need be concerned with," the sword spoke into his mind.

More mysteries and questions.

The strange man turned away again and started to melt into the shadows that were now everywhere, thanks to the onset of dusk. Jared watched him and he tensed when he saw him stop and turn to face him one final time.

"Since this little encounter gave me some pleasure, I will leave you with a small reward." He paused for a moment before speaking again. "Your brother is not dead."

The last word was spoken just as the Musketeer phased out of existence, more like a whisper falling over Jared like a slight wisp of wind. To Jared, however, it hit with the force of a thunder bolt.

Steven was alive? The revelation left him with conflicting emotions. On one hand, he was happy his brother was not dead; but on the other, he was terrified of what he could and would do.

He started to sit up when a thought burst into his mind like a Mack truck, causing him to jump up. If Steven was still alive, then anyone who knew what he was would be in danger.

"Oh God, Dana."

ana awoke to darkness. Why was her room so dark? She sat up and looked around. Everything seemed the same. Her IV was beeping away steadily, the chair was still in the corner, and her table was still cluttered with used Styrofoam cups and tissues.

The familiar smell of disinfectant permeated everything. Well except for her; she really needed a shower. She lifted her arm, sniffed her shirt, and immediately pulled away, wrinkling her nose and coughing.

Oh yeah, she was ripe all right.

All in all, everything appeared to be normal, yet something felt wrong. She couldn't put her finger on what it was, but something was definitely off. The air felt heavy and oppressive. So much so that the lights in her room seemed to be muted and dimmed.

She sat up, squinting her eyes, trying to bring everything into better focus. A strange haze seemed to hang in the air all around her. She waved her hand back and forth, attempting to brush it away. Nothing.

Maybe she just wasn't completely awake yet. She rubbed her eyes. *Oh God, that felt good*. When she was finished, it took a few minutes for her eyes to adjust back to the normal light spectrum. Nope, still there.

"What the heck?"

It had to be the pain medication making her groggy. That was the only logical explanation. She reached out and pushed the button for the nurse. No reply. The nurse usually responded pretty quickly, day or night. That was strange.

She swung her feet around and gingerly stepped out of bed. Her legs wobbled and she reached out for the IV. It clattered noisily as she all but fell into it, trying to keep her balance. The racket echoed in the oppressive silence, making it seem louder than it had been.

She froze. Her heart was suddenly beating out of her chest, and she was overcome by the sudden urge to bolt. She quickly scanned the room, her eyes frantically darting back and forth. The silence did not like being disturbed.

She shook her head, trying to clear the fog. "What the hell is going on?"

The sound of her own voice caused her to jump. It seemed to echo back at her as if the noise could not pierce the strange mist. A sudden wave of terror washed over her with such force that she fell to her knees. Something in the darkness had heard her, and it was coming for her.

Waves of fear washed over her, and the impulse to run was so unbearable she nearly did.

As quickly as the fear had come, it was gone. Replaced by a voice and an overwhelming sense of surrender.

"It is too late. You are already dead. It is too late. Eternity awaits," a voice suddenly whispered in her mind. *"Lie down and sleep, for eternity awaits."*

Her eyes suddenly felt heavy, and she sagged. She was so tired. The voice continued its mantra. *So tired.* With each word, her eyelids slowly began to close.

Yes, the voice was right. She was already dead. Flashes of pain from a strange shadow weapon to her stomach ran through her mind. She saw herself lying in the cool grass. Yes, she had died that day. All that was left for her was to close her eyes and go to eternity.

A flash of light so bright it hurt suddenly burst into the room. The intensity of it knocked her over and she threw one of her arms up to shield her eyes. Someone was screaming.

As quickly as the light had come, it was gone. She lay on her back, breathing heavily, her eyes closed and her arm still held over her eyes. All was quiet again. Even the strange voice she had heard in her head was gone.

After a few seconds, she dared a peek. The room was dark again. The oppression, however, was gone just like the voice. No mist either. A constant steady whine from her IV machine and her own breathing were the only noises in the room. Everything seemed to be back to normal.

She stirred and felt a slight sting in her arm. When she looked to the area of the pain, she noticed that her IV had been pulled out.

Famine

When she tried to get to her feet, she was beset by a sudden fit of coughing that sent her back to her knees.

Was her throat raw? Had the voice she heard screaming been hers?

"Good, you're awake," a male voice intoned from somewhere over by the door. "About time. I broke the enchantment, like, five minutes ago. Don't think I can take them by myself."

Dana snapped her head in the direction of the voice and her mouth instantly dropped open. Standing by her door with his back to her, peering around the door jamb into the hallway, was a man. A man dressed in a white hospital gown that barely covered bright red boxers, and a body covered in so much hair he could have been mistaken for a sasquatch.

The man turned his head, revealing clever dark brown eyes and a handsome face that looked like it hadn't been shaved in days. He gave her a look that screamed, "What are you waiting for??" and jerked his head to one side, beckoning her towards him.

Dana just stared at him.

The man rolled his eyes. "God," he groaned. "Are you going to come over here or not? We don't have all night. If we don't act soon, people are going to die."

"Who the heck are you?"

The man put a finger to his lips and shushed her angrily. "Be quiet, for God's sake," he whispered harshly. "Do you want them to hear us?"

The scene was so absurd she was sure now she was dreaming. It was the only thing that made sense. She had to be dreaming. Of course, most people didn't know they were in a dream when they were dreaming, and she was definitely aware. Or at least she thought she was.

"This is so very confusing."

"Not really," the man replied. "It's pretty straightforward. We gots a vampire infestation."

"A what?" she asked incredulously.

He shushed her again, this time more forcefully. "Keep your voice down."

Okay, if he shushed her one more time she was going to jam her IV pole into his backside.

"There are no such things as vampires," she replied calmly.

The man rolled his eyes again and looked up at the ceiling. "Really? This is what you give me to work with? Seriously, you should have just let them have her. Yeah, yeah, I know. Every life is important. You got a plan and all that. Yada, yada."

Dana blinked and stared. Yup, this guy is crazy. He must have escaped from the psych ward. She should probably restrain him or something and then go get help.

She got to her feet, her own gown barley covering her toned legs, and drew it tight around herself, suddenly becoming very aware she was not wearing a bra. She walked towards the man, tying her robe closed as best she could.

The man continued to mumble to himself as she reached him and stood next to him. She was about to put her hand on his shoulder but stopped. The strange mist that had been in her room was in the hallway.

She gasped.

Famine

The man turned and clamped a hand over her mouth. It startled her and she glared up at him angrily. He met her gaze.

"Will you be quiet already?"

She mumbled indignantly and then sighed before reaching up and pulling his hand away from her mouth.

"Okay, okay," she whispered. "I will be quiet. But, dream or not, if you put your hands on me one more time I am going to break something vital. Got it?"

He shot her a withering look before nodding and turning back to the hallway. She inched as close to him as she could without being inappropriate and followed his gaze.

Through the haze she could see the nurse's station. It appeared to be empty. There were papers scattered everywhere and a clipboard lying on the floor directly in front of the desk. A red light was blinking on the phone, waiting to be answered. It was too quiet, and the place seemed to be completely void of life.

"Where is everyone?" she whispered. "There should be at least one nurse around."

He pointed at the floor next to the nurse's station. "See the hand sticking out? The nurses, along with everyone else on this floor, are most likely unconscious."

Dana squinted in the dim light and then saw it, too. Sure enough, there was a hand peeking out from around the nurse's station. It wasn't far from where the clipboard lay, explaining why papers were scattered all over the floor and desk. She had most likely fallen asleep and dropped them.

"I can't see the vamps, though, but I'm sure they're down there. Put up a sleeping spell on this entire floor. Not their usual MO, brings too much attention. I'm guessing they're looking for someone."

"Who?"

"Not sure. If I had to guess, I would say you. Just my luck that I'm here when vamps decide to attack. Stupid angel. I'm going to kick him in the nuts next time I see him. Fine, it's not his fault, but I can't kick you in the nuts, now, can I?"

Dana closed her eyes and rubbed the bridge of her nose. She was starting to get a headache.

She took a deep breath and then interrupted his mumbling. "Why do you think it's me they're after?"

He shrugged. "Because you were the one God told me to break out of the spell. I figure He has a plan and all that."

Dana was stunned. *God told him? What does that mean? Is that who he thinks he's talking to?* This whole thing was getting more absurd by the minute.

She was about to ask him to clarify, when a movement at the end of the hall past the nurse's station caught her attention. She squinted, trying to make out exactly what it was. The only light she had for illumination was a red flickering exit sign that gave the scene an eerie horror movie vibe.

There was a sudden displacement of the mist, as if some unseen force had walked through it. She gasped as the fog stirred and shifted, pulling back to reveal a tall man dressed all in black.

Famine

The swirling mist that covered the entire hallway masked the man's features, making it impossible for her to identify him. The man turned his head slowly, scanning his surroundings, and her breath caught in her throat when she saw his dark-red-glowing eyes.

As she silently watched, he unexpectedly crouched down and lifted his head slightly, closing his eyes and sniffing the air like a predator tracking its prey.

"Mistress, our target is on this floor," the man said softly, never rising from his crouch.

There was another slight movement just behind the crouching man and then the mist itself began to swirl and twist. It made no sound and continued spinning faster and faster until it formed into the outline of a woman.

The mist suddenly stopped its churning, but the outline of the woman remained fixed like some kind of shadowy apparition fashioned from the haze. Dana could make out the dull red glow of two eyes staring out from the specter. They seemed to bore into her from down the hallway, as if the creature knew she was watching.

Pain erupted in her mind and she gasped, doubling over and clutching at her suddenly throbbing head.

Waves of overwhelming agony washed over her, driving her to her knees as a women's voice echoed in her mind. "Hello, Dana. It is nice to see you again."

The last thing she saw before blacking out from the pain was the half-dressed crazy man's face hovering over her, mouthing words she was too disoriented to understand.

Jeremy hovered over the prostrate form of Dana. What had happened? One second, she was up right and coherent and then, poof, she was flat on her back.

He bent down and whispered as loudly as he could. "Are you all right? Did they do something to you?"

No response.

He snapped his fingers in her face a few times but got no reaction. Frustrated, he contemplated slapping her to try and jolt her awake but chose to lift her head up and pry open one of her eyes instead. Her pupils constricted instantly, showing her brain was still functioning, but that was all. She gave no other response to the stimuli.

"Crap."

A crash came from somewhere down the hall, followed by a low hiss. Jeremy whipped his head in the direction of the noise, accidentally dropping Dana in the process. Her head hit the floor with a loud thud.

He grimaced. "Double crap."

Jeremy held his breath, listening. Had they heard him drop her? If they had, then they would most likely move in the direction of the noise. He figured he only had a few seconds to prepare before the vamps located them.

He decided getting the unconscious woman out of harm's way was his first priority. He didn't know who she was or why the blood-sucking candy-stripers were after her, but he wasn't about to let them have her without a fight.

Grunting and cursing under his breath, he reached down. managing to get his arms up and under Dana's. He straightened his back, lifting her slightly. Ignoring the excruciating pain erupting pretty much everywhere in his body, he dragged her away from the doorway and farther into the small room.

"You couldn't just let me have one week without some kind of life-threatening situation, could you?" he managed to grunt between gasps for air.

For all his complaints, God knew him better then he knew himself. Knew that he would never look away or back down when someone, no matter how small or seemingly insignificant, needed his help. Sure, he would gripe the entire time, but deep down inside it was just who he was.

Jeremy knew what it was like to feel powerless and lost. To feel forgotten and thrown away. Unlike so many who had experienced what he had, he refused to allow his pain to make him bitter and angry. To drive him farther away from people.

One blessing that had come from all of the hardships he had encountered was the ability to truly see others. He didn't look away and pretend not to see like most people did. No, Jeremy was the kind of man who met the ugly of life head on and refused to blink.

Just as he managed to pull Dana behind the long plastic curtain that divided the hospital room, the air suddenly seemed to get heavier. He could feel a powerful and oppressive presence quickly approaching them.

He lowered Dana to the floor as quietly and gently as he could and crouched down next to her. It was impossible to see anything in the dim light, but he knew that the malicious presence he felt wasn't far away.

There was the slightest sound of someone's feet shuffling just on the other side of the curtain and Jeremy stifled a curse. One of the vampires was in the room with them. Darkness fell on the screen, eclipsing what little light was coming through it as the silhouette gradually materialized on the other side of it.

The vampires were in the room, and all that separated him from them was a thin layer of plastic. Maybe if he was quiet they would get bored and just leave. Nah, no such luck. That kind of good fortune never ever happened to him. If something could go wrong, it would. That was his life.

Ready or not, he knew he was going to have to fight. Even if they managed to kill him, he still wasn't going to let them take the woman. Who knew, maybe he'd get lucky and take a few of them out before they murdered him.

He caught some motion out of the corner of his eye and snapped his head in the direction of the movement. A clawed hand appeared on the curtain and slowly started to move it. The metal hooks that hung the fabric from the ceiling clacked softly together as the creature deliberately drew it to the side, exposing them.

All Jeremy could make out in the darkness was the shadowy silhouette of a tall man with long gangly arms and glowing red eyes. He squinted in the low light, trying to get a better look at what kind of vampire it was, and defensively moved in front of Dana, putting himself between her and it.

The creature didn't attack, but simply stood and studied them. Its shimmering eyes moved from Jeremy to Dana and then back to Jeremy.

After a few seconds of silence, it spoke in a surprisingly human voice. "If you walk away now, I will let you live. We do not wish to kill you; all we want is the woman."

"Oh, is that all? Just the woman. Let me get right on that."

The creature cocked its head to one side and squinted. Apparently, it had been hunching, because it slowly rose to its full height, which was at least three inches taller than it had been a moment ago. It let out a low growl.

Jeremy grimaced. Pale skin and glowing red eyes, check. Human-looking, check. Big sharp teeth and claws, check. Oh crap, it was a *strigoi*. Yep, he was definitely going to die.

Well, at least lose a limb or two, but either way it wasn't going to be pleasant. Dying with his butt showing was not the way he ever thought he would go. Well, it wasn't one of his top ten guesses anyway.

Maybe it would bite him and try to turn him. Was that even the way it worked? It certainly worked that way in the movies. Of course this wasn't the movies, and he really had no idea how the whole process functioned. Oh well, God would most likely not let that happen anyway. He hoped.

With a quick prayer to the Almighty Jeremy shifted his feet into a fighting stance, preparing for the inevitable skirmish and his demise. With a smile he lifted his hands up front of his face, closing them into fists and getting into a defensive stance.

He could feel divine energy rising up from within as a visible surge of pure holy power exploded forth, surrounding him with an aura of soft white light that caused the vampire to shy away from him warily.

Jeremy steadied himself. "We gonna do this, or are you just going to stand there and hope I keel over dead from staring at your ugly face?"

The creature grinned, its lips parting to reveal elongated, razor-sharp canines. It rolled its neck and rotated its arms, which made audible cracking sounds, and raised its clawed hands into a combative stance.

Jeremy grunted. "Go easy on me. I'm already a bit dinged up."

The statement was true. For all of his bravado, Jeremy was still injured from his fight a few days earlier with an evil immortal being known as the Musketeer. This entire time he had been gritting his teeth, ignoring the constant pain he felt in torso from his not quite mended fractured ribs.

Thanks to the frequent communication with God, Jeremy mended faster than most people. It was impossible to be in contact with the power of the Almighty as much as Jeremy was and not be healed. But the process wasn't instantaneous like a miracle, but more of a gradual progression of healing over time.

The creature studied him warily, the grin never leaving its face. With impossible speed it quickly lunged at him, claws attempting to rip into his flesh. Jeremy turned slightly, flinching away from the attack.

There was a flash of light and the creature let out a shriek of pain. It quickly jumped back, pulling its injured hand away from the burning light and clutching it against its chest protectively. Fine tendrils of smoke gently drifted upward from the creature's injured hand and there was the distinct acrid smell of burning flesh.

Jeremy smirked. "Not so smug now, are ya?"

The creature bared its teeth and hissed.

Jeremy's victory was short lived, however, as two more vampires stalked into the room. They moved forward and flanked their wounded companion, their shining red eyes burning with anger.

Jeremy threw his hands up in the air and dramatically rolled his eyes.

"Seriously?" he whined. "One wasn't enough? After this is over, You and I are going to have a serious discussion, whether I live through this or not."

Steeling himself, he readied himself to confront the two new threats, when a sudden wave of pain took his breath away. He swayed on his feet for a few seconds before reaching out and grabbing the side of the bed for support. He gritted his teeth and closed his eyes until the pain subsided.

Thankfully the vampires were still too cautious of him to take the opportunity to rush forward and disembowel him.

Thank God for small mercies.

"Well, that sucked," he grumbled. "Don't suppose you have an aspirin, do you?"

"Give us the girl," demanded the first vampire again, this time with a whole lot more venom.

"What happened to the 'and we will let you live' part?"

It bared its fangs and growled. "The time for that has passed."

Jeremy smirked.

"The time for that has passed," he parroted in a deep, mocking tone. "Seriously, did you just watch a Vincent Price movie or something?"

The creature hissed and lunged at him again. There was another flash of light and more burning flesh. This time, however, the creature's hand actually caught on fire.

It hopped around, screeching and flailing its burning appendage. Its brothers hissed furiously but stayed just out of arm's reach of the still-glowing Jeremy.

Guess they're smarter than their friend, the undead matchstick.

Jeremy put his finger up to his mouth and looked to the side like he was lost in deep thought. "How does the saying go again? Oh yeah, the definition of insanity is doing the same thing over and over again, expecting different results."

The vampire let out a long, low, inhuman growl and bared its fangs again. The fire that had engulfed his hand had dissipated, and Jeremy watched in dismay as the charred flesh slowly mended itself. Within a matter of seconds, the skin had returned to its normal pale, almost porcelain, appearance.

Jeremy groaned and sighed deeply. "Great, healing factor, and it's better than mine. This is going to take forever."

None of the vampires dared get to close to Jeremy for fear of being burned by the holy light. It bought him some time to think. He had to get the woman out of harm's way, but he had no idea how he was going to do that.

Maybe he could just keep goading them into attacking him. Sooner or later the light would do enough damage to destroy the creatures. Of course, that was only if it lasted long enough. He never knew with this sort of thing.

No, that wasn't going to work again. He could already see that the vampires were done making that mistake. He didn't know how they planned on getting past his defenses, but he could see their evil little brains working behind those beady, glowing eyes.

He had to do something and quick or they were both going to die. Well, at least undie if the legends were correct. Either way, he wasn't drinking anyone's blood in an erotic fashion like in the movies. No way, no how.

If any of these blood suckers even looked at him in a seductive way, he was going to shove his foot so far up their butt they would be crapping pieces of him for weeks.

The warning registered in his body before it hit his brain, and he was moving before he even knew what was happening. It was like that sometimes. Almost as if someone else was controlling his body for him.

He dove to the side just in time to avoid one of the hospital chairs. It crashed against the wall and then ricocheted to the right. Two more came hurling towards him and he felt the wind on his face as one of them missed him by mere centimeters.

He wasn't quick enough to avoid the other, however, and it clipped him on the side of the head. Stars exploded behind his eyes, and he stumbled. He shook his head, attempting to get his eyes to work again. As soon as his vision cleared, however, he was met by the sight of something big flying towards him.

Was that a hospital bed?

"Oh, crap."

The bed hit him square in the side of the chest, directly in his still-tender ribs, and he felt them splinter. He heard himself scream as the world around him erupted in agony.

His stomach lurched as he was launched through the air. He smashed into the far wall, leaving a deep dent in it before sliding unceremoniously to the floor.

His only thought was of the unconscious women. He had to get to her. If he didn't, she was going to die. Or worse.

Nausea and vertigo washed over him as he tried to move, causing him to lurch to the side. His legs buckled and he fell, facing the unconscious women. He tasted blood and bile, and the fluid filled his mouth, causing him to gag and cough violently.

The pain from his hacking nearly made him black out, but he managed to stay conscious. It was no good. The damage to his body was too severe and he was unable to move. All he could do now, as the vampires closed in on the helpless women, was watch.

Tzedakah teleported them directly into Dana's room. There was a blinding flash of light and then the room slowly materialized in front of him. It was kind of like how an old tube TV turned on. The image slowly came into focus until the complete picture was visible on the screen. With the sword, however, it was all done in three dimensions instead of two. It was very disorienting, but remarkable at the same time.

Jared watched as the hospital room manifested around him. At first everything was monotone and without form, and then splashes of color burst forth as the indistinct shapes formed into a hospital room. At least, what used to be a hospital room.

The space was in complete disarray. What lights were still functioning flickered, and there was broken furniture scattered everywhere. A fine mist of drywall dust hung in the air like fog, covering everything with tiny white particles.

Someone lay on the floor, unconscious, next to a turned over IV stand that squealed noisily. Two men dressed like bikers hovered over the prostrate form, while a third stood facing the other direction. *Was he holding a hospital bed like a baseball bat?*

There was a huge indentation in the wall that seemed to have been made by something large. When he saw Jeremy lying stunned on the floor, he knew what had made the dent in the wall.

What was he doing here, and where was Dana?

The vampires were so focused on their prey that they hadn't noticed him yet, so he took the time to inspect the scene. His dark gaze showed him everything, and when he looked at the three men who had attacked his friend, what he saw shocked him.

To his eyes they looked like emaciated corpses. Not decayed and rotting like a zombie, but thin and wan like a person who was dying of starvation.

Sunken eyes darted back and forth with a look of frantic desperation driven by an all-encompassing hunger. They looked like meth addicts so far gone on drugs that they would do anything for their next fix.

To mortal eyes, the creatures appeared as perfect human specimens. But to the dark gaze, they were revealed as pathetic starving creatures who were completely enslaved to a hunger that could never be satiated.

"Ow, that hurt," Jeremy groaned. "I can't believe you just hit me with an actual hospital bed. You should be proud, that's a first for me."

The vampire tossed the bed over his shoulder and it clattered noisily, coming to rest directly on top of the other bed in the room.

"Any last words, human?" it asked.

As it spoke, Jared finally noticed just who the woman was that lay on the floor, and he gritted his teeth and growled. Tzedakah flared to life in his hands, vibrating in concert with his rising anger.

Jeremy looked past the creature and met Jared's eyes. He grinned. "Ha. You're all so very screwed."

Jared moved so fast even the vampires' supernatural eyes couldn't follow his movements. He had cleared the distance and struck the nearest vampire three times before Jeremy had even finished speaking.

The vampire didn't even have time to scream before Jared cut him down.

It instantly incinerated, its body turning into a smoking pile of ash. The distinct smell of charred flesh permeated the room and tiny black particles of burnt skin fluttered gently in the air where the creature had been standing.

The second vampire's eyes went wide as the shining blue light of Tzedakah rushed at it through the floating ashes of its brother. He managed to bend backward just in time to avoid the strike. The blade cut through the creature's shirt but missed its body.

Famine

Jared followed up his initial thrust with a sweeping kick at the creature's legs. It anticipated the movement and fell backward, using the momentum of the fall to pull its feet up away from the strike.

It landed softly on its hands, and in one fluid movement flipped back upward to land on its feet in a fighting crouch.

Jared, however, had never stopped the momentum of his sweep, but continued to turn his body with his leg. He spun and whipped his foot around, smashing it into the center of the creature's chest.

The impact was so loud that it sent out a mini shock wave. The sound of the creature's bones shattering followed next like the steady rap-rap of a machine gun. It hit the far wall so hard that it actually flattened like a cartoon character.

Gore and viscera exploded out of every orifice, splattering the ceiling and the floor. It hung on the wall like some grotesque piece of modern art before igniting into flames and disintegrating like its brother.

Jared slowly turned his head to look at the third vampire. The darkness in his eyes writhed and twisted hungrily. His mouth was a thin line, and he didn't speak. The power of Tzedakah was physically palpable, and it poured out of him in intense waves of spiritual pressure that caused ripples in the air around him.

The creature met Jared's gaze and didn't flinch. Apparently, his display of absolute and overwhelming force hadn't impressed him. At least, if it did, he was doing a good job of hiding it.

The creature growled, and with blinding speed reached down and plucked Jeremy from the floor. Its strong arms wrapped around Jeremy's throat, causing him to audibly choke as it held the wounded man in front him like a human shield.

"Destroy it!" shouted Tzedakah into his mind. "Obliterate the abomination."

Powerful emotions rose up at Tzedakah's words, threatening to overcome Jared's independent rationale. He gritted his teeth and forced them and the will of the sentient sword back down.

"Destroy it!" Tzedakah's thoughts were more insistent this time, and they physically hurt, causing him to double over.

"No," he growled through gritted teeth. "It has Jeremy."

"The sacrifice is acceptable," it pushed back, even harder. "The abomination must not be allowed to continue."

The vampire eyed him warily, unsure of what was going on. It tightened its grip on Jeremy and he gasped in pain, his eyes slightly losing focus.

Anger flared up inside Jared at the sight of his friend's pain and he slowly rose to his feet. This thing, whatever it was, had his friend. It had also tried to hurt Dana. For that, he was going to make it pay.

"Okay," he said, "We do this together, but Jeremy is to remain unharmed. Is that understood?"

Before he was even done speaking, the consciousness of the sentient sword flooded into him, making him gasp.

Famine

Near unlimited power and a thousand lifetimes of knowledge surged through his body in an instant.

He had seen the creation of the very universe itself. He had seen mountains crumbled to dust by the ravages of time. Empires had risen and fallen, yet he remained. Nature itself changed, but he remained constant. He was Justice, and nothing could escape his judgment.

The change in Jared was instantaneous and could be felt physically. The air itself seemed to bow to him, and the floor creaked and cracked under the weight of his presence.

The vampire's eyes darted frantically back and forth as it searched for a way of escape. It backed up until it touched the wall.

"Stay back," it stuttered, "or I will kill the human."

Jared said nothing in reply. His body seemed to flicker slightly, going in and out of focus and he lifted Tzedakah and casually rested it on one shoulder.

"Did you hear what I said? I will kill..." The creature's words were cut off in midsentence as his arms suddenly slipped from his shoulders and fell to the ground.

The vampire stared at its severed limbs in horror and confusion. He stammered incoherently as Jeremy, now free from his grip, stumbled away from him and out of harm's way.

Jared flickered again and the creature blinked twice as it began to smoke. There was a look of complete confusion on its face as its head slipped from its body, igniting into flames as it fell.

He watched the creature burn for a few seconds before slowly turning his head and fixing his gaze on Jeremy. The light from the burning creature flickered across Jared's features, making him look like a demon from hell.

"Why does everything have to be cut so close?" Jeremy croaked, rubbing his injured throat. "You sure took your sweet time."

His words caught in his mouth when he saw Jared's face. He swallowed and slowly got to his feet.

"You okay?"

Jared said nothing.

"Jared?" he asked, his voice cracking a bit.

Jared didn't reply but removed the sword from his shoulder and slowly pointed it at Jeremy. The darkness in his eyes writhed and twisted, seeming to reach out toward Jeremy.

"Jeremy Wagner," Jared intoned in a voice that was no longer his own. "You have been judged and found guilty."

"Oh, crap," he stammered, shying away from the glowing blade. "This is not good."

Famine

Jeremy continued to back away from the gleaming sword until his back hit the wall. He sucked in his gut and attempted to flatten himself like a cartoon character. The eerie blue-black glow of Tzedakah illuminated his features, highlighting every crease.

There was nowhere for him to go. He had retreated as far as the little room would allow. His eyes darted past Jared. Maybe he could make a run for it. Make it past the glowing blade before it killed him.

Yeah, that would happen. He may have been fast in his youth, but time and battle had worn down his agility. Sure, he was still faster than most men his age, but even in his prime he was no match for the speed of the freaking avatar of Justice.

I mean, come on, he hadn't even seen Jared move when he had decapitated the vampire using him as a human shield. This whole situation was so unfair, and he was going to let God know exactly what he thought about it when he saw Him. Which, it seemed, was going to be sometime in the next few seconds.

Jared pressed the glowing blade to Jeremy's chest, the darkness in his eyes writhing and dancing, reaching out towards him. Oh God, this really was the end. Jeremy turned his head to look at the unconscious woman who lay only a few feet from him. At least he had been able to protect her. It wasn't much, but it was enough.

He sighed slightly and smiled faintly, turning his gaze back to face Jared.

"Make it quick. I think I've earned that at least."

Jared nodded slightly and then drew his hand back to strike. Jeremy closed his eyes and scrunched up his features, his head subconsciously moving to one side. He whimpered softly in anticipation.

Nothing happened.

A few more seconds passed and still nothing. No stabbing pains. No burning in his chest. No smell of blood or loss of consciousness. He risked opening one eye, his head still tilted to the side, away from the glowing sword.

Jared was still standing in front of him with the sword tip pressing against his chest. His hand, however, was trembling slightly. His brow was furrowed, and he was gritting his teeth so hard that they were making loud popping noises.

Jeremy opened up his other eye and relaxed slightly. The sword was still dangerously close to his chest, but for some reason Jared hadn't struck. Not yet anyway.

"Jared?"

Famine

No response.

Jeremy waved one hand back and forth in front of his face. The only response he got was a slight tightening of the jaw. If he kept this up, he was going to shatter his teeth completely.

"Jared? You in there, buddy?"

Jared's voice came out in a low growl. "I told you he wasn't to be harmed."

Jeremy exhaled, releasing the breath he had inadvertently been holding. His stomach extended slightly, causing Tzedakah's blade to dig a little into the flesh of his sternum. He felt no real pain thanks to the adrenaline coursing through his veins, but he could feel a small trickle of blood start to run down his chest.

"Dang it, man. Snap out of it," he huffed, sucking his gut in again.

Jared blinked once but his shoulders visibly relaxed, and he unclenched his jaw. The arm holding the glowing sword, however, didn't move.

"Listen, man, I know you're in there and that you can hear me." He tilted his head slightly in the direction of the woman lying on the floor.

"There is a woman hurt just over there and we need to get her some help. I'm not sure how bad she is, but if we can just put this whole *judgment* thing on hold for a few minutes, I'm sure she would appreciate it."

"And," he mumbled, "so would I."

Jared turned his head to look at the woman on the floor and the rest of his muscles visibly relaxed. He lowered his arm, gritting his teeth as he did. The arm wavered slightly at first, but it wasn't long before Jeremy could let out the breath he'd been holding.

Before the air had finished leaving Jeremy's lungs, Jared was at Dana's side. He knelt down and gingerly lifted her head, resting it on his folded knees.

He watched as Jared hesitantly reached out and brushed a stray hair away from the woman's face. She stirred slightly at his touch, and he froze in place.

"Hey, man, is something wrong?"

No response.

Jared tensed suddenly and clutched at his chest as if he was having a heart attack or something. He groaned audibly and fidgeted, gritting his teeth against whatever it was that was affecting him.

What in God's name was going on?

"Jared, are you okay?"

He reached out to his friend and laid his hand reassuringly on his shoulder. As soon as he touched him, he instantly felt that something was wrong. Physical waves of tension pulsed out from Jared, passing through Jeremy like surges of lightning.

He gasped and instantly let go, doubling over slightly and breathing heavily.

"What in the world just happened?" he sputtered.

Jared slowly opened his eyes and gazed down at the motionless woman in his arms. Jeremy watched curiously as he stared at her. Well, this was weird. Did he know her? What was it he was seeing when he looked at her?

As if reading his thoughts, Jared spoke. "I see...nothing."

Famine

"What do you mean by nothing?"

"I see nothing but her," he said softly, never taking his eyes off of the unconscious woman. "No past or future, simply the present. I see her in this moment and only this moment."

"Okay. So, is that a good thing or a bad thing?"

"I'm not sure," he replied, "Nothing seems to be disrupting my connection to Tzedakah. I can still feel him in my head. I have defied him before, and it felt...different."

"How so?"

"It's hard to put into words," he continued. "When my connection to Tzedakah is disrupted, it feels like he's shouting at me from far away. I can hear him speaking, but I can't understand what he's saying. It feels like I'm slowly sinking into water and getting farther and farther away from him."

"Kind of like drowning?"

"Exactly," he said, nodding his head. "Like I'm drowning, and my life is slowly fading away."

"And this time it feels different?"

"Yes, because, if anything, my feelings are stronger and more substantial. It's almost as if Tzedakah is feeling exactly what I'm feeling, but that can't be."

"Why?"

"Because..." Jared said, shaking his head in frustration. "As far as I have experienced, he doesn't feel anything at all except anger at injustice."

"And what are you both feeling now?"

"Love," he replied softly.

Jeremy blew out a long breath and ran a hand through his unkempt hair.

Who was this woman and who was she to Jared? God had definitely wanted him to come to her aid, and the vampires were certainly after her. Well, he may not know exactly who she was, but one thing was becoming very clear to him: this woman was important.

At least he had the answer to one question that had been nagging at him: Jared hadn't showed up at just the right time to rescue him but had come for this woman.

He crossed his arms and snorted, glancing disapprovingly up at God. "I guess I don't merit a superhero rescue, do I?" he mumbled.

Jared either hadn't heard him or didn't care and made no response. God ignored him as well.

He sighed and looked down at the woman. She was very beautiful, even haggard and bruised like she was.

"Who is she?" he asked.

It took a few seconds before Jared replied, "Dana."

"Okay. So, who is Dana? You obviously know her."

Jared gently brushed another stray hair away from her eyes. "My ex-partner and the love of my life."

Jeremy sputtered incoherently for a few seconds before finding his voice again. "She's what?"

Jared sighed and glanced up at him. "The love of our life."

"Okay. So she is, or rather was, your girlfriend. Wait a minute, did you just say ours?"

Jared furrowed his brow and looked up at Jeremy. "Did I?"

"Yeah, man, you just said *ours.*"

He looked away from Jeremy and stared off into the distance.

"No," he said, firmly shaking his head. "It's only me."

He paused again. "Or is it?"

Jeremy shrugged and waved a hand dismissively. "Whatever. Either way, she needs medical attention and fast. Plus, I'm pretty sure these guys were just basic henchmen."

"What do you mean?"

"I mean that these guys were lightweights compared to what I saw in the hallway before the attack."

He ran his hands through his hair again and shuddered. "That thing, whatever it is, is no *strigoi.*"

Jared's expression became vacant again and he stared off into nothing. Jeremy had seen this expression before, when Jared and the sentient sword had had conversations telepathically in the past.

The darkness in Jared's eyes suddenly snapped to life. It writhed and twisted angrily as if the darkness were trying to claw its way free of the sockets.

His head whipped around to stare at the open door. As he did, Jeremy followed his gaze and saw the silhouette of a woman standing there. The presence of the creature radiated waves of oppression that caused the lights in the room to visibly dim.

Jeremy grimaced as he squinted in the low light. "Speak of the devil."

Jared was fast, at the door in the blink of an eye. The creature, however, was just as fast and was already halfway down the hallway.

He stepped out into the corridor and examined the retreating creature. It looked like a dark cloud as it flowed gracefully away from him. When it reached the end of the hallway, it stopped and formed once again into the vague shape of a woman. It just stayed there, watching him. Waiting.

"Stay with Dana," he instructed as he turned his dark eyes on Jeremy. "Keep her safe."

"What?" was all he heard Jeremy say before he was gone.

He flew down the hallway so fast that his passing caused the papers on the nurse's station to scatter in his wake.

Famine

His thoughts went to the unconscious medical staff, but Tzedakah assured him that they were unharmed. Once the vampires were all destroyed, their spell would lift and all they would suffer would be headaches and an inability to remember what had happened to them while they were unconscious.

As soon as he reached where the creature was, it transformed once again into mist and flowed away from him and into the next hallway. Once in the room beyond, it passed through the opening at the bottom of a closed door and out of view.

The vampire seemed to be one step ahead of him, making it difficult for him to get a good read on it. Tzedakah was strangely silent about the creature. Of course, he was pretty sure all he would have to say about it was *kill it*. Or something similar.

He decided he would go through the doorway slowly and with his guard up. The door creaked as he pushed it open, echoing in the wide-open space beyond. The light from the room he was in illuminated the dark entryway to a stairwell.

Any lights that had been in the stairway were completely out, and all that was visible was being lit by the light coming from the open door.

If Jared were still human, the oppressive darkness would have made him feel anxious. He could feel the looming presence of the creature watching him, but he didn't feel fear. All he felt was the pulsing of Tzedakah in his hands and the absolute certainty that he could handle whatever this creature could dish out.

He closed the door, plunging the stairwell into complete darkness. His eyes instantly adjusted to the blackness, and he saw everything as if it were daytime. The creature was a few floors up from him. It was once again in the shape of a woman and it stared down at him, waiting patiently.

It seemed to want him to follow it. At least he thought that was what it wanted him to do. If it had simply wanted to flee, it could have done so at any time. Instead, every time he got close to the creature it moved just far enough away from him that he couldn't catch it and then waited for him to catch up before moving away again.

Strangely, he didn't sense malice from the vampire. Yes, there was an overwhelming sense of wrongness to it like it somehow didn't belong in the world, but no sense that it wanted to harm him.

Of course, he could be misreading the situation entirely; it was a vampire, after all, and vampires were predators that fed on human beings. The other vampires had radiated evil. This one, however, only gave off the sense of danger any predator would.

"Don't be fooled by it," the sword said in his mind. "It is evil regardless of how it appears."

Jared continued up the stairs until he was almost upon the vampire again. Once again, the creature dissipated and moved away from him and farther up the stairs.

"I am pretty sure your world view is fairly narrow," Jared said out loud.

"What do you mean?"

Famine

"I mean, to you everything is black and white. There is no grey."

"Something is either evil or it is not. There is no in between. There is no *grey,* as you put it."

Jared harrumphed. "See, narrow view. You don't leave yourself anywhere to go. Everything is absolute, but life isn't like that. Life is messy and many-faceted. Sometimes a thing can do evil but not necessarily *be* inherently evil."

The sword didn't speak for a few seconds, and when it did it was a bit subdued.

"You speak of humans."

Jared nodded his head. "Among other things."

"I have existed for countless centuries. I have seen the beginning of man and I will see their end, and I can say with absolute certainty that there is no grey in their nature."

The sword fell silent and didn't speak again as they continued to follow the vampire up the winding stairs.

Once they had reached the top floor and had nowhere else to go, the creature again turned into mist and slipped under the closed door to the roof.

Jared slowed to a stop when he reached the door. Just like before, he wasn't going to recklessly run through. He may not sense that the creature meant him harm, but Tzedakah was right. It was a vampire, after all, and very dangerous.

He placed his hand on the bar and slowly pushed the door open. It clacked noisily and he grimaced. So much for stealth. Of course, he was fairly certain that it already knew he was there, so it really didn't matter anyway.

Still cautious, he slowly moved out and onto the roof, letting the door close behind him. The night was clear and the moon was bright. It illuminated the rooftop, casting dark shadows everywhere.

The vampire was standing at the edge of the building, waiting patiently for him. This time, however, the creature had fully materialized into the shape of a beautiful women wearing an elegant white gown that barely covered her ample curves. The dress fluttered in the wind, revealing shapely legs and full breasts.

She was pale, with long, flowing golden locks that seemed to glow in the moonlight. Her eyes were the lightest shade of blue and they flashed playfully as he drew close to her. She licked full lips that were the color of ripe apples and smiled, revealing long white fangs.

Even though he was not quite alive, the absolute beauty of the vampire still affected him. She exuded lust and desire, and it called out to his base nature with every movement she made. All he wanted to do was to go to her and have his way with her.

"Good Lord," he thought. *"If I were still mortal, there is no way I could resist her."*

His heart thumped in his chest as he drew closer to her. Desire for her threatened to drive out every other thought in his mind. He gritted his teeth against the obvious mental assault and pressed on.

Just when he thought he was about to give in, Tzedakah intervened. The overwhelming urge to go to her and ravage her instantly vanished. It was as if Tzedakah had simply switched off a light and that part of him ceased to be.

Famine

The woman frowned and cocked her head, sensing that something in his demeanor had changed. She stuck out her lower lip and pouted playfully.

"This is new," she purred. "No one has ever been able to ignore my charms so completely. I find it intoxicating."

Jared said nothing but continued to walk towards the woman. Once he was a few feet from her, he stopped. Tzedakah glowed brightly and hummed angrily in his hand. It wanted to destroy her. He could feel it almost as strongly as he had felt the lust from the vampire.

He was about to oblige the sentient sword, when something about the woman gave him pause. He couldn't put his finger on it. She seemed familiar somehow, like something from another life.

It clawed at the back of his mind like an itch he just couldn't reach. He examined her as Tzedakah pressed him to strike.

"Just hold on a minute," he said audibly. "Let me think."

It hit him then, and his eyes went wide with recognition.

"Jasmine?"

The woman smiled, but her eyes didn't share the sentiment. "Hello, Jared. It's been a while."

He said nothing. He was too shocked to speak. The sword was uncharacteristically silent as well. If he didn't know better, he would have thought that Tzedakah was just as stunned as he was.

Of course that couldn't be true, since the sword cared little for humans or their relationships. All the sentient sword was concerned with was justice, plain and simple. Nothing else mattered. No amount of pain or explanation could deter it. Justice was black and white, and there was no room for compromise.

Jasmine watched him patiently, her head cocked slightly to one side. The fake smile on her face did little to hide the absolute hatred that burned in her ice-blue eyes. She crossed her arms, pushing her breasts up and causing them to almost spill out of the low-cut dress.

Famine

This time, however, it had no effect on him. None at all, and that concerned him a little. He pushed the worries to the back of his mind. He would deal with them and their implications later.

Jasmine had been the love of his life. At least, so he had thought. She was everything he had ever wanted. Stunningly beautiful, charming, successful, and the desire of every male from Binghamton to Scranton. That was until she had just up and left him out of the blue.

Well, according to his friends and family it really wasn't all that surprising. He had apparently been emotionally distant and neglectful for years before she had finally left. In fact, he had supposedly given the attention that should have gone to her to his partner, Dana.

Whatever. They were all just overreacting. She had broken his heart. He was the victim here, not her. Of course, the events of the last few months had actually reinforced how Jasmine had been feeling.

The truth was that it had been easy for him to let her go. Her leaving had actually been one of the best things to ever happen to him. It had enabled him to finally stop lying to himself and admit that he loved Dana.

Also, he had to admit to himself, that here she was standing before him and all he could think about was if Dana was okay. Maybe he really hadn't ever truly loved her.

"Nothing to say?" she asked, snapping him out of his thoughts. "It's not as if you haven't seen me for months or anything like that."

"A lot has happened in the last few months."

"I know," she replied, her voice softening a bit. "I went by your parents' house when I heard you had died. Even though you had broken my heart, I still loved them as much as I loved my own parents. I couldn't go in, of course, but I was worried about them."

Jared didn't respond but just stood watching her. He noticed that he wasn't breathing and could easily have been mistaken for a statue. Moreover, his feelings seemed more distant than they should have been.

Self-retrospection aside, he should be having stronger emotions from seeing her. Why wasn't he more concerned with what happened to her? She was a vampire, after all. What had actually happened to her in the months since she left?

She shook her head and scowled. "Still just as articulate as ever. I bet if it were Dana standing here, you would have a lot to say."

The darkness in Jared's eyes came to life and writhed violently, and his fingers tightened on Tzedakah's hilt.

"Now, that gets a reaction out of you," she snarled. "I go missing for months and come back to you a monster, and no response. Mention your precious Dana, and you're ready to kill. Nothing changes with you, does it?"

She was right, of course. Jared sighed and his shoulders hunched slightly. He relaxed his grip on Tzedakah but kept his hand resting on the pommel of the sword as it hung from his belt.

In response to his change in posture, Jasmine's eyes softened. She ran a hand reflexively through her hair and glided closer to him until they were standing face to face.

Famine

Her feet never touched the ground, and her gown and hair still waved as if being moved by some unseen wind. He didn't pull back as she searched his features.

He desperately wanted to feel something, and he supposed he did, just not what he knew she wanted. Instead of the heartache of losing her, all he felt was regret. Regret that he had hurt her, and even that seemed like a distant memory.

It apparently showed, because her face fell and she turned away from him, pulling her arms around herself tightly. Tears formed at the corner of her eyes, and the urge to pull her close to comfort her was overwhelming.

He started to reach out for her but stopped and withdrew his hand. Nothing he could say would be enough. He had hurt her, and no matter what he told himself, he had done it intentionally.

Deep down he had known what he had been doing to her, and he had been too much of a coward to stop. He had tried to convince himself that he had loved her, but in actuality his heart had always belonged to someone else.

Neither of them spoke for what seemed like a long time.

Jasmine finally broke the silence. Her voice was barely a whisper. "Did you even try to look for me?"

Jared sighed. "I called you and left a thousand messages, but you never answered. I eventually reached out to your mother, and she told me you no longer wanted to see me. That you didn't even want to speak to me. That you had gone off with someone else."

She turned on him angrily. "And you just let me go. Just like that. With some strange man I had just met."

"What was I supposed to do? I had no idea where you'd gone or who you had gone with. Your mother wouldn't tell me anything, and all I knew was that you didn't want anything to do with me anymore. I was devastated."

She snorted. "Really? You moved on pretty quickly for someone who was *devastated*."

On the word 'devastated' she made air quotes with both her hands.

Jared said nothing.

Scowling, the vampire floated a few feet away from him and glowered at him with ice blue eyes that burned with hatred.

When she was a sufficient way away, Jared felt somehow different. He couldn't put his finger on how, but he knew that something changed when she withdrew from him.

It was then that he heard the sword calling to him in his mind. The voice was distorted at first, like he was hearing it while immersed in water. Then, with the suddenness of an explosion, it flooded legibly into his consciousness.

"It is manipulating your emotions," Tzedakah screamed. "It is using your suppressed guilt to try and disrupt our bond."

Jared narrowed his eyes. "I guess it worked."

"Not entirely," the sword replied. "But it did take me a few seconds to reach you. Seconds that could have been disastrous."

Famine

Jasmine's growl brought their attention back to her. She was hovering higher in the air and her ice blue eyes appeared to be glowing. The sneer on her lips revealed that it was no secret he had broken whatever hold she had managed to place on him.

"Was it thoughts of her that enabled you to shrug off my influence? I bet it was," she snarled. "The ever-present Dana. Even when she isn't here, she somehow is."

So, she didn't know about the sword. If she did, she wouldn't have wasted her time trying to manipulate his emotions. All she knew was that he was somehow still alive, but not how he was.

A strange white aura appeared around her hands, and small tendrils of frost snaked up and around her hands and arms. Waves of cold emanated off of her, leaving small patches of frost on whatever it touched.

In response to her sudden aggression, Jared drew Tzedakah and moved into a defensive stance.

"Why are you here?" he asked.

She sneered. "Why do you think?"

"Dana," he replied matter-of-factly.

Her eyes sparkled with a wicked gleam, and she smiled broadly at the mention of Dana's name.

"Perhaps."

Jared growled softly in response and Tzedakah's glow brightened, driving away some of the encroaching darkness.

"Oh," Jasmine laughed. "Are you going to try and kill me? You may find that harder to do than you think. I am not the week little girl you left sitting by herself at the Number Six."

Jared narrowed his eyes but said nothing.

She bared her fangs and snarled. "There is something that has been bothering me, though. How did you manage to defy death? I would say that you faked your death, but that really doesn't make a whole lot of sense. Plus, I went to your funeral and the grief I saw on your parents' faces was far too real to have been a show."

The darkness in Jared's eyes writhed and reached out towards Jasmine, but he still said nothing.

"I bet it was her, wasn't it?" she spat. "Your love for her conquered even death. Of course, we both know that's nonsense."

She balled her hands into fists and her face contorted into something inhuman and visceral.

"Oh, I saw her there. She was sitting next to your parents and sobbing and crying like she had just lost the love of her life," she mocked. "How pathetic. She should have moved on from you years ago. She would have been better off if she had."

"Like you did?" Jared retorted.

Before he had even finished speaking, Jasmine was upon him. He felt his clothing and flesh tear as she raked at him with her fingernails. After each strike he felt strangely cold, as if she were cutting him with icicles instead of fingernails.

"I did move on from you!" she screamed.

Her attack had taken him by surprise and had put him on his heels. She was fast, almost as fast as he was, and he was barely managing to fend her off. She struck again and again, and each time he just managed to deflect her strikes.

Famine

While feinting a strike to his head, she suddenly struck at his midsection with her free hand. The gambit would have worked if she had been faster, but he sucked in his stomach and arched his back, narrowly avoiding the strike.

The momentum from the attack took her head dangerously close to the hand that held Tzedakah, and he saw his chance to strike. He slammed the pommel of the sword hard on her exposed temple.

At least, he thought he had. Instead of feeling the resistance of tissue and bone, his hand passed harmlessly through the place the skull should have been. The force of his strike carried him forward and he stumbled, unable to adjust to the sudden lack of expected resistance.

Jasmine had transformed into an icy cold mist, making herself intangible just as he was about to make contact. Jasmine in her fog form danced and swirled around him, leaving trails of frost on his clothes and skin.

Even though he was not technically alive, the cold still affected him. As the vaper continued to churn around him the temperature decreased, and his movements gradually began to slow. He swung futility at the flowing mist, but it was like trying to hit a cloud.

Jasmine formed into the vague shape of a woman, two glowing orbs of light burning in the fog where her eyes should have been. He could feel waves of malice and hatred boring into him as she glared at him.

She laughed as a gust of arctic wind rose up and buffeted him. She mocked him and taunted him, and her voice came to his ears with each gust, becoming louder and more intelligible with each blast.

"I will kill her," it whispered. "I will put her out of her misery before you can ruin her, too."

Jared gritted his teeth and snarled as he pushed against the wind. He had no idea how she had come to be a vampire and, truth be told, he didn't really care. She was monster, an abomination, and he was going to destroy her.

Tzedakah glowed even brighter in his grip and the wind seemed to flow around him, creating a bubble that gave him a reprieve from the buffeting gale. He was still freezing and his movements sluggish, and frost now covered his face and most of his body.

Rage and determination surged into his consciousness, and when he looked at her he no longer saw Jasmine. All he saw was a monster, a blight on the world. A creature that fed off of the life of others. A murderer.

He raised the glowing blade in the air and growled, "Enough!" And a pulse of pure energy surged forth from the sentient sword and slammed into the outline of Jasmine.

Jasmine screamed as blue energy arced around her like lightning in a storm cloud. Everywhere the electricity touched turned black, as if the mist was being burned by the power. As soon as the energy subsided, the hazy form flickered and coalesced back into a flesh and blood woman.

Jasmine hunched over and, breathing heavily, tried to move towards Jared, but her legs buckled, and she fell to one knee. She scowled at him, her face a twisted mask of impotent fury.

"No more hiding," Jared growled. His voice was ethereal and hollow and seemed to be emanating out of him

Famine

rather than being spoken from human vocal cords. "This ends now."

The spiritual pressure around Jared increased exponentially as he slowly walked towards Jasmine. The very air around him seemed to warp at his passing, as if one were looking at the world through a prism.

Jasmine's wide eyes darted back and forth, looking for an avenue of escape. They came back to rest on the encroaching Jared, and she could not tear them away from him. It was like looking at some ancient god. The power and pressure he projected was like nothing she had ever experienced before.

"What are you?" she breathed.

Jared said nothing in response but continued his slow, deliberate advance.

She shied away from him as he drew closer and put her arms up defensively in front of her. It was futile and she knew it. She had power, more power than she had ever imagined was possible, but what was coming for her now was on a completely different level.

Jared was nearly on top of her, and her mind screamed for her to run, to get away. Still, she couldn't tear her eyes away from the horror that was before her. Terrible, great, and emanating the wrath of a cosmic being, she was transfixed by Jared's power.

Those dark eyes seemed to bore into her very soul. The darkness reached out for her, threatening to consume her. She could feel it strip away all of her mental defenses. It accused her and judged her. Laid her bear before its gaze. There was no hiding from it. No excuses. She knew instinctively that it saw everything. Saw her for what she was. A monster.

Every lie she had ever told herself from when she was young to this moment, every justification, was obliterated in that gaze. She had become a monster long before she had been turned into a vampire.

Tears formed in her eyes as Jared lowered himself until they were eye to eye. The darkness that had replaced his baby blues writhed and reached out for her. She instinctively shied away, pressing her back so hard against the cement of the roof's edge that it drew blood.

She saw in her periphery the glow of the iron-wrought sword as it inched towards her. She felt the cold touch of metal as the blade rested on her sternum directly between her breasts. Still, she couldn't tear her eyes away from that horrible gaze.

"Jasmine Lassiter," Jared said calmly in that ethereal voice that seemed so alien to the man she had known.

"Daughter of Mary Ann and John. Vampire. Abomination. You have been found guilty."

Her face was awash with dark blue light, but all she could see was the darkness writhing in those eyes. All she could feel was the guilt of what she had done, what she had become.

She was a monster. She had sacrificed her humanity and become something that never should have existed. She was an echo of a power long forgotten and dormant. A power that had led to the near destruction of the world.

As she stared up into Jared's face, she searched it for the man she had known. The man she had loved. He may have been a fool and he may have hurt her, but deep down he was a good man. A kind man.

What she saw there now was someone she didn't recognize. It was like she was looking at a completely different person. A doppelganger of the man she had known. There was no mercy, no pity or kindness, only the absolute certainty of judgment and death.

Her heart sank at the realization that this thing before her was no longer the man she had known. Just like her, he had died and come back something else. A monster in his own right.

She was going to die and there was nothing she could do about it. Desperately she tried to tear her gaze away from the pools of nightmare black that held her, but she couldn't. Her mind raced as she tried to think of a way of escape, but the dark gaze muddled her thoughts.

She thrashed and struggled as the hateful blade slowly pushed forward. Panic gave her strength and she clawed at

Jared's face with her nails. He swatted her fingers away with his free hand as he slowly slid the glowing blade into the exposed flesh of her chest.

"No!" she screamed, more in defiance than pain. "Noooo!"

Frantically she grabbed the blade with both hands in a desperate attempt at stopping it from sliding any farther into her body. Ignoring the searing pain in her fingers, she managed to slow it enough to buy a few precious seconds.

Pain and fear muddled her thoughts, making it nearly impossible for her to think. Her muscles burned and she knew that the supernatural strength she had been given at her new birth wasn't going to be enough to save her.

Her only chance was to reach Jared somehow. To break through the monster to the man underneath. She gritted her teeth and used her remaining power to try and manipulate his emotions just as she had done earlier.

"Jared, stop," she said as calmly as she could. Her voice wavered slightly from the strain in her muscles and the pain in her sternum. "This isn't you. You were a cop, for God's sake, not a murderer. You don't have to do this."

The only response she received was renewed pain as the sword slid a few more centimeters deeper into her flesh.

"Jared, please," she whispered as her strength failed, her hands dropped to her sides and her eyes lost focus.

It was no use. He was beyond reasoning. Beyond emotion. Nothing she said was going to cause him to stop.

She felt the cold bite of steel as Jared pushed the sword a little closer to her heart. The pain was not gone, but it seemed to be far away like she was experiencing the echo of an event that had already happened.

She wondered what death would be like. She was a vampire, after all. Was Hell and damnation what awaited her, or would she find mercy? She had been a Christian once; at least, she went to church with her parents when she was young.

She hadn't been especially faithful as an adult, but she had still believed in her heart that there was a God. Tried to live in a way that didn't hurt anyone. Tried to be a good person.

Of course, she had given up her humanity and become something else. She had embraced the ancient power that was offered to her. A power that defied the will of God.

Maybe He would understand. Maybe He would show her mercy even though she had chosen to let go of her humanity to become something else. Something more.

The truth, however, was that she wasn't sorry. She had found a new life. A life filled with experiences that dwarfed the life she'd had as a human. Every feeling, every emotion, all of life was now somehow...more. The constraints and limitations that had been placed on her by her humanity were gone, replaced by strength, power, and the freedom to use those gifts. To live in any way she saw fit.

Her head slid to the side as she slumped, and she looked up at the man she had loved. The man who she now realized had become a tool of the God who hated her for throwing off His limitations and becoming more.

It was only a matter of heartbeats before the blade reached her heart and it would be over. She managed to focus her eyes and she fixed them on those black holes that had replaced his eyes and met them with defiance.

"I regret nothing," she hissed through gritted teeth. "You are the monster here, not me."

She refused to look away, and braced herself for the end.

Nothing happened.

She blinked a few times and squinted in confusion. What was he waiting for? Was he trying to torment her? No matter how much he had changed, she couldn't bring herself to believe he had become a sadist. No, something was off.

It was then she noticed that his arm was trembling slightly, as if he was fighting himself. Almost as if he was fighting against some external power that was trying to force him to do something he didn't want to do.

Maybe he had chosen to stop himself. Maybe she had reached him somehow. She shifted her body to the side slightly, away from the weapon. It didn't move with her.

She allowed herself to hope. Maybe she wasn't going to die today after all. She had no idea what had caused him to stop, but she wasn't going to look a gift horse in the mouth.

She held her breath and inched away from Jared as fast as she dared until she had completely extricated herself from the sword. As soon as she felt the pressure of the blade release, she flung herself as far away from the glowing weapon as she could.

The instant she began to move, the blade shot towards her again. This time, however, it stopped just short of reaching her. Jared's hand was noticeably shaking now, and she saw that his brow was furrowed and his jaw set and tight, as if he was straining against some heavy weight.

"No," he growled through gritted teeth.

When he spoke this time, his voice was different than it had been before. It was still ethereal and hollow, but it sounded more like the Jared she knew. Not the thing that had just tried to kill her.

He turned to look up at her and his face was a mask of pain. Those nightmarish black eyes continued to writhe and reach for her, but she no longer felt hatred emanating from them.

She decided to take a chance and reached out to touch his face. He didn't shy away from her, but his hand continued to shake from the strain of holding the blade at bay. As she moved closer the sword seemed to follow her, but Jared managed to hold it firm.

His face was cold. Too cold to be the flesh of a living person. Was he like her? There was much she didn't know about this new world she had been born into. Perhaps he was just another creature like her. Born of the others. A child of the forgotten ones.

Perhaps she could convince him to come with her. If she reached out with her power and once again manipulated his emotions, maybe she could do more than just escape.

It was obvious that he was powerful. Maybe even more powerful than her master. If he could be convinced to join them, then she would be adding a powerful ally to their cause.

Famine

She made up her mind and once again reached out with her new abilities. Subtly, she attempted to influence his emotions.

"Jared," she purred softly, her eyes glowing. "I can offer you something more than power. I can offer you freedom. Freedom from the restrictions of mortality. Freedom from the tyrannical and oppressive morality of the human world."

She couldn't tell if her words were reaching him, but his face did seem to soften a bit as she spoke.

She continued. "All you have to do is come with me. Walk away and leave your old life behind. Leave her behind."

As soon as the words left her lips, she knew she had made a mistake. Jared's face darkened and he let out a low, ominous growl. The blade in his hand erupted with light, and this time he didn't try to stop it as it surged towards her.

Tzedakah struck the wall where Jasmine had been only a second before, throwing up sparks and leaving a long gash in the concrete. Jasmine had narrowly avoided the strike by once again turning into mist and making herself incorporeal.

Jared growled as she shot off into the night sky, fleeing his wrath and her just judgment. He raged after the fleeing specter, hurling bolt after bolt of arcane energy into the night sky.

Each blast illuminated the surrounding area like lightning strikes. If anyone had been looking on, they might have thought a storm was brewing.

Jared jumped up onto the ledge of the rooftop and watched as the cloud of cold surged across the horizon and towards the Susquehanna River and the outskirts of the city proper.

Famine

He should never have stopped Tzedakah from killing her. She was no longer the girl he had known. She was a monster and had come here to harm Dana. He couldn't afford to allow his feelings of guilt and regret to get in the way of what he needed to do anymore.

For his part he had loved her once, even if it wasn't as he should have. If he was honest with himself, he still did care for her, but those were feelings from another life. Here and now in this new reality such attachments were a detriment and could no longer be entertained.

Does that include how I feel about Dana?

The thought gave him pause and left a knot in his stomach as he watched Jasmine growing smaller on the horizon. Was his inability to let go of Dana something he couldn't afford as well? Was it part of an old life that he needed to let die?

"You can contemplate such things at a later time," Tzedakah said, breaking his reverie. "The abomination will escape if we do not pursue it immediately."

"I know," he shot back, irritated.

He stood there for a few more minutes, thinking, then sighed deeply and nodded his head in internal resolve. "Okay, Tzedakah, let's go get her."

With that said he jumped off the rooftop, did a flip in midair, and landed on his feet on the ground below. As soon as his feet touched the earth, he shot off like a blur in the direction Jasmine had fled.

The trees, houses, and buildings moved past him so fast that his surroundings began to distort into one continuous stream of indistinguishable shapes that all appeared to merge into one long singular entity.

The lights became streaks of color, and it felt to him that his feet were moving so fast that they seemed to be hovering over the ground instead of running on it.

It was a strange sensation, and it left him feeling a bit disoriented at first. Before long, however, his mind and his muscles adjusted to the speed, and it became less disconcerting and actually quite exciting.

Especially when he hit the river, and it didn't even make a dent in his momentum. He actually ran right over the surface of the water like it was solid ground.

"I could get used to this," he said out loud.

"There are great many things we can do when we are in unity."

"Like what?" Jared asked as he took a tight turn and nearly lost his footing. "Crap! Better keep my focus on the road."

"Anything is possible if it is…required."

Jared ducked a tree branch and zipped in a zig zag through a housing development, jumping a few fences and even a large doghouse that left the occupant in a fit of loud barking.

"Anything?" he asked dubiously. "And what does, *if required*, mean?"

"We are not constrained by the laws of the mortal realm." Tzedakah answered. "So, anything your imagination can think of is technically possible. If it is needed, that is."

Famine

"Wait a minute," Jared responded, making sure that he kept an eye on the fleeing Jasmine. They were closing the distance fast and would soon overtake her.

"So, can I fly?"

"If the situation requires it, Yes."

"If I can fly, why are we chasing her on foot?"

"Because this is what you decided to do. It is what your subconscious imagined when you thought of chasing the abomination. So therefore, we run."

Jared absorbed the information Tzedakah had given him silently as he continued to move through the countryside, getting closer and closer to the fleeing Jasmine.

He was almost upon her, and the rage and anger that he had temporarily suppressed came rushing back to the surface. She was a monster, an abomination, and this time nothing would stop him from ending her.

There was no discord between the two of them, they were in perfect unity on this. Both of them wanted to destroy her. Jared, to protect the people she may harm, and Tzedakah to bring justice to a creature that deserved judgment.

Jared slowed as he watched Jasmine descend into a large crop of trees. He could sense her just up ahead and he quickened his pace in anticipation.

As he drew closer he passed a small, slightly dilapidated farmhouse that was hidden deep in the woods and far away from the hustle and bustle of the city. At first it didn't register as anything special, but as he passed it he felt the overwhelming urge to stop.

Something was wrong with that house. He could feel it. Like a stain on the world that didn't belong. Before he realized what was happening, he had stopped and was staring transfixed by the unremarkable home.

"What in God's name," Jared whispered. "I suddenly feel dirty, like I haven't showered in days. It's as if I am covered in so much filth that it would take years to wash it all off."

Tzedakah didn't respond with words but began to vibrate so hard that Jared thought the sentient sword would shake right out of his hand. Whatever was in that house certainly had him all riled up.

He stood transfixed for a few more seconds before shaking his head and clearing his thoughts. Whatever was in that house didn't matter right now and would have to wait. Jasmine was the immediate priority, and took precedence. They could always come back and deal with whatever was in this house when they were done with her.

He turned in the direction where he had seen Jasmine land and started to quickly move that way. At least, he tried to move that way.

What in the world is going on? My legs won't move.

"Tzedakah, what are you doing?"

No response.

"Tzedakah, we need to get over there," he said, pointing with his free hand in the direction where Jasmine was. "Whatever is going on in this house can wait till we have delt with Jasmine."

"No, the abomination can wait," the sword replied.

Famine

Jared gritted his teeth and growled. "No, she can't. If we don't deal with her now, she could return later to hurt Dana, and I won't allow that."

"Jared, this is more important."

"No, it isn't," he retorted angrily.

"Yes, it is," the sword replied.

Jared tried to move his legs again and even tried throwing his torso in the direction he wanted to go. Nothing he did worked. Tzedakah simply would not allow him to leave.

He had to get to Jasmine, didn't he understand that? They could always double back to this stupid house after they were done.

Jared closed his eyes and allowed all the frustration and anger of the last few days to build up inside of him. He may not be in control of his destiny anymore, but he would be damned if he was going to allow this talking piece of metal to stop him from protecting the woman he loved.

He opened his eyes and slowly lifted the glowing blade till it was at eye level with him.

"Let go of my legs right now," he said softly, a hint of menace in his voice. "Or I swear I will find the largest rock I can and plant you in it like Excalibur and leave you there to rot."

Jared felt Tzedakah release his legs and he stumbled forward, nearly falling as he did.

"Jared, people will die if we do not help."

Jared snorted as he turned away from the house and stalked off in the direction of Jasmine.

"Don't try to manipulate me. I know you don't care if people die. You consider humans expendable. All you care about is justice, plain and simple, and nothing else."

The sword went silent, but he could feel urgency emanating from it. With each step he took away from the house the pressure grew in intensity, until it threatened to overwhelm him.

He gritted his teeth and exerted his will against the mental onslaught, attempting to drive Tzedakah's emotions out of his head.

Nothing was going to keep him from Jasmine. He had to protect Dana no matter the cost. He didn't care what kind of atrocities were being committed in that house. All he cared about was keeping her safe, and Jasmine was an immediate threat to that.

"Jared," the sword said softly. "You must stop and go back. People are going to die if you do not."

Jared swatted a low-hanging branch out of his way and kicked at a patch of brambles as he continued to move in the direction he sensed Jasmine was.

"I don't care," he exclaimed, but his voice lacked conviction.

"Jared, please," the sword pleaded.

This last statement caused Jared to pause in mid-step. He blinked a few times and his mouth dropped open.

Please?

Tzedakah never said please. At least, not that he could remember anyway. Usually, if he wanted Jared to do something he just simply took him over and made him. In fact, if what was going on in that house was so urgent, why hadn't he just done so?

Jared closed his eyes and shook his head.

No. It doesn't matter. Dana is my first priority. Once I'm sure she's safe, then I can worry about other people.

His resolve renewed; he continued towards the monster who had threatened the woman he loved.

For all I know, it's just some kid smoking crack or something trivial like that. To Tzedakah every sin is a major one. In fact, he would probably kill a toddler for stealing a piece of candy.

Even though he had rationalized his decision not to help, he couldn't stop himself from looking over his shoulder at the small farmhouse. Was he making the right choice?

Dana was no longer in immediate danger, after all, and Tzedakah seemed so...upset, if that was even the right word for what he was sensing from the sentient sword.

"Jared," Tzedakah said, suddenly frantic. "The children will die if we don't go back right now."

The children? Wait, there are children in danger back there?!

Suddenly an image flashed in his mind of a boy of about twelve with a shock of bright red hair, standing defensively in front of a little girl who looked to be about ten with messy blonde hair. The girl's eyes were wide with fright, and her pudgy cheeks were stained with tears.

The little boy was brandishing a small metal baseball bat, waving it back and forth in an attempt at warding something off. The girl's nightgown was torn, and she was clutching the tattered pieces of the garment across her exposed body, trying in vain to cover herself.

All thoughts of Jasmine and Dana fled as he watched the scene unfold in his mind. The image suddenly winked out before whatever it was that the boy was trying to defend against came into view.

"Jared," Tzedakah pleaded again. "They are going to die."

Jared took one last look in the direction he knew Jasmine was before turning on his heels and speeding off in the opposite direction.

"Not if we have anything to say about it, they won't."

Famine

Jasmine swirled through the night sky as fast as her powers would allow. Whatever it was Jared had become, there was one thing she knew for certain: he was far more powerful than her. Maybe even more powerful than the one who had made her.

She kept glancing behind as she fled from the hospital, scanning the horizon for any signs that she was being followed. Even in her mist form, she could still feel her heart beating hard in her chest. He had almost killed her, and she wanted to get as far away from him as she could.

Why had he let her go? Was he tormenting her? Playing with her before he killed her, like a cat with a mouse? Certainly, he was angry that she had threatened his precious Dana, but cruelty had never been in his character before. Of course, he was no longer the man she had known. He was something else.

She wasn't sure he was even human anymore. When she had touched his cheek, it felt so cold. Like touching a corpse. She shuddered at the memory. No, whatever he was wasn't human. Not human, but also not like her. He had become something else entirely. Something new and unknown, and that frightened her.

Perhaps the White Lady would have the answers to her questions. Certainly, Durgala had to know something, even if Lady Musume did not.

Of course, she had gone to the hospital against both their wishes, and she had no idea how they would react to her disobedience. Especially since her action had led to the deaths of three of their warriors. Either way, she would soon find out. She could sense both presences not far away.

As she flew she scanned the ground below, searching for them. She was struck by how small everything looked. She had long ago passed from the bright lights and grey hues of the city to the soft shades of green and rolling hills of the countryside, and she was once again reminded of just how beautiful Upstate New York was.

Those who had never lived in or visited here thought New York was just one huge city. They had no idea that most of the state was beautiful rural country. The Empire State was home to two major mountain ranges, a thousand lakes and rivers, and miles and miles of uninhabited forest.

It truly was a breathtaking place that always seemed to be overshadowed in the public consciousness by the relatively small section of the state that was New York City, Long Island, and its surrounding boroughs and counties.

Famine

As soon as she flew past a lone farmhouse that was hidden away by a large grove of trees, she saw a small meadow that was surrounded by enormous oak trees. It was a veritable island of grass in a sea of trees.

When she drew closer to the grotto she knew that her master was there, since she could sense his distinct power emanating from it. With one last look behind to make sure she hadn't been followed, she quickly floated down to meet them.

While she gently descended, her body slowly solidified back into its original form. She completed the transformation, becoming solid again just as her left foot touched the soft grass.

Instantly she saw a blur of movement out of the corner of her right eye. As soon as her subconscious registered the movement, the smell of rotting flesh reached her.

Reacting out of instinct she turned slightly, and with blinding speed reached out and plucked the clawed hand that had just tried to rip her face off out of the air.

An angry hiss escaped her lips as she wrenched the wrist of the creature, downward and hard. She was rewarded by the sound of bones splintering and a loud howl of pain from the creature.

The pathetic being writhed in pain at her feet, trying in vain to escape her viselike hold. It pleaded with her for mercy, but she tightened her grip even harder at its pleas. Jasmine snarled and glared at the thing with eyes full of disgust and malice. She hated the wendigo, but she knew that if she killed him it would mean her death as well.

Not wanting to face the wrath of her masters, but needing to punish the creature for its insolence, she decided that it no longer needed the hand she was holding.

She sneered down at the stinking rotting creature as her hands began to glow pure arctic white. The creature's eyes went wide with terror when it realized what was about to happen and it thrashed wildly trying to free itself from her grasp.

"No, Mistress," it croaked, its words becoming incoherent croaks of pain as tendrils of white frost formed on its wrist and then slowly made their way towards its captured hand.

Before long, the wendigo's entire hand was completely frozen. She glared down at the pathetic creature who whined like a wounded animal. With a final short flick of her wrist the wendigo's hand snapped clean off.

The creature fell backward and drew its wounded appendage to its chest. It folded its thin body around the injured arm and turned itself protectively away from Jasmine.

She stood over the wendigo, who was rocking back and forth and whimpering loudly. The blue-white glow that emanated from her washed over the pathetic creature, causing it to squint from the brightness.

"That is enough," a man's voice commanded from behind her.

At the sound of the voice her eyes went wide, and her face drained of any remaining color. Her heart felt like it was going to beat right out of her chest, and every muscle in her body instantly went rigid.

Famine

She exhaled slowly, trying in vain to calm herself. She didn't want to show fear in front of him. He never reacted well to fear. Of course, he reacted even worse to insolence, so fear was probably a better option for her anyway.

Pull yourself together, girl. You're acting like a teenager who just got caught sneaking back in after curfew. He may not be pleased, but he wouldn't hurt me. Would he?

She closed her eyes, gritted her teeth, and managed to bring her wayward muscles back under control. After a few long seconds she felt the tension leave her, and she sighed softly before opening her eyes.

Nayati still lay at her feet, groveling, and she had to fight the urge to kick the creature. Better judgement won out, though, and she slid her hands down the sides of her dress to remove any wrinkles and then reflexively fixed her hair instead. With one last long sigh, she turned around to face the speaker.

She wasn't completely certain that he wouldn't punish her for disobeying him, but she was certain that he wouldn't kill her. That was something at least.

Vladmir Durgala stood in the darkness, his bearlike arms crossed over his broad chest. His full lips were pursed, and his prominent brow was furrowed. The black cloak he wore over his seven-foot muscled frame flitted slightly in the wind, revealing black jeans, knee-high leather boots, and a tailored white dress shirt.

"Vell, vat do you have to say for yourself?"

Jasmine contemplated lying to him, but she was certain he already knew what she had done. He always did.

God, this really was just like being a kid. In a way it was. Afterall, he was the one who had made her so, in a way, he was her father.

Which was very weird for her, since she had been very attracted to him when they first met. In fact, it was that attraction that caused her to go with him in the first place. She still was, but her desire for him had changed.

Sure, he was dashingly handsome, and he exuded masculine charm and sex appeal, but once she had been turned her feelings for him had gradually changed from lust to devotion. She still wanted him, but her feelings of devotion for him now far outweighed her romantic desires.

No, lying to him was a bad idea. She would admit her disobedience and hope that her punishment wasn't too severe. She had always done the same with her biological father in her former life, and she saw no reason to change now.

The truth was, she wasn't sure she could lie to him even if she wanted to. He always knew what she was thinking, like he could see inside her head.

She lowered her gaze and slumped her shoulders. "I'm sorry, Master."

He stared at her for a few long seconds before sighing heavily and uncrossing his arms. He shook his head slightly, his long raven hair flowing around his angular face like water around an island.

"Vy must you always be so impatient, Kicsi?"

She looked up at him but avoided his piercing ice blue eyes. She knew full well what would happen if she looked into those eyes.

Famine

"I don't know. I guess I take after my maker."

She smiled sheepishly and batted her eyes at him. Lying might not be an option, but using her feminine wiles certainly was.

She walked slowly towards him, allowing her hips to sway back and forth seductively. Pushing out her chest to emphasize her breasts, she licked her cherry red lips and smiled.

"Can you blame me, my love?" she purred. "You know what she did to me. What she cost me."

He raised one eyebrow and pursed his lips, never taking his eyes off her as she gently walked her fingers up the exposed part of his chest.

He shook his head slightly and sighed. "I know what you are trying to do, Kicsi, and it will not work."

She drew close to him and put her lips directly next to his ear. "Are you sure?"

Vladmir closed his eyes and shuddered involuntarily. A sound of remembered pleasure escaped his lips and he smiled slightly.

"Kicsi," he scolded gently. His tone lacked conviction, however. "Your tricks do not verk on me."

He was clearly enjoying himself. Maybe she would be able to get by without being punished after all.

Seeing that he was responding to her advances, she slowly moved her hand up and rested it on his cheek. He tilted his head slightly, allowing his face to sit in the palm of her hand.

"Vy do you care about such things?" he asked, not opening his eyes. "Is your new life not enough to satisfy you?"

"You know it is," she replied.

"Then why are you so obsessed with this Dana. Revenge is something I understand, but she is no longer of any consequence to you."

Anger bright and hot welled up inside of Jasmine at the mention of Dana's name. All fear of punishment fled, and she forgot just who it was that stood before her.

"No consequence?" she growled, pulling her hand away from his cheek. "No consequence! How dare you make light of what she did to me!"

Vladmir didn't lash out at her but simply stood, shaking his head like he was dealing with an infant throwing a tantrum.

"Little miss perfect knew exactly what she was doing. She always managed to find some way to get between us."

She began to pace back and forth, waving her arms in the air angrily. "Oh, I had a rough day and need to talk. Oh wait, don't go over to Jasmine's tonight, I am sick, and I need you. Yeah, that little bitch knew exactly what she was doing."

Vladmir rolled his eyes and sighed.

"Jasmine, my dear, you really must let this go. In a hundred years you will not even remember that she existed."

Jasmine narrowed her eyes and scowled. "I very much doubt that. I ran into Jared at the hospital, and he's like us. At least I think he is."

113

Famine

Vladmir's eyes flashed with surprise. "Vat did you just say?"

At the tone of his voice Jasmine froze and turned to look at him. As soon as she saw his eyes, she knew she had made a mistake.

Swallowing the fear that was now starting to grip her, she backed away slightly. He didn't move towards her, but she knew he didn't have to. All he had to do was simply wave a hand and she would be writhing on the ground in pain.

She began to speak but he held up one finger, indicating for her to be silent. She instantly obeyed, her heart beating so loudly she was sure he could hear it from where he was standing.

He continued to hold up his finger as he slowly moved his head back and forth, searching for something. He returned his gaze to her and spoke softly, his voice thick with menace.

"Where are the three warriors you took with you?"

"I...they," she stuttered, unable to find her voice.

As she continued to flounder, his eyes suddenly shot to her chest. She self-consciously looked to the area he was glowering at and saw to her surprise that the cut Jared had given her earlier was still bleeding. Why hadn't it healed?

"Did he do that to you?" he asked, his voice showing an unusual amount of apprehension.

"Yes," was all she could manage.

"How?" he demanded. "Vith vat?"

She swallowed and withered under his intense gaze. "With...with a sword," she finally managed to say.

"Did he kill the others?"

She nodded.

He closed his eyes and gritted his teeth. He didn't speak for several seconds, but just stood there as if he was uncertain of what to do next.

Jasmine was still very much afraid, but she was also curious. She had never seen him like this. Was it possible that he was frightened at what she had described? Had she been right before, when she thought that Jared might be more powerful than him?

Before Jasmine had time to contemplate further, he opened his eyes. She could tell that he was calmer, but she could still sense the anger seething just under the surface.

"Do you have any idea vat your disobedience has just caused?" he said softly.

She shook her head.

"Of course, you don't. You are still just a child. You run headlong into the world without any clue of the dangers that lurk there."

He sighed and massaged the bridge of his hawk-like nose. "I always knew this day may come, but I had hoped we would have more time to prepare for it."

"Prepare for what?" she asked.

He shook his head. "Not here. It may still be nearby. Ve will discuss this further when we are safe from spying eyes."

He turned away from her and melted into the shadows.

"Nayati, pull yourself together and come."

She watched as the wendigo rose and, still holding its injured appendage, followed its master into the shadows.

What had he meant? Was Jared that much of a threat? It was obvious that he was something different from them;

but if not like them, then what was he? Had her reckless actions put all their plans in jeopardy?

She hoped not, but the way Vladmir had reacted to her news scared her. What was it he wasn't telling her? She hoped that when they arrived back at the compound all her questions would be answered.

With one last look around to make sure no one had seen them, she turned and followed him into the darkness.

The closer Jared got to the farmhouse, the more the feeling of being filthy intensified. Also, the closer he got to the home, the more dilapidated it appeared to be.

Was it this decrepit when he passed it earlier? He couldn't be sure, but something in his gut told him no.

With each step closer, he watched as the paint cracked and peeled and the white of the walls rotted to a dingy grey. Holes appeared in the black tiles on the roof, and he watched as the glass from one of the windows suddenly cracked. A few pieces of it fell to the ground but made no sound as they hit the dry earth below.

He had no idea what was happening. The structure seemed to be rotting away in front of his eyes. There was also an overwhelming sense of wrongness emanating from the residence that made him uneasy. It drove away the light, leaving the building shrouded in a thick oily haze.

"What in the world?" he whispered.

Famine

"You are seeing the truth of this dwelling," Tzedakah said into his mind. "Nothing can hide from our eyes. We see the world as it truly is, and not how it perceives itself to be."

"Even inanimate objects, such as houses?"

Reaching the window he was sure he had seen break, he tentatively reached out and ran his fingers over the glass. It was solid. The glass still appeared jagged and shattered, but it felt smooth and undamaged to his touch.

"They aren't alive, so how can they perceive themselves to be anything at all, let alone anything other than what they are?"

Continuing to move around the house, Jared noticed that even the grass was wilting and dying wherever it touched the building. The house's influence did have its limits, however, since it only appeared to be able to affect an area of about a foot from itself.

"Everything that is created has a purpose. That purpose is decided by those who created it. Even if the purpose of the thing is changed, the echo of what it was designed to be remains."

Jared frowned. "That doesn't answer my question."

"When humans and other sentient beings look upon this place, they see a home. A dwelling place for a family. This is what it was built to be."

The sword paused as if it was searching for the right words. Jared continued around the house till he reached the back door. He tried the knob, but the door was locked.

"The rest of the world sees a house, a home, because that is what it was designed to be. It is what it perceives itself to be," the sword continued. "But we see the reality of what

118

it has become. A place of filth and pain. We see the truth that it tries to hide. That it has been corrupted."

A muffled scream followed by a shout brought Jared's attention back to the reason for them being here. It sounded like it had come from somewhere in the basement of the house.

"So much for subtlety," he said as he drew back, preparing to kick down the door.

As soon as his foot hit the wood, however, it passed through it like it wasn't even there. He stumbled slightly and suppressed a startled shout as his whole body phased through the door.

"What just happened?" he whispered, putting his hands out to steady himself.

"Stealth is required if we wish to save the children unharmed," Tzedakah explained. "If I had allowed you to break down the door, we would have alerted it to our presence. I felt that this was a better alternative."

Shaking his head slightly to reorient himself he peered into the darkness, scanning the area for any signs of danger. They were in a small kitchen.

The room was clean, with dishes drying in a rack by the sink and a small bowl of fruit in the middle of the modest kitchen table. Moving past the table, he walked into the next room.

It was a living area with a couch and loveseat placed facing a large TV that was hung on one of the walls. This room, too, was clean and well kept. Moving from room to room on the first floor, Jared found each area to be clean

Famine

and filled with the usual furniture and accoutrements one would expect in a home.

If he wasn't watching the house decay and rot around him, he might have thought that Tzedakah had made a mistake.

A picture on the wall caught his attention, and he moved closer to get a better look at it. It was a portrait of a family. A middle-aged, slightly overweight balding man smiled back at him with his arm around a pretty blonde woman who Jared assumed was his wife.

They both rested their hands on the shoulders of two children. A little boy who looked to be about eleven and a little girl of about eight. The children were smiling, but Jared could tell that their eyes didn't share the sentiment. They were not the happy family this picture wanted to perceive them to be.

As he continued to examine the photo, he watched in fascinated horror as the man's face transformed into something that looked like it came out of a child's nightmare. The boy's face fell and the little girl's contorted into a silent scream.

Another muffled shout snapped him back to reality and he leapt into motion, literally running towards the source of the sound. It was louder this time, and he was certain it was coming from somewhere in the next room.

"We need to find these kids right now," he hissed.

The next room was where the front door opened to the main hallway. Whipping his head back and forth, searching for the source of the shout, he noticed a staircase that led to the upper floor.

His gaze swept to the stairs and he peered into the darkness, searching for anything out of the ordinary. Even total darkness was no problem for him since his new eyes allowed him to always see everything unimpeded.

"They are not up there," Tzedakah replied to his unspoken thoughts. "They are down there."

The arm holding the sentient sword rose on its own and pointed at a small door under the stairs Jared hadn't seen. It was cracked slightly, and he noticed that there was soft light coming from it.

Tzedakah's glow seemed to grow in intensity, as if the blade was mirroring the same sense of urgency that was churning away in his own gut. They had to move quickly if they wanted to save these kids.

Save them from what?

Tzedakah hadn't really given him anything to go on other than the fact that the children were in danger. Given the way the picture had changed, he knew that whatever was waiting for them wasn't going to be pleasant.

He was certain they could handle what they found down there, but it would certainly be nice to have all the information for a change.

Grunting, Jared grimaced and rolled his eyes. Given his interactions with the blade up till now, he was pretty sure that was never going to happen. Seeming to know exactly what Jared was thinking, he could almost feel the sentient sword projecting his own annoyance back.

He reached the door and gently pushed it open. The voice of what Jared assumed was the little boy from the portrait instantly became audible.

Famine

"If you come any closer, I will hurt you."

A man's voice, gruff and slurred, responded, "If you don't give me that bat right now, boy, I am gonna beat you to death with it."

Leaving the door ajar, Jared quietly crept down the steep stairway toward the commotion. There was a small wall at the bottom of the stairs blocking his view of the rest of the basement, and he couldn't see what was going on in the next room.

It was then that he heard a small whimper. Was that another child? The girl from the picture perhaps. Or was it someone else?

"I won't let you touch her," the boy said, his voice shaking.

"Is that so," the man replied, his voice dripping with venom. "Think you're a big boy now, do you? Think you're old enough to take on your old man?"

There was no response from the boy other than the sound of his hands tightening on the grip of the bat he supposedly held.

"Danny, it's okay," a little girl said, her voice cracking and frightened. "He will hurt you if you don't give him the bat."

"He will hurt *you* if I do," the boy replied.

The man laughed at that. It was a hateful, spite-filled laugh that sent chills down Jared's spine.

"Oh, I'm not gonna hurt you, darlin'," the man said, his voice suddenly soft. "You're my special girl. Daddy would never hurt you."

Jared instantly felt dirty. It was the exact same sense of filthiness he had experienced when they first approached the house.

"But I will hurt Danny if he doesn't put down the bat."

Suddenly the girl screamed, "Danny, no!"

Jared heard the distinct sounds of a struggle, and he moved closer to the doorway to try to get a view of what was going on. The boy cried out in pain and Jared heard the loud clatter of something metal hitting the concrete floor.

"I warned you, boy," the man said. "Now I'm going to have to teach you a lesson."

Jared could hear both children sobbing, and he gripped Tzedakah so tightly his knuckles turned white. Rage, hot and ferocious, welled up inside of him and he gritted his teeth so hard he thought they might shatter.

As if it felt the same, Tzedakah's brightness grew to the intensity of a miniature star. The sword was vibrating so fast that Jared found it difficult to hold on to it.

It was then that Jared heard another voice, one that he hadn't noticed earlier. The voice was low, raspy, and inhuman. How had he missed it before?

"You must kill the boy," it muttered softly. "He doesn't understand and can no longer be trusted to keep silent about your forbidden love for the girl."

What in God's name was that? It wasn't human that he was sure of.

"We must move now," Tzedakah said, his voice uncharacteristically thick with anxiety. "We are out of time."

Famine

Agreeing, and unable to contain himself any longer, Jared stepped around the wall and into the basement.

ophia's eyes shot open, but she didn't move. Her heart was beating so fast that the pulsing of it in her ears was nearly deafening. Something had awoken her. A strange noise perhaps, or something scurrying in the darkness.

Slowing her breathing, she tried to calm her raging heart. Still not moving, she decided that if whatever had awoken her wanted to harm her, then pretending to be asleep was her best chance.

Her plan seemed to work, and when nothing came for her, her heart started to slow, and her breathing returned to normal. Just when she thought she had gotten herself under control, fire erupted in her leg.

Biting her lip to keep from screaming, she slowly shifted her gaze to her legs. She exhaled gratefully when she saw nothing was there. She was alone in the small cell.

I can't believe I'm reduced to playing dead like an opossum. I feel like a kid again, jumping at every movement and sound in the darkness. Afraid that the bogeyman is waiting in the shadows to come and kill me.

The bogeyman was real, though, and she had met him. Something had awoken her, and in this place that was never a good thing. She may be angry with herself for feeling like a scared little girl, but it was those very emotions and her response to them that had kept her alive.

Making sure she was indeed alone, she grimaced and whimpered slightly as she turned over adjusting her position. The muscles in her right calf had cramped up while she was tensed up and that was the source of her sudden pain.

Thanking all that was holy it wasn't something else, she gritted her teeth and gently massaged the offending muscle until the tightness subsided.

It took a few minutes for her eyes to adjust to the darkness, but when they did, she saw that she was still alone in the small cell. After her failed escape attempt, she had been separated from the other children and placed here for punishment.

The little room was barely big enough for her to stretch out in and was surrounded on three sides with iron bars. The floor was made of cement, and dirty with dark stains where some form of liquid had sat till it had dried.

She shuddered when her mind wandered to what the stains could be and how they had come to be here. She shook her head, driving away the dark thoughts, and gingerly slid herself backwards till she was sitting with her back against the wall.

Dwelling on the unpleasant things that could happen to her would only make her more afraid, and she couldn't afford to allow herself to be distracted. She had to keep her wits about her and her mind free of fear if she wanted to survive this nightmare.

The wall she was now sitting against felt like it was made of stone, and a sturdy metal door that was always locked sat in the middle of it. The only other objects sharing the little room were a pot for her to use as a toilet and a filthy brown sleeping bag.

A narrow hallway stretched around her cell, leading from the main compound to the room that held the other side of the metal door. There was a small, barred window directly in front of her. Delicate tendrils of moonlight streamed in, providing a small amount of light. They illuminated the area, revealing fine particles of dust that danced like little pixies in the beams.

"Even in this place of horrors, there is beauty," she thought out loud.

A tear slowly dropped from one of her eyes, leaving a streak in the filth that stained her cheeks. Yes, there was beauty, but there was also horror. If only she hadn't tried to escape. If only she had been a good girl and done what she was told.

Try as she might, she could no longer hold back the thoughts of the farmer and his family. They had been murdered because of her. She could still hear their screams echoing in her mind. She shut her eyes and put her hands over her ears, trying to suppress the phantom wailing.

Famine

It didn't work and, unable to hold back the guilt and shame any longer, she placed her head between her knees and wept.

When she no longer had any tears left, she sat back up against the wall. She was exhausted and her stomach hurt from sobbing and lack of food. Her lips were cracked, and her throat was raw from crying. She moved her tongue around in her mouth, trying to create enough saliva to relieve the dryness. None came.

Sitting in the darkness, watching the beautiful moonlight dance of the dust fairies, she suddenly went rigid. Squinting, she peered into the shadows near the window.

"Who's there?"

Nothing. The silence was absolute and all she could see was the continued frolicking of the dust particles. Certain she had seen something move in the shadows, she slowly got up and quietly made her way towards the window and whatever was lurking there.

A thousand horrors flew through her mind, and she couldn't stop her heart from racing as she drew closer. Had they sent some new terror in to torment her?

Certainly, they had kidnapped her and the others for a reason. They wouldn't just kill her, would they? Of course, she had disobeyed them, and making an example of her might serve more of a purpose than keeping her alive.

Squinting from the low light, she scanned the area around the small window. She saw nothing but her dust fairies. No darker shape lurking just beyond the light. No nightmare waiting to torment her.

She exhaled long and slow, forcing the anxiety out with her breath. Feeling her heartbeat slowing she closed her eyes, willing her emotions to return to normal. It was just her imagination. A hallucination caused by hunger and dehydration, nothing more.

"Why are you in here?"

She jumped at the sound and let out a strangled cry. Her throat was too hoarse to muster anything more than a croak. For once, being dehydrated worked in her favor, since her scream would have woken the entire complex. As it was, however, the noise was barely more than a whimper.

Panic overcoming her, she fell onto her backside in a sitting position. Frantically she scooted herself backward along the floor and away from the voice. She didn't stop moving until she felt herself bump into the sturdy metal bars of the far cell wall.

"Shhh..." came a soft hiss from the darkness. "They will hear you."

Sophia blinked, staring into the darkness. Her heart still felt like it was trying to force its way out of her ribcage, but the shock of the moment was starting to ebb and she could feel herself calming down a bit.

Whoever or whatever this was, they didn't seem to be hostile. Of course, she knew full well the kinds of monsters that roamed these halls, and more than a few of them liked to toy with their prey.

"Sorry I scared you," the voice intoned from the darkness. "I didn't mean to."

Finally calm enough to notice, Sophia realized that the voice was that of a little girl. But that couldn't be, since as

Famine

far as she knew all the other children were locked up in the stables. Had one of them escaped?

"It's okay," she replied gently, trying not to spook the girl.

"Why are you in here?" the voice asked again. "No one ever comes in here."

Sophia grunted as she shifted her weight forward, away from the uncomfortable bars.

"I was...bad," she said, using simple words that any child would understand.

"Oh," replied the voice.

Sophia got to her feet and stretched. Trying not to be obvious, she nonchalantly gazed into the darkness, attempting to get a look at her mysterious visitor.

"May I ask your name?"

No reply, just silence.

Sophia still wasn't entirely sure that the girl wasn't a hallucination. After all, she had been deprived of food, water, and sleep for about a day now, and she hadn't had much of them before she had attempted to escape. Maybe she was finally losing it.

"Are you still there?" she asked.

"Yes," replied the girl.

"That's good," Sophia said gently. The girl seemed a bit skittish, and she didn't want to frighten her away.

There were a few seconds of silence before the girl spoke again.

"What did you do that was bad?"

Sophia smiled slightly.

"I escaped."

"You did?"

Sophia could hear the surprise in the girl's voice. No one escapes the compound. Well, physically at least. Death was always a constant companion here, and suicide a tempting way of escape from the nightmare.

"Yeah," she said, squinting into the shadows and trying in vain to get a glimpse of the girl. "I almost got away, too."

Sophia watched as two delicate, porcelain-colored hands materialized out of the shadows and reached out to rest on the bars.

"Really?" asked the child, her voice quivering slightly. "How?"

"Well," she said, a sly grin spreading across her face. "Give me your name and I'll tell you."

More silence.

"Kathleen," the girl finally replied. "But everyone calls me Kat."

"Well, Kat, I have small hands, you see."

She held out her arms to show the girl. Wincing from the million small cuts and bruises that lined her skin, she rotated her wrists.

"See, small hands and narrow wrists. When they put the cuffs on me I extended my fingers, causing my hands and wrists to get a little bigger. When they had gone, I simply closed my fingers and made my hands as small as I could. Then, *pop*, off they came."

She flexed her fingers, demonstrating the technique. The little girl let out a small gasp when she saw the mangled skin around her hands and wrists.

Famine

Sophia looked down at the raw, lacerated flesh, grimacing. One corner of her mouth quirked in an ironic half smile as she remembered just how painful it had really been getting those shackles off.

"Well," she said softly, "I guess they didn't just pop off, but they did come off."

Still smiling, she glanced up at Kat and her breath caught in her chest. Her hands flew up reflexively and she flinched backward, banging her head against the steel bars painfully.

To her horror, watching her through the bars across the small room was the emaciated white face of a little girl of about ten.

Her long, dirty, jet-black hair hung from her head like straw and stuck to her cheeks in matted clumps. Her thin, pale blue lips were parted, revealing long, wicked-looking fangs.

"Oh, God," Sophia gasped. "You're one of them. You're a vampire."

It wasn't the gaunt, corpse-like appearance of the girl that had startled Sophia, but rather it was the little girl's eyes that had frightened her. Massive, glowing-red orbs unblinkingly gazed at her from across the room.

These were the eyes of a predator. The eyes Sophia knew all too well. Unconsciously, her heart began to race as her fight or flight instinct kicked in.

Surprisingly, Kat showed no response to her sudden panic. With an unnatural stillness that unnerved Sophie, the little girl simply continued to watch her from across the room. If she was upset or thrilled by her terror, she was doing a good job of hiding it.

When Kat didn't move to attack her, Sophia realized that the little girl wasn't going to. Not yet anyway. Could it be possible that she wasn't one of the vampires that had kidnapped her? It would explain why she was down here hiding.

Famine

Maybe she had been turned by accident. She certainly was young. Too young to be of much use. If she was an unintended consequence of feeding, maybe instead of killing her they had simply set her free.

Too small to fend for herself amongst the others, she would eventually starve and die on her own. Problem solved without getting their hands dirty.

That wasn't a very comforting thought, however. If she was indeed starving, then she was very dangerous. Hunger made even normal humans desperate.

Whether she was one of the kidnappers or not, she was still a vampire. The little girl may not have attacked her yet, but she was still a threat, and Sophia knew she had to be very careful.

"What happened next?" Kat asked, breaking the silence.

It took Sophia a few minutes to compose herself and find her voice again. When she finally did, it cracked as she spoke.

"Uh...once I got the cuffs off," she continued, forcing her train of thought back on track. "I...I waited for dawn and then made a run for it."

Kat shifted slightly and finally blinked. It didn't make her look any less like a monster, but it did make her seem less like a lion sizing up its prey.

"I guess you didn't make it," Kat said, a hint of disappointment in her voice.

Sophia sighed and ran her hands through her matted hair.

"Nope. They caught me at the edge of the forest near a..." Her voice seized in midsentence as the memory of the previous night brought all the guilt and pain flooding back.

Wiping a few stray tears that had fallen despite her attempts to stop them, she cleared her throat and continued. "Near a small farm. The family there came out to see what was wrong. I tried to warn them, but..." Her voice trailed off again and she grew silent, unable to relive the horrible massacre.

Her silence was explanation enough. Kat nodded her head in acknowledgment that she understood the unspoken implications.

No one escaped the monsters that lived here. No one.

The conversation lapsed into a sullen silence, neither of them knowing what to say next. Sophia was strangely comforted by the little vampire's presence. It seemed like ages since she'd had someone else to talk to.

Sure, the other kids were always around, but most of them just cried. Those that didn't just sat quietly with dead, vacant eyes. No longer able or willing to beg for mercy or fight.

They were the ones that scared Sophia the most. The cries she understood. She had cried the first day as well. Being nineteen and a junior in college, most of the children here were younger than her. Too young to really understand what was happening to them.

The Hollows; that was what she had come to call the kids with that hundred-yard stare. They had given up. They had accepted their fate. There was no longer any hope in

Famine

their eyes, and that horrified Sophia. They were just shells of their former selves. Hollow.

An oppressive sense of despair grew in her heart. It was only a matter of time before she, too, would succumb to hopelessness and become hollow.

She hung her head and slumped forward, resting her head in her hands. It was only a matter of time. In the end she would die, or worse. What was the point of continuing to hold on to hope? No one was coming to help them, and if they did, they would face the same fate as the farmer and his family.

Rousing herself, she shook off the crippling thoughts. No. That would not happen to her. She wasn't a frightened little girl. She was a fighter. She had worked hard to get where she was. An all-state field hockey captain and one of the top students in the state.

No, she was a warrior, and she never gave up. Never. It didn't matter what she had to do; she would get out of this hell hole.

She gingerly stood to her feet, wincing at the pain in her head from where she had knocked it against the bars.

"If you don't mind me asking," she said, giving Kat a sideways glance. "Where did you come from?"

Kat blinked slowly and then looked away. "Sidney. I think."

Well, that answered one of her questions. Kat hadn't come here with the vampires. Like her, she had most likely been kidnapped and then turned by accident. It was probably wise not to ask, though.

Thinking of a better follow-up question, she asked, "Kat, how long have you been here?"

Kat blinked a few times before turning back to look at her. She cocked her head to one side and her eyes took on a far-off gaze.

After a few seconds of thought, she suddenly fixed her gaze on Sophia.

"A very long time."

Sophia scrunched her forehead. "How long?"

"I don't know. I can't remember."

Kat looked away again as she spoke, avoiding Sophia's eyes. She was clearly uncomfortable answering questions about herself.

"If you don't want to talk about it, I understand," Sophia said gently.

"It's okay," Kat replied, still not looking at her. "I don't mind."

Sophia ran her teeth over her lower lip and sighed. No matter what Kat said, Sophia could tell she was apprehensive. She scrunched up her face as she scrutinized the little girl. She had to be tactful about how she proceeded if she didn't want to push her away.

"Well, can you remember anything about your family? Your mother, father, or maybe brothers and sisters?"

Kat's brow furrowed and Sophia noticed that her lip was quivering.

Crap.

She had stupidly jumped right to a question that was obviously going to be painful for her. What was she thinking?

Famine

"I'm sorry," she said softly. "I didn't mean to upset you."

Kat sniffed and ran a hand over her eyes. She blinked rapidly before turning her head slightly to look at Sophia.

"It's okay. I just haven't thought about them in a long time. They seem like a dream to me now. You know, like when you wake up and everything you just dreamed is all fuzzy."

Sophia nodded.

"It's like that when I try to think of them," Kat continued. "I can sort of see them and remember them, but not really. Like a dream that's all over. All except..."

She trailed off and turned her head away again. This time, however, Sophia could feel her retreating internally. It was very clear that whatever she had been about to say was something she didn't want to relive.

Sophia understood that feeling all too well. Especially when she thought about the farmer and his family. Shuddering involuntarily at the memory, she pushed it from her mind and continued.

"Well, then, maybe there is something else you can remember," she said, changing the subject. "Like what events were happening in the world at the time you were...taken?"

Kat seemed to brighten up a bit, her dark mood lifting slightly.

"I don't know." She shrugged. "You mean like who won the World Series and stuff like that?"

"Sure," Sophia replied with a smile. "Anything you can remember. It will give me a good idea of how long you've been here."

"Umm..." Kat murmured to herself, her eyebrows rising slightly. "I think the Mets won the World Series last. I remember my dad let me stay up late to watch the games. I don't really care about baseball, but if I told him I wanted to watch the games then I got to stay up past my bedtime."

The Mets? It has been over thirty years since they won! 1986, if I remember right.

Sophia's mouth dropped open, and she just stared at the little girl. She didn't know what to say. She had to be mistaken about the Mets. She had to be. There was no way she had been here over thirty years. Had she?

Regaining her composure, she decided to ask some follow-up questions for clarification.

"Kat, do you remember who the President was?"

Kat thought for a minute and then shook her head.

Of course not, you idiot. She was like, eight, when she was kidnapped. You've got to think of something an eight-year-old would know.

Her eyes lit up and she smiled. Snapping her fingers and then pointing at Kat, she said, "I've got it. What was your favorite cartoon?"

Every kid watched cartoons, and every generation had their favorites. Her favorite had been *Sponge Bob* along with around eighty percent of kids her age. Her dad's had been *Super Friends*. Every kid had their favorite, and she was betting so did Kat.

Famine

Kat's red eyes seemed to brighten. "I like *She-Ra*. She's my favorite. I wanted to be just like her. A powerful princess who protected people."

She smiled a big smile at the memory, and it made her look a lot more like a little girl.

"I used to run around my yard with a stick as a sword," she continued, whipping her hand through the air as if she was brandishing a blade. "Me and my brother would play He-Man all day long after school."

She stopped abruptly at the mention of her brother. Tears welled up in her eyes once again and her bottom lip began to quiver. She quickly looked away when she noticed Sophia looking at her.

Sophia waited a few seconds before speaking again. "What was your brother's name?"

Sniffing loudly, Kat wiped her nose on one of her sleeves. "Mike."

"Was he younger than you?"

"No, we were the same age."

Sophie blinked a few times. "He's your twin brother?"

She nodded.

"Looks just like me, but a boy."

Wow, she had a twin brother. Maybe he was still alive out there somewhere, waiting for her to come home. It was possible her family was still looking for her.

Sophie really didn't follow baseball, so she could be wrong about the last time the Mets had been in the World Series. So that was not a very good measure of how long Kat had been here.

She kind of remembered her mother mentioning She-Ra, but her parents still watched cartoons as adults so that wasn't much help either. Maybe Kat could remember something that had more of a concrete date to it.

Before she had a chance to ask another question, Kat's eyes went wide and she snapped her head in the direction of the door to the main living area.

"What is it?" Sophia asked, subconsciously lowering her voice to a whisper.

"Someone is coming," Kat replied quietly. "I have to go. I'm sorry."

Kat drew her hands back and seemed to melt into the shadows like a wraith. The last thing to disappear were Kat's haunting red eyes. They seemed to linger in the air for a few seconds before finally fading away.

"Wait," Sophia hissed after here. "Who's coming?"

"Mother," came her reply. It was more of a whisper in the wind than a voice, and it sent chills down Sophia's spine.

Jared stepped out of the shadows and into the low light of the basement. He was standing only a few feet from the man he assumed was the father.

The boy was lying protectively over the little girl, his small arms covering his head from the blows that he knew would inevitably come. Even if he died, he was determined to protect his sister.

The little girl was crying, and her dirty face was streaked with tears. She was grunting and breathing heavily as she tried to push her brother off.

"No, Danny. He's going to hurt you if you don't get away."

Danny ignored her pleas and stayed where he was. His red and white striped t-shirt was ripped at one arm, and his red pajama pants stretched and slid around on his frame as he repositioned his legs for a stronger hold.

"Kill him already," the strange voice he had heard earlier hissed.

It didn't take long for Jared to locate the source of the mysterious voice. Attached to the father's large frame was a hideous, snakelike creature.

Black as the night and covered in scales, the monster's long worm-like body was wrapped around the large man's torso. Two small, batlike wings fluttered absently each time the coils contracted.

The head, which was humanoid with massive bulbous yellow eyes and two small ebony horns, was positioned directly next to the man's left ear. Its forked, yellow tongue flicked with each hissing word it spoke.

"Do it. Do it now. You know you desire to."

This time when the creature spoke, Jared noticed that both the demon's and the man's eyes glowed the same sickly yellow.

The father scowled and let out a low growl in response to the creature's beguiling spell.

"If you don't move right now, boy, I'm going to kill you."

He twirled the bat and smacked it twice in his palm for emphasis.

"I'll give you to the count of three to move."

As Jared took in the scene, his eyes fixed on the big man. Before he knew what was happening the dark gaze activated, and he was instantly transfixed.

The world around him gradually slowed and then came to a stop. Jared couldn't tear his eyes away as every hidden moment of the man's life unfolded before him.

Famine

He was not the children's real father, but rather their stepfather. He had married their mother after their true father had been killed overseas while in the military.

At first, he was a caring and good stepdad, and they had loved him. What they didn't know, however, was that the man hid a dark side, and after a year of happy marriage his relationship with their mother changed.

It started with him increasing the depravity of what he asked his wife to do. She agreed and even enjoyed it at first, until his desires became more and more violent and humiliating. Insecure, afraid, and feeling trapped, the woman gave in to his ever-growing sexual appetite until all her dignity was gone. In the end, there was nothing left of her but a hollow shell that resembled a person.

The children saw the bruises and watched as their mother changed and became distant, until she was no longer emotionally there. She turned into a ghost, gliding through life as an echo of her former self. Then, tired of the mother, the man turned his eyes on the daughter.

It was at this time that the creature came. Drawn by the man's depraved imaginations, it had wrapped itself around his soul—intensifying his emotions and driving him farther and farther into wickedness. What had only been passing thoughts now turned into overwhelming compulsion. No, it hadn't controlled the man but rather pushed his emotions, encouraging him into more and more vile actions.

Knowing what was coming Jared growled and tried to force away the images, but Tzedakah wouldn't allow it. His stomach lurched and rage welled up in him as he was forced to watch as the man repeatedly did unthinkable things to the little girl.

For the rest of reality, it was only a fraction of a second, but for Jared it felt like an eternity. He had seen enough, and he silently pleaded with the sword to stop the images.

It refused, and the images continued to come.

"No!" Jared's mind screamed. "Please, I can't watch anymore."

He tried to move, but his limbs wouldn't obey him. He had to get away, had to make the images stop, but his body refused to move no matter how much he fought. Still the images flowed, until his mind couldn't take it any longer.

Then it happened, like someone had thrown a switch somewhere deep in his subconscious. Every thought, every objection, fled from his mind, and all that remained was calm, cold fury. Jared the man, the cop, the human being, was gone and all that was left was Justice.

The disturbing images ended, but Jared didn't notice. His eyes were fixed on the man. No, the vile monster. This creature was not a man, not a living, breathing, human being. He was a monster. A monster that had eluded justice for too long. A monster that needed to be destroyed.

Time reasserted itself and the world snapped back into motion. This time he didn't oppose Tzedakah but allowed the sentient sword in willingly. Somewhere deep in his subconscious he knew he should protest, or at least ask more questions, but he was beyond that now.

"Okay, boy," the man spat. "I warned you."

The little girl screamed, and the boy closed his eyes and whimpered softly in anticipation but never moved.

Famine

The man raised his arm, and with a wicked sneer drew his arm back to strike. Jared moved then, too fast for mortal eyes to see, and placed himself between the man and the children.

He raised Tzedakah with one arm, and with a resounding clang stopped the metal bat midflight. Startled, the man's face screwed up into a mask of confusion and the little girl's screams caught in her throat.

To the other people in the room, it seemed like Jared had materialized out of thin air. Terrifying and emanating an aura of wrath that was palpable, Jared looked like a spirit of death.

"What the?" said the man.

The darkness in Jared's eyes writhed angrily, reaching out towards the man. He said nothing in reply but turned his head to look down at the huddled children.

Sensing that something was happening, the boy dared a quick peek. His face went pale when he saw Jared watching him. The soft blue glow of Tzedakah added to the ethereal effect, making Jared look even more like a terrible spirit from the netherworld.

A low growl thrummed deep in Jared's throat, and he turned his attention back to the father. The man's face was pale with fear, and sweat had begun dripping down the sides of his fat face.

The man swallowed.

"Who the hell are you and what are you doing in my house?"

Jared regarded the man coldly, but still said nothing.

"No," hissed the creature. "No. No. No."

Jared had forgotten about the creature that had latched onto the man, and he shifted his eyes to examine it.

As soon as his eyes locked on the thing, he knew instantly what it was. An Alastor, a demon of lust. He didn't care what its name was, it was of no consequence. It was nothing more than a nuisance.

He flicked his free hand and Tzedakah flashed. A muzzle of blue energy appeared over the creature's mouth, silencing it. The Alastor thrashed its head wildly, trying in vain to dislodge the muzzle.

Tzedakah thrummed in his hand, and he could feel power flowing from it and into him. Jared flicked his hand again and the creature's wings burst into blue flames and disintegrated. It fell to the floor, flailing in agony.

With a final twitch of his fingers, blue-glowing chains snaked up from the floor and wrapped themselves around the creature. They continued to tighten around the demon until it finally exploded in a cloud of sickly yellow mist, leaving only a faint trace of brimstone that lingered stubbornly in the air.

Without expression he turned his eyes back to the man. None of the mortals could see what had just happened, but he did notice that the man seemed to stand a little taller as if a weight had been removed from his shoulders. The yellow glow in his eyes had also subsided.

Blinking rapidly, he stumbled backward and nearly fell over. The man grabbed his head with his free hand and his eyes glazed over as he stared blankly at Jared.

"What?" he sputtered. "What?"

"Franklin Wadsworth," Jared heard himself say.

Famine

His voice was strange and ethereal and no longer resembled that of a human. It was the voice of a wraith. The voice of death. The voice of the Spirit of Justice.

"You have been judged and found guilty."

Jared's voice brought the man back to his senses and he sneered. He raised the bat and pointed it at Jared.

"Mister, I don't know who you are, but if you think you can walk into my house and threaten me, you've got another thing coming.'"

The darkness in Jared's eyes writhed angrily, and he set his jaw.

"For the defilement of the innocent, for the abuse of your wife and your stepchildren, and for many more sins, I sentence you to death."

Jared's words hung in the air with a dreadful sense of finality, and the man's face went instantly pale.

Franklin's eyes went wide, and his breathing quickened. Like an animal that senses doom is at hand, his eyes darted back and forth as if looking for an avenue of escape.

"W-W-Who are you to judge me?" he whimpered, the hand holding the bat shaking uncontrollably. He gripped it with both hands in order to keep himself from dropping it.

"I am Justice," was Jared's simpe reply.

The man gritted his teeth and growled, breathing in and out heavily.

"Justice? Ha!" the man spat, regaining a measure of courage. "You're like all the rest. Like the teachers and cops. You don't understand our love and you never will. You call

JW Kiefer

it immoral and evil, but it's nothing like that. I love the girl and she loves me, and what we do is pure and right."

He spat on the floor and glared at Jared, but his hands still shook as he adjusted his grip on the bat.

Jared said nothing.

"Nothing to say to that? Self-righteous people like you never do. If you don't believe me, just ask the girl."

He lifted the bat and pointed it at his stepdaughter.

"Tell him, darling. Tell him how much you enjoy what we do."

Jared turned his gaze back to the two children. They were both still on the floor, but now the little boy had placed himself in front of his sister.

He had one hand out protectively and the other reaching backward, covering his sister. His eyes were wide with fear, but his mouth was set in a grimace of resolve.

All Jared saw of the little girl were her terrified eyes as they peered out at from behind her brother's shoulder.

She whimpered and shied away from the big man, burying her face deeper into her brother's shoulder.

Jared had seen enough, and he turned his gaze back to Franklin. He raised Tzedakah and pointed it at the man. The sword's glow grew in intensity, and it vibrated violently in his grip.

"Darling," the man whimpered, his voice pleading. "Come on, Sandra, tell him. You know you love me, and I love you. Tell him. Please."

The girl broke out into uncontrollable sobs at the man's words.

"Sandra," he growled, "Tell hi..."

149

Famine

The man's words were cut off before he could finish his sentence. His mouth continued to move, but no words came. His eyes darted back and forth until they locked on the little girl.

They remained focused on Sandra as a thin red line appeared on his neck. His eyes never left the girl as his head slowly slipped to one side and fell to the floor with a sickening splat.

Blood spurted from the stump as the body unceremoniously dropped to floor in a heap. The air was filled with a sweet, metallic sent as blood poured from the gaping wound, pooling around the corpse.

Jared stood with his sword arm held outward. His movements had been too fast for mortal eyes to see, and the man had never seen the strike that had killed him.

It was a merciful death and one the man didn't deserve. Somewhere deep in Jared's mind he knew he should be appalled at what he had just done. He wasn't even shocked, and that worried him. No, all he felt was grim satisfaction.

He sighed and lowered Tzedakah, turning to look at the children.

Danny's face was white as a ghost and his eyes were wide with horror and fixed on the dead man lying just a few feet away from him. His mouth was locked open in a silent scream, but no sound would come.

He turned his face to look at Jared, who had taken a few steps towards him, then seemed to come to his senses. Pushing his sister even farther behind him, he stuck out his chest.

"D-D-Don't come any closer," he stuttered.

Jared got down on one knee till he was eye level with the boy. Tzedakah's glow softened as he looked the boy in the eye. Just as he was about to speak, a loud shriek came from behind him.

Jared turned his head slightly to see who or what was screaming. Standing at the bottom of the stairs was a middle-aged woman. Her brown hair hung down around her face in a jumbled, uncontrolled mass, and her dark eyes were full of panic in the low light of the cellar.

Her pink nightgown rustled slightly as she took a step forward. One pale hand, its fingernails bitten down to nubs, was held up to her mouth. She was gaunt, her cheek bones hollow and sunken. This woman had seen much in her life, and it had taken its toll on her.

Her eyes were locked on the corpse that lay only a few inches from Jared. He followed her gaze, noticing the growing pool of blood that he was now kneeling in. Somewhere deep in his mind he knew he should shy away from the liquid, but he didn't.

The woman turned her gaze to the children. Her eyes filling with fear as she raised one hand toward Jared.

"I don't know who you are, mister," she begged softly. "But please don't hurt my babies."

She moved a few steps closer, her bare feet making soft plopping sounds on the cement floor. Both her hands were held up now, and she crouched slightly as if she was trying to calm a wild animal.

"You can take whatever you want. I won't stop you. Just leave my kids alone."

Jared turned his head to look at the children. Danny was breathing heavily and still held his sister behind him protectively. Sandra's blue eyes and a few strands of her golden hair were all that was visible from behind her brother.

Jared frowned and turned his head back to the woman. He knew her name instantly. Cecelia. She was the children's mother. Tzedakah was oddly silent, but his glow increased slightly as the women took a few steps closer.

"Please, I'm begging you. Let my children go."

She got down on one knee and beckoned to her children.

"Danny, Sandra, come here, babies. It's okay. The man won't hurt you. Just come here to Mommy."

The kids didn't move.

Cecilia's breathing increased and her voice grew a little more frantic. "Children, please, it will be okay. The man will let you past him."

She glanced at Jared, her eyes pleading. "Right, mister? You won't hurt them, will you?"

Jared squinted at the woman and then turned his head slightly to look at the children.

Famine

Why hadn't they gone to their mother? He wasn't going to hurt them. Of course, if he had shown up at his house and killed his father when he was their age he would probably be locked up with fear as well.

The mother began to sob quietly, unable to control her emotions any longer. Her voice grew more frantic with each passing second.

"Please, babies, just come here. It will be okay. I promise. Mister, please tell them you won't hurt them."

Jared slowly stood up. The woman went rigid, and her breathing became erratic. He could feel the raw pain and terror pouring off her, and it was beginning to influence him. The cold certainty of Tzedakah drained away as he watched the mother, and the kindhearted Jared slowly returned.

The magnitude of what he had just done still hadn't sunk in, but he was beginning to feel more himself. He sighed and his shoulders relaxed. He stepped away from the children, careful to avoid the corpse of their stepfather.

A surge of anger and revolution played across his face as he walked past the dead man. No, dead monster. He still hated the man for what he had done. He may be coming back to himself, but his feelings on what he had done to the man—no, what needed to be done—hadn't changed.

He shook his head and then turned his dark eyes to the children.

"It's okay," he said, his voice soft and ethereal. "I won't hurt you. You can go to your mother."

The kids still didn't move. Eventually, Danny tore his gaze from Jared and looked at his mother. His lower lip began to quiver, and he could no longer stop the tears.

Rubbing his eyes so he could see better, he slowly inched towards his mother, making sure his sister was always between him and Jared. As soon as they reached her, they instantly threw themselves into her arms and all three began to weep uncontrollably.

Jared sighed as he watched the little family. Danny was clutching both his mother and his sister, still placing himself between them and him. Even now, he was brave enough to try and protect them. Sandra was crying and had her face buried in her mother's chest.

"It's okay now, babies," she cooed softly. "It's okay. It's all over. You're safe."

Yes, Jared thought to himself. *They are.*

But would they be okay? They had endured something no child should ever have to endure. They had seen things no child should have to see. No, there would be lasting consequences.

Sure, he had stopped their stepfather. Stopped him from hurting them ever again, but at what cost? He had murdered the man right in front of them. No adult, let alone a child, could see that and not be scarred for life.

He still had no doubt that what he had done was right. At least, he thought he was sure. Was it Jared that was sure, or Tzedakah? Could he even tell the difference anymore?

He raised the glowing blade till it was only inches from his face. The blue-black glow from the sword illuminated his face, washing away all color.

Famine

"We are going to have to have a long talk after this," Jared whispered. "A *very* long talk."

He pursed his lips and sighed, looking up from the sword to the reunited family. As soon as he locked eyes on the mother, it hit him. The dark gaze.

It struck with such intensity that it took his breath away. He staggered to one side and had to reach out to a nearby wall to steady himself.

"No," he breathed. "No."

"Yes" replied the sword coldly. "We are not finished here."

Time began to slow around him, and he knew what was coming. He fought against Tzedakah, mentally throwing up every protest he could, but the sword destroyed them all. It broke down every mental wall he erected, leaving him bear to what he knew was coming.

Cecilia had not been a bad child. She had done her best to obey her parents. Sure, she was rambunctious, as any child could be, but overall she was a good kid.

Jared watched as she opened presents on Christmas mornings. Reveled in the smell of baked cookies and spiced hot cider. Watched as she had snuck into her parents' room when she was old enough to know Santa wasn't real. Stealing a glimpse of her and her siblings' presents.

Tzedakah seemed to notice the times she lied or disobeyed. He felt every twinge as he watched her every misstep. Jared mentally chastised the sentient sword for finding such trivial things disturbing.

The scene changed; she was a young woman now. A cheerleader in high school. She desperately wanted the attention of one of the baseball players. Sam was his name, and he was handsome. He felt his heart flutter with hers when he asked her out on their first date.

Jared continued to watch as the couple got married young. Watched as their two children came. Felt the same joy at seeing their first steps and hearing their first words. She was not a perfect woman, but she wasn't evil.

Then it happened. Terrorists had attacked New York City. Sam's father and mother both worked in the Towers, and both had lost their lives there. Sam needed to avenge his parents' death. Needed to do something. So, against her wishes, he joined the army and went away to war. Went away and never came home.

Jared gritted his teeth, trying to push away the waves of grief and hopelessness that washed over him. Tried not to watch as Cecilia lost herself in her sorrow and turned to drugs and alcohol. Became abusive.

Just when he thought she would break and destroy herself and her children, he came. Franklin had driven away the pain and made life bearable again. She got help with her addictions and was able to love her kids again. He loved her and her children through the worst parts of her recovery.

Then it happened, gradually and not all at once. Franklin began to change. He became more and more sexually depraved. Forcing her to watch porn and to do things she found demeaning. At first it wasn't so bad, but then it turned violent.

Jared knew this was when the demon had latched onto him. After a few minutes of watching Franklin beat, mentally torment, and rape her he pleaded for the visions to stop. They didn't and only became more and more vile.

Years and years of torment eventually wore the woman down, until nothing was left. Nothing but a hollow shell. Her beauty faded, leaving a husk of a woman. If Jared had hated Franklin before, what he was seeing only validated those feelings.

What was Tzedakah doing? This woman was a victim. Sure, she had been abusive to her children, but mentally not physically. All she was guilty of was being absent and not being a very good mother, nothing worthy of judgement.

Then it happened. One night she awoke, to find her husband was gone. Slowly she rose and silently walked out to look for him. She found him in Sandra's room.

At first, she wanted to run into the room and kill the man, but just as she was about to burst in she stopped. Maybe the answer to her endless torment was before her. Maybe, if she simply walked away and pretended not to see, he would finally leave her alone.

Making up her mind, and sick inside, she slowly closed the door and went back to her room. She laid back down but couldn't sleep. She could hear her daughter's sobs coming down the hall and covered her head with her pillow, trying to muffle her daughter's cries.

She was a terrible mother, she knew, but she just couldn't do it anymore. If her daughter was the price she had to pay for her sanity, then so be it. She closed her eyes, but sleep didn't come. Sleep would never come easily again.

"Oh, God, no!" Jared cried. "No! Please, God, no!"

The change came then, just as it had before. All pity and empathy fled, leaving only hatred at the injustice she had committed. The injustice she had turned a blind eye to and allowed to happen.

The world snapped back to life around him and he took a deliberate step toward the woman. Tzedakah burst to life in his hands, waves of brilliant blue-black light illuminating his features.

He raised the sentient sword and pointed it at the woman. The darkness in his nightmare- black eyes writhed and seethed, reaching out towards the woman as if it would suck her in.

"Cecelia Wadsworth," he said, his voice more of a rasping wind than a human voice. "I find you guilty of the injustice of allowing your children to be abused by their stepfather, and many more sins that need not be named."

His words, even though ethereal, rang throughout the room with such terrible finality that the woman froze. Both children's faces went pale, and they turned to look at Jared. They had seen what he had done to their father and knew what was about to happen.

"What?" Cecelia replied, fear making its way into her voice.

Danny turned and placed himself between his mother and Jared. As brave as ever, the little boy trembled, and Jared noticed that wetness had appeared in the front of his red pajama pants.

Even though he was obviously terrified, the little boy would not move. Would not run away.

Famine

"Mom," he stuttered. "Run. Take Sandra and get away."

Jared took another step towards the little family.

"Cecelia Wadsworth, I find you guilty of unjust acts, and actions leading to unjust acts. I sentence you to death."

Jared raised Tzedakah, but the boy would not move. Would not leave his mother.

"Mom," he pleaded, his voice still cracking. "Get Sandra and go."

"What are you talking about?" she replied. "I'm not leaving you."

Sandra continued to cry, her sobs loud and uncontrolled.

"Danny, what are you doing?" she asked between sobs. "Don't! He'll kill you."

Jared felt Tzedakah's anger toward the boy for getting in his way. Didn't he understand that this needed to be done? Didn't the boy understand what his mother was?

Jared growled and raised his hand, planning on knocking the boy aside. How dare he come between him and the unjust.

The boy did not move but closed his eyes and flinched, waiting for the blow. It never came. The boy's courage had somehow reached Jared through the torrent of Tzedakah's emotions. Through the raging whirlwind that was Tzedakah's need to bring justice.

The boy opened his eyes and saw Jared's hand only inches from his face. His breathing was still fast and heavy, but Jared could see the relief and confusion on the boy's face.

"Go," he growled through gritted teeth, his voice still hollow and ethereal. "Take your mother and sister and get as far away as you can."

The boy was too frightened to move, and he just stared at Jared.

"Go!" Jared shouted. "I can't hold him for much longer."

Sandra, still crying, also knew what was about to happen, and she grabbed her mother's night gown and started pulling.

"Mom," she pleaded. "We have to get out of here now."

Confused and usure of what was happening, Cecelia's maternal instincts finally kicked in. She scooped both her children up and, with a strength born of desperation, made a beeline for the stairs.

Jared screamed as Tzedakah's fury slammed into his mind like a freight train. He stumbled to the side and nearly fell over as waves of emotion poured over him.

"What are you doing?" he accused. His words were physically painful for Jared, and each word was like being struck with a hammer.

"She doesn't need to die!" Jared shot back. "She was as much a victim as the children."

"She stood by while her husband abused the girl. She allowed it to save herself. What greater evil can a mother commit than to allow her children to be defiled in her stead?"

Jared moaned as more waves of agony swept over him. He realized Tzedakah wasn't trying to hurt him; he had simply opened so much of himself to him that Jared felt just

Famine

how powerful Tzedakah's emotions were. Just how powerful the need to bring justice was.

The more he fought against it, the more painful it would be. He lived because the sword willed it. He didn't truly understand it all yet, but he did know that the sword needed him. Not just as a host, but it needed for him to understand. Understand why they did what they did. Why it existed.

Jared tried to understand, but he couldn't just let Tzedakah kill the children's mother. Yes, what she had done was unforgivable, but she was a victim, too. He had to understand that. Jared had to make him see.

"Tzedakah, she's a victim, too," Jared said softly. "Don't you understand? Yes, it was unforgivable what she did, but she was broken. Broken by the same monster that abused the girl. Can't you understand that?"

Tzedakah was silent, and Jared thought that he had managed to reach him. Thought maybe he had helped him see that not everything was black and white.

"I am sorry, Jared," Tzedakah said, genuine regret in his voice.

And then the world went black.

ophia watched as the small room filled with a familiar white mist. She hugged herself with both arms and vigorously rubbed up and down, trying to fend off the growing chill.

The sound of her teeth chattering echoed in the little room, and each breath hung in the air like little frozen clouds. Tears stung her eyes as a blast of frigid air whipped through the room, causing her hair to lash about her head and into her eyes. The cold made her sluggish, and she was shaking so hard it was impossible for her to brush it away from her face.

Just when she thought she would pass out from the cold, the wind subsided and a modicum of warmth returned. Sighing with relief she shifted her weight, allowing her shoulders to relax.

Famine

She wasn't alone any longer. The wind had gone, but it left something in its place. Something worse. She felt the creature's eyes boring into her without even looking at it.

She didn't have to see to know what it was that had come. It was the thing Kat had called 'Mother'. She knew her as Lady Fuyuko, the White Lady. The creature she hated most in this God- forsaken place.

"Who was here?" asked Fuyuko. "The faint smell of someone else lingers in the air."

Sophia grunted, shifting her weight, but didn't reply.

She felt the woman's eyes fix on her and bore into her. An unpleasant pressure slowly grew in her mind, causing her head to throb.

"I asked you a question, child."

Sophia gritted her teeth and refused to answer. She wasn't going to give her the satisfaction of an answer. Not after what she had done to the farmer and his family.

Pain flashed over her, hot and intense, and she screamed. The world went red, and she forgot about the cold and her nakedness. All that existed at that moment was pure, white-hot agony.

She didn't really know how long she had been screaming or when she had stopped, but her throat was dry and raw as if she had been shouting for a long time. Smacking her lips, she tried to drum up saliva to relieve the pain in her throat, but she had none.

She was lying on the floor face down, but she had no memory of how she had gotten there. She planted her hands and tried to push herself up, but a sudden wave of nausea sent her tumbling back to the ground.

"Child, why must you try my patience so?"

Sophia turned her head in the direction of the voice and saw two perfect bare feet, their manicured toes clenching slightly. The porcelain skin of the Asian vampire glowed softly, creating a near-translucent appearance.

Grunting, Sophia pushed herself over until she was lying on her back looking up at the woman. Everything hurt, especially her head.

She placed one arm over her eyes and groaned. "I guess I'm just a glutton for punishment. It's why I joined the cheer squad."

Fuyuko exhaled loudly. Sophie was still covering her eyes, but she could imagine the look of disappointment on the woman's face. It made her smile. It was a small victory, but in this hell she took what she could get.

"Honestly, love, I do not know why you persist in your insolence. Your stay here would be far more pleasant."

"Like I said," Sophia replied with a hint of sarcasm in her voice. "I'm a masochist."

"No, my dear," the vampire said softly. "Trust me on this, you are not. But you may learn to become one in time. Everyone breaks eventually. Everyone."

If Sophia wasn't mistaken, this last word was spoken with an underlying sense of sadness. She shifted her arm just enough to allow one eye to peek out.

Fuyuko was not looking at her and her eyes were vacant. The woman's mind was obviously somewhere else. Her brow was furrowed and her eyes sad, as if she were reliving some long-ago event that still haunted her.

Famine

Sophia furrowed her brow and chewed on her lower lip. This woman was obviously a monster, she knew that all too well. But at times, she seemed to be almost human.

Sophia moved her arm and tried to sit up. Pain shot through her head, sending more waves of nausea. She burped and choked but held on to what little she had in her stomach.

It took her longer than it should, but she eventually managed to sit up and prop her back against the bars. Panting from the exertion, she sat with her eyes closed and one hand massaging her temples.

When she finally managed to recover enough to look around, she noticed that Lady Fuyuko was watching her.

Their eyes met and Sophia couldn't help but notice how beautiful the vampire's eyes were. Almond-shaped and so light a hue of blue that they almost appeared translucent. Her long lashes never seemed to move even when she blinked, which wasn't often, and appeared as if they were made of delicate icicles.

They were so big and lovely. She had never seen their like before. Like little pools of freezing water that she wanted to lose herself in.

So deep. I wonder how far they go.

She wanted to find out. Wanted to swim in them until she drowned. Her heart ached with a longing that took her breath away, and she gasped.

Lady Fuyuko smiled, and it was like the sun had just broken through the clouds on a gloomy winter's day. She was so lovely. Her teeth gleaned like pearls and her lips were the color of fresh roses. The faint, crisp smell of arctic air caused Sophia to smile at memories of winters long past.

"So lovely," she heard herself murmur.

Lady Fuyuko glided straight through the bars as if they were illusions and hovered over Sophia. She moved until her face was so close to Sophia's that she could feel her breath on her neck, and she shivered involuntarily when it touched her skin.

Lady Fuyuko's eyes grew so enormous that they eclipsed the world. Everything else faded away and all that remained were those haunting eyes. So big. So blue. So fathomless. So beautiful.

"Now, child," Lady Fuyuko purred. "Who was here? You can tell me. I will not be angry with you."

Something deep in her subconscious objected. A small voice that cried out in warning in the back of her mind. But those eyes. So big. So wonderful.

"I...I..." she heard herself stutter.

"Yes, child," purred Fuyuko. She reached out and gently brushed the fingers of her right hand against Sophia's cheek. "You can tell me. You want to tell me, do you not?"

"It was..."

But before she could finish her sentence, a man's voice boomed into her subconscious.

"Enough!"

Sophia and Lady Fuyuko gasped in unison from the sudden intrusion. The world snapped back into focus around Sophia, and she felt her stomach lurch in protest.

Groggily, she looked around and found that she was still sitting against the bars of her cell. The salty, musky smell of perspiration hung in the air, and she shivered as the cold of the room once again reasserted itself.

Was she wet? Yes, she was covered in a slick layer of sweat that ate up the cold like a sponge. She drew her legs in and hugged herself, trying to drive away the cold. The throbbing in her temples returned, and she groaned and had to squint her eyes from the pain.

"Orokana otoko," Lady Fuyuko spat.

Sophia turned her head towards the noise, closing one eye and scrunching her brow as she did. Lady Fuyuko was standing just outside of her cell, one hand resting against the bars and the other massaging her temples.

"I swear," she moaned. "Even after a thousand years that man still has no understanding of his own mental strength."

"Do I not?" asked the voice from before. "Perhaps I do and simply wanted to make a point."

Fuyuko let out a low hiss in reply. She shook her head, trying to clear the fog left from the broken mental spell.

It was then that Sophia noticed they were no longer alone. Where the door to the outer rooms should be there was now a dark shape. Light seemed to bend away from it like a school of fish avoiding danger.

Sophia watched as the darkness moved into the room. It flowed like mist until it came to rest directly before her cell. With each graceful movement, the darkness shifted and contorted until it was replaced by a huge bear of a man.

Sophia's heart began to race, and her breath caught in her chest. Blinking rapidly at the pounding in her temples, she couldn't prevent her eyes from going wide in terror.

The man turned his head and looked down at her with a grimace. He pursed his full ruby-red lips and scowled. His bright blue eyes seemed to bore into Sophia's very soul and she cowered, trying to push herself through the bars.

Sophia may have hated lady Fuyuko, but she was a kitten compared to the man who just materialized. Lady Fuyuko was certainly a monster, but this man, Lord Durgala, was a monster of biblical proportions.

"Did you have to intrude so abruptly?" Lady Fuyuko asked through gritted teeth. "You could have killed the girl."

The man raised one eyebrow and turned his head slightly toward the White Lady. Sophia gasped for breath as soon as the man's gaze was broken, and she realized she had been holding it.

The pressure of the man's presence didn't go away, but it did diminish slightly when his direct attention was drawn away from her. She slumped down, too exhausted to move, and simply listened as the two monsters talked.

Lord Durgala waved a hand dismissively. "The girl is of no consequence. If she dies, she dies."

Fuyuko shook her head. "Ever the fool. Tell me, oh great one, how long do you think we can keep this place a secret? How long can people go missing before someone takes notice?"

"Ve are careful and always have been. Never taking more than is necessary and never being impatient or impulsive."

He shook his head. "No, Fuyu, it has been one for almost a hundred years and will continue to be a secret until we no longer have need of it."

Famine

"Yes, but this age is different. They have technology that rivals the elder days," replied Fuyuko with a bit of scorn in her voice. "The girl already escaped once, and what had to be done was messy and loud and will undoubtedly bring the attention of the local authorities."

"Fuyu, do not worry. I am a diplomat, and I own this land, which places it under diplomatic protection. They would not dare invade my private sanctuary. Their laws prevent them."

"As they did in Romania?" she asked.

The man's eyes grew hard. "Do not test me, witch. You are easily replaced."

Fuyuko's eyebrows shot up and she sneered. "With the blonde child? I think not."

"She is more powerful than you realize, Fuyu. Already she can do things that it takes most of us decades to learn. My gut tells me that she is the one we have been searching for."

"She is a child," Fuyuko spat back, turning on the man. "Do not let your lust for the girl's ample...assets cloud your judgment."

Lord Durgala let out a low chuckle. "Jealousy does not become you, Fu."

"Nor does infatuation you."

The big man raised his massive hands in a placating gesture. "Peace, Fuyu. I am not taken with the girl's beauty. I simply have hope that this time we may have finally found the right one."

Fuyuko sighed.

"You have said that a thousand times, and a thousand times you have been wrong."

"True," the big man grunted. "But all I have to be is right one time."

He put his hands down and gently rested them on Fuyuko's shoulders. She turned her head away from the man, her lips pressed together, and her brow furrowed.

"Fuyu, you know what my goal is. No, what my dream is. That has never changed. Everything I do, no matter how cruel, is for our kind. For our children and for their children."

Fuyu sighed and looked up at the man. He smiled reassuringly down at her.

"Trust me a little longer, Fuyu. I feel—no I know—that this time it will be different. No more skulking in the shadows. No more feeding in dirty barns surrounded by cattle. No, we will once again take our place as the rulers of this world."

He gently put one hand under her chin and lifted her face toward him. "No more dead children in the snow."

A single tear gently fell from her eye and meandered down her cheek. Before it reached her chin, it froze in a perfect teardrop of crystal.

"Okay," she said after a few seconds of silence. "But we will need to be careful for a while. The death of the farmer and his kin will undoubtedly bring attention."

Vladmir grimaced.

Fuyuko's eyes narrowed, and she stepped back a pace. She searched his face for a few seconds before speaking.

"What is it you are not telling me?"

Famine

Sophia noticed that Lord Durgala's face went dark, and he grimaced. He pursed his lips and turned away from Fuyuko.

Something had happened. Something directly related to her escape attempt. She was sure of it. She had to know what it was.

Sophia quietly edged closer to the place where the big man stood so she could hear better. Her fear of the man was gone, replaced by a growing spark of hope that maybe her escape attempt was not in vain after all.

"Vladmir," Lady Fuyuko snapped. "Answer me. What has happened?"

The big man growled. "Nothing that need concern you."

The woman's eyebrows shot up and she crossed her arms and raised her chin.

"Really? Well, I *am* concerned."

He didn't meet her gaze, but Sophia could feel his anger rising. It was a growing pressure that threatened to crush her mind.

Gritting her teeth, she fought the panic that threatened to overwhelm her. She had to keep calm. Had to find out what he was hiding.

Fuyu swept her gaze slowly back and forth around the room as if she was looking for someone.

"Where did you go?" she questioned. "When I came here to see if the girl was sufficiently punished, you were not in your usual chair."

Vladmir narrowed his eyes and turned to look at the woman. "I was called away on a pressing errand. Like I said before, it is nothing for you to be concerned about."

Fuyuko scoffed. "Come to think of it, your new toy was gone as well. Now I understand."

Vladmir gritted his teeth. "You understand nothing, witch."

"You always insult me when I hit close to the mark. What is it you are trying to hide from me? Certainly, it was not a simple tryst with your new lover. You know I do not care about such things."

Vladmir continued to glower but said nothing.

"When I came into this room, I sensed another presence. It quickly faded, but I could not tell who it was. Was it your new whore?"

Vladmir let out a low, throaty growl.

"Fuyu, why would I care to hide if Jasmine came here? She could kill the girl, and I would not care one bit. The presence you felt vas that blasted winter child. She is still alive and running about the castle, causing mischief."

Fuyuko blinked a few times, and her mouth dropped open slightly. "Katherine is still alive?"

"Yes. I did not have the heart to kill her. She is one of yours, after all."

So, Sophia thought to herself, she had been right about Kat. Even though they knew about her, maybe she could still be of help to her and to the other children. That is, if she even cared about such things anymore.

Fuyuko shook off the temporary bewilderment. "That aside, something happened you are not telling me about."

Famine

"Come on," Sophia hissed under her breath. "Just spit it out already. Tell me what I need to know. Tell me what it is that distresses your mind so."

Vladmir shifted uneasily. "Let it go, Fuyu; I have it all under control."

Fuyuko narrowed her eyes and searched his face again. "Do you, now? If it is nothing to be concerned with, then why do you need to have it under control?"

He sighed heavily and ran a hand through his dark mane. "Jasmine got a little impatient."

"What does that mean?" Fuyuko asked.

He looked up at her and grimaced.

"She was still angry about the woman who stole her man in her past life and went to get revenge. She took three of our warriors. Only she returned."

Fuyuko's eyes went wide, and she clenched her fists.

"She did *what*?!"

"Fuyu," Vladmir said placatingly. "Ve have all made mistakes. You know what it is like when you are first turned. All the emotions that go along with it. It is hard for anyone to control."

Fuyuko shook her head. "No, after what happened the other day, we cannot afford to have her trapsing around killing anyone she sees fit. It will bring too much attention."

Vladmir grimaced and set his jaw. "I know, Fuyu, but her mistake may have greater consequences."

"The three dead warriors?" Fuyuko asked. "Certainly, the woman she went after does not have the power to kill them."

"No, she does not."

"Then who did?"

Vladmir's expression turned grave.

"I do not know."

"But you suspect."

He sighed again and rubbed the bridge of his nose. "Let it go, Fuyu. I vill handle it."

The temperature in the room plummeted and Sophia began to shiver uncontrollably. Her breath came out in tiny clouds, and she had to strain to hear what her captors were saying over the uncontrollable chattering of her teeth.

"It was him, wasn't it?" Fuyuko said in a soft, menacing tone.

Vladmir grimaced and turned to the woman. He stood to his full height and then seemed to become even taller. His large frame dwarfed the angry woman in both physical and spiritual presence.

"I believe so," he replied, his voice commanding. "And hear me on this, Fuyuko. You *will* not investigate this matter. You *will* let this go. Do not test me on this, or you will face the consequences."

Fuyuko glared at Vladmir but said nothing.

The air in the room was so cold now that Sophia was only moments from passing out. Who was this person that had killed three vampires? They obviously hated, and from what she could sense from Lord Durgala, possibly feared him. Maybe the mistake of the pretty new vampire would bring help.

Lord Durgala's booming voice knocked her out of her thoughts, which had become sluggish from the cold.

"Do you understand me?"

Famine

Fuyuko nodded, but her face was a mask of rage.

Oh, she knew this man and hated him. That made Sophia smile. More than likely this man wasn't going to be any help. After all, if he had so much power, why hadn't he destroyed this horrid place sooner?

Still, the look of absolute hatred and rage on Lady Fuyuko's face made her day. *Here in Hell, after all*, Sophia thought as darkness finally took her, *you took a win wherever you could get it.*

All there was, was darkness. All-encompassing darkness. An oppressive blackness that seemed to swallow all life. There was nothing. Everything had ceased to exist.

Jared's heart sank.

"No," he whimpered. "No..."

He could see nothing. Feel nothing. Hear nothing. The only thing he was conscious of was his own body, which felt cold. Unbearably cold, as if all warmth had been sucked from the universe.

His heart began to beat faster and faster, and his breathing quickened until he thought he would explode.

"No!" he screamed.

His voice started out soft at first and then steadily grew, until it was one long unintelligible bellow of despair.

He had no idea how long he had been screaming. A minute. An hour. A day. Perhaps a year. Time had no meaning here. He stopped, but the knot in his stomach remained.

"No. Time doesn't exist here in the void," he spoke aloud, though the words seemed to falter and fade as if they could not or would not exist audibly here in the void.

Maybe this is Hell.

"Perhaps," came a reply to his thoughts.

He could not distinguish whether it was his own mind that had spoken or something else. There was no sound. No air to carry the vibrations. Just a word that formed in his head.

I am dead. That I am certain of.

"You are."

Replied the voice again. Coming from inside himself, but not himself. He didn't know how he knew. He just did. Knew it as surely as he knew that the void was the absence of light and life. The absence of everything. The absence of the universe.

Is this the end?

"No," replied the voice.

Jared fell silent. His thoughts were muddled. He couldn't think. When did he come here? Had he always been here? No. The void was not his home, not where he belonged.

He grimaced and squeezed his eyes shut. It didn't make a difference that there was no light to see by, but it was an instinctual reaction to his frustration. He raised one hand and lightly tapped his palm to his temple. Another instinctual movement.

What was I doing? I know it was something important. Something outside of the void.

No matter how hard he tried, he couldn't grasp the thought. It was there, taunting him, just outside his reach. It was important, that he was sure of. Why couldn't he remember? It was like the void devoured even his memories.

"Your time here does not need to be unpleasant."

The voice again. This time from outside his mind. He whipped his head back and forth, his eyes searching. No good; the darkness was total, or he thought. "Perhaps I am blind."

"You are dead," said the voice. "Dead men do not see."

Who are you?

No reply.

Jared waited in silence. Waited for the mysterious voice to speak again.

Just when the fear that the speaker had decided to abandon him to the void threatened to bring back despair, there was a brilliant flash of light.

Jared had to raise his hand to shield his eyes from the radiance. They began to water, and he had to squint and turn his head slightly in order to look at the light.

It was more than just uncomfortable; it was painful, and his head throbbed. Just when he was about to break and look away, the light slowly faded to a bearable level.

Jared slowly lowered his hand, wary that the light might return.

What he saw was a sword floating in the void directly in front of him. Its tip was facing downward, and it glowed a soft blue-black that seemed to drive back the nothingness of the void.

It lingered angrily just outside of the light, waiting to reassert itself.

The iron-black blade bobbed slightly, and Jared noticed that pommel of the weapon was the face of a women wearing a blindfold. The face glowed a bit brighter than the rest of the weapon, and he could feel its intense gaze upon him.

Jared squinted and watched in horrible fascination as the hilt, which was in the shape of a hand, began to flex and come alive.

It slid away from its place holding the blade, revealing another appendage. This one also began to move until both became long arms that hung below the face.

There was no sound, but the movement was jerky and unnatural as if the appendages were made of metal, and he imagined the noise of grinding metal on metal. As the arms continued their upward and outward movement, the blade split in two and extended to form long legs.

When the metamorphosis was finally finished, a creature about the same height as Jared hovered before him. It was humanoid in shape and appearance but had hard angels and sharp edges.

Jared's mind had begun to clear as he watched the sword transform. At least he knew who it was that floated before him. Or rather, what it was.

"Tzedakah," Jared growled softly.

The head tilted to one side, and he swore he could see faintly glowing eyes under the blindfold that covered its face.

"What the hell have you done?"

"Only what was necessary."

Jared snorted, and his lip curled into a sneer.

"Putting me back here in the void, even though you know what it does to me?" his voice cracked slightly. "Was necessary?"

"You would not listen. You were being unreasonable."

"You could have simply taken over. You didn't need to..." He waved an arm outward, gesturing to the void, and shivered. "Put me in here."

The sword didn't speak, but Jared was sure he noticed its mouth twitch slightly at one corner. A very human gesture, unusual for the normally emotionless creature.

"I felt you needed reminding."

Jared's eyebrows shot up.

"Are you punishing me?" he accused.

His voice came out at a higher pitch than he intended. "You are, aren't you?"

"I am not. You simply would not listen, and I needed you to understand. I felt this was the best way to get your attention."

As Tzedakah spoke, all his memories came rushing back. Jasmine, the dilapidated farmhouse, the man he had killed, and the mother and her children.

Oh, God. The mother.

Jared gritted his teeth and literally shook with uncontrolled rage. When he spoke, his voice was low and menacing.

"What...did...you...do?"

"What needed to be done," it replied, and Jared was sure that he detected a hint of anger in its voice.

"Let me out of here right now."

"No, not until you calm down."

Jared fixed his gaze on the sentient sword.

"You mean, *not until you're done*."

Tzedakah didn't respond.

Tzedakah's silence was the straw that broke the camel's back, and he lunged for the metal man's throat. The sword twisted out of the way, its arms twirling around completely like a helicopter's blades.

One of the metal arms struck him in the side of the head, causing him to see stars, but he managed to grab a hold of the other arm as it rushed by. His weight slowed the rotation down enough for him to get his free hand around Tzedakah's throat.

Tzedakah's shook off Jared's other arm and balled his hands into fists. He rained stunning blows down upon Jared's exposed head. Jared gritted his teeth and refused to let go.

He deflected a vicious downward strike that was intended to break his arm, the blow sending painful shockwaves through his arm. He managed to dodge backward just in time to avoid the other fist as it flew at his face. It grazed his chin but did no real damage.

Before Tzedakah could get his fists back around to strike at him again, Jared threw all his weight forward and slammed hard into its torso. He managed to get his other hand around Tzedakah's throat as well and wrenched it close to his body, restricting its movement.

"Now," Jared said through gritted teeth, "let me out."

Tzedakah thrashed wildly in his grasp. Its legs, that were formed from the business end of the blade, bent upward and bit deeply into Jared's back and side. Fire erupted where the blade sank into his flesh, but he refused to let go.

"Let me out!" Jared screamed.

Tzedakah didn't respond but continued to twirl and thrash, trying to shake Jared off. Pain continued to erupt along his entire back and side as the legs repeatedly tore into his flesh. He pushed past the pain and held on.

Just when he thought he couldn't hold on any longer, there was a flash of light, and he found himself back in the tangible world.

He blinked his eyes and shook his head to drive away the disorientation. There was still blackness in his peripheral vision, the remnants of the void that still stubbornly held on. It would eventually dissipate. The nothingness couldn't linger long in the same space as the substance. They were like matter and antimatter; one could not exist in the presence of the other.

Once he was able to orient himself again, he saw that he was in the farmhouse's living room. The couch was thrown to one side and the coffee table was smashed.

Famine

When he moved one foot, he heard the distinct crackle and pop of glass breaking. He moved his leg and felt it brush up against something hard. It was one of the table lamps that had been sitting on one of the end tables. It was smashed.

The living room was destroyed, presumably from a fight. Or a slaughter. Jared grimaced as he took in the scene. There was no blood that he could see, so that was a good sign. Maybe the woman and her children had escaped.

He felt sick when he thought about what he had done before he blacked out. Sick over what he was going to do to the woman. That was why Tzedakah had put him in the void and why he had made him fight his way out. He needed to get Jared's consciousness out of the way.

As soon as he thought of the sentient sword, he realized that he was gripping something with both hands. He released the grip of one hand and lifted the object with the other.

The sentient sword glowed softly in his grip. Blood glinted in the low light, and he grimaced. Maybe it wasn't her blood. Maybe it was the stepfather's instead. Deep down, though, he knew it was just wishful thinking.

He stared at the weapon for a few seconds before a sound from the other room caught his attention. Turning towards the noise, he slowly walked in the direction of the sound. Once he had reached the boundary of the hallway, he saw bare legs lying on the floor.

His stomach dropped as his fears were realized. Tzedakah had not spared the woman. The closer he got, the stronger the sickly-sweet coppery smell of blood grew. He noticed that the woman's legs were bent awkwardly and that one of her slippers had come off.

He didn't want to, but he knew he had to look. To face what he had done. At least, he told himself he had to check on the children. Tzedakah wouldn't have harmed them, they were innocent. Well, not physically anyway; what he had done to their parents would certainly scar them forever. No child could see the horrors they had just witnessed and come out of it unscathed.

Putting his hand on the wall to steady himself, he paused before swallowing and then stepped out into the hallway.

The woman's eyes were fixed and lifeless. There was red all over the floor, but it was just in one area on her nightgown. A small area directly in the center of her chest. Directly where her heart would be.

At least he had made it clean and as painless as possible. That was something anyway. A bitter comfort, but a comfort nonetheless.

He raised Tzedakah and glowered at it. His feelings for the blade and what it had made him do raged inside his chest like a storm. He wanted to hate the thing, but he couldn't. At least, not completely.

Was he furious? Yes. But in its own way it was right. By its logic, it was the only true course of action. Jared was conflicted. He was beginning to understand how Tzedakah thought, to understand it more. But that didn't make what they had done any easier to reconcile.

He still thought that there had to be a better way. Tzedakah saw the world as black and white, but it just simply wasn't. Yes, the woman was wrong. She had allowed the children to be abused, but she was also a victim.

Did she deserve to die? On a basic level, yes. Still, the weapon had to be able to see things from all sides. To understand why people did the horrible things they did. To make allowances for the circumstances that drove them to make the choices they made. To be understanding.

Jared realized, however, that Tzedakah and its logic was as rigid and unyielding as the metal it was formed from. Maybe that was how it should be. He certainly couldn't do what was necessary. To make the hard choices no matter how distasteful they were. The fact that he couldn't kill his murdering monster of a brother was proof of that.

The same rustling sound he had heard earlier knocked him out of his contemplations.

He turned toward the sound just in time to see someone duck behind the large armoire by the front door.

He was there in an instant, Tzedakah drawn and ready to strike. Before he struck, however, the distinct sound of whimpering and crying stopped him. Danny was crouched protectively in front of his sister, his eyes wide with terror. The little girl was weeping uncontrollably.

Not wanting to scare them further, Jared backed a few feet away and put his arms up, palms outward. The girl kept crying, and Danny's only response to Jared's placating gesture was frightened eyes fixed firmly on the glowing blade in his hand.

Jared tried to bend down to touch the boy to let him know he meant him no harm, but the boy shrank from his touch, and the girl let out a terrified scream.

He quickly backed a few feet farther away. The little girl stopped screaming, and Jared swore he could hear both children's hearts beating.

"I'm not going to hurt you," Jared said softly, once again realizing that it was not his voice but the soft, raspy, ethereal voice of a spirit.

"If you try to hurt my sister, I will..." Danny stammered, his words trailing off into stuttering sobs.

Jared wanted to say more. Something that would comfort the children, but he had nothing. To them he was a monster. They didn't understand that what he had done had been necessary. That he had saved Danny's life. Had saved Sandra from a life of abuse and degradation.

All they saw was the monster who killed their parents. Maybe they were right. Maybe he was nothing more than a monster. Looking at their frightened little faces, he thought maybe he was.   A bogeyman who comes in the night to kill and destroy.

He sighed and turned away from the children. Certainly, their stepfather had been a monster. Maybe in her own way the mother was, too. But in the end, so was he.

He opened the front door. The soft glow of dawn's light washed over him, and he paused. He turned to l*ook back at the children. They were still watching him with terrified eyes.*

No, he thought as he shut the door and walked away. *I may not be a monster, but I am certainly not one of the good guys.*

The world slowly came into focus and Dana was immediately struck with how bright it was. Squinting at the sun beaming through her window, she raised one arm and placed it over her eyes.

"Ugh," she groaned. "Who brought the sun closer?"

ZZZZ...

What in the world? Is someone snoring?

She slowly lifted her arm and peeked out in the direction of the noise then jolted up and snapped her head in the direction of the source of the snoring. A half-naked man was slumped in the chair near the window.

"What?" she asked out loud. "Who?"

The man let out a snort, scratched at his chin, and then yawned. He shifted in his seat, smacked his lips, and then scrunched up his unshaven face and squinted.

"I see you're finally up," he said, failing to suppress another yawn. "I guess I fell asleep waiting for you to regain consciousness.

Dana's mouth hung open, and she just stared at the man as if he had been speaking a foreign language.

Jeremy cracked his neck and then arched his back. The nearly see-through hospital gown he wore barley covered all his unmentionable parts, and Dana had to suppress a gag as she saw how hairy he was.

Was he a man or a sasquatch? Her eyes went wide as sudden realization dawned on her.

"Wait, you're that guy from my dream last night."

Jeremy raised one eyebrow and smacked his lips again.

"That's me," he chuckled, scratching his midsection. "The man of your dreams."

Dana scrunched up her nose and grimaced. "A nightmare maybe."

Jeremy put his hands up and lurched backward as if he had been slapped.

"Hey, now, is that anyway to talk to the guy who just saved your pretty little butt?"

"My what now?" Danna snapped, swinging her legs out of the bed and taking her blankets with them.

She dropped to the floor as an alarm suddenly started blaring from somewhere to her left. She didn't know who this guy was, or why he was in her dream last night, but she was certainly going to find out.

"I don't know who you are or why you're in my room, so you'd better start..." Her voice trailed off as the room suddenly began to spin. "Start... I don't feel so good."

189

Famine

She swooned and then promptly fell back onto the bed. Her bare legs dangled off the side, and she realized her gown had shifted to where it was now around her waist.

A vague thought flitted into her mind as she lay there watching the swirling patterns that danced in front her eyes. *My panties are showing.* She blushed and then tried to reposition her gown.

Her head throbbed with each movement, and after a few unsuccessful tries she gave up. After all, whoever this guy was had seen them already anyway.

The man's face suddenly intruded on the dancing lights and stared down at her. He was still squinting.

"I wouldn't try that again if I were you. At least not for a while anyway. The side effects of a mental attack can be rough"

"A what?" she slurred drunkenly.

Jeremy unceremoniously swung her legs back onto the bed. She groaned as he did, and they landed hard, causing the bed to bounce slightly.

Jeremy sighed as he gently placed her blanket over her legs, covering her up.

"A mental assault."

She blinked and stared at him. She obviously understood what he had said, but there was no way she had heard him clearly.

"Wait a minute," she said, shaking her head to try and drive away the fog. "I'm pretty sure I misheard you."

He raised his eyebrows and grinned. "Really?" he said with a smirk. "Then let me say it slower. You were hit with a mental assault."

He spoke slow and deliberate, as if he was talking to someone who was developmentally disabled.

Dana rolled her eyes. The vertigo was beginning to subside, and she felt her head beginning to clear.

"You're a bit of an ass, aren't you."

Jeremy huffed and returned to his chair by the window. It groaned in protest as he slumped heavily down onto it. She watched him curiously as he rested his head on one of his hands and then slumped his broad shoulders.

The strange intruder was handsome in a rugged way, with high cheekbones that were shaded with a few days' worth of stubble. Full brows accentuated eyes that were a deep brown, slightly sad, and seemed older than they should be.

He noticed her looking at him and smiled. It was a warm smile that reached his eyes, which looked upon her with worry. Whoever this man was, he seemed to be genuinely concerned about her.

"I'm still not sure you aren't crazy, but I do appreciate your help getting back into bed," she said with a small smile.

She repositioned herself so she was sitting up and noticed that her stomach didn't hurt as much as it had. Whatever it was they had given her last night not only knocked her out but miraculously lessened the pain of her injury.

Lessened was too feeble a word. It had damn near irradicated it. How was that even possible? There was no drug she had ever heard of, legal or illegal, that could do that.

Famine

Dana prodded at her wound, but still the pain was minimal. It was more of a stretching or tenderness than outright pain. She scrunched her face up and removed the bandage covering her stab wound just enough to allow for a quick peek.

Her eyes went wide, and she pulled it down the rest of the way. She ran her hands over the place where she had been struck and felt new scar tissue. That wasn't possible. The injury was too new, it shouldn't be this far along for another week at least.

She noticed the man watching her and blushed when she realized just how much of her stomach was showing. She instantly lowered the gown and covered herself back up.

"They must have given me something strong last night to help me sleep, because I had the strangest, most vivid, dreams."

"Yeah, mental attacks do that to me as well," the man said with a snort, thankfully not mentioning her display. He did raise one eyebrow, though, obviously curious about what she had been doing.

She glowered at the man. "Okay..." she replied skeptically. "Since you're here in my room, claim to have saved me and don't seem to be going anywhere, can I ask your name?"

He shrugged. "Sure."

Neither of them said anything for about a minute. Dana felt her face begin to flush.

"Well?" she demanded.

"Well, what?" the man said, suppressing a grin.

"Oh my God, you are annoying," Dana huffed. "What is your name?"

"Oh," he replied, his eyes alight with mischief. "Jeremy. Jeremy Wagner."

"I'm Dana."

"I know."

"How?" she demanded. "I just told you."

"Nah, you told me in your...dream." Jeremy used air quotes again to highlight the word *dream*.

"Oh, God," she huffed, rolling her eyes again.

At that moment she became aware of the fact that she was incredibly thirsty. Rolling her tongue about in her mouth to try and drum up some saliva, she glanced around, looking for her water.

After a few seconds her face went white. This wasn't her room. At least, it wasn't the room she had been in last night. Everything was backward.

As far as she recalled, her bed had been on the other side of the room. The chair and table were completely different colors, and the bathroom was all wrong as well.

"Wait a minute," she said, comprehension dawning on her. "Why am I in a different room?"

"Because the other one blew up," Jeremy answered dryly.

"It did what?"

"Blew up." He paused and squinted one eye. "Well, not really, but that's what everyone else here believes. It was actually destroyed by..." He paused again; this time lost in thought.

After a few seconds he sighed heavily and grimaced.

"Let's just say that it was destroyed and leave it at that."

"By what?" she questioned dubiously.

Jeremy sighed and turned away.

"So, why were you in here anyway?' he asked, changing the subject. "Some perps rough you up or something?"

"Hey," she retorted, "You aren't going to just brush off my question like that. Wait a minute, how did you know I'm a cop?"

Jeremy groaned. "A little birdy told me. Can you answer my question now?"

Dana gave Jeremy a glare that could boil water.

"Ugh," Jeremy groaned, throwing up his hands. "Fine, God told me. You know, the big G...O...D. The man upstairs. The Almighty. Yahweh. Jehovah. Jesus."

"Really," she replied dubiously. "I find that hard to believe."

He shrugged.

"I really don't care what you believe. It's true, nonetheless. You can thank me for healing your stomach as well."

He rolled his eyes and then looked skyward. "Fine, she can thank *You* for it. All I did was place my hand on her and be Your conduit. Geesh, I know I can't actually heal anyone. But, come on. Where would she be if I hadn't been here?"

Dana blinked her eyes a few times and stared at Jeremy. Healed her? But that was impossible. If she had thought him mad before, this had clinched it.

Of course, there were a lot of Christians who believed in the supernatural. But she had always brushed off those claims as falsities or misinterpretations. It was like when a person was believed to have been raised from the dead but was actually in an undiagnosed coma.

She did consider herself a person of faith, but it had its limits. Of course, what she had witnessed over the last few days and the fact her injury was healed were glaring contradictions that she couldn't reconcile.

Also, who in the world was he talking to? Certainly, it couldn't be God. Could it? A thousand questions raced through her mind, and she was just about to fly into a tirade, when she stopped herself.

She still wasn't certain Jeremy didn't belong in the loony bin, but she was convinced he was telling the truth. She was so certain of his sincerity that it scared her. How did she know? She hadn't the foggiest, but she did. She knew it as clearly as she knew her own name.

She thought back to all her experiences from the last few days. The murdered girls, the revelation of Steve being a serial killer, Johansson's lies, and Jared's death.

Oh. God. Jared is dead.

How could she have forgotten? Memories of how he had touched her face before he died washed over her. The look in his eyes as he tried to warn her about his brother. The breaking of her heart as she watched the light drain from his eyes.

All the pent-up emotions she had been suppressing burst through her barriers like water overflowing a dam. All the pain, rage, and sadness slammed into her with such force it took her breath away. They overcame her carefully crafted walls and her eyes filled with tears. Just like when the world became too hard when she was a child, she pulled her legs up to her chest, hugged them, and began to weep.

Dana unexpectedly became aware of strong arms wrapping around her. She started to pull away, but they gently and insistently pulled her in. Too weary to fight, she allowed Jeremy to draw her into his strong embrace. He said nothing but simply held her while she cried.

Jared teleported directly to the base of the hospital where the window to Dana's room looked out. The window was utilitarian, with no frills. Much like the rest of the hospital, which was built for function and not form.

The sun was rising steadily and was now breaking through the tree line across the street, casting long shadows. The red light from the many fire trucks that had responded to the unexpected incident last night flashed from one side of the building. The hustle and bustle of the first responders and the hospital staff was thankfully concentrated on the area of Dana's old room and not on the side of her new one.

He pushed himself deeper into the long shadows, doing his best to be inconspicuous.

"I can mask us beyond any ability for mortal eyes to detect."

Jared grimaced as Tzedakah's voice filtered through his mind. The sentient sword's voice in his head was still slightly disconcerting. They appeared just as his own thoughts did, and sometimes it was hard for him to discern where his thoughts ended and Tzedakah's began.

He growled under his breath and continued to stare up at the window. He was still angry with Tzedakah and didn't want to talk. Of course, he really couldn't ignore the sword if it wanted to press the issue.

He sighed heavily. "Fine. Do it then."

The world around him suddenly shimmered slightly and the light beaming down on him seemed to bend and refract as if it was flowing through a prism. He could still see, but now everything appeared as if it were being viewed through a veil.

"No one will be able to see us now."

Jared said nothing but continued to stare upward. He noticed that the window to Dana's room was open a crack. The voices of people talking drifted downward, but he couldn't make out the details of the conversation coming from within.

"Would you like me to amplify the dialogue?"

Jared rolled his eyes and huffed. Obviously, Tzedakah wasn't picking up on his annoyance and had no intention of shutting up, so he might as well make use of it. He didn't have to be civil about it, though.

"Yes," he replied curtly.

Immediately the voices became audible and completely clear.

"Thank you," he heard Dana say. Her voice was raw, as if she had been crying.

"No problem," a man replied.

He recognized the voice to be Jeremy's. So, he had stayed with her. That was good. At least she would have some protection if anything else came after her.

From what he had experienced of the man, he knew him to be honest and true. Also, he had never met anyone who radiated the presence of God with such strength. Wherever Jeremy went, it seemed God went as well.

"You all right now?" he heard Jeremy say. "My side is starting to cramp up."

There was a muffled sound, a grunt, and then a loud thump.

"Hey, why'd you do that?" Jeremy moaned.

"Because you're an ass," Dana growled. "I'm sure it's not the first time a woman has hit you."

A wide smile made its way across Jared's face, and he shook his head as Jeremy mumbled something under his breath.

If he had been in the room, he would have cautioned Jeremy. Dana's temper was legendary. Jeremy, on the other hand, was a bit of a curmudgeon, so he doubted anything he said would have stopped him.

"What can I do for you, dear?" came a different voice. It was warm and sounded like the voice of an elderly woman.

"Is there any way I can get some water?"

Dana's voice this time.

"Of course," replied the woman. One of the nurses, Jared guessed.

"Is there anything else you need?"

Famine

"No, not really. I'm just very thirsty. I feel like I haven't had anything to drink in ages."

"Well," the woman replied warmly, "that is to be expected. You were sleeping for quite some time."

The sounds of shuffling and the peeping and chirping of an IV machine replaced the conversation that had hit a lull, so Jared allowed his thoughts to turn inward.

Feelings of self-loathing for being unable to protect her, anger at his brother for hurting her, and regret for not being able to be there for her churned inside him.

Also, jealousy. He was surprised to find that he was harboring a small spark of jealousy toward Jeremy who, in his own idiotic way, was able to be there for her.

"It should be me, not him," he snarled.

A man in a set of scrubs suddenly came around the corner, a cigarette dangling from his lips. He squinted and peered in Jared's direction.

"Hey, is someone out here?"

Jared went completely still. He knew that Tzedakah had said no one would be able to see them, but it was impossible to suppress years of human instinct.

He internally berated himself for his childish outburst as the man scanned the area for a few more seconds before taking a long drag off his cigarette.

"What's the matter?" another man's voice interjected.

"Thought I heard someone talking."

"Probably just one of the firefighters," the other man opined.

"Yeah, probably."

The man took one last look around and then left.

Jared blew out the breath he had been holding. At least he would have if he needed to breathe. One of the benefits of being dead.

He didn't even need to breathe to speak. His voice just seemed to flow out of him like an ethereal echo from a spirit. It no longer came from his vocal cords, but from somewhere else.

Just like his freezing in place, he supposed holding his breath was the instinctual human part of himself that had yet to die as his body had. Maybe in time that would fade as well.

How much of himself would he lose? He already felt his emotions becoming less intense, less human. As far as he knew, he was essentially immortal. Would he live forever? What kind of changes would occur after centuries? Would he be able to hold on to the parts of himself that made him human, or would he become as soulless as Tzedakah?

He shuddered.

Will I even be me anymore?

"Why are you in here?" he heard the nurse say. Her voice was stern, as if she were speaking to a wayward child, and it brought Jared back from his thoughts. "How many times do I have to tell you to get back to your own room?"

There was another thump and then Jeremy shouted, "Hey, I was comfortable!"

"Go be comfortable in your own room," the nurse scolded.

There was more grumbling from Jeremy and a snicker from Dana.

Famine

Jared heard the nurse leave as Jeremy continued to grumble. The only other noise he heard was the continual beeping of the IV drip.

"I guess I better go back to my cell and get some clothes on before Nurse Ratched there has my head," he heard Jeremy say. "I'll be back in a few."

"Back?" Dana asked. "I do appreciate you checking up on me, though I still have no idea why you did, but I can take it from here."

"Sorry," Jeremy responded with a grunt as if he was standing up. "I promised a friend I would stick close to you. Well, more like was ordered, but I figure I'll do it anyway."

"What friend?" Dana demanded suspiciously.

"I told you." He replied. "A little birdy. Kind of a grumpy, scary little birdy, but a little birdy nonetheless."

"Wait a minute," Dana protested. "You can't just leave me hanging like that. What little birdy?"

There was the sound of a chair creaking and then the sound of footsteps receding.

"Hey!" Dana shouted. "What birdy? Come back here right now and explain yourself. I still have a million other questions! Like why were you in my dream last night?"

Jared smirked as Dana let out a string of curses after Jeremy. He was in for a world of hurt when he got back. Dana was the fiercest person he knew when she was angry, and she would most certainly make him pay.

The sound of a ring tone split the air. He knew the tone very well and it sent a stab of pain through his heart. It was Dana's.

"Hey, Aunt Giana, how are you doing? I assume Dad called you. Don't worry, I'm fi..."

Her words were cut off instantly and Jared could hear her breathing increase. When she spoke again her voice was controlled, but worried.

"Okay, Aunt Giana, I need you to calm down. I can't understand what you're saying. Okay, that's better. Now, what happened? Are you and Uncle Frank all right?"

There were a few moments of silence where all Jared could hear was Dana's breathing and the unintelligible sounds coming from the phone.

"Okay, okay. Have you contacted the police yet?"

More silence as Dana listened to her aunt's response. Jared could tell by the subtle nuances of her voice that she was shaken. She was good at hiding her anxiety from others, but he knew her too well, having been her partner for years.

"All right, I know. You did all you could do for now. It's perfectly okay. You know you can always call me, and I will always be there to help."

More silence as Dana listened.

"Aunt Giana, how long has Sophia been missing?"

He heard her let out a controlled breath.

"She said she was coming home for the weekend to do her laundry and stuff. and that was three days ago? Why am I just hearing about this now?"

The pitch in her voice went up an octave, as she was no longer able to completely control her anxiety.

"Yeah, I understand, but hurt or not I would have wanted to know right away. It's okay, what's done is done.

it's just, three days is a long time, and if I had known sooner I could have done something already."

The sound of a bed creaking and then the loud, continuous beeping of an angry IV machine came from the room.

"Aunt Giana, when did you notify the police?" she said, and then let out an exhale of relief. "No, you did the right thing; the sooner the better. Who did you talk to? Okay, she's a good officer. She's in charge of the missing persons unit."

There was the muffled sound of Dana moving around and then a woman's voice.

"Miss Campbell, you really shouldn't be out of bed. You still have a ways to go before you're fully recovered."

Dana ignored the nurse and continued her conversation with her aunt.

"Miss Campbell," the woman continued to protest.

"All right, it will be okay. Tell Uncle Frank I'm on my way. I'll be there as soon as I can check myself out of here. No, don't worry about me, I'm fine. It was just a scratch. Okay, I love you, too."

After Dana hung up an argument ensued with the nurse that Jared knew the poor health care worker wouldn't win. He felt bad for the woman, but any pity he felt for the nurse was eclipsed by the worry he felt for Dana's family.

"If I remember correctly," said a voice from directly behind him. "Isn't Sophia Dana's cousin?"

Reflexively he drew Tzedakah and whirled around to face the intruder. How had someone managed to get the drop on him? Tzedakah should have warned him long before anyone got this close.

His jaw dropped when he saw who it was that had spoken. Standing before him, dressed in a black hoodie and ripped jeans, was his brother, Steve. The hood hid his face, but there was no mistaking the man who had killed him and had done his best to kill Dana.

"Well, don't just stand there gawking. Come give your little brother a hug."

W ell, nothing to say to me, big brother? I guess that's expected. You always were the strong, silent type. Always afraid or incapable of telling people what you really think. Always keeping your true emotions bottled up."

He chuckled and reached into his pocket and pulled out a cigarette and lighter. Jared tightened his grip on Tzedakah until his knuckles were white, but he didn't make a move towards his brother.

Steve lit the cigarette, took a long drag, and then shook his head as he exhaled.

"I always figured it was because you were so insecure that you were afraid that, if you did, people wouldn't like you anymore. It's the real reason Jasmine, left you know.

"You were so afraid of being rejected that you never showed her how you felt. If I had been you, I would have...well, let's just say she would definitely have no doubt about how much I liked her."

Jared narrowed his eyes. Steve's words were meant to goad him. To make him so angry that he would lash out without thinking. It's what he did. He was a master at it. Always managing to find that one sore that still wasn't quite healed and stick his finger in it.

Jared relaxed his grip on his sword, but not his stance.

"Are you even capable of loving someone other than yourself?" Jared asked calmly.

Steve laughed as he exhaled, and it sent him into a fit of coughing. He raised the hand with the cigarette and pointed it at Jared.

"Good one. See? You can do it if you try."

Tzedakah was strangely quiet. The last time he had faced Steve, the sword had all but taken over his body in his attempt to get him to kill Steve. Why was he silent now?

In response to his thoughts, he heard Tzedakah whisper in his mind, "Be careful; he is no longer the brother you knew."

No kidding. He was a freaking psychopath. Jared already knew that. He knew that the brother he had loved and grown up with was just a façade. Or rather maybe it was Steve struggling to suppress the monster within. Either way, Jared had seen firsthand what his brother was capable of.

"No," Tzedakah said. "That is not what I am speaking of. Look closer."

Jared concentrated and let the dark gaze activate. Unlike when he looked at others, he didn't see the evil things that Steve had done but rather a dark shadow wrapped around him. No, it was more like it had rooted itself in him like some kind of parasite. Jared could see it as black

Famine

tendrils that seemed to be invading every area of his brother's body.

He shuddered as two red eyes suddenly opened in the blackness over his brother's head. They glared at him hatefully with unrestrained malice. Waves of power emanated from the demon like electricity, and Jared realized that the creature that held his brother was no ordinary demon.

Steve licked his lips and smiled.

"Oh, I can feel you scanning me like a tricorder from *Star Trek*. It feels weird."

"What in the name of God has that thing done to you?" Jared breathed.

The more he looked at the monster his brother had become, the more revolted he felt. His skin suddenly felt like it was trying to crawl off him, and for the first time since he had died his stomach churned.

It was as if Steve had become the antithesis of everything Jared was. Like they were antimatter and mater. Neither could exist in the same space.

He became acutely aware, however, that this time it wasn't Tzedakah he was feeling. No, this time it was his own emotions. His own sense of loathing and love. If anything, his internal conflict seemed to be interfering with his link to the sword.

That was what the sword had really been warning him about. Not that Steve and his demon in and of themselves were the greatest threat. No, it was the fact that Steve had this strange effect on his relationship with the sword.

JW Kiefer

Steve flicked his cigarette away and spread his arms out wide.

"What makes you think it did anything to me? Maybe it simply showed me what I truly am. Removed all the barriers that held me back."

Even though Steve's words were delivered imperiously, there was something else in his tone. Something not quite right, as if Steve didn't quite believe what he was saying. Or rather, perhaps, was unable to say. Maybe like him, he was not completely in control of himself.

"Why are you talking to it? Kill it now before it can do even more damage than it already has," Tzedakah whispered.

His voice seemed strange, softer, strained somehow. It was then that he realized Tzedakah hadn't been whispering, Jared just couldn't hear him as clearly.

"By the look on your face, I can tell that the thing you hold in your hand wants you to kill me," Steve commented, snapping him back to the moment. "Did you ever stop to think why? I mean, besides the obvious that is."

"I don't need him to give me a reason to kill you," Jared said quietly.

Even though his voice held conviction, in his heart he was unsure. He still loved his brother; even though he had become a monster, deep down he was conflicted.

Steve raised his eyebrows. "Oh, is that so? You couldn't do it before, not even when I tried to murder your precious Dana. What makes you think you can do it now?"

Famine

Jared growled then lunged at his brother. All his caution, all of his doubts, fled in the face of overwhelming rage.

"Don't you speak her name!" he snarled.

Steve grinned and stepped to the side, avoiding Jared's thrust. He was quick, quicker than he had been the last time they faced, and he easily avoided the strike.

Jared was caught off guard as Steve grabbed his wrist and twisted. The force of the move would have shattered a normal person's wrist, causing them to drop their weapon, but Jared's enhanced strength and durability allowed him to counter the move.

Instead of his bones breaking, Jared used the force of the movement to launch himself forward into a flip that wrenched his hand free from Steve's grip. He landed lithely on his feet and then quickly reversed his grip on Tzedakah, and with blinding speed he pivoted and swung a powerful slash at his brother's midsection.

Steve bent backward until his body was parallel to the ground, his feet never moving, and the blade passed harmlessly over him. He snapped back upward and the hood he had been wearing fell away, revealing his face.

Steve's once-handsome features were now twisted and altered. One half of his face was elongated and ash grey. Large fangs protruded from a mouth that was far too large for his face, and one eye looked like it belonged to some feral beast. It glared hatefully at him, glowing bright red with malice.

The rest of his features were normal, with his remaining ice-blue eye filled with what looked like pain. The hateful smirk on that side of his face also appeared forced, as if he were wearing some kind of mask.

Jared balked when he saw his brother's twisted features, and that momentary lapse in concentration left him wide open for Steve's fist. The downward blow hit him squarely on the right cheek, with such force that it plowed him straight into the ground.

Steve followed up with a kick to his head that caused an explosion behind his eyes. He then let loose with a flurry of kicks that slammed into his exposed flank.

"If I recall," he grunted between kicks, "you were a lot faster last time. More powerful. What happened?"

Jared grabbed Steve's ankle as he came in for another kick and turned his entire body over. The force of the movement lifted Steve into the air and Jared flung him off to the side and away.

The fight had started drawing attention, and the last thing Jared needed was a crowd. With a crowd came police, and with police came trouble. As much as he wanted to stop his brother, he didn't want anyone being hurt collaterally from their battle.

Thankfully, up till now most passersby had paid them only a cursory amount of attention. Tzedakah's glamor had kept him hidden for the time being. Jared knew, however, that the longer their fight continued the sooner that would eventually change.

"Tzedakah!" Jared called. "Get us away from the city."

And, he thought, away from Dana.

"No, you don't!" Steve bellowed, his voice bestial and guttural. "No magic tricks. Just us."

Famine

Jared looked up just in time to see tentacles of dark energy surging towards him. With no time to think, he dodged to one side and then rolled. The earth shook from multiple impacts as the dark energy repeatedly slammed into the ground, barely missing him as he moved.

They sent flecks of dirt and debris flying in every direction, hitting anything in their wake. Moving faster than thought Jared ended his roll and leapt into a run, narrowly avoiding the missiles.

He lunged at Steve, Tzedakah tracing a line of light in the air. Steve, however, twirled to the side, away from the glowing blade. He lifted one of his hands, and the shadows there coalesced into a spike that he sent flying at Jared's exposed flank.

Jared, even though his connection was weakened, was still fast enough to dodge the oncoming spear. He turned to one side just enough and brought Tzedakah down, severing it. As soon as he did, the shadow weapon dispersed.

Never slowing, he followed up with a backhand swing at Steve's head and then a downward slash. Steve threw himself backward and deftly avoided the blows. Never slowing his momentum, he turned and started running.

"Catch me if you can!" he called over his shoulder.

Without hesitation, Jared gave chase. Steve always seemed to be one step ahead of him as they jumped over fences and ran through back yards. He reached out to Tzedakah for speed, but the sword seemed unable to comply. At least he thought it was doing all it could, considering their shaky connection.

As the pursuit dragged on through one back yard to another, they left dogs barking and angry people shouting in their wake. Jared watched as Steve scaled the high wooden picket fence that marked the barrier to the next yard. He followed, clearing the tall fence with a single leap.

Just as Jared reached the top of the fence, he looked down. Directly below him on the other side, sitting next to a swing set and surrounded by toys, sat a small child.

Jared had to twist in midair to avoid landing on the tot. The maneuver saved the child but took him close to the sturdy wooden swing set. His foot slammed into the playset, causing him to flip around in midair. He heard the wood crack, and he grimaced. He spun wildly for a second before managing to right himself and land on his feet.

The child, a little boy of about three with curly dark hair, stared wide-eyed at him. He had a rubber dog protruding from one side of his open mouth that he held tightly with both hands.

Jared stared back at the child, scanning him for any signs he had been hurt, before turning and following Steve. He couldn't help smiling as the little boy's sudden bursts of laughter followed him into the next yard.

Even in the darkest times, one could find joy. He had no idea why the little boy's laughter had moved him so, but it did. Shoving past the dullness in his emotions to, for the briefest of moments, cause his heart to come alive again.

It was short lived, however, as he cleared another tall fence to find Steve waiting for him. He held a teenage girl tightly from behind, her eyes wide with terror. One of his

Famine

hands was in the shape of a gun and it rested directly against one of the girl's temples.

"Okay, big brother, let's play a little game."

ana peered out the open window as she pulled on a pair of jeans. She could have sworn she had just heard what sounded like impact explosions. After the last few days, she no longer took anything for granted. If something sounded like an explosion then, no matter how unlikely it was, she knew she should check it out.

The sun was directly in her eyes, and even with squinting she could barely see anything. The ground did seem to be chewed up a bit, and there were a few people milling around, but nothing out of the ordinary. Maybe she had been mistaken.

She heard someone come into her room, so she turned away from the window. Whatever it was she had heard, she didn't have time to investigate. Her family needed her. It had already been a few days, and the window of opportunity for finding her cousin was quickly closing.

Famine

She let out a groan when she saw who it was. Jeremy stalked through the open door, looked her up and down, and then grimaced.

"You're not ready yet?" he grumbled. "Seriously, I left, like, ten minutes ago."

She rolled her eyes and turned to grab her leather jacket, which was still on the chair where the nurses had placed it.

"I told you I don't need your help."

Jeremy snorted and crossed his arms. The long, tattered, brown trench coat he always wore pulled apart as he did, revealing dark jeans and a New York Mets T-shirt.

"Well, you really don't have a choice. I'm coming along whether you like it or not."

She turned and stared up at the man, meeting his annoyed gaze.

"I could have you arrested, you know."

Jeremy raised one eyebrow. "For what?"

"For stalking, impeding an investigation. Any number of things," she replied coolly. "I honestly don't need a reason. All I have to do is make a call. They might not be able to keep you for long, but they can hold you for twenty-four hours."

Jeremy narrowed his eyes. "Then do it, Nancy Drew."

Did he just call her Nancy Drew? Not even Jared would dare talk to her like that. Who did this guy think he was?

Dana's cheeks flushed a bright red, and she crossed her arms and planted her feet. If it was a war of wills he wanted, then he would have it. He had no idea who he was messing with.

The two glared at each other from across the small room, neither of them giving an inch. Both were stubborn. Extremely stubborn.

Jeremy slouched suddenly and yawned. Then he scratched his head absently and rolled his tongue around in his mouth and began to loudly suck his teeth.

God, he was an annoying man. She could feel her face beginning to heat up again and she gritted her teeth. If he thought she would be the first to give in, then he had another thing coming.

Thoughts of all the horrible things her cousin might be going through suddenly ran through her mind. She didn't have time for this, and every second she wasted with this buffoon was a second less than her cousin had.

She gritted her teeth. "Fine. I won't stop you from coming along, but let's get one thing straight right now. You do what I say, no exceptions."

Jeremy raised an eyebrow and pursed his lips. He stared at her for a few seconds before speaking.

"Okay, deal. But I am *not* getting you coffee or anything like that, got it?"

She pushed past him, avoiding eye contact, and walked out the door. Jeremy sighed and shot an annoyed glace Heaven-ward before turning and following her.

She took off in a brisk walk, ignoring everyone they passed. So far no one had tried to stop them, but it was only a matter of time before someone realized they were technically not supposed to leave.

The two companions made it out of the hospital without incident and were soon standing in the parking lot.

Famine

"You have a car?" Jeremy asked, scanning the parking area.

Dana chewed her lip. "No. I was air-lifted here."

Jeremy sighed heavily. "Okay, I don't. No need for one in the city. Besides, I'm fairly certain I was delivered here by angel. I was hurt badly, so I don't remember much of what happened. We could call an Uber."

Dana shook her head. "No need, Aunt Giana said she would be here in a few minutes. Wait a minute, by *angel*?"

Jeremy glanced at her out of the corner of his eye. "Yeah, and he's going to hold it over my head forever. I can't believe I needed *him* of all creatures to rescue me. I'm never going to hear the end of it."

Dana blinked a few times and then turned away, rolling her eyes. *This is going to be fun. My cousin is missing, and now I'm being followed around by an obviously insane person. At least it couldn't get any weirder. Could it?*

A large white SUV screeched into the parking lot, knocking her out of her thoughts. It came to a jarring halt directly in front of them. The front passenger door flung open, nearly hitting Jeremy.

Aunt Giana stared out at her, her eyes red and cheeks swollen. "Dana, thank God. Your Uncle Frank has been out every day and most nights looking for Sophia. I'm sorry I called you in the hospital, but we didn't know what else to do."

"It's all right," she replied reassuringly as she and Jeremy got into the car. "Like I said, I wish you had called earlier."

Before the doors were even closed, Giana mashed the gas pedal. Jeremy yelped in surprise and Dana was flung backward in her seat.

"I know, dear," the woman said, her voice cracking a bit. "We didn't want to trouble you until you were fully healed. Sophia is a grown woman, and we figured she would turn up eventually, but after a day with no word we started to think the worst."

Dana fumbled with her seat belt, her eyes darting continuously from it to the road. "I'm glad you finally did," she said, subconsciously flinching as her aunt nearly hit a parked car. "Has my dad been helping with the search?"

"Yeah," she replied as she turned the steering wheel hard to the left. "As soon as he knew you were stable and out of danger, he came to help. I don't think he and Frank have slept much in the last few days."

Aunt Giana glanced in the rearview mirror and frowned. "Who's your friend?"

Dana turned and looked at Jeremy. He had managed to get his seat belt fastened, and his knuckles were white from how hard he was clutching the sides of his seat.

"A colleague," she replied, giving Jeremy a look that said "play along". "He's actually a private investigator who specializes in missing persons. I called him as soon as I heard, and he agreed to meet me at the hospital."

Jeremy chuckled and reached into his pocket and pulled out a card, his free hand maintaining its death grip on the seat. He handed it to Dana.

She took it and her eyes went wide. The card read: 'Jeremy Wagner Private Investigator NY State License number 11000055555'. There was also a telephone number, address, and in smaller letters at the bottom it read, "Reasonable Rates. Specializing in Missing Persons. Satisfaction Guaranteed."

Her mouth dropped open as she looked from him to the card and back up at him again. He shrugged.

"Wait," she whispered. "You really are a private investigator?"

He chuckled and then nodded.

"What was that, dear?" her aunt asked, distracted.

"Nothing," she replied, pocketing the card and turning back to face the front of the car. She shot Jeremy a suspicious glance as she did, and he winked. Her face flushed and she gritted her teeth.

"Okay, Aunt Giana, tell me everything you know."

"Well," she began, "Sophia called and said she would be home for the weekend. Her laundry was starting to pile up and she needed a break from her roommates. I guess they're kind of wild and are always staying up late drinking and hanging out with boys."

Dana chewed her cheek as she listened. She knew that despite what her aunt thought, her cousin was no saint. She certainly wasn't promiscuous by any means, but she had done her fair share of partying. Her detective brain went into overdrive as scenarios of what could have happened flitted through her mind.

"When she didn't come home that night we were a bit concerned, but after a day of no responses from our calls and texts we started to worry."

Her voice cracked. "That's when we called the police."

"I assume that's when you were directed to Detective Bermudez?"

Her aunt sniffed and nodded. "Once I told them I was your aunt they sent us to her. They all but jumped when they found out we were family."

Dana smiled. "Yeah, one of the perks of being a relative to a police officer. Honestly, though, we take missing persons cases very seriously nowadays."

She changed the topic. "Have they found anything? Are there any leads?"

Giana shook her head, wiping away a few stray tears. She looked awful, like she hadn't slept in days.

"No one has found anything. It's like she just vanished."

Dana turned away and looked out the window. They had gotten off eighty-one and were now on Front Street, heading out of the city. Her aunt and uncle lived in the country, which posed a bit of a problem. There were plenty of places out here where people could go missing and never be found.

The Southern Tier was not a place where people vanished often. Sure, you had a few here and there. Hunters going out and never returning. Kids disappearing from the playgrounds. An occasional serial murder, but nothing like other states.

A vivid picture of Steve popped into her mind, along with the mutilated remains of a young girl. She gritted her teeth and balled her hands into fists. At least she had killed the son of a bitch. That was one monster that was never again going to cause a family to lose a loved one.

Famine

Her thoughts reflexively turned to Jared and the overwhelming sadness came knocking again. She missed him so much. It wasn't fair. Just when he had begun to see her, really see her, he was taken from her.

She shook her head and wiped away a stray tear. Her cousin's time was running out and she needed to have all her focus if she was going to find her. The grief had to wait. After all, she knew the deep hole Jared's death had left in her heart would never go away. There would be time enough to be sad once Sophia was safely back with her family.

She caught Jeremy watching her out of the corner of her eye. Despite the fact that he was obviously a bit mad, she was starting to like the man. Behind all the gruffness was a genuine concern for her.

She doubted his story about a friend telling him to stick close to her. More than likely, he had simply seen someone in need and decided to help. That was a rare thing these days. Most people just looked the other way and pretended not to see.

She smiled to herself and whispered, "Maybe the rest of us are the ones who are mad."

"What was that, dear?" her aunt asked.

"Nothing," she replied. "I was just thinking out loud."

They turned onto another road and Dana could see about twenty cars up ahead, all parked off to the side of the road. People were scurrying back and forth as a big man wearing a flannel shirt, boots, and faded jeans stood in the road, barking orders.

He turned as they slowed and coasted up next to him. His broad smile belied the weariness in his eyes as he bent down and rested his hands on Giana's now-open window.

His cropped salt and pepper hair brushed up against the top of the car door, and dimples appeared on his unshaven face as he smiled in at the group. Dark circles from days of little to no sleep caused his deep blue eyes to appear sunken.

"Anything new?" Giana blurted before the man had a chance to speak.

He sighed heavily and shook his head. "No. We've been scouring the area, mostly sticking to the main roads. We figured if she broke down or got into an accident then that would be where we would find her."

Giana's face fell and he gently placed a massive hand on her shoulder. "Don't worry, Gia, we'll find her. It's just a matter of time."

He turned to look at Dana and his eyes brightened. "I'm glad to see you up and around, baby girl. You had me worried there for a while."

"Hi, Daddy," she replied warmly. "It's good to see you, too."

Before the two could finish their reunion, someone started yelling.

The teenager looked like she was about to scream. Her eyes became frantic and they darted back and forth, looking for help that wouldn't come. Her lower lip began to quiver, and a lone tear broke free and made its way down one cheek.

Steve leaned in and whispered something in her ear, his eyes never leaving Jared's. She nodded slightly and Steve relaxed his grip. Jared narrowed his eyes as Steve smiled and patted the girl's arm reassuringly.

"That's a good girl. If you keep this up, I might even give you a cookie."

Jared narrowed his eyes and Tzedakah pulsed in agitation. Brother or not, this time he wasn't going to walk away.

"You know," he said to the girl, "I used to love playing games when I was a kid. Do you like games?"

The girl sobbed quietly but said nothing. He shrugged and turned his eyes back to Jared.

"Do you remember family game night?" he continued idly. "It seems like another life now, after all that's happened."

He smiled wistfully as he spoke, his eyes taking on a far-off look. "I can still smell the popcorn Dad always popped. You know, with that old air popper we had? The smell of melting butter and generic movie theater salt was heavenly. Well, at least on the surface anyway. We both know what it was like underneath."

Jared shifted slightly and Steve tensed, his grip once again tightening around the girl. She whimpered loudly and more tears began to make their way down her face.

Steve shook his head. "Not yet, big brother. The game has just started."

"This isn't a game," Jared replied menacingly, his ethereal voice adding to the effect.

Steve's eyebrow shot up and he smirked. "Isn't it?"

"No," he replied. "People don't exist simply for your amusement."

Steve shook his head. "Even after all that's happened to you, you still don't get it."

He sighed heavily. "Big brother, I'm the least of their worries. I'm Just a little shark in a big ocean. The real monster we should all be fearing is the one that created this ocean. His malevolence makes me look like a goldfish."

"Destroy the blaspheming creature," Tzedakah growled.

Famine

"If I move now, he will kill the girl," Jared replied softly.

"That is acceptable."

Jared's blood ran cold as he felt Tzedakah's indifference to the girl's fate. He gritted his teeth and growled under his breath.

How could Tzedakah even suggest such a thing? It was unthinkable. No rational human being would even consider sacrificing the girl. Of course, the sword wasn't human, and it was single-minded in its desires. Kill the wicked and bring them to justice, no matter the cost.

Jared noticed his brother smirking and watching him. "It told you to kill me even if it means sacrificing the girl, didn't it?"

Jared made no reply, but the look on his face spoke volumes.

Steve laughed loudly, but his laugh quickly turned into a fit of coughing. Jared saw his chance to move, but before he could his brother quickly recovered and the moment passed.

He waved the index finger of his free hand, the other never leaving the girl's temple. "Not yet. We're just getting to the good part of the game."

"What do you want?" Jared snarled.

"I want you to admit what I already know!" he snapped. "That life is nothing more than a game for God's amusement. That all of us *precious* humans are nothing more than toys for Him to do whatever He wants with. Just look at that sword of yours. He doesn't give a rat's ass about any of us. You included. Does that seem like the creation of a loving God?"

Jared blinked a few times and raised the sentient sword up to his face. Tzedakah pulsed and vibrated in his hands, its blue-black glow washing over his features.

All the suppressed rage he had been stifling towards the sentient sword stormed inside him. It threatened to burst through the hollow numbness that had gradually replaced his human emotions.

Steve watched, a satisfied smile on his lips. "I knew you were beginning to see. It was only a matter of time. That thing is using you. It doesn't care about you any more than God does. To them you're nothing more than a tool to be used and then thrown away."

Was Steve right? Certainly, he had his doubts. Especially over the last few days. He felt like all he had been doing for the last few days was trying to hold on to some semblance of himself. To his humanity. Minute by minute, he could feel it slipping away. Being replaced by the empty, cold numbness. Being replaced by a monster.

Thoughts of Dana's smile invaded his melancholy. Her deep brown eyes appeared before him, and his heart skipped a beat. Oh, how he missed her. Missed the smell of her skin and the taste of her lips.

"Jared!" Tzedakah's voice thundered into his consciousness.

He gritted his teeth and blinked his eyes rapidly. The world seemed out of focus. He shook his head, trying to drive away the fog. What had happened?

"Jared, you need to be careful. His words are poison."

Famine

Jared returned his gaze to his brother and saw the satisfied smirk on his face. The terror in the captive girl's eyes, however, snapped him back to the moment and he straightened.

"He is trying to break the connection between us," Tzedakah said.

"He doesn't have to try hard to do that," Jared snapped.

Tzedakah was silent, but Jared could sense his apprehension. Had he given him the thoughts of Dana that had brought him back from his lethargy, or had it come from somewhere else? Either way, it had done the trick.

Whatever it was Steve had planned for him, he knew it wasn't going to be pleasant. No matter the cost, he was going to save that girl. He was certain of that. Regardless of what the sentient sword thought, he wasn't going to stop being the man Dana had loved. That man wouldn't let the girl die.

Steve chuckled. "Trouble in paradise?"

In response, he raised Tzedakah into a defensive posture and planted his feet.

Steve smiled broadly. "Okay, then, I guess you're finally ready to play."

Jared surged forward and Steve's smile broadened. A small voice in the back of his mind screamed at him. Something wasn't right. Either Tzedakah or his subconscious had picked up on something he hadn't seen. He quickly redirected himself and moved out of his brother's reach.

As soon as he switched locations, he noticed the slightest twitch of the wrist his brother was using to hold on to the girl. He squinted his eyes and spotted a small black strand of shadow moving away from the hand. It blended in with the natural shadows of the area, and if he hadn't shifted his position he never would have seen it.

"Okay, big brother," Steve said with a twinkle in his eyes. "Let me explain the rules."

Steve lifted the arm slightly, his other hand never leaving her temple. He twitched his two middle fingers and Jared's stomach dropped as a small bundle wrapped in a blanket floated out of a nearby window.

A small cry escaped from the blanket-wrapped child and Jared growled. He didn't have to be a rocket scientist to know exactly what it was his brother had in mind.

"So, the game we are going to play today," Steve continued, "is called, 'Are you fast enough?' Or 'Cruel choice'. I'll let you decide which it will be."

He drew the child closer and then snapped his fist closed. The child screamed as the tendrils of darkness constricted around it like a python. The girl next to him became hysterical and she lifted her arms to reach out for the infant.

"Davey!" she wailed.

Steve wrenched her backward as the cries of the child were cut off and replaced by gasps for air.

"Now, now, you'll spoil the game if you move," he said into her ear.

Famine

"Let me make myself totally clear," he continued, his voice soft and cold. "If you so much as twitch again, I will kill the child. Nod if you understand."

She nodded, her chest heaving with sobs.

He patted her shoulder. "That's a good girl."

He turned his eyes back to Jared who watched with narrowed eyes, his lips pressed into a tight thin line.

"Okay, now, here are the rules. I plan on killing both of these innocent children. Well, innocent is relative I guess, but you get the drift."

He waved his hand dismissively in the air before continuing, "So, since I'm willing to bet you're not fast enough to stop me completely, this leaves you with a choice. Which one are you going to save?"

Jared shifted in place and mentally reached out to Tzedakah. "Are we fast enough to stop him?"

Tzedakah was silent for a second before finally saying, "No. Not as you are now. Our connection is...weak."

Jared gritted his teeth as he thought. He had to stall for time while he came up with a plan.

"I remember the M&Ms," he said suddenly.

Steve cocked his head in confusion. "What M&Ms?"

"The ones Mom always used to get when we watched movies."

Steve blinked a few times before replying, his voice was slow and hesitant. "Yeah, Dad got them for her every time, even when we didn't have money for them."

"That's what I remember most. The smell of chocolate," Jared continued, his mind working frantically to find a solution. "No matter how small the bag, she always shared them with us. I still have to get them every time I go to the movies. It used to drive Dana nuts."

Steve nodded slightly, the wistful smile returning. He sighed heavily. Jared's mind raced with every possible scenario. Every one of them ended with either both or one of the children dead.

"Think, Jared," he berated himself internally. "There must be a way. If speed isn't the answer, then what is?"

Steve chuckled, bringing Jared's attention back to him. "All this talk of M&Ms makes me want to get some candy. Maybe I will when this is over."

He released his death grip on the infant long enough to allow a ragged gasp of breath and long wail to escape. The teenage girl shrieked and Jared tensed as Steve closed his hand, once again strangling the child's cries.

"As much as I enjoy reminiscing, I think it's time for you to stop stalling and make your choice."

Oh, God, there's nothing I can do. One or both are going to die. What's the good of having all this power if I can't even save one child?

Jared brought the glowing sword to his face and grimaced. If he could toss it away, he would. The sword might hold unlimited power, but it was only the power to destroy.

"Soulless monster," he snarled in his mind.

"No," came Tzedakah's soft reply. "I am not."

Jared blinked. "What did you just say?"

"I am not soulless."

Neither spoke for what seemed like hours, though it was only a fraction of a second.

Famine

Tzedakah was the first to break the silence. "Do you trust me?"

"How can I trust you?" Jared replied. "After all you've done? You're as much a monster as Steve."

"No," he said. "I did what was necessary to save the children at the house."

"By killing their mother?"

"Yes," he replied simply. "I did what I felt was needed to protect them. Trust me, Jared. I wish to save these two just as much as you."

Jared shook his head in uncertainty.

Steve had finally reached his limit and he clenched his fist harder. The infant boy in the blanket choked and gurgled and the girl sobbed.

"Jared," the sword called frantically. "Let me in and I will save them, even if it means allowing the abomination to escape."

Jared set his jaw as soon as Tzedakah's words entered his mind. That was all he needed to hear. The blade may not care if humans lived or died, but one thing it wasn't was a liar.

He nodded slightly as he opened himself up and felt Tzedakah's consciousness flood into him. They surged forward, their choice made.

Dana and Giana jumped out of the car as soon as they had pulled over to the side of the road. A short middle-aged man wearing denim overalls and a flannel shirt was waving from the tree line.

"Did you find something, Ed?" Dana's father called.

The man's face was white. He swallowed hard and reflexively looked back the way he had come.

"Um...yes, but not pertaining to Soph."

Dana's father furrowed his brow and crossed his arms. "What do you mean?"

"I-I..." the man stammered and then shook his head. "I was checking the dirt road to the Walker Farm, seeing if maybe she had broken down and tried to make it there."

He ran his hand through his matted dark brown hair. "Jim, I...I don't know what to make of what I saw."

Famine

Jeremy finally extracted himself from the car and walked up to them. Dana glanced at him but continued to focus on the conversation.

Uncle Frank walked up at that moment, his brow knit in concern. "What's the matter? Did you find Sophie?"

Dana's father turned and put his hand on Frank's shoulder.

"Not yet. Ed here said he found something down at the Walker Farm, and he was just explaining it."

"Was it Sophie?" he asked, his voice rising slightly. "Oh God, Ed, if it's Sophie and she's hurt or..." His voice trailed off. He composed himself and continued. "Or worse, just tell me."

"Frank," Dana's father said, squeezing his shoulder reassuringly. "It isn't Sophie, but it's obviously something. Let's hear what he has to say and then go check it out before we jump to any conclusions. Okay?"

He turned back to Ed and nodded for him to continue.

Ed cleared his throat. "Well, like I said, I don't know how to describe what I saw. It's like nothing I've ever seen before. If I had to guess, it looks like a pack of wild animals attacked their German shepherd. It was all torn to shreds.

"I thought it strange that it was just left there, so I called out to Hank, but there was no response. It was way too quiet, so I approached the house and saw the door was open. As soon as I stepped into the house, the smell of death hit me, and I panicked."

He swallowed hard and grimaced before continuing. "Jim, there was blood everywhere. I was too scared to stick around to see if anyone needed help."

JW Kiefer

Dana blinked a few times as her mouth dropped open. Everyone else just stood speechless, unsure of how to respond. Jeremy, on the other hand, sighed and groaned.

"Death and carnage. Why does it always have to be death and carnage?"

Dana turned to him and punched him in the arm hard.

"Ow! What was that for?" he grumbled.

She gave him a look that said "shut up and be quiet" before turning back to the stunned group.

"Sheesh," he mumbled. "You didn't have to hit me."

"Ed, I need to see the scene," she said, drawing all eyes to her. "Can you take me there?

He nodded. "It's not far, just a five-minute walk down the trail."

Nodding back, she turned to address the rest of the group. "This is an active crime scene, so only I go with Ed. I can't have anyone else coming along and contaminating the area before the forensic team arrives."

A few of them began to protest and she held up her hand to silence them. "No exceptions, understand? I doubt that whatever happened there has anything to do with Sophia, but just in case, I need to preserve as much evidence as possible. The fewer people around, the less contamination."

She nodded to Ed, grabbed Jeremy's arm and started pulling him towards the tree line.

"Hey," he protested. "You said everyone had to stay here, so what do you need me for?"

"Just shut up and come on."

Famine

"We'll continue to search the main roads and let you know if we find anything!" her dad called after her. "You be safe, baby girl, and keep us posted!"

"I don't understand," she heard Uncle Frank say as she pulled Jeremy protesting into the trees. "What did Ed find?"

"I'm not sure, Frank," her father's gradually fading voice followed. "But I do know it wasn't Sophia."

"Are you sure?" Frank replied.

Even though the voices were growing increasingly hard to hear, her father's sigh was audible.

"Yeah," he replied, his voice growing fainter but still audible. "Let's continue to focus on the main roads and trust Dana to handle what Ed found. I promise she'll let us know if she finds anything."

It didn't take long before the conversation and the sounds of the search party faded, replaced by the serene atmosphere of the forest. Birds chirped joyfully, and there was a gentle breeze that caused the leaves to rustle and dance.

She exhaled deeply, taking in the familiar scents of the countryside. It calmed her and sent fond memories of her childhood dancing through her mind. She had grown up here and had always loved the wild, untouched country. Some of her fondest memories were of her and her friends roaming these same forests and meadows.

Unlike kids today, she didn't grow up with cell phones and video streaming. No, she had played outside and knew by the streetlights coming on that it was time for her to return home.

She caught Jeremy watching her in her periphery.

"What?" she grumbled, rolling her eyes.

He raised one eyebrow and smacked his lips. "Nothing. I was just wondering why you forced me to come along."

"I didn't force you," she protested. "I just nudged you in the same direction I was going."

"Okay," he huffed. "If that's what we're calling it. Then why did you *nudge* me along?"

"You know," she replied, waving an arm skyward. "That thing you claim to be able to do."

"You know I'm not a psychic, right? I can't just make it happen on command."

She sighed. "Yeah, I know, but I just figured that you might be able to get something from... you know."

Jeremy raised his eyebrow again and shrugged. "Worth a shot. Oh, and 'God' is the name you're looking for."

"Whatever," she continued dismissively. "I can't seem to get rid of you, so I might as well put you to work."

Ed had moved ahead a few yards, and he turned and waved back to them.

"It's only a little farther. If you look closely, you can make out the top of the house through the trees."

They continued in silence until the stench of something dead hit them like a Mack truck. She placed one hand over her nose and mouth and Jeremy fell into a fit of coughing.

"What in God's name?" he exclaimed.

Before he had finished his sentence, they spotted the dead dog. The carcass was surrounded by a swarm of flies and alive with a horde of writhing maggots.

Jeremy gagged at the sight of the eviscerated animal, but Dana was used to such things. Decaying blood and gore had been strewn everywhere. The whole area smelled foul and putrid.

Ed hadn't stopped when he reached the dead animal but had instead quickly made his way to the house. He was standing tense by the front door, his face ghostly white.

They left the carnage behind and slowly walked towards the house. Her eyes scanned every inch of the yard as she approached, her detective brain looking for anything out of the ordinary.

She saw what appeared to be tracks leading from the carcass of the dog to the house but was unable to distinguish if they were human or animal. It had to be some sort of animal. No human could have killed the dog that way. Could they?

Of course, everything she had believed to be true about the world had been challenged over the last few days. She reached down and reflexively touched her impossibly healed stomach. She looked up at the strange man who had claimed to have done it. He was walking slightly ahead of her and didn't notice her watching him.

Yes, the world no longer made sense. Everything she thought was impossible was beginning to be challenged in her thinking. The rational, ordered world she had always known, she was now completely unsure of.

She shook away the thoughts and focused her attention as she drew next to Ed and the once- again-gagging Jeremy. The stench of death had increased exponentially as they drew closer to the wide-open door to the house.

Ed, his face now turned from white to green, said, "I think I'll just stay out here if it's all right with you."

Dana nodded as she peered into the house. The smell was so strong that even she had to fight hard not to gag.

"Me too," Jeremy started to reply, before his words were cut off by Dana yanking on his arm.

"Oh no, you don't," she barked. "You're coming in with me."

Jeremy grumbled loudly but followed her into the shadow-filled house.

Beams of sunlight shone through the windows, illuminating a large living area with an overturned brown leather couch and broken furniture strewn across the room. Blood and gore literally covered everything.

The signs of a struggle were obvious, and she was unsure how to proceed. She didn't want to contaminate the scene, causing precious evidence to be lost, and she knew that the less she touched the better.

Her heart stopped and her breath caught in her chest when she saw the little arm. It was sticking out from under the overturned sofa.

Throwing caution aside, she surged forward. Jeremy shouted in protest as she dragged him along. As soon as they reached the couch, she let go of his arm and dropped to her knees.

"Help me lift this!" she exclaimed. "There's a kid under here!"

Jeremy didn't hesitate, and he pretty much threw the couch aside in his haste. It crashed to the floor, knocking a lamp off one of the tables that was still standing.

Jeremy's face went pale, and he closed his eyes and exhaled slowly when he saw the tiny body. Dana gritted her teeth and balled her hands into fists. She rubbed them hard on her thighs, fighting back tears.

The only way they could tell it was a little girl was the tattered remains of the white dress she was wearing. She had been torn apart and was barely recognizable as a human being.

Dana was frozen in place, and she barely noticed Jeremy's hand as he gently rested it on her shoulder. She turned and looked up at him. His lips were pressed together into a thin line and his eyes were soft as he looked down at her.

"Why?" she heard herself say as she turned to gaze at the child again. She reached out and gently touched the little girl's fingers. They were lifeless and cold.

"What kind of monster would do this?"

He shook his head. "I wish I could say I don't know, but this is not the first dead little girl I've had the misfortune of seeing. Nor my first monster."

He straightened, removed his coat, and then gently draped it over the girl's body. Dana let out a ragged sob as she let go of the little hand and rose to her feet.

They stood together just staring at the little covered body until Ed broke them out of their trance.

"You guys okay in there?"

Dana looked up and noticed Jeremy watching her. His eyes were filled with concern, but they were also hard with anger.

"Are you okay?" he asked.

She nodded, a look of grim determination on her face. Grimacing, she turned on her heels and pulled out her cell.

"I'm fine," she replied, walking towards the door, the phone already to her ear. "But whoever or whatever did this won't be when I get a hold of them. Of that, you can be damn sure."

Steve's smile widened as Jared surged forward. He was trusting Tzedakah to keep his word, but deep in the back of his mind he still had doubts. How could he trust the sword? Even when it was being honest with him it was never really telling him everything.

The mysterious Musketeer figure was a perfect example. He too had a sword, and it didn't take a genius to see that Tzedakah hated it. That they hated each other. Could it be that Tzedakah was not the only one of his kind? He pushed all the questions to the back of his mind as he lunged. This was no time for him to be distracted or for the connection between the two of them to be interrupted. If they were going to save the children, then they both needed to be completely on the same page.

Steve's finger twitched and the girl screamed as dark energy coalesced at her temple. Too slow. They were too slow and weren't going to make it. He had to make a choice. The teenager or the infant.

No, I can't. How can anyone make such a choice? Tzedakah promised he would save both, but I guess he overestimated his abilities. Well, I have to make a choice or he will kill both of them.

"Jared," the sword's voice echoed in his mind. "Trust me and let go of your doubt."

He blinked rapidly and then looked around. He was still moving forward but the rest of the world wasn't. It had simply...stopped.

The girl's eyes were closed, and her mouth hung open in a silent scream, but she was frozen like a statue. Likewise, the child was suspended in midair, the shadowy tendrils that held it halted in place.

The whole scene was kind of like a movie that had been paused. It was as if Tzedakah had simply reached out and stopped reality in its tracks.

"How..." he stuttered.

"It was necessary," was the sword's simple reply.

Jared fixed his eyes on his brother and growled. This time he was going to end his reign of terror for good. This time he was going to kill him. Tzedakah was right, people like him couldn't be allowed to live. All they brought to the world was pain and misery. They needed to face justice.

He swung Tzedakah and severed the tendril of darkness that held the infant. It instantly dissipated, but the child didn't fall. It continued to hang suspended above the ground.

Famine

He grabbed it, cradling it safely in one arm and then in the same fluid motion he spun and swung Tzedakah upward, intending to sever the arm holding the girl. Before Jared's strike could land, however, the darkness in his brother's finger surged outward, knocking the blow off course.

The sudden unexpected pressure to the blade knocked Jared to the side, putting the tip directly in the path of the girl. Thinking fast, he twisted his body so the sword wouldn't hit her. Instead, he plowed into her, knocking her out of Steve's grasp.

As soon as they were out of danger, the world snapped back to life. Steve turned instantly and shouted curses at Jared. His voice had changed and was now much lower and sounded more like an animal's than a human's.

"Amelnakru, I will destroy you!" he bellowed.

Jared got to his feet and placed himself between Steve and the children.

"Run," he said to the girl as he handed her the screaming infant. His eyes never left his brother, who glared hatefully at him.

As soon as the children were safely away, he allowed himself to relax a bit. Tzedakah had come through just as promised.

"Why must you always interfere?" Steve growled. "Eons pass and still you are a thorn in our side."

Jared furrowed his brow as he listened to Steve rant. Tzedakah vibrated angrily in response.

What in the world is he talking about? Eons? Steve hasn't been alive for even thirty years. What is going on with him?

Steve's sudden roar brought Jared back to the moment. It sounded like the bellowing of some great beast and couldn't have come from human vocal cords.

As he watched, shadowy tendrils of energy began to seep out of Steve's skin. It was as black as tar and in seconds it engulfed his brother, covering him completely in a shroud of darkness.

Bat-like wings sprouted out from his back and two glowing red eyes emerged from the inky blackness to glare daggers at Jared. The place where his face should have been parted and formed into a great maw filled with razor-sharp teeth.

This was something new. Last time he had morphed into a half-human/half-demon creature, but this current transformation was on a whole different level.

"The Musketeer promised me you would be taken care of," the creature bellowed. "But of course, he lied. I should have expected it. Deception is his nature."

Musketeer? Was he the guy who had attacked me earlier? The one who had a sword like my own?

"Stay alert," Tzedakah hissed. "You are no longer dealing with just your brother."

Jared narrowed his eyes and pursed his lips.

That was obvious. What *was* he dealing with, though? It was apparent that this creature was what was responsible for Steve's newfound power, but what exactly was it and what was it doing to him?

Famine

Tzedakah was silent on the matter, and Jared rolled his eyes and sighed. What did he expect? It never volunteered information and getting the sword to give up anything was like pulling teeth.

"I guess there are some things one must do themselves," the creature said, looking past Jared. "But first."

It lifted its hand and pointed a finger at the fleeing children.

"Die..."

Jared spun just in time to see the girl drop. There was no scream. No sound at all. She just simply stopped moving and crumpled to the ground. She lay face down, the other child underneath her and hidden from sight.

The girl was still. Too still. Jared knew that she was gone. The child in her arms hadn't cried out when she fell on it, and Jared knew deep down that he too was dead.

Rage welled up from Tzedakah, and it mixed with Jared's own growing anger to form a hurricane of fury. The darkness in his eyes writhed as he turned his head to glare at his brother and the monster inside him.

He raised Tzedakah and pointed it at them. "You will die for that."

"You have said that before, and yet here I still am," it snarled back.

The uncertainty from earlier was gone. Jared could no longer tell where he began and Tzedakah ended. Their thoughts and feelings were so intertwined it was almost impossible to distinguish between the two.

"No matter how long it takes. No matter how many generations pass," Jared heard himself say. "I will end you."

"Empty words that mean nothing. Prove it with action," it growled. "If you can."

Jared charged forward, Tzedakah glowing so brightly he could feel its heat. The world slowed to a crawl, and he knew instinctually that it had not slowed down but that he was simply moving so fast that the world around appeared to be in slow motion.

He jumped when he was a few feet from the creature and twisted in midair, using the momentum from the maneuver to launch a wicked two-handed downward blow.

The Steve monster slapped it aside with one hand while simultaneously landing a fierce blow to Jared's now-exposed flank. The hit sent him careening into the wall of a nearby home.

The siding dented and cracked, revealing the drywall underneath. A cloud of white particles slowly drifted around him, and the metal creaked as he removed himself from the human-size dent he had made.

Before he had a chance to get his bearings, warning bells sounded in his mind. He lunged to one side, narrowly avoiding another blow from the creature's fist. He continued into a roll as dirt and wall particles peppered his body from multiple impacts that he narrowly avoided.

The thing was extremely fast, and Jared just barely managed to stay one step ahead of the creature's continued onslaught.

Jared ducked a right cross and then blocked a jab from the creature's left. He winced at the crack it made when it connected with his forearm, but the deflection gave him an opening.

He took advantage of it, thrusting Tzedakah hard at its exposed midsection. To Jared's astonishment, the shadowy energy that surrounded Steve formed into a third arm that deflected the blow.

The energy arm snaked up and over the blade, wrapping itself around Jared's forearm. He jerked backward hard but was unable to free himself from the creature's grasp.

It pulled him close until their faces were almost touching.

"I have you now," it said triumphantly.

Jared saw stars as Steve hit him squarely in the jaw. His head snapped backward painfully and then he was pulled back forward just in time to meet yet another blow.

Punch after punch slammed into Jared. Some to his head and face, others to his torso and midsection. Dazed from the continuing hits, Jared was unable to react to the monster's furious attack. He felt himself slumping in the creature's grip, his hands dangling limply at his sides.

Tzedakah screamed in his subconscious, but he couldn't make out what it was saying. The blows didn't stop, but they did slow. At least it seemed like they did. He couldn't be sure since he wasn't even sure if he was still standing.

His jaw exploded as another punch rocked him. He felt the creature pull him close again and could feel its hot breath on his face. It stank of rotten eggs and burning earth.

"I have to say," it growled, "I am disappointed. Every other bearer I have faced was far stronger than you. I guess this generation truly is the weakest. I will have to commend Azazel. His designs to infiltrate your education system and pop culture appear to be working. I know Moloch enjoys the constant sacrificing of your unborn to him."

Jared heard the thing speaking but couldn't concentrate enough to really understand it. At least it had stopped hitting him.

The world spun as Jared felt himself being lifted higher. He heard the creature grunt and felt his stomach lurch as the ground flew up to meet him. The sound of his bones cracking and the feeling of his tendons tearing replaced all other sensations as his body slammed into the earth.

Stunned, he lay staring up at the clear blue sky. Impossibly, he still held onto the sentient sword. Though his grip was tenuous, he could still feel it pulsing angrily.

Thankfully, he continued to sense Tzedakah in his subconscious. The sword's words were garbled and unclear, but he could clearly feel its emotions and its will.

His serene view of the clear sky was eclipsed by the dark shape of his demon brother's form. Glowing red eyes glared down as the monster loomed over him. Jared could feel Tzedakah's will and power growing in him with every second, and the fog from before was starting to lift.

"I have to admit," it continued, "your brother is strong. It took years of manipulation to break him and to mold him into what I desired him to be. You should feel slightly proud of him. If not for me, he may not have become the monster you know."

Jared gritted his teeth and narrowed his eyes as his hand tightened around Tzedakah's pommel. White-hot rage surged up from within him, intensifying his connection with the sword. The confirmation that his brother hadn't simply chosen to be a monster, but that he had been pushed down that path, silenced his internal turmoil.

He may not want to kill his brother, but destroying this creature was something he and Tzedakah agreed on. All Tzedakah's resolve poured into Jared, mixing with his own, and with it all its power.

Snarling, Jared slammed his fist into the side of the creature's head. The darkness wavered and Steve's human face appeared for a fraction of a second before it disappeared from view.

A noticeable shockwave rippled out from the place where his fist had connected. It smashed into the surrounding area, shattering glass and sending anything that wasn't anchored down flying.

He jumped to his feet and dashed after the flying form. Alarms blared, dogs barked, and the chatter of raised voices followed him as he moved. The trail of destruction left in the creature's wake made it easy for Jared to track where it had gone.

He found it lying tangled up in a metal jungle gym in the middle of a playground. The metal rods that made up the structure were twisted and bent around his brother's form. A few of the rods were broken and were now impaled in his flesh.

Thankfully no children were around, but the usual joggers and pet walkers either stood dumbfounded or ran screaming from the grizzly scene. He could hear the clicking of cell phone cameras from the onlookers who hadn't fled, and sirens blared from somewhere in the distance.

The darkness that had encompassed his brother's body was slowly receding. It left the mangled form looking more human, but still not quite. Half of his features were still enlarged and monstrous. One red eye was still visible, but the other was ice blue.

Both eyes tracked him as he approached. It didn't take him long to reach the tangled form, and he slowly raised Tzedakah until it was only inches from his brother's face. The glow from the sword washed over his brother's features, giving it a blue sheen.

"Well, big brother," Steve said, his voice a mixture of demonic and human. "What are you going to do?"

He suddenly grimaced and jerked and contorted, as what seemed to be waves of pain shot through his body.

"He will do nothing," growled the demon as Steve's consciousness was forcefully overpowered. "His love for you will prevent him."

The creature contorted again and Steve reasserted control, the human blue eye pained but focused.

"Oh," he said, his voice now more Steve than monster. "For certain last time we met, but I wouldn't be so sure of that now. Right, big brother? You still torn on what to do with me?"

Jared narrowed his eyes and gritted his teeth. He said nothing, but his arm wavered slightly.

Famine

Steve grinned and laughed. The sudden motion caused him to cough violently, and he growled as waves of pain wracked his body. When he had finally calmed, his breathing was shallow and labored.

"Jared," he managed to whisper through gasped breaths, "just kill me already. If you don't, I will just keep coming after Dana. This thing inside of me has its own plans, and I will probably lose myself to it soon, but I will make damn sure I kill her before I do."

Jared's eyes focused menacingly on Steve, and they bored into him like daggers. The trembling in his hand ceased and he drew it back to strike.

The taunting smile never left his brother's face as Jared moved to attack, but something in Steve's eyes made him hesitate. They seemed almost peaceful, as if he wanted to die. That went against everything he had always known about his brother. Why would Steve want to die?

Steve saw Jared's hesitation and this time both his eyes flashed with anger.

"Do it, you coward!" he spat. "Or do more people have to die before you grow some balls?"

What game is he playing? he thought to himself. *Something seems off.*

Steve's face suddenly twisted and contorted as the demon tried to reassert its dominance. Steve's features switched rapidly between demon and human, neither one managing to take complete control.

There was definitely something wrong, but before he could put his finger on what exactly it was Tzedakah's presence invaded his consciousness.

252

"Steve Cadrette," he heard himself say in the now-familiar ethereal tone. "And the betrayer Azrael..."

What was he doing? He had to stop Tzedakah. Something was off. They were missing something important, and he was certain that Tzedakah's single-mindedness was driving them to make a mistake.

Before Tzedakah could finish the statement, however, there was a flash of violet-black light and he felt the arm holding the sword being knocked aside.

He spun with the force of the push and quickly turned back around to face his brother, Tzedakah at the ready. He was met by the smiling face of the Musketeer instead.

All Jared could do was watch as he raised his rapier in a salute, and with a wink and a nod both Steve and he vanished in another flash of violet-black light.

Steve was dropped unceremoniously on the ground. They were in a clearing surrounded by trees. Sunbeams hit his face, and he lifted one hand to shield his eyes. The sun was low in the sky and would soon set.

"That went well."

He turned to look at the man who had spoken. He was standing with his hands on his hips, watching him.

Steve stood and brushed himself off as the Musketeer sighed and stroked his goatee. The Frenchman continued to look at him, his expression thoughtful. The wounds that Jared had inflicted on him were already closing and he could feel his strength returning. There certainly were perks to being possessed.

"Well," he continued, "as well as could be expected, that is."

Steve could feel the anger from the entity inside him. Feelings of hatred, fear, and betrayal surged through him, making it hard for him to distinguish which were the creature's emotions or his own.

As if the Musketeer could sense the demon's feelings, he smiled and said, "You don't agree, Deces?"

Before he knew what he was doing he was lunging at the man, the dark energy seeping out of him to form a large, wicked-looking scythe. His swing hit nothing but air, and he stumbled slightly from the lack of expected resistance. The Musketeer had vanished.

He felt cold steel on his throat an instant later. Steve swallowed and the motion of his Adam's apple caused the razor-sharp blade to leave a thin line of blood on his skin.

"As much as I would enjoy killing you," he whispered jovially, "there is still too much I need you for. Our timetable is moving along nicely, and even though your showing in the fight was a bit...disappointing, it had the desired effect."

Shockingly he could feel the demon's fear of the Musketeer's threat. If it was scared of the Musketeer, he reasoned, maybe he should be, too. The creature's thoughts flitted rapidly through his mind, and he realized it wasn't the man himself it feared but the blade. The blade that was very much like the one Jared wielded.

The Frenchman, however, had yet to do anything more than make playful, idle threats. It was obvious that it wasn't out of charity that the Musketeer had saved him. He wanted something from him, but what that was he still didn't know.

"And what effect was that?" he growled, doing his best not to move too much lest he deepen the cut on his neck.

Famine

"Why, to rattle our dear Jared," he replied, removing the rapier from Steve's throat and waving it around with a flourish to emphasize his point.

"He may have beaten you soundly, and with only one punch I might add, but he now fears that you will kill the love of his life. As pointless as love is for him, he seems to be unable to let go of her, and we shall use that to our advantage."

Steve narrowed his eyes and glanced sideways to look at the Musketeer.

"What exactly are we planning that we would need an advantage for?" he croaked, reaching up to rub his throat.

The Musketeer released him and stepped back a few paces.

"Why, we are playing a game, my dear Steven," he answered, using the same phrase Steve had used earlier. "The second greatest game ever played by mankind, and the stakes are higher than you know."

'Well," he paused, the darkness in his eyes dancing with what Steve could only describe as joy. "At least part of you knows anyway. The rest of you will catch up in, how you say... à l'heure? Ah yes, in time. You would think after all of these years I would have a better grasp of your language."

He flipped his hand dismissively and turned away from Steve to examine his surroundings. He tapped one finger on his lips as he did. What was he looking for? They were deep in the woods and there was no one around for miles.

The stench of rotting flesh hit him out of nowhere and he had to fight the urge to wretch. His eyes watered as he scanned the surrounding woods, trying to locate the source of the disgusting odor. The Musketeer seemed unphased by the scent and raised one eyebrow, as if curious by his discomfort.

A creature the likes of which Steve had never seen before stepped out of the tree line. It was mottled gray and tall, with long lanky arms and legs. It moved around on all four appendages like an animal and wore tattered and dirty clothes that seemed too big for its emaciated frame. It stopped a few feet from Steve and clenched and unclenched its fingers and toes which were capped by wicked- looking claws.

The thing fixed its beady, black, marble-like eyes on Steve. They seemed to gleam with unrestrained malice as it hungrily licked its cracked lips. The creature was obviously ravenous, and it had that frantic, desperate look all starving animals had.

If Steve hadn't known any better, he would have thought the beast was a reanimated corpse. Of course, after his experiences over the last few days, it wouldn't have surprised him.

Steve reached out to the demon for power, readying himself for a fight. He could feel the black energy surging up from within and his own features twisting and contorting, becoming more bestial. His bones popped and cracked painfully as they rearranged and transformed themselves into the half-human/half-demon form he had used when he fought his brother.

To Steve's surprise the thing didn't attack. It simply continued to stare at him like he was a delectable piece of meat. It was unsettling, and he shifted uncomfortably. What was it waiting for?

"Where is your master?" the Musketeer asked, breaking the tension.

"He will arrive as soon as the sun sets," the thing replied, its eyes never leaving Steve.

The Musketeer smacked his lips and sighed. "Very well, I suppose it can't be helped. But it really is bad form. We both know that he can move in the day just as easily as he does in the night."

The creature shrugged and its skin made a sound similar to someone crinkling parchment paper. It turned its head and smiled at the Musketeer, revealing long-needle like teeth that were stained with blood and gore. Steve could smell the thing's rancid breath from where he stood, and he wrinkled his nose in disgust.

"Master comes and goes at his pleasure, but the mistress Musume cannot walk in the daylight."

The Musketeer's eyebrows shot up. "He is bringing the White Lady. How very interesting."

The wendigo shrugged again. "My master brings his entire court. At least, those who currently reside here at the farm."

"I suppose he has questions?"

The wendigo shrugged again but said nothing.

The Musketeer sighed and waved his hand dismissively. "Well, I can see I will get no answers from you. You may go. You stink of death, and I can no longer stomach the smell."

The wendigo bowed deeply and flashed Steve another menacing smile before melting back into the shadows. Even though the wendigo had left, Steve could still feel its hungry eyes watching him from somewhere just outside his field of vision.

I wonder if the women I killed ever felt me watching them. Felt my longing to murder them, to have my way with them. Of course, unlike this horror, I never desired to eat anyone. Kill them sure, but not eat them. That's just...wrong.

"It is simply its nature," came a hissing-soft reply in his mind. "The creature is no longer human. It has transcended humanity to become something more."

Steve was silent as the demon continued. "To him mortal man is the same as the prey animals you consume. Do you find it distasteful that someone eats a steak even though it was once a living being?"

"A cow is not the same as a human," Steve protested.

The demon laughed. "I would wager that the cow might feel differently."

Steve had to admit the devil had a point. Of course, he wasn't going to become vegan or anything, but to the wendigo humans were prey just as cows were to humans. Of course, cows hadn't once been human the way the wendigo obviously was. If the stories he had heard were true, then cannibalism was what caused someone to become one in the first place.

"No," replied the demon. "The yearning for human flesh is born from an internal transformation. Once this begins, the desire for human meat becomes unbearable. And once the creature gives in, there is no going back."

Steve narrowed his eyes, and his heart began to beat faster as a thought struck him.

"Will this same transformation happen to me?"

The demon was silent for a long moment and Steve gnashed his teeth in frustration.

"Demon, will I become like the wendigo?" he growled.

"No," it finally said. "But you have already sensed that you are changing."

Steve nodded and he noticed the shadows growing long as twilight set in. He had more questions for the entity, but it would have to wait. The sun was about to set, and whoever or whatever they were waiting for would soon be arriving.

He walked up next to the Musketeer, who was thoughtfully caressing his beard. He glanced at Steve out of the corner of his eye.

"Did you and Azrael have a good chat?"

So that was its name. Azrael.

Jared had said the same name earlier when he had tried to kill him, and now he knew why. He could sense an apprehension from the demon, as if it didn't want him to know its true name.

Before he had a chance to contemplate why, the last rays of sunlight disappeared below the horizon, leaving them in darkness. His demon-enhanced eyes instantly adjusted to the deepening blackness, and he became acutely aware that they were no longer alone.

He sensed the vampires before he saw them. They seemed to materialize out of the shadows like wraiths and surrounded them. He counted no fewer than ten, with more outside his field of vision.

If the Musketeer was afraid, he didn't show it. He simply stood, looking bored as one of the largest men Steve had ever seen approached them. He was flanked by two women—one of Asian descent and glowing a soft blue; the other pale, buxom, blonde, and strikingly beautiful.

To call the man a giant might not be completely accurate, but Steve reckoned he must be close to seven feet tall. His long, dark hair was parted at the forehead to reveal a slender golden crown.

"Renault," he said cooly. "Can you explain vhy Tzedakah is here in New York killing my children? Think carefully before you speak, Frenchman, for if your answer displeases me you will sorely regret it."

Sophia turned over in her cell and winced. Everything hurt. She arched her back, trying to crack it, but the muscles in her abdomen seized from the motion, forcing her to curl up in agony.

She thought her teeth were going to shatter from how hard she was gritting them, but after what seemed like hours the pain finally subsided. The cramping had only lasted for a few seconds, but to her it had felt much longer.

Apparently, she had been holding her breath the whole time, because tiny black dots swam in front of her eyes. She took in a long, ragged breath, her head spinning from the surge of oxygen.

"I guess I'm dehydrated and low on potassium," she rasped. "That's the only thing I can think of that would cause involuntary muscle cramping."

Her voice sounded harsh and hollow to her. God, she was exhausted. At least she was being left alone in here. Out in the general population, she had been constantly harassed. They all were, even the children.

She shuddered at the thought. It was violent, yet sexual at the same time. Not all of the vampires enjoyed hurting them. Some, like the White Lady, cared for them almost as if they were her children. At least as much as one could care for a creature they saw as food.

Her stomach suddenly lurched and growled in protest, and the hollow pit in her stomach sent waves of nausea through her.

How long had it been since she ate? It seemed like she had been confined here for weeks, but it had actually only been a day or two.

Even before her failed escape attempt, they had fed her little. All of the prisoners were fed once a day, and never much. This was to keep them weak. The weaker they were, the easier they were to control.

Also, their bites carried some kind of toxin. On adults it had an aphrodisiac effect, but for children it acted more like heroin. It numbed the mind and the senses, and made them completely compliant and submissive.

She shuttered as the euphoria she had experienced flashed through her mind. It was like nothing she had ever experienced before. Sure, she had done a little weed, but never anything harder than that. If the high from drugs was even a fraction of what a vampire bite was like, she understood why it was hard for people to leave. They were literally addicted to the thing that was killing them.

The vampires didn't want to kill them, necessarily, at least not through starvation anyway. They needed them alive. Needed them for food, and if that food source was too high and addicted to run away then all the better.

The thought of what she knew was even now being done to the children enraged her. Bile filled her mouth, and she choked and coughed, turning on her side as she did.

How dare they do this to them? They weren't cattle. They were human beings, damn it.

She slammed her fist into the concrete floor and felt the skin around her knuckles tear. Ignoring it she slammed her fist into the floor again, this time reveling in the pain. It fueled her fury and drove away the weariness in her mind.

Gritting her teeth, she rolled over and tried to stand. Her legs shook as she did, and she had to grab the bars of her cell to keep from falling. It took all her remaining strength, but she managed to pull herself to her feet.

She rested her head against the bars, her eyes closed, breathing heavily. Anger was all well and good, but her body was too weak to do anything about it. She needed food and water, and she needed it now.

"Calm down, Sophia," she said to herself. "Going off halfcocked won't do anything but get you killed."

When she had composed herself, she looked around the little cell to see if maybe someone had left her some food or water. Nothing.

Judging by the lack of light streaming in from the little window, it was dusk. It would be night soon and maybe they would finally let her out. Or kill her. Either would be better than another night sleeping on this hard floor.

"What I wouldn't give for a Spiedie right now."

"What's a...Spiedie?"

Sophia jerked at the sound of the voice and lost her balance. She fell unceremoniously backward and landed hard on her rump. Two red eyes stared back at her from the other side of the bars.

Sophia sighed and rubbed her backside.

"Kat, if you don't stop sneaking up on me like that, you're going to give me a heart attack."

The little vampire was silent as Sophia gingerly got to her feet and made her way over to her. Kat never blinked or moved but stood completely still. The lack of movement was unnatural and unsettling. The hairs on Sophia's arms stood on end, and she shivered.

Even though she looked like a little girl she was, after all, a predator. And Sophia's subconscious knew it. She was pretty sure Kat wouldn't hurt her, but she still had to be very careful nonetheless.

"What brings you too my neck of the castle?" she said with a faint smile.

Kat cocked her head to one side. "This is not a castle. It's a camp. At least, it used to be."

Sophia's eyebrows shot up. "How do you know that?"

She shrugged.

"There are cabins, a playground, and other stuff you find at camp. I'm pretty sure Mike and I..."

Her voice cracked. She swallowed and cleared her throat before continuing. "I'm pretty sure we went here one summer. It was run by a church, I think. I remember swimming in the river."

"Makes sense," she replied.

Famine

Sophia yawned and leaned heavily against the bars. Her eyelids suddenly felt like they were made of lead, and she had to blink them to keep them from closing.

"I don't suppose you have anything to eat or drink?"

Kat shook her head.

"Oh well, was worth a shot."

She turned so her back was against the bars and slid down until she was sitting on the floor.

"You never answered my question, by the way."

The little vampire made no sound as she joined Sophia on the ground. She sat quietly for a few seconds with her legs crossed and hands in her lap before shrugging.

"I just wanted to see you again. The others are scared of me. Especially the children. None of them will talk to me."

Sophie nodded slightly. "Can you blame them? If I wasn't so tired, I might be too scared to talk to you as well."

She shot Kat a lopsided smile.

"Of course, I would be your best friend forever if you could rustle me up something to eat and drink."

Kat furrowed her brow. "I'm sorry. If I could, I would."

Sophia sighed and waved her arm dismissively. "No worries."

Kat suddenly gasped. Sophia's eyes snapped open, and she whirled around, her head moving back and forth, scanning the darkness. Nothing seemed out of the ordinary.

"What's wrong? Is someone coming?" she whispered.

Kat didn't respond, and Sophia noticed that the vampire's eyes were fixed on one of her wrists. She looked down reflexively and noticed the subtle glint of something metallic on her skin.

JW Kiefer

Kat's eyes were the size of saucers as Sophia moved her arm into the waning light so they could get a better look at the shiny object. Sophia smiled wistfully at the thin silver bracelet with a running shoe charm she wore on her right wrist. I had been a gift from her father for placing first in All-State's.

She really wasn't sure why they had allowed her to keep it. At the time she supposed it was because they didn't like silver. A fear of silver was a staple of vampire lore, so it made sense.

She shook her wrist and sent a kaleidoscope of silver illumination skipping across the little cell. Both of them smiled and their eyes were bright as they watched the phantom spheres of light dance.

Even here in Hell there is beauty.

After a few minutes Sophia lowered her arm and the little orbs disappeared. She could feel Kat frowning at her, but she just didn't have the energy to keep her arm up any longer.

They fell into silence again, but it was an amiable silence. The gloom and despair that usually permeated the cell had been temporarily driven away by the reflection from her bracelet.

Sophia broke the silence first.

"Can I ask you something?"

Kat nodded.

"What happened to your brother?"

Kat was silent for what seemed to Sophia to be an eternity. She knew Kat was apprehensive about the subject of her brother, but she was curious. Maybe he had escaped and that was why Kat had been interested in her own failed attempt.

If he had managed to escape, maybe she knew how he had. It was worth a shot. Even if it caused Kat to clam up and possibly leave. She liked the company of the little girl, but finding a way out of this Hell-hole was crucial. Not only for herself, but for all of the other captives as well. If she didn't, they were all going to die here.

She was about to press the issue when Kat finally replied.

"He's dead."

Sophia's heart dropped into her stomach. So much for that line of thinking. She would have to find another way of escape.

"I'm sorry, hon," she said with a sigh. "Did he die here?"

Kat nodded and blood-red tears formed at the corner of her eyes. "We were both taken at the same time. I had gone into the woods near the playground to go pee. That was when I was taken. Mike heard me scream and came to help. That's when they got him, too."

Sophia's expression was one of sadness and horror as she listened. What had started out as a fun day on the playground had turned into a nightmare. They had been tied up and thrown into a large van and brought here.

The trip had been very disorienting since they had been blindfolded and gagged. As soon as they arrived at the camp, they had been thrown into what looked like an animal pen alongside other frightened children.

They were left there to fend for themselves for what seemed like days. There was nothing to eat or drink, and the nights were cold. The twins clung to each other for warmth and support until the vampires had come for them.

"Back then," she said, her eyes haunted, "they didn't even try to keep us alive or comfortable. They simply came for us one at a time, dragging us off kicking and screaming."

Sophia felt anger and horror rising up inside as she listened to the little girl's story. She barely noticed the pain of her nails digging into her palms. She was clenching her fists so hard she was drawing blood.

"The children they took never returned. We were all so scared. We had no idea what was happening to them. I couldn't stop crying, but Mike held me close and told me it would all be okay."

She paused for a second and sighed deeply.

"Sometimes," she went on, her voice haunted and soft, "they would take one of us at night while we slept. We would wake up in the morning to find someone missing. That was even scarier than when they came in the day.

"No one wanted to go to sleep, because they were scared they would disappear in the night. We were all so tired and hungry. Mike promised me he would stay awake while I slept and that helped me sleep. I know he fell asleep after me, but it made me feel safer."

"He was a good brother," Sophia stated during one pause.

Kat nodded, wiping tears from her eyes. They left crimson streaks on her cheeks, adding to the horror of her story.

Famine

"It wasn't long before they came for me. Mike tried to stop them, but they hurt him. They took me away, washed me, gave me a nice dress, and then took me to a large bedroom where there was a very tall man with blue eyes waiting for me.

"He asked me to come sit on the bed next to him. I didn't want to, but something in his eyes made me want to. I couldn't stop myself from going to him, and he made me turn around so he could look at all of me. It felt dirty and wrong, but I couldn't stop it from happening."

Sophia's emotions went from horror to rage and back again as Kat continued. After the man had inspected her, another had come to get her. He was not nice, and he tore her dress and beat her as he fed off her.

He seemed to like it when she screamed or cried and hurt her more whenever she showed fear or pain. Eventually she passed out from shock and blood loss, and it was over.

The lump in Sophia's throat prevented her from speaking as tears made their way down her cheeks. All she could do was sit and stare as Kat met her eyes.

"How long was it before you...awoke?" Sophia asked when she could find her voice again.

"Not long," she replied softly. "They hadn't expected me to turn, so they dropped me outside where they kept all the others who had died. I awoke on a pile of them."

"Were you scared?"

Kat shook her head.

"Not scared, hungry. So hungry. I could smell the children in the pens. They smelled like food. Before I even knew where I was, I was in the pen with them."

Sophia gasped and put her hand to her mouth. "Oh, God," she breathed.

Kats eyes were haunted as she stared at something only she could see. She nodded as another tear broke free and streaked down her cheek.

"He smelled so good, and I was so hungry. The boy sat up as I was standing over him. He jumped up and hugged me. I knew he was talking to me, but I couldn't hear anything other than the rushing of the blood in his veins. Before I realized what I was doing, I had killed him."

She fell silent, her lip quivering.

"It was Mike, wasn't it?"

She nodded and turned away.

"I couldn't stop myself," she whispered. "I was so hungry."

Sophia reached out and drew her close. There was no way for her to completely wrap her arms around Kat with the bars between them, but she did the best she could.

"Kat, I am so sorry. If I had known, I wouldn't have asked."

They stayed like that for a long moment before Kat pulled away. She sniffed and smiled at Sophia.

"It was long time ago but, unlike my parents, I can still remember it clearly."

Before she knew what she was doing, Sophia had removed the bracelet her dad had given her and handed it through the bars to Kat.

Kat's eyes went wide, and she looked from the bracelet to Sophia then back to the bracelet again.

"Are you sure?" she breathed excitedly.

Famine

Sophia nodded and then grabbed one of Kat's wrists with both her hands and placed the little bracelet on it.

Kat pulled it close to her face, her eyes alight with excitement. She smiled broadly and then tried to hug Sophia through the bars. It was awkward and Kat was much stronger than a young girl should be, and she crushed Sophia against the bars painfully.

"Ow," she groaned. "Take it down a notch before you break a rib."

There was a commotion in the other room and it drew Sophia's attention, but after a few seconds she realized that no one was coming to bother them. When she turned back to Kat the girl was gone.

She rubbed her hand through her hair and sighed. She wasn't sure she trusted the little vampire, but when she was sharing her story, she seemed sincere. It was a sad story, but one that rang with truth.

"I should have shown her mercy and ended her life the moment I realized she had turned."

Sophia's eyes shot open, and her heart raced as she slowly turned to face the person who had spoken. She knew the voice well and shivered involuntarily even though the temperature in the room hadn't changed.

The White Lady was looking in the direction Kat must have fled, her eyes distant.

"I know that children like her cannot thrive in our world. Yes, they may survive for a time, but in the end their fate is always the same."

Sophia said nothing but reflexively shifted away from the beautiful vampire. Fuyuko didn't respond but continued to stare off into the darkness.

"I think," she said with a pause, "maybe she reminded me of my own daughter. Of course, all children do. Every mother who has lost a child would say the same."

She sighed and then turned her ice blue eyes on Sophia, freezing her in place. She felt like a statue, as if the beautiful vampire could turn people to stone with a look. Those haunting eyes seemed to grow bigger, and she felt herself being drawn into them.

"Now, my dear, Lord Vladmir has finally decided your fate," Fuyuko said calmly.

All Sophia could do was watch in fear as the White Lady opened the door to her cell and slowly advanced.

"Let us not keep him waiting, shall we?"

Vladmir's ice-blue eyes bored into the Musketeer, who simply matched his gaze with his usual grin.

Neither man spoke, but stood staring at each other from across the field. After a few seconds had passed, the massive vampire turned and bowed slightly to Steve.

"Lord Azrael," he said in reverence.

Without warning Azrael took over his body, and the voice that came from him was not his but the demon's.

"Vladmir," it replied, nodding slightly in acknowledgement.

As if that was all the attention the vampire warranted, the demon receded, and Steve was once again in control.

"I hate it when you do that," he hissed softly. He felt Azrael's indifference and it infuriated him, but there was very little he could do.

As much as he hated being overpowered by the demon, he did learn one thing. Apparently, it was no ordinary devil. The honor the vampire showed it was confirmation.

The formalities over, the big man turned his attention back to the Musketeer. He crossed his brawny arms over his chest and glared at the much smaller man.

The tension from the vampire was palpable, but the Musketeer met the bigger man's gaze with his characteristic smile.

The Frenchman tapped his lips with one pointer finger. "Tzedakah here in New York? I had no idea."

Vladmir was on him in an instant and he wrapped one of his massive fists around the Musketeer's throat. He lifted the still-smiling man until he was eye level with him.

"Do not think I will spare you, Renault. You are merely a husk for the sword. You are one of many and not the first I have dealt with. You promised me that your counterpart would not interfere with our plans and yet, he does."

The Musketeer's smile widened to a maniacal grin, showing just what he thought about the vampire's threat. The darkness in his eyes writhed and twisted anxiously, reaching out towards Vladmir.

"Careful, Prince," he chuckled. "Avlah does as he pleases. Your Council's petty machinations only interest him as long as they continue to...how you say? Ah yes, amuse him."

Vladmir growled and squeezed. The Musketeer's only response was to allow his chuckle to escalate into a full-blown cackle. This infuriated the vampire, and he lifted the man higher and cocked his arm like a football quarterback.

He halted suddenly as the tip of the Musketeer's rapier appeared centimeters from his left eye. Steve hadn't even seen the Musketeer draw the weapon. Neither, apparently, had the large vampire prince who stood frozen, staring wide-eyed at the glowing blade.

Both the White Lady and the blonde vampire snapped into motion. They were stopped instantly by the raised hand of Vladmir. He shook his head slowly and the two women retreated a few paces, but did not relax, continuing to glare menacingly at the Musketeer.

"As entertaining as a battle with you and your children would be, let us not hinder the goals of the ruling Council anymore then we need to, shall we?" the Musketeer said calmly. "Afterall, you can ill afford to lose more of your children. Nor, might I add, they you."

Vladmir narrowed his eyes, and then gently lowered him to the ground. The Frenchman cricked his head back and forth, cracking his neck, and then fixed his rumpled tunic.

"Much better," he said with a smile. "Now that this unpleasantness is out of the way, let us discuss where the Council's plans currently lie. I see you have brought the supposed Chosen One."

Vladmir turned to look at the blonde woman, who stood passively a few steps behind the prince. A small smile graced her face and Vladmir's eyes shone when he looked at her.

The pale Asian woman who stood next to her, on the other hand, was glowering at the Musketeer as if she wanted to rip him apart.

Her lips curled into a snarl, and she spat, "How can you trust this obutsu? He is no better than the other one."

Vladmir sighed, closed his eyes, and then rubbed the bridge of his nose.

"Fuyu, you know as well as I that we need Renault to deal with Tzedakah."

"I will deal with him myself," she retorted.

"Sister," he replied patiently. "Now is not the time for this. Ve will discuss this when we return to the farm."

"No," she spat back. "We will deal with this now. The Shogun took everything from me, and I will have my vengeance."

"Enough!" he bellowed, and even Steve could feel the power of his displeasure. The demon in him, however, seemed unphased by the outburst.

"You will hold your tongue, or I will rip it out of your mouth. Is that understood?"

The tension in the little vale rose again as the two vampires squared off. Lady Fuyuko was the first to give in, nodding and crossing her arms as she looked away. Her face remained a mask of anger, but she acquiesced.

Vladmir glared at her for a few more seconds before turning back to the Musketeer. He beckoned to the blonde, who gracefully moved to stand next to him.

Steve blinked a few times when he saw her. He knew this woman, he was sure of it. She was the kind of beautiful that no man could forget, but for the life of him he couldn't remember where he knew her from.

Then it hit him. She was Jared's ex-girlfriend, Jasmine. The one that had finally had the guts to dump his sorry ass.

Famine

Now *this* was an interesting development. An interesting development indeed.

He turned to look at the Musketeer, who noticed his gaze and winked.

So, he knows who she is as well. I would wager that this whole meeting was orchestrated just so he could get a good look at her. I don't know what he has up his sleeve, but I would bet my left arm that it isn't going to be pleasant for Jared.

He smiled to himself at the thought of his brother suffering and felt the demon respond in kind. The demon may be taking him over but at least they shared a few things in common. Their desire to bring misery being one of them. Their hatred for God another.

The Musketeer smiled appreciatively and the darkness in his eyes danced. He sauntered up and grabbed Jasmine's wrist, lifting her hand to his mouth and kissing it gently. She smiled back at him with a look of pleasure on her face.

For the briefest of moments Steve thought he saw a flash of recognition in her eyes. It was gone just as quickly as it had come, but Steve was certain he had noticed it. The Musketeer had sparked something in the woman, but what it was he didn't know.

"My lady, it is a distinct pleasure to make your acquaintance," he said, removing his hat with a flourish and then bowing.

"The pleasure is all mine," she replied, stifling a little chuckle of delight.

"This is Jasmine," Vladmir said, pride in his voice.

The Musketeer replaced his hat and moved back a step. He nodded in approval and then turned to Vladmir.

"The Shogun is dead," he said. "I killed him days ago."

Fuyuko gasped and the Musketeer looked at her, nodded, and then saluted her with his sword. Steve could see the rage once again rising in her face, and apparently so did Lord Vladmir. Gritting his teeth, he turned and gave her a glare that would stop a runaway train. She instantly fell silent and returned to sulking quietly.

The Musketeer turned his gaze back to Vladmir and continued. "The one who killed your warriors is Tzedakah's new pet. I will deal with him in my own time, but I can assure you he will not hinder the plans of the Council."

Steve noticed recognition flash in Jasmine's eyes again. It was minor, but he saw it. He was pretty sure the Musketeer noticed it as well, but the other vampires seemed oblivious.

The conversation they were all having was obviously far more enlightening to the beautiful vampire than she wanted to let on. She, like the Musketeer, was hiding something, but what was it?

Vladmir crossed his arms and nodded. "I will trust you to handle Tzedakah, Renault, but if she is who I think she is then we will be moving soon and we cannot afford to have him interfering. If I truly am correct about her, then the time of the Awakening is upon us."

Besides," he continued, turning to glare at both women, "recent events may necessitate us to abandon New York and return to Europe. Between Jasmine's childish tantrum at the hospital and Fuyu's ill-advised slaughter, we have attracted too much attention. It will not be long before someone else takes notice. I fear our time here is over."

The Musketeer nodded. "Will the other covens follow suit?"

Vladmir furrowed his brow. "I am unsure. Certainly, the other high lords who journeyed to the New World will at least attend the Awakening."

He sighed and rubbed the bridge of his nose again. "I assume that most will leave their forces here to be used in the events that will follow. I cannot be certain, there is still much for the ruling Council to accomplish, but it would be prudent to have as much strength here as possible. My forces, however, will return with me."

The Musketeer nodded. "Well, I have much, how you say sottises? Ah yes, mischief to manage, so I will bid you *au revoir*."

He turned to Jasmine and bowed low again. "My lady, it was delightful."

She giggled a girlish giggle and curtsied. He smiled broadly and then turned to Lady Fuyuko. He gave her a sympathetic smile.

"I am truly sorry, my dear, to have robbed you of your vengeance, but it is the reason I exist after all, is it not?"

If looks could kill, the one she gave him would have slain him where he stood. He just shrugged it off and turned his gaze back to Vladmir.

"Prince," he said fixing his hat. "As always, a pleasure. Give my regards to your master. That is, if you manage to accomplish what you are setting out to do."

The vampire lord nodded, and the Musketeer turned away with a flourish and headed over to where Steve stood.

Steve watched as the vampires melted into the shadows. The last to go was Jasmine, who lingered. She watched the two men, her brow furrowed in thought for a few more seconds before she, too, disappeared into the night.

"Well, that was enlightening," the Musketeer said. "Did you recognize the girl?"

Steve nodded. "Jasmine Lassiter. The lovely girl who broke my brother's heart."

The Musketeer laughed. "It is oh so delicious, is it not? Did you notice her face when she saw me?'

"Yeah," he replied, somewhat confused. "She seemed to recognize you. Have you two met before?"

He shook his head vigorously. "No, my dear garcon, but I would wager a hundred livre that she has met someone like me. Can you guess who that might be?"

Steve thought for a moment before it hit him.

"Jared," he replied excitedly. "She's seen Jared. She didn't recognize you per se, but your eyes. You have the same eyes."

The Musketeer jumped in place, throwing his arms out to his sides and doing a little jig.

"Yes indeed!" he exclaimed. "If I had to guess, I would say that the little incident at the hospital involved him. It is also why the vampires are so, how you say, effrayé? Ah yes, spooked is the correct word, I believe. They fear her little tryst has brought Tzedakah down on them."

Famine

"You didn't know who she was beforehand?" Steve asked.

The Musketeer shrugged. "I had my suspicions, but as soon as I saw her, I knew for sure. Especially after her reaction to me."

"So, this whole meeting was just to verify she was his ex?"

"No. No. My dear Steven. I did promise to keep my counterpart off their respective backs, so their anger was justified. I had no idea that the woman Vladmir had mentioned was your brother's lover, but if I am correct, and I always am, your brother spared her life at the hospital. After I deduced that, I wanted to know why."

He put one index finger next to his nose and winked. "And now I do."

Well, that's food for thought. Maybe she tried to kill Dana. That would explain why Jared was so jumpy when he showed up at the hospital. Of course, it could have just been him. He did try to kill him, after all. Actually, did kill him.

Steve smiled at the memory.

"Come, Steven," the Musketeer said, turning and swiping his rapier downward in the sky, a large tear in space appearing where his blade cut through the air. "We have much to do."

Steve took one long look back at where Jasmine had been before turning and following the Musketeer through the portal.

Dana watched as a large group of State Police officials swarmed over the farm. Her family had left the area after being cleared by the Staties, and that left her and Jeremy alone to watch the ant farm.

She ran her hand through her hair as a pair of uniformed troopers approached. It felt greasy and a bit gnarled. Like her, it really needed a long hot shower and some TLC. How long had it been since she washed it, or even taken a shower for that matter?

The man in the lead, the commanding officer, she supposed, smiled. He was handsome in the guy next door kind of way. Fit and tall with dark brown eyes that looked weary, but warm.

"Officer Campbell?" he asked.

"Detective Campbell," she corrected, a little harsher than she intended.

"Detective; sorry, ma'am." He sighed. "It's been a long day. You know how that goes, I'm sure."

Dana nodded. "Yeah, been a hard few weeks for me as well."

Jeremy snorted. "That's the understatement of the year."

Dana shot him a withering glare as the second officer, a younger man who looked like he was born from the unholy union of a bull and a human, stepped forward.

He glared down at Jeremy, who was about two inches shorter than the behemoth.

"We were talking to the detective. When we want your input, we'll ask for it."

One of Jeremy's eyebrows rose so high she thought it would shoot right off his forehead.

"Is that so?"

Dana got between the two men before it could escalate into something unnecessary.

"Okay, boys, let's take the testosterone down a notch. We're all friends here."

"Jenkins," the other trooper said, his voice hard. "Stand down."

The younger nodded and took a few steps back but never took his eyes off of Jeremy. They both continued to glower at each other.

Dana relaxed and turned back to face the older trooper.

"Sorry about my friend here. He doesn't play well with others."

"Hey," Jeremy protested. "He started it."

"Oh my God," she sighed. "I'm sorry for my idiot friend, here, Trooper..."

"Captain," the man replied. "Captain Fox. No need to apologize—what you guys stumbled on here would put anyone on edge. It's shaken us up as well. This is not something you see up here. The city maybe, but not here."

Dana nodded. "Yeah, been a lot of this kind of horrible going around lately."

"You talking about the East Side Stalker murders in Binghamton?"

She rubbed her neck and nodded. "Yeah, they were my cases. Mine and my partner's..."

She stopped short, her voice cracking. She gritted her teeth as Jared's dying face flashed through her mind, threatening to overwhelm her. With an effort of will she pushed the emotions back into the box she had locked them in. Now was not the time for this. Her cousin was still missing and the sooner they got through all of this, the better. There would be time to deal with it all later.

"Anyway," she said, changing the subject. "I suppose you have some questions for us."

He nodded, his eyes sympathetic. "Sorry about Detective Cadrette. It's always hard losing someone, especially a partner."

She smiled wearily. "Thank you, Captain."

Captain Fox nodded back and then pulled out a small notebook and pen. He flipped it open and rifled through the pages till he found one that was blank.

"Being a detective, I'm sure you know the drill. You don't have to talk to us if you don't want to, but the quicker we get this out of the way the quicker we can rule you two out as suspects."

Jeremy looked like he was about to say something stupid, so she shot him a warning glare. He took the hint and closed his mouth but couldn't resist sticking his tongue out at her before returning to his staring contest with Jenkins.

"It's okay. We have nothing to hide."

"Okay, then let's start with the obvious. What were you doing way out here in the country?"

"My cousin recently went missing and I came out here to help look for her," she replied, reflexively crossing her arms. "My aunt and uncle don't live too far from here and we have been scouring all of the possible routes she may have taken to get home."

He nodded. "We were informed shortly before arriving that Miss Esposito's family had filed a missing person report. Is this why Mr. Wagner is accompanying you?"

"Yeah, he's a friend and a private investigator. I called him in as soon as I found out she was missing."

It was a lie, but not a complete one. She really did need his help, and he really was a private investigator. Hopefully Captain Fox wouldn't dig any deeper into their relationship. If he did, it might raise a few questions.

Remembering Jeremy's card in her pocket, she pulled it out and handed it to him. He read it and then looked at Jeremy. He eyed him for a few seconds before nodding and handing it back.

"So, now that we've established the reason you two are out here," he continued, "why exactly did you end up here at Stafford's' farm? It isn't off any of the main roads and not a place where your cousin would likely be. It seems kind off odd that you were looking for her here."

She fidgeted slightly and glanced over at the house. Her face went white as two workers slowly brought out a small, covered body and put it into a large van that said *Chenango County Medical Examiner* on it in large red letters.

Captain Fox turned his head slightly to see what she was looking at and grimaced. No one spoke and the atmosphere of the small group was heavy as they watched the body of the little girl disappear into the van.

After a few more seconds of silence, Dana cleared her throat and turned everyone's attention back to the interrogation.

"One of the searchers, Ed Menta, was investigating the houses in the area just in case she had gone to any of them for help. He knows I'm a police officer, so as soon as he discovered the scene he ran back to get me. That's when we arrived."

He flipped a few pages and then read. "That would be Mr. Edward Menta of Smithville Flatts?"

She nodded.

"Is this when you notified authorities of the incident?"

She shook her head. "No, he didn't know how to describe what he had seen, so he led us here to show us. He was understandably in shock and unsure of how to respond to what he had witnessed."

Famine

Captain Fox frowned and pursed his lips. He looked at her for a few seconds before closing the notebook and putting it back into his breast pocket.

His face softened and he smiled wearily.

"I believe you, Detective Campbell, and your story matches with everyone else we talked to from your group."

He turned to Jeremy, who was still in a starring match with Jenkins.

"You have anything to add?"

Jeremy raised a finger as if he was about to speak, but another glare from Dana made him think better of it. Instead, he just shook his head and shot the Captain a smile that looked strikingly like the grin of a cat who had just eaten a pet bird.

Fox raised an eyebrow and shook his head slightly before turning back to Dana.

"Of course, whoever takes over this case may still have questions for you two, so it would be appreciated if you both stayed where you can be reached. You know how it goes."

She nodded and turned to look at the house. More bodies were being taken to the van and what seemed like a hundred technicians scurried about the house and yard. All four of them were silent, their faces grim and haunted.

"Hell of a thing," Fox murmured, breaking the silence.

She nodded, never taking her eyes from the house. The sun was low in the sky, and it cast shadows everywhere, giving the large home a more ominous feel. The whole place felt wrong, as if it were stained somehow. Despite the hustle and bustle of constant activity, the house seemed silent and still.

JW Kiefer

There would be no more family dinners filled with laughter and conversation. No more nightly games or bedtime stories. All of that was annihilated. Destroyed by an act so horrific that it was near inconceivable.

At least it should be. She knew better, though. Since she had put on the badge, she had become all too acquainted with the terrible things the monsters of this world were capable of.

"Well," she said breaking the silence. "If there's nothing else, we need to get back to searching for Sophia."

He nodded. "I would offer help, but we're strapped as is, and with this on our plate..."

"I completely understand," she said, cutting him off with a dismissive wave. "If you would, however, put a shout out to all your guys to keep an eye out for her, I would appreciate it."

"Of course," he replied with a smile. "Now, if you two would kindly leave my crime scene, we can get back to work and all be home by dinner."

Without another word, he turned on his heels and shouted for Jenkins to follow him. Dana watched the two officers leave, her eyes narrowed and a scowl on her face.

"Oh," he said, turning back one last time, his face slightly sterner than it had been. "If I were you, I would look elsewhere for your cousin. She isn't in this area, and I can't have you or any of your people snooping around out here until we have this sorted out. Do I make myself clear, Detective?"

Dana's face flushed and she squinted her eyes and glared at the captain. After a few second standoff she finally nodded, and he turned on his heels and left her there, glaring daggers.

Well, that went from friendly to dismissive fast. If I didn't know any better, I would think they were trying to get rid of us.

Jeremy sauntered up next to her, a matching scowl on his face.

"I really don't like that guy."

"Jenkins?" Dana asked, never taking her eyes off of the retreating officers.

"No, the other one," he snorted. "Jenkins is just a sad guy who was forced to realize that the world isn't high school, and no one cares how many touchdowns he scored or nerds he stuffed into trash cans."

"No, the good Captain," he said, running a hand through his hair. "He gives me a strange vibe. Could be God, my gut, or the Mexican I ate for lunch. They all feel the same sometimes. Either way, I'm pretty sure he isn't what he seems."

Dana rolled her eyes.

"Is everything a conspiracy to you?" she scoffed. "Next you're going to tell me he's a vampire or some kind of ghoul."

"Could be," he replied seriously. "But ghouls smell like death, and he smelled like after- shave and testosterone."

"Oh my God," she groaned, shaking her head.

"What?" he asked, throwing his hands out defensively.

She rolled her eyes again and turned away from the house and started off back the way they had come.

"Come on, Van Helsing, let's get back to the others before it gets too dark."

Jeremy followed, grumbling and shooting her dirty looks. Before they had gone far, however, Jeremy stopped. He was staring intently at something on the ground just inside the trees.

"Hey, hold up a sec," he called, bending down to examine it.

Dana came over to see what it was he had found and gasped.

"That's Sophia's!" she exclaimed, dropping to one knee next to him.

She reached out with trembling fingers and picked up a small silver bracelet. She dropped it into one palm and raised it up to get a better look at it.

She had to squint her eyes in the dying light, but there was no mistake. It was Sophia's. Her father had given it to her after she placed first at All-State's.

Jeremy put his head directly next to hers and stared down at the bracelet. His breath was warm and smelled like peppermint.

Had he brushed his teeth? When had he found time to do that?

"You sure?" he asked.

She nodded.

How had it gotten here? Was what happened at the farm somehow related to Sophia's disappearance?

She shuddered at the thought and her heart began to beat a little faster. What if whoever had done this had killed her, too?

Jeremy must have read her mind because he put his hand on her shoulder and said softly, "I'm sure she wasn't in the farmhouse when it happened. More than likely, she came through here long before it happened and dropped it unknowingly."

Dana scowled and gritted her teeth and closed her fist around the silver band. She clutched it to her chest and rose. She stared off into the woods, her mind racing with all sorts of terrible thoughts.

"Dana, this doesn't mean anything more than we know she came through here."

Dana shook her head and gritted her teeth in impotent fury. She knew he was trying to comfort her. To give her hope. But something deep in her heart was shouting a warning. Her cousin was in terrible danger, and she had to get to her. Had to do something.

But what? She had no idea where to even start looking, and the local law enforcement seemed uncooperative. Then it hit her, and she whirled on Jeremy.She lifted the bracelet up to him and said, her voice nearly a shout, "You specialize in missing people! Take this and do your thing and find her!"

He furrowed his brow and lifted his hands. "My what?"

"You know," she replied. "Talk to God or use your psychic powers. That's what you do, isn't it?"

He sighed and his eyes turned soft. "Dana," he said gently. "That's not how it works. I can't just snap my fingers and make things happen. God talks when He wants, and I listen. He chooses the time and place, not me."

"Then what are you good for?" she snapped coldly.

She turned away from him to start off back the way they had come when she noticed the slight opening in the trees directly where they had found the bracelet. She walked up to it and peered into the growing darkness as Jeremy grumbled to himself behind her.

To her surprise, there was a path hidden behind the undergrowth. It led away from the house and into the forest. Could Sophia have come this way? Without explanation she pushed aside the low hanging branches of the tree that covered the opening and stepped into the darkness.

Jeremy ground his teeth and shook his head. He lifted his face to the sky as he jumped to his feet.

"Can you believe her?" he growled as he plunged into the darkness after her. "I save her from vampires, wander around getting bitten by all manner of woodland creatures while trying to help find her cousin, and this is how she thanks me. Unbelievable."

Famine

It became harder and harder to see as the sun went down, and Jeremy tripped more times than he could count as he followed Dana further into the dark forest.

He was pretty sure this was how most fairy tales started. Two people wandering blindly through the woods at night. Hanzel and Gretel, Little Red Riding Hood, and every other Grimm Brothers story he had heard always took place in a dark forest at night, and not one of them ended happily. Well, it wasn't quite night yet, but close enough for the analogy to fit.

He shuddered involuntarily as the forest came alive with all sorts of strange sounds that were foreign to his city-born senses. The whole environment felt unnatural to him, and that unsettled him. The sounds and smells of the city he knew and was comfortable with, but this? This was something he wasn't equipped to handle. Every little sound, smell, or shadow had him on edge.

As he moved yet another low-hanging branch aside, a bug the size of a Volkswagen smacked into his face. He swatted at it, frantically flailing his arms and slapping his face until it finally flew off. Most likely to go harass a moose or some other animal. Did they even have moose in New York State? It did butt up against Canada. So maybe.

It felt like they had been walking for hours, and Bugzilla was the last straw. He was tired, hungry, and everything hurt. Especially his feet. They felt like they were on fire.

He walked miles every day in the city, everybody did, but apparently hiking in the great outdoors worked different muscles entirely. His poor body was screaming at him in protest, and he had reached his boiling point.

"How long are we going to stay out here?" he hissed, swatting futilely at another bug that was dive-bombing one of his ears. "I can't see a thing, and every critter in creation seems to want a piece of me."

Dana ignored him and continued forward. She had her cell phone out and the flashlight app on. Surprisingly it was very bright, and they could see at least five feet in whatever direction it was shining. Unsurprisingly, however, all it showed was more trees.

Jeremy sighed and then flinched as a branch suddenly smacked him in the face.

"Hey," he cried. "Watch where you're flinging those things. You could've put my eye out."

Famine

Jeremy's face flushed and he balled his fists. He was about to continue his tirade, when she mumbled, "Sorry".

She sounded so disheartened and dejected that his anger melted. God, if he were in her place would he being doing anything less? No. He, too, would be jumping at any lead no matter how small or insignificant it was.

It was obvious that she was starting to lose hope, and his heart went out to her. He really wished he could just snap his fingers and bring her cousin back. Sure, God could, but He never really did things that way. At least not in Jeremy's experience.

They continued on in miserable silence as every pest in the greater Upstate area assaulted them. He swatted at them futilely and continued to lumber along after Dana. It felt like they had been walking for hours, but a quick check of his watch told him it had only been about forty minutes.

He stopped suddenly as every hair on his body stood on end. Someone or something was watching them. Narrowing his eyes, he scanned the surroundings. He couldn't make out a thing, and that put him even more on edge. Everything just looked like black shapes in the darkness.

Dana had noticed his sudden stop and was staring at him, her brow furrowed.

"What is it?" she asked.

He put his hand up for her to be quiet and felt the icy glare that she gave him in response. Before she could protest, he shushed her. The heat from her anger was almost palpable and he grimaced, straining to hear or see anything out of the ordinary.

Nothing. Whatever it was had moved away. He could still feel it lingering somewhere in the shadows, but it was no longer close enough to set his senses tingling.

Maybe it was an animal or something. Certainly, there were predators like black bears and coyotes out there. Could that have been what he'd sensed? His instincts told him otherwise. He knew all too well the horrors that lurked in the darkness, and whatever it was that was out there felt suspiciously like one of them.

"Are you going to tell me what it is that's gotten you all spooked?" Dana asked.

Jeremy scanned the area one last time before shaking his head.

"It's nothing, just something felt off."

"Kind of like a psychic impression?" she asked, her voice thick with sarcasm.

"Something like that," he growled.

Dana turned away and snorted. "I thought it didn't work that way."

Jeremy rolled his eyes. Sad or not, she was really starting to make him angry. With a deep sigh he continued after her but was unable to shake the nagging feeling that they were being followed.

Of course it could just be his imagination, but he had learned to listen to that small voice in the back of his mind. Especially when it was trying to warn him of danger.

Before long they saw a light up ahead. It was small at first and off in the distance, but it was unmistakably man-made. Dana's pace quickened and Jeremy almost had to run to keep up with her.

'Hey, wait up," he wheezed. "I'm not in as good a shape as you."

She ignored him and continued on. Did she just pick up her pace? That little punk did. Well, then she could just face whatever it was that was up there by herself.

He had half a mind to just walk away and let the vampires or whatever else was hunting her have her. Of course, God would never let him, and he had promised Jared he would keep her safe. And, he thought begrudgingly, she was starting to grow on him.

It wasn't long before the woods parted, revealing a large chain link fence with barbed wire at the top of it. Every few feet there was a sign that said, 'No Trespassing. Intruders will be prosecuted'.

"What the?" Jeremy said, scowling.

Dana ran her hand against the fence's links. It was clean and well maintained, but weathered and old.

"Some kind of compound?" she murmured.

"Yeah, but why out here?"

"I don't know," she replied, peering into the area beyond the fence.

Jeremy came and stood next to her, his brow furrowed. "If I didn't know any better, I would think this was some kind of prison."

Dana nodded. "Yeah, but that can't be. The only jails in the area are located at Sheriff's Department offices."

Jeremy felt eyes on them again and he whirled around. Dana yelped and jumped back as he instinctively threw his hands up into a defensive posture. His heart was beating double time, and he squinted into the darkness, searching for the mysterious watcher. Whatever it was, it was close. Very close.

"What's the matter?" she whispered, her own eyes scanning. He noticed her duty weapon was in her hands and in the ready position. "Did you hear something?"

He shook his head.

"Then what?"

He didn't answer. He had no idea what he was feeling. All he knew was that there was someone or something watching them. The hairs on his arms were acting like he had a million volts of electricity going through him, and every subconscious alarm bell in his mind was going off like Fourth of July fireworks.

"Wait a second!" Dana exclaimed, pointing to a large tree just inside the fence line. "Look over there."

He looked in the direction she was pointing and winced. Sitting on one of the tall trees and barely visible was a black video camera. Not the generic kind you buy at an electronics store, but one of those industrial cameras only used by government agencies and such. It was well camouflaged, and he was impressed she had noticed it.

The whole situation screamed secret government facility, and Jeremy's detective bells were ringing deafeningly. Even so, it wasn't the mysterious cameras or whatever lay behind the creepy fence that was the cause of his growing sense of unease. Something else was out there in the darkness.

Pushing his worries to the back of his mind he turned to the camera, screwed up his face, and waved. Whatever was out there would show itself or it wouldn't, but either way he was done trapsing around in the dark, creepy forest.

"Hey, mysterious person on the other side of the camera!" he shouted. "Any chance you saw a college-age blonde run through here?"

"What are you doing?" Dana hissed.

"What does it look like I'm doing?" he growled, thrusting his hands up at the camera. "They obviously know we're here. And with all of these cameras around, it would be impossible for them not to have seen something. I don't know about you, but I'm done trudging around here in the dark and cold. If these guys saw something, then let's ask them and then get the hell out of here."

Dana sighed, peering into the darkness past the fence. She winced slightly and gingerly ran her fingers over her stomach.

Jeremy grimaced. Her eyes were shadowed, but he could tell she wasn't doing well. She was doing her best to hide it, but he knew she was still very much in pain. Not only emotionally but physically. Even with God's usual help *he* still wasn't completely healed, and she had nearly been gutted only a few days earlier.

"I don't think they are going to be very cooperative," she mumbled.

"What gives you that idea?" he snorted. "All of the friendly *No Trespassing* signs? Clearly, they just love visitors."

She pointed towards a shape in the distance.

"Is that a building?"

Jeremy came up and stood next to her. He peered into the gloom and squinted.

"Could be," he murmured. "I can't tell for certain but, given the cameras, it's a good bet."

She nodded and then pushed away a stray lock of hair that had fallen into her eyes. Jeremy couldn't help but glance over at her. She really was beautiful. Still a pain in the butt, but lovely nonetheless. In spite of himself, he really was starting to like her.

She noticed him glancing at her and scowled.

"What?" she demanded. "Do I have dirt on my face or something?"

He frowned, crossed his arms, and raised one eyebrow. *Yep, definitely a royal pain in the ass.*

"Something like that," he growled. "If it is a compound then let's go find the front door and knock."

She looked back at the shape in the darkness and then down the fence line. She was quiet for a few seconds. Jeremy looked at his watch and fidgeted.

"I guess it's worth a shot," she finally said.

Jeremy sighed audibly and turned and started walking briskly in the direction that appeared closest to the building-like object.

"About time," he grumbled.

Before he could get another complaint out, he was suddenly blinded by a bright light shining in his eyes.

"Hey," he snarled, throwing his hands up. "You trying to blind us?"

Reflexively he pushed Dana behind him, putting himself between her and whoever was shining the light on them. He expected her to protest, but she pushed closer to him instead.

Well, this is new, he thought with a smile. Before the emotion could take root, however, he shook his head slightly and grimaced. *That's enough of that; get your head in the game.*

"Identify yourselves," a gruff voice said from behind the light.

"You identify *your*self," Jeremy replied.

"This is private property," the man barked back. "Can't you read the sign? Now I will ask you one more time, who are you and why are you prowling around?"

He felt Dana push past him and his first impulse was to stop her, but he knew that would be a mistake. Anyway, she would probably break his arm if he tried.

"My name is Detective Campbell, and this is my colleague." She raised one arm and the light glinted off the badge she held in her hand. "We're here on police business. Are you security? We would like to talk to whoever is in charge here."

The light shifted slightly toward Dana, illuminating the silver badge she was holding up. It stayed there for a few seconds before finally being lowered toward the ground. It took a minute for his eyes to adjust and all he could make out was that the person holding the flashlight was large and man shaped.

"Detective Campbell," said a familiar voice from the darkness. "Let's drop the lies, shall we? We both know you aren't here on police business."

It was then that Jeremy recognized the big man holding the flashlight and scowling at them unpleasantly. Deputy Jenkins sneered nastily as Captain Fox slowly walked up to stand next to the big man.

He shook his head and looked at them like a disapproving teacher. "Detective, what in the hell are you doing? I thought I made it very clear that it was time for you and your friend to leave."

Dana ground her teeth. "You know damn well what I'm doing, Captain."

He put his hands on his hips and shook his head. Deputy Jenkins growled slightly and seemed to be hunching like a cat ready to pounce.

Dana shifted her gaze to Jenkins and her hand reflexively went to her pistol. Jeremy could see her stiffen and her face become hard.

Her intuitions were good, he realized. She instinctively knew something wasn't right and so did he. The feeling of dread that he had earlier pushed to the back of his mind was now front and center and shouting at him.

"Whoa now," Fox said, raising his hands. "No need for that. We're all friends here."

He put his hand on Deputy Jenkins' shoulder. The deputy visibly relaxed but didn't take his eyes off of them. His gaze unsettled Jermey. He knew that gaze; had seen it on countless monsters, both human and non-human.

"Are we friends?" she asked, her hand remaining on the handle of her weapon. "As far as I was taught, friends don't sneak up on each other in the dark."

Fox's expression hardened. "Detective, need I remind you again that you are out of your jurisdiction? This is my county, and my tolerance for your shenanigans, police officer or not, has reached its limits."

Jeremy swallowed and shifted his eyes back and forth between the two law enforcement officers. He didn't like Fox or Jenkins and knew there was something off about them, but the Captain did have a point. They were creeping around in the woods at night and possibly trespassing to boot.

"So, now if you please, why are you and your friend here sneaking around this property after I explicitly directed you to leave and go home?"

Dana narrowed her eyes. "I repeat, you know why we're out here."

"Detective, your cousin isn't out here. No one is, especially this late at night," he said, his expression softening. "I understand your frustration, I really do, but snooping around on private property isn't going to help you find her. I told you I would look into it as soon as possible, and I meant it."

Fox sighed and removed his hand from Jenkins' shoulder.

"You're actually lucky we were still around and are the ones who responded to the trespass call. If it had been any other deputy, they might have shot first and asked questions later."

Dana shot him a look but relaxed slightly. He noticed, however, that she still kept her hand resting on her belt, not far from her gun. She turned and looked toward the mysterious property.

"What is this place?" she asked.

"None of your damn business!" Jenkins snapped.

Jeremy took a step forward, putting himself between the officers and Dana. Jenkins sneered at him and closed his hands to fists.

Jeremy grinned and winked at the big man.

"You looking for a fight, big boy?"

"Oh, yeah," Jenkins answered with a nasty grin. "I've been wanting to beat the shit out of you since we first met."

"Really? Well then come over here and do it. I'm waiting."

"Gentlemen," Captain Fox commanded, "that will be enough."

Jenkins seemed to freeze in place, his muscles trembling as if straining against some unseen force. Jeremy also felt as if some invisible hand had suddenly risen in front of him, hindering his ability to move.

Was the Captain using magic? No, that wasn't it. He could see magic and knew when it had been cast. Even invisible spells were visible to him. Usually, anyway. Everything was always subject to God.

No, the Captain's command had simply been that powerful. Very few creatures, both light and dark, had that kind of authority. Cold began to seep through his body and he shivered slightly. Who or what was Captain Fox?

Dana hadn't acknowledged Jenkins' outburst and was still casually staring towards the building shape in the darkness. So, she was unaffected by whatever it was that held them in place. Interesting.

"Some kind of compound?" she mused out loud, still ignoring the now-fuming but still seemingly frozen Jenkins.

Fox shook his head. "You're like a dog with a bone, aren't you? Detective, this is private property, and I am not at liberty to discuss it. Least of all with people who skulk around in the darkness like thieves."

She turned and looked at him. "Thieves? Is that what you're going with? You know very well we aren't thieves. What exactly is going on out here, Captain? I have lived here my whole life and never heard of any facilities like this being built in Chenango County. Perhaps I should do some digging myself. Maybe get a warrant and proper permission and all that. I'm sure if I dig deep enough, I'll find something interesting."

The captain smiled but his eyes were hard. "Campbell, we can do this the hard way or the easy way. You can either walk out of here with us willingly, or we can put you in handcuffs and take you out the difficult way. Honestly, I prefer the easy way but that's entirely up to you and your friend here."

He turned to look at Jeremy and waves of dread washed over him. He staggered as the unseen force that had held him suddenly dispersed.

"Are you all right?" Dana asked, moving over to grab him before he fell.

He shook his head and grimaced.

"Yeah, just felt faint. Probably low blood sugar or something. I haven't eaten all day."

Jenkins looked white as a ghost as well, but he remained on his feet. Obviously, he was feeling the same effects but was handling it better. Jeremy glared at Captain Fox, who impassively stared back at him.

Were his eyes glowing red, or was it a trick of the light? This guy was definitely not what he seemed. They were in danger, and he had to convince Dana to leave. The sooner they got away from these two, the better. Whatever they were, it had become painfully obvious he couldn't handle them. He was already feeling better, but playing faint was probably the only way to get Dana to leave. And they needed to leave *right now*.

Dana helped him stand but kept one arm on his back for support. He noticed the look of concern on her face and his cheeks flushed. He looked away and cleared his throat.

"You okay, Mr. Wagner?" Captain Fox asked.

"I'll be fine." He coughed. "Just a little dizzy is all. Low blood sugar, you know how it is."

The way the corner of one side of his mouth rose into a grin let him know the good Captain wasn't fooled by his display in the slightest.

"Very well then. If you two would be so kind, we can escort you back to the road and to the rest of your group."

He didn't wait for them to respond but turned and walked away, trusting they were going to follow. He stopped when he reached Deputy Jenkins and turned slightly.

"Oh, and if I were you, Detective, I would forget about this place. Do what you will, but if I were a betting man I would wager that you'll find digging here to be harder than you may think."

Dana gritted her teeth but said nothing. She turned back and her eyes softened as she looked at Jeremy with concern.

He avoided her gaze. She was indeed starting to grow on him. Too much, and he was going to have to deal with that before it became a problem.

She was, after all, Jared's girl. Jared the all-powerful unmerciful spirit of justice and vengeance's girl. His growing feelings aside, he didn't want to kick that hornets' nest if he could help it.

Of course, Jared was a zombie, wasn't he? Could the undead even have relationships? Well, he wasn't really a zombie, but certainly his state of being would make it impossible for him to have a normal life.

He glanced at her as they followed Captain Fox, Deputy Jenkins taking up the rear. She noticed his gaze and smiled.

He blushed again and turned away, pretending to cough. Yeah, he was definitely going to have to push that down. Down so deep no one was ever going to dig it back up.

****

Kat watched them go, the moonlight glinting off her red eyes. The small troop walked around a bend and out of sight. She waited for several minutes before dropping down, not making even the slightest sound as she landed on the soft earth.

Her gamble had worked. The policewoman had found the bracelet just like she had hoped. And just like she had hoped, she had followed it back to the compound.

Everything had almost met with disaster when the other two men had shown up. Thankfully, they had been too distracted by the intruders to notice her hiding in the trees.

She shuddered at the thought of them. They were the worst of their kind. Cruel and merciless. Thankfully, they had clearly been ordered not to make a scene, or the pretty policewomen and her friend would be nothing more than red streaks in the snow and her desperate plan over.

If they had discovered her, she doubted they would have hurt her. All of the creatures here knew that if they laid a finger on her, Mother would rip out their hearts.

No, her fears were for the human girl Sophia she had met in the cell. She was kind to her and had even given her a gift. Kindness was something she had not experienced in ages, and it had brought back emotions she thought long dead.

It was impossible for her to save herself from the terrible darkness, but maybe she could save Sophia. It was a long shot, she knew, but hope was stirring inside her. Not a hope for herself, but a hope that maybe, just maybe, someone could escape this place.

She glanced once more at the location where her fragile hope had gone before sighing deeply and turning away. A movement in the darkness caught her eye and she was on it in a flash.

It was a small rabbit, its tiny nose wiggling frantically as it tried to free itself from her grip. Its chest rose and fell rapidly, its heart beating fast from fear. After a few seconds it gave up and went still, its little nose still twitching.

Famine

No, not even the tiniest of creatures escape this place, she thought to herself as she bit into the rabbit's neck. It was a pity it had to die, but she had to eat just like everyone else. After all, if she had the will to kill herself, she would have long ago.

She dropped the corpse of the animal to the ground and took one last look in the direction the policewomen had gone before melting into the shadows.

Maybe this time will be different. Maybe this time hope will prevail.

The night was dark, the moon hidden by clouds. Jared walked around the small clearing where he had last seen Jasmine. The previous few days were a blur.

Steve was indeed still alive and was changing in ways he didn't understand. The strange man dressed like a musketeer had opened up a whole new can of worms he had no idea what to make of. Dana was okay but seemed to be running headlong into danger. At least Jeremy was with her, so that was something.

And vampires existed, and Jasmine was one. Vampires. Sure, he was raised in a Pentecostal home and had always been told about demons and angels, but vampires? If they existed, what other legends were real? Was Bigfoot real?

Jared stopped to listen, but all he heard were the usual signs of the forest. The rustle of things scurrying in the underbrush, the creaking of branches as the wind blew through the trees, the cracking of twigs and the breathing of something big not far off in the darkness. Was it a Bigfoot? No, it was most likely a bear or some other normal creature.

"I can enhance your hearing if you like," the sword offered.

Jared ignored it. His fight with Tzedakah had rattled him. It was becoming increasingly clear that the sentient sword was a monster. Maybe *monster* was too harsh a word, but that was the way he felt.

In his previous life he had been a police officer and had seen a lot of horrible things. Sure, he had wanted to beat a few perps to death for what they had done, but everyone knew that wasn't justice. It was vengeance. Or was it?

In truth, he wasn't sure anymore. After all, the sword was in fact the living embodiment of justice. How could its actions be anything but? He wished Sanctuary was here to ask. The angel, even though he was usually late to the party, had always seemed to have the answers.

Where had Sanctuary gone? Last time he saw him, he had been with Jeremy. He wasn't at the hospital. If he had been, Jared was sure he would have intervened.

"The angel is not in the vicinity," Tzedakah said into his mind. "If you have questions, I can answer them."

Jared grunted. He was still angry with the sentient sword and didn't want to talk to it. Besides, it would probably just lie to him or cryptically refuse to answer his questions.

"I never lie," it replied simply.

Jared grunted again but didn't respond, continuing to quietly examine the area. Nothing seemed out of the

JW Kiefer

ordinary. Tzedakah could probably show him where she had gone, but he wasn't going to ask the bastard for help.

Just when he was about to give in and ask the sword for assistance, warning bells went off in his mind. With supernatural speed he ducked and turned, slashing backward at the unseen assailant he had sensed.

His blade hit only air as the would-be attacker burst into shadows. The darkness flew a few paces away and then solidified into a very large man with jet-black hair and cruel, ice-blue eyes.

"I knew you would come here," the man stated in a deep, thickly accented voice. "Despite his assurances, I knew I could not trust that bastard Renaud. Of course, he is a creature of chaos after all. The man who trusts such a creature is a fool, and I am no fool."

Jared narrowed his eyes and shifted Tzedakah into a two-handed grip. Power emanated from the man in visible waves. His eyes, though blue, glowed a slight red. He smiled, revealing long ivory fangs.

"It seems," he stated with a sigh, "that I must deal with you myself after all. I cannot let you interfere."

"Interfere in what?" Jared asked. He never took his eyes off the vampire even though he was secretly scanning the area for any other threats. He sensed none. The vampire was apparently alone.

"Be careful," Tzedakah warned. "This abomination is no ordinary monster. He is ancient and powerful."

"More powerful than you?"

"No, but you are not ready for such a battle."

"You gonna take me over again? Send me back to that...place?" Jared's voice quivered slightly as he spoke. Even though his tone was defiant, he couldn't hide his fear of returning to the darkness.

The sword was silent as the big man crossed his arms and squinted his eyes. *Yeah, that's what I thought. Not going to rule it out, are you? Well, just so you know, I'm still not going to just let you do things I believe are wrong without a fight. You can count on that.*

"You are not what I expected," the vampire said, pursing his lips and cocking his head. "I had heard that the Shogun was destroyed and another had taken up the mantle, but your aura is...chaotic. I had feared that this would be a fight I could not win, but now? Perhaps Fortune has shined on me."

"You didn't answer my question."

The vampire frowned and his eyes burned with intensity. "And I shall not. The less you know, the less likely you are to interfere."

Jared grimaced. "No big villain monologue? Okay, then what do you want with Jasmine?"

Vlad chuckled. "She is destined for a great purpose. A purpose that she will step into soon. Sadly, however, you will not be around to see it."

Jared narrowed his eyes, and he could feel Tzedakah reaching into his subconscious, attempting to connect with him. The connection was tenuous at best due to his subconscious aversion to the sword.

If he had been a normal human, he wouldn't have been able to track the vampire's movements. Thankfully, he wasn't.

Vlad was fast. Very fast, but with Tzedakah's strength he was faster. He dodged the punch that would have turned his face to mush with ease. The vampire followed up the blow with a flurry of punches that Jared just as deftly evaded or deflected.

The onslaught continued and Jared soon found himself being driven backward. Both men's arms were indistinguishable blurs. At first, the vampire's attacks had seemed to be coming at him in slow motion, but now each attack was increasing in speed. Was the vampire getting faster or was he getting slower?

Could he get tired? He didn't feel tired, but he soon found himself barely managing to hold the vampire at bay. Tzedakah screamed in his mind, but he sounded like he was shouting at him from across a great distance.

Pain erupted from his shoulder as the vampire landed a blow, raking him with his claw-like fingernails and tearing his flesh along with his clothes. He staggered and just barely managed to raise the glowing Tzedakah to deflect the other clawed hand that was meant to rip his throat out.

He didn't, however, have the time to dodge the powerful kick that followed. It slammed into his stomach and lifted him about two feet off the ground. Before he could recover, the vampire smashed both his fists into his torso and sent him careening backward.

He braced himself for the inevitable impact with the trees. It never came, as a shadowy blur suddenly flew down at him from the sky and hit him with a blow that sent him crashing to the ground. The shock wave from the impact sent earth and rocks scattering in all directions.

Jared groaned as he lay motionless in the small crater his body had created. Dust and particles hung in the air, distorting his view, and he could no longer see the vampire. All light slowly shrank as a veil of darkness enveloped him.

Tzedakah glowed brightly and he gingerly stood up and looked around, holding the blade out defensively. It illuminated the area directly in front of him, driving back the oppressive darkness but not dispelling it completely.

"I have fought others like you," said a voice from somewhere in the blackness. "But I must admit you are the weakest. Had the Shogun lived, I am sure he would have defeated me with ease and possibly brought all our plans to ruin."

"Yeah," Jared said, grimacing. "I'm hearing that a lot lately. Sorry to disappoint you."

"It is no disappointment. I feel fortunate that it is you and not him. Perhaps the Almighty has made a mistake. I never thought it possible, but he did choose you after all."

Jared gritted his teeth. The vampire was right. He was the wrong choice. The sword, God, or whoever was responsible for him being here had made a mistake. He couldn't be what they wanted him to be. He couldn't be a merciless killing machine for the universe. He didn't want to be a monster like Tzedakah.

A sudden movement in his periphery made him turn and put his sword up. As quickly as it had come, it retreated into the darkness. Jared tightened the grip on Tzedakah and turned again as another blur buzzed past him. This time it left a small scratch on his cheek.

"Do you long for death?" Vlad asked from the shadows.

Jared said nothing as he continued to turn in a defensive circle, his eyes scanning for any signs of movement.

"Failed constable. Failed boyfriend. Failure as a friend. Failure as a son and brother, and now, failure as Justice."

Jared narrowed his eyes. How did this thing know so much about him? Could it read his thoughts? Either way, what he was saying was true. He was a failure.

Another blur of motion, but this time behind him. He whirled and slashed wildly at the black shape as it flew past but hit nothing. His arm felt heavy and his movements sluggish.

He heard the tearing of cloth as the vampire's claws ripped his coat, and he contorted just in time to prevent the talons from reaching his flesh.

"Tzedakah," Jared hissed. "If you're going to do something, now would be a good time."

Two more flashes of movement in his periphery and more sounds of tearing material, but each time he just managed to avoid being injured. It was taking everything he had to stay even a small step ahead of the impossibly fast vampire.

"Jared!" Tzedakah shouted. He sounded like he was miles away. "You must let me in!"

Jared growled and swung wildly as the vampire tore past him again. This time he heard the comforting sound of claws on metal as he deflected the vampire's strike and he smiled.

Ha. I got your rhythm now.

His smile faded as the vampire launched a flurry of attacks, each one faster than the last. He managed to intercept only a handful, and the sound of tearing cloth and rending flesh filled his ears as he was thrown around and around by the onslaught.

Flashes of darkness and pain filled his world. It was like being in a blender. Each time the darkness passed, the vampire's claws did their work. Time and time again he was sent spinning, only to be hit from the other side and sent reeling in the other direction. This went on for what seemed like hours before abruptly coming to a stop.

Jared teetered on his feet, his free arm dangling at his side. The clothes and the flesh on one arm were shredded. In spite of the vampire's fury, however, he still held Tzedakah. He shakily lifted the sword into a defensive position and set his feet.

The darkness around him seemed to gather and draw closer. Waves of despair surged out of the blackness. The heaviness was intense, and it drove him to one knee, causing his sword arm to drop a few inches.

Failure. Mistake. Disappointment. Murderer. Monster.

Jared closed his eyes and gritted his teeth against the mental assault. Despair gripped his heart, and he barely noticed as his other leg gave way. His head lolled forward as he collapsed to his knees. The blackness that swirled where his eyes should be dimmed and stopped their churning.

He was so tired. Tired of failing. Tired of fighting. Tired of hurting. Tired of the loss and tired of the pain. He was so tired of it all, and most of all he was tired of being a monster.

Tzedakah's glow dimmed until it was nothing more than a glimmer, flickered rapidly, then blinked out.

So tired, he thought. Maybe it's time for me to just die.

Jared was motionless, his eyes vacant as Vlad slowly walked out of the shadows and came to stand over him. He sneered, the glow from his red eyes washing over Jared making him seem like he was covered in blood.

"Easier than I thought," he murmured, raising his hand to strike. "Not even you can save someone from the misery of their own soul, Tzedakah. Perhaps you will find another vessel in time to stop what is coming. Either way, his journey ends here."

As he raised his arm to strike, a soft light from the sky caught his attention. He glanced upward and saw what looked like the glow from a blazing fire somewhere just outside his sphere of darkness.

Vlad's eyes widened in terror as his spell was suddenly shattered by a massive fireball. It streaked down from the heavens and slammed into the ground, launching dust and debris everywhere.

Vlad, who had managed to jump out of the way just in time, shielded his eyes from the burning intensity of the light. He growled in pain as his exposed flesh was seared by the fiery light.

Jared seemed to wake up as if from a dream and shook his head, trying to drive away the fog in his brain. He had to squint, as the light from the fireball was so bright it even hurt *his* eyes.

"What??" he exclaimed as the light dimmed slightly and the dust from the impact settled.

He sagged in relief when he saw what, or rather who it was, that had crashed between them. Standing in the crater, his massive wings shielding Jared, stood an enormous angel. He turned and looked down at Jared and smiled, his golden eyes blazing with holy light.

"Sorry I'm late," he said with a wink. "But I guess that's to be expected."

Jasmine threw her free arm up, shielding her eyes from the intense light as she cowered from the burning brightness. It seemed to invade and obliterate even the slightest hint of darkness, and she nearly fell from the tree she was perched on in her attempt at evading it.

The bare branches of the big oak did little to protect her from the light, and tendrils of smoke erupted from her skin. The acrid smell of burning flesh and hair stung her nostrils and she gritted her teeth from the pain. Thankfully, the barrage didn't last long.

As soon as the sphere of light receded, she repositioned herself to a more stable location. The branches shook from her weight and the few remaining leaves that had resisted autumn's cold snapped and fell.

Her white gown caught on a branch as she moved, revealing long shapely legs and porcelain skin. A few stray strands of her flaxen hair tumbled into her blue eyes when she pulled the dress free, and she nearly fell again as she swatted them aside.

So much for vampire grace. I guess even undeath can't free me from my family's genetic clumsiness.

Returning to her vigil, she watched as Vlad got up and dusted himself off. Smoke still wafted from his exposed skin, but overall he seemed unfazed.

"Well, that sucks," she hissed. "I thought for sure Jared would be a match for Vlad, but he pretty much kicked his butt. Not even the light from that angel did any real harm to him."

She cursed and slammed her fist into the tree's trunk, sending another wave of wayward leaves sailing to the ground. She had followed Vlad when he left the compound and was overjoyed to see Jared, hoping he would kill him.

All of her plans hinged upon Jared being able to kill Vlad. She had been certain that he could by the way Vlad had freaked out after her encounter with him at the hospital.

She gingerly touched the small cut on her neck that still hadn't healed. Vlad was far more powerful than her. More than likely, she would never reach the same level of ability, even though he continued to assure her that she was some kind of chosen one.

Chosen for what? No one had actually explained that part to her, and every time she brought it up Vlad dodged the question. If she was so important to the vampire cause, then why wouldn't he explain it to her? She should have been ecstatic and excited about what was ahead, but she wasn't. All she felt was this growing cold dread.

The feeling of anxiety aside, she loved being a vampire. It was like she was some sort of god now. The power and enhanced senses and emotions. Every single sensation was a thousand times more potent. Even though she knew Vlad was hiding something from her, she still wasn't going back to her old life. This one was way too much fun.

Her lips curled into a lascivious smile, and she ran her tongue across her fangs as she thought of Jared. Oh, what she would do if she got her hands on him. She had always loved being with him, but now she bet every kiss and every touch would be so much more superb.

She shook her head, driving away the thoughts. It was a moot desire anyway. Even the intervention of that angel didn't seem to be enough to stop Vlad, and that terrified her. Before this night was over Jared would most likely be dead, and she would not only have lost him a second time but be without a card to play against Vlad.

In truth, she was unsure which thing bothered her more. She had been so angry with Jared for allowing that whore, Dana, to come between them, and she wanted revenge, but her desire to get away from Vlad was just as strong. Maybe even stronger.

"Well now, this is something I have not seen in a century," Vlad said, his voice bringing Jasmine back to the events unfolding in the clearing.

"Sanctuary, it has been a very long time."

Vlad turned his head back and forth as if looking for something.

Famine

"Where is that pitiful band of disciples you always have around? I hope that nothing unpleasant has happened to them."

Jasmine watched as the angel snarled and the flames from his two blades increased in intensity in response. Vlad must have hit a nerve.

"Leave now," the angel growled. "Or I will turn you into a pile of ash."

Vlad smiled, bearing his ivory fangs. "My dear Sanctuary, there is no need for such hostility. After all, we have not spoken in years. Surely you will not deny me my pleasantries."

The angel narrowed his eyes but said nothing.

Vlad sighed then waved his hand dismissively.

"I guess it is truly of no real importance. If they were killed, you would simply replace them like an old pair of worn-out shoes. And they say I am the monster."

Sanctuary twirled his flaming swords and slammed them together, sending sparks flying in all directions. He locked them into a defensive stance and narrowed his eyes. The smell of what seemed to Jasmine to be some kind of incense rose up from the flaming weapons.

She choked and had to suppress a fit of coughing as she breathed in the scent. The smoke smelled like roses and was more beautiful than even the most expensive perfume. Despite that, it stung her nose and throat as if it were poison.

"One more word," the angel said coldly, "and this will be where you die. This time for good."

Vlad sneered and raised an eyebrow. "You inger are all the same. Self-righteous and overconfident just like your master. Perhaps if it were simply me you would prevail. But, sadly for you, I did not come alone."

Jasmine watched as Vlad lifted both arms and stretched them outward. She gasped as puffs of smoke erupted all across the clearing. The acrid scent of sulfur filled the air as twenty vampire warriors materialized, all arrayed in full medieval battle attire.

The vampire soldiers quickly surrounded Jared and Sanctuary. The metallic clinking of steel armor rang out as the monsters drew their swords or lowered wicked-looking pikes. In unison as if choreographed, they all raised broad shields and leveled their weapons toward the two men, creating an impenetrable wall around them.

The corner of Vlad's mouth rose slightly. "I may be arrogant," he said, "but I am no fool. And only a fool would confront the Spirit of Justice alone. Even if he is still nothing more than a pup."

Jasmine cursed under her breath. If she had any doubts that Jared would survive, the sudden appearance of twenty of Vlad's warriors dispelled that notion.

Where had they all come from? I didn't sense a thing. Nothing at all.

So many vampires should have set off her danger sense like a tornado siren in Kansas. Was Vlad so powerful that he could shield so many of them from being noticed? If so, she really was in trouble. Not even the angel seemed to notice they were being surrounded.

Famine

Jared gingerly getting to his feet brought her attention back to what was happening in the clearing. He moved until his back was against the angel's and raised his sword. Blue energy exploded from the iron blade bathing the area in azure light.

He bared his teeth and the empty dark pits that had once been his eyes burst to life, writhing angrily and reached out towards the vampires. It felt to Jasmine as if they would suck all existence in and annihilate it like miniature blackholes, destroying everything that had the misfortune to encounter it.

"I don't know about you," he snarled, his voice ethereal and frightening, "but I have had enough of monsters and arrogant assholes for one day."

His anger was so palpable that she shivered involuntarily and slightly shied away. The combination of holy power and unadulterated and unquestioning wrath encompassed the entire area.

She noticed sweat on some of the warriors' brows and all of them fidgeted and glanced uncertainly at each other. Even Vlad was visibly shaken by the immense power the two were radiating. No, not power, but the absolute and unquestioning understanding that judgment had come, and no one would escape its fury.

Vlad gritted his teeth, smiled, and crossed his arms. He straightened and waved one hand dismissively.

"Quite the display, but it is nothing I have not seen before. Tzedakah and I are old adversaries and, well, I have killed my share of Sanctuary's disciples. It will take more than anger and parlor tricks to frighten me."

Jasmine noticed that Vlad's minions' postures changed. Their eyes hardened, and they set their jaws and reaffirmed their grip on their weapons. Even here up in the trees she felt Vlad's confidence in her mind calming and reassuring her.

Had Jared used some kind of spell on them? If he had, Vlad had broken it. Probably not, it was most likely the same kind of mental pressure Vlad generally employed.

She had learned the hard way that powerful supernatural beings all created a spiritual pressure by their presence. Sometimes it could be hidden or suppressed, but it was an attribute they all shared. And when unleashed it could be oppressive, agonizing, and downright terrifying.

She shook her head, absentmindedly curled a lock of hair between her fingers, and sighed. If Vlad was strong enough to dispel the effects from the spiritual pressure of two powerful supernatural beings, then what hope did she have of defying him let alone destroying him?

Her countenance fell as the realization hit her that Jared was doomed, and with him her carefully crafted plans. Fire flashed in her eyes, and she compressed her lips so tightly they almost disappeared.

She glared down at Vlad, her eyes blazing with hatred, and dug her fingers into the tree's trunk so hard she cracked the bark.

"Shit," she cursed. "What do I do now?"

A thought struck her, and she straightened, narrowing her eyes and chewing her lower lip.

Famine

"Perhaps," she mused, "before Vlad murders them, Jared and the angel will weaken him enough for me to kill him. He wouldn't expect it. Not from me."

She doubted Vlad would kill her if her murder attempt failed. He needed her too much. At least so he said. In truth, she speculated, she really had nothing to lose. Perhaps if her plan failed the other sword-wielding guy would be willing to ally with her. What was his name? Renault?

Her attention was so completely focused on Vlad, Jared, the standoff going on below, and her thoughts, that she failed to notice the subtle shaking of the tree as a slender figure alit next to her.

A shiver ran through her, and her flesh broke out into goosebumps as a familiar cold female voice whispered, "I would be careful of voicing your thoughts aloud, child; he can hear you even from here."

Jasmine swallowed and then grimaced. She didn't dare turn to face the person who had spoken.

"Lady Fuyuko," she said with a nod of deference.

The beautiful vampire grinned faintly, her light blue lips parting to reveal her ivory fangs.

Her eyes sparkled. "I noticed you had gone and decided to see where you had run off to. I should have guessed you would come here. After all, this is the last place you saw your love."

Jasmine narrowed her eyes and pressed her teeth together so hard they made audible cracking sounds.

One of the White Lady's eyebrows shot up. "Oh, have I hit a nerve? It appears the *princess*," she spoke this last word with obvious contempt, "is still throwing a temper tantrum over her scorned lover."

Jasmine snarled and her eyes blazed red with hatred, but she didn't dare strike out at the much older vampire. She was pretty sure she wasn't powerful enough yet to take her, plus Vlad had made it abundantly clear that fighting amongst themselves was expressly forbidden. At least for the royals. He cared little what the lower classes did.

Jasmine forced her face into a serene mask. She may not be strong enough now, but she soon would be. At least, if her assessments of her conversations with Vlad were correct.

The time was quickly approaching for her to ascend, and when she did Vlad had assured her she would be more than a match for the hateful Asian bitch. She had no idea what it all meant, but Vlad was completely certain it would be soon.

She was nervous about it and couldn't shake the sense that he wasn't telling her everything. Vlad always brushed off the subject every time she brought it up, so she was still in the dark about the specifics of the process.

Lady Fuyuko chuckled and turned to look at what was happening below. Her laugh grated on Jasmine's nerves, and she fought the urge to backhand her. Oh, unsure or not, the first thing she was going to do after she ascended was knock Lady Fuyuko down a notch.

Her head exploded as Lady Fuyuko let out a loud hiss, sending out a violent psychic barrage of hatred and rage that nearly knocked Jasmine from the tree. She had to close her eyes and grit her teeth in order to suppress the scream that was forming in her lungs.

"You!" Fuyuko shrieked.

Frost formed on Jasmine's exposed flesh and her breath condensed in the air as the waves of cold emanating from the White Lady chilled her to her core.

It took all her strength to keep her footing when the tree shook violently as Lady Fuyuko planted her feet and shot downward like a rocket.

The entryway light popped to life and the wooden boards of her old porch creaked as Dana wearily stepped up to her front door.

She sighed, squinting as the brightness sent her head pounding. Fumbling in her pockets for her keys, she heard them jingling just beyond her reach.

Curse this jacket. A hole had ripped in the inside of her right pocket about a year ago and her keys were always finding their way into it. Her keys and pretty much everything else she dropped there. It was like the Bermuda Triangle of clothing.

Jeremy stepped up and huffed, tapping his foot and scowling just as she finally managed to pull them free. The inside of her pocket was dragged out with them, and she cursed as the sound of tearing cloth signified that her snagged keys had just made the hole bigger.

"You gonna let us in or what?" Jeremy complained.

Famine

She was too tired to get irritated at his perpetual crankiness, so she ignored him. After a few seconds of fumbling, Jeremy grumbling the entire time, she got the door open and stepped inside. The familiar scents of her home instantly washed away all of the anxiety of the past few days.

Exhaling loudly, she flipped the light switch on the wall next to the door and dropped her keys onto the little table there. Other than a thin layer of dust, it was exactly as she had left it.

"Home sweet home," she sighed, throwing her coat onto the back of a chair and plopping down on her cream-colored couch. She snuggled in contentedly, gathering all the large throw pillows to herself until all that was visible were her feet and the top of her head.

The sound of Jeremy closing the door interrupted her perfect moment and she lifted her head above the pillows to scowl at him. He had removed his brown trench coat and placed it next to hers on the chair.

He looked around the room as he untucked his shirt. "Nice place you have here," he said. "Could use a good dusting, though."

She rolled her eyes. "Sorry, my maid is currently out of town."

He snorted. "Yeah, it's hard to find good help these days. You should see my place. My maid hasn't done a thing in...well, in never. I don't know why I keep paying her."

This time it was her turn to snort back a laugh. Even though she found him absolutely infuriating, the little joke had managed to lighten her mood a bit. He turned and smiled warmly at her. She found herself automatically returning his smile, her cheeks flushing slightly.

He really was handsome, in a floppy and unkempt kind of way. Like that celebrity that made a living playing a grumpy, down on his luck guy who is always just one step away from rising to his potential. Women were suckers for guys like that. Jared had been a guy like that.

Her smile slowly faded as the grief came flooding back. Blinking back tears, she buried her face in one of the pillows. No way she was going to let Jeremy see her cry again. Plus, she didn't have time to fall apart. They both needed to get some rest so they could continue the search for Sophia in the morning.

Jermey cleared his throat. "You got a bathroom I can use?"

She pointed in the direction of the stairs, her face still obscured by the pillows. "First door at the top of the stairs." Her voice was a bit strained, but if he noticed he didn't let on.

"Thanks," he replied, turning and heading up the stairs, leaving her alone with her thoughts.

The couch seemed less comfy and the lights in her living room seemed dimmer. It was as if every time she remembered Jared the world itself became a little less bright somehow. It was probably her imagination.

She sniffed and wiped her eyes. They had to be sunken, beet red, and rimmed by dark circles. She haphazardly attempted to fix her wayward hair, but quickly gave up. God, she was tired.

Famine

I don't remember a time when I was this exhausted. Not even during finals week in my last year of college, and I think I only got about two hours of sleep a night for two weeks then. Of course, no one in college tried to eviscerate me. Well, just Mr. Billings in calculus, but that was mental and not physical.

Sighing, she got up, scattering the pillows in all directions, and stumbled into the kitchen. Usually a bit of a clean freak, it barely even registered to her that most of them had fallen on the floor.

She ignored them. She'd get them in the morning. If not then, later. Who cared anyway? It wasn't like she was constantly having visitors stop by. Not even her dad came over much these days.

Why do I care so much? In the grand scheme of things, it's not like the cleanliness of my house matters.

With a shrug she banished her musings and bent down to open up the fridge. Frowning and gaging slightly, she instantly regretted her decision.

"Oh God," she croaked. "What is that smell?"

It only took a few seconds to locate the source of the rotting odor. Some left-over Chinese which was now a putrid shade of dark green glared up at her ominously. Ignoring it, she pulled out a can of Coke. Using her foot, she closed the door while simultaneously popping open the soda.

One never really paid attention to thirst until they had a chance to rest. When they did, it hit them in the face like a runaway train. This was the case for her, and she guzzled down the Coke in a single breath.

"I needed that," she breathed out.

She put the empty can on the counter and then pulled out another. Not seeing an additional Coke, she grabbed a can of grape for Jeremy and then walked back into the living room.

Her body definitely needed water, but it also needed sugar, so another Coke was exactly what the doctor ordered. It didn't take long for the sugar and caffeine to hit her system, and she was already feeling more awake and alive.

She heard Jeremy thumping loudly down the stairs before he lumbered into the living room.

"That for me?" he asked, pointing at the can of soda sitting on the glass end table.

Before she had a chance to answer he scooped it up, popped the top, and noisily started guzzling it down.

Dana raised one eyebrow. "Yeah, and you're welcome."

Ignoring her, Jeremy plopped down in the chair that held their coats, leaned back, and closed his eyes. Dana watched him curiously as she continued to sip her drink. Every time she thought she might be warming up to him, he did something that made her rethink her feelings.

"So, what's our next move?" he asked without opening his eyes.

She took another sip of her Coke. "I was thinking I would go into the station tomorrow and see if my Captain could maybe reach out to the County Sheriff and find out more about that compound. I can't shake the feeling that it's related somehow to Sophia's disappearance."

He grunted. "From the reception we received from those two goons, do you think that's wise? By the way they acted, it seems to me that the local sheriff knows exactly what's going on over there. I mean, one of them was a Captain for God's sake."

She didn't respond right away but stared at her drink, lost in thought.

She trusted Captain Jackson. He was a standup guy and an honest cop who had always treated her and every other officer under his command fairly. Even if the local sheriff's department was involved in something fishy, he certainly wouldn't be.

"Yeah," she said, drawing out the word. "I trust him, and I think he can help."

Jeremy sucked his teeth, and she grimaced. Oh, how she hated it when he did that.

"Okay, but we should probably have a back-up plan just in case," he stated.

She blinked as a thought hit her and she started to say something but then stopped herself. Jeremy noticed and sat up.

"What?"

She waved her hand dismissively. "It's nothing. Just a thought is all."

"Well," he encouraged. "Spit it out."

She paused for a few seconds before answering. "I know a guy who may be able to help, but I don't trust him. At least, not completely."

"Ok, what's his name?"

"Johansson."

"Just Johansson? Is he another cop or something?"

"Not exactly," she replied, finishing her drink and setting the can on the table next to her.

"Okay," Jeremy growled, throwing his hands up in an irritated manner. "Then what is he?"

She rolled her eyes. "He's an FBI agent, okay? You satisfied?"

"You had that in your arsenal this whole time and you're only now mentioning it?"

"Like I said," she replied through gritted teeth, "I don't trust him."

"What did he do to make you not trust him?"

"It's complicated," she stuttered. "And I really don't want to talk about it."

"But if he's a federal agent he certainly would be more help than a local police officer, even one as high ranking as a Captain."

"No," she stated flatly. "Not unless I have no other choice."

"Seriously," Jeremy sputtered. "This guy must have done something real terrible to cause you to be so petty."

"What did you just say?" she asked, jumping to her feet.

"You heard me," he said, also getting to his feet and meeting her glare with one of his own.

"You have some nerve," she growled.

"Me?!" he replied incredulously. "I'm not the one who is stubbornly dismissing the best card we have to play."

"What do you know about it?" she yelled, her voice rising and her hands flailing. "Why are you even here anyway? It's not like you care about my cousin. You don't even know her, or me for that matter."

He gritted his teeth, closed his eyes, took a long deep breath, and exhaled it slowly. "Okay," he finally said before retreating and once again flopping back down into the chair. Slumping in the chair, he massaged his forehead with one hand. "No FBI agent, but I think that's a mistake."

Continuing to shoot daggers at him with her eyes, she eventually followed suit and returned to her place on the couch.

God, he's so infuriating. It's like he knows exactly what to do to get under my skin. Maybe it's because I know he's right, but I'm still not going to give Johansson the satisfaction of me asking him for help. Not after the way he blatantly kept me in the dark about what he knows about how Jared died.

Jeremy's unexpected snoring brought her back to the moment. Was he asleep? Really? She looked up and saw that he was slumped to one side, his cheek resting on one of his hands and his mouth open slightly. The rhythmic rising and falling of his chest confirmed that he was indeed asleep.

All of the anger that had been raging in her evaporated and she sighed. Her eyelids felt like iron weights as her body suddenly reminded her just how exhausted she was.

Quietly rising from the couch, she retrieved the big brown blanket she kept draped over the back of the sofa and gently placed it over him.

She furrowed her brow as she fixed the blanket and bent closer to his mouth, smelling his breath. His breath smelled of spearmint. When had he put gum or a mint in his mouth? Thoughts of her grandfather fluttered through her mind. He always smelled of spearmint. Spearmint and Old Spice.

Strange that those memories should surface now, especially with everything else that was happening. She couldn't deny that the smell of spearmint made Jeremy more attractive somehow. Maybe it was a subconscious thing, like when a guy wore the same cologne as a woman's father.

Smiling, she fixed the blanket so it covered him better and then, shaking off the thoughts, turned and headed towards the stairs. It was late and she wanted to take a long shower before finally getting into bed.

He was right about Johansson, and if the captain couldn't help her, she would seriously consider reaching out to him. But *only* if the captain couldn't help.

For someone who only met her a few days ago, Jeremy had gone above and beyond to help her. Heck, she wouldn't have if she were in his place. Certainly not to the extent he had. For all of his annoying idiosyncrasies, he really was a good guy. She stole one last look at him and brushed away a stray hair before turning and moving up the stairs.

J ared, above!" shouted Tzedakah.

He looked up just in time to see a blue comet hurtling towards him. Lunging to one side, his feet were moving before his mind had time to register what was happening.

Debris flew in all directions as the missile struck the ground exactly where Jared had been standing only moments before. The sound of rock hitting metal rang out as debris peppered the vampires.

The unmistakable scent of burning earth was all that remained of the particles that flew towards the angel. The holy fire that surrounded him was a perfect shield, incinerating everything that tried to penetrate it. He stood unfazed as the dust settled, eyes blazing, jaw set, one blade pointing at the new intruder and the other directed at Vlad.

"Fuyuko," Vlad commanded, crouching, one arm raised defensively in front of his face. "Do not interfere."

Ignoring him, Fuyuko glared at Jared, her eyes burning with rage. "You," she uttered, her voice cracking with unrestrained fury.

What in the world? Who the heck is this? Do I know her? Well, whoever she is, she definitely hates me for some reason.

"She hates *me*," Tzedakah explained in his mind.

Was there a hint of sadness in his tone? Or maybe regret? That can't be, he doesn't feel those things. He doesn't feel anything. Especially not towards a vampire.

Jared tightened his grip on Tzedakah and pressed his lips together. "Yeah, well, that seems to be the general sentiment everyone has after meeting you."

Tzedakah didn't respond to his barb. A persistent feeling of sorrow continued to linger in Jared's mind. Slightly distracting, it wasn't an overwhelming sensation but more of an echo or deep ache in his soul. Kind of like a festering wound that had scarred over but not healed.

"Fuyuko," Vlad spoke, his voice softer this time but commanding. "I understand how you feel, but you need to let me handle this."

"Know how I feel?!" she snapped. "Don't patronize me, Vlad. You know nothing of how I feel."

Vlad's expression hardened and his eyes blazed scarlet. The surrounding horde all hissed audibly and shifted in place as waves of fury flooded from him. Jared winced as well, his subconscious screaming of imminent danger. Even Sanctuary seemed to be gritting his teeth against the mental onslaught.

Famine

"My patience for your insolence is thinning," he responded coldly, his voice nearly a whisper.

Lady Fuyuko's face paled, and her shoulders bowed as if under the weight of some invisible pressure. Gritting her teeth against Vlad's mental assault, she refused to back down. Jerkily, she slowly forced her head around until she was facing Vlad.

"Rokudenashi, if you do not release me," she snarled through gritted teeth, "I will destroy you."

"Enough!!" he thundered, and the White Lady fell and slammed face-first into the ground as if struck by an unseen hand.

The rest of the vampires seemed to be affected by the invisible force and they all dropped heavily to their knees. The sound of clattering metal filled the air as a few of them were unable to hold on to their weapons or shields.

The sudden cracking sound of breaking branches followed by a loud thud invaded the silence. Vlad turned, and his expression darkened even further when he saw a beautiful woman rising unsteadily from the underbrush.

Trembling and shaking her head, her golden locks whirled back and forth wildly as she stumbled drunkenly into the clearing. Her long, form-fitting gown was smudged and torn at one side, revealing long, shapely legs. Squinting, she glanced up at the gathering, her deep blue eyes vacant as if stunned.

Jared's mouth dropped open. "Jasmine?"

The beautiful vampire seemed to regain her senses at the sound of his voice. Her eyes clearing as she turned to look at him, she nodded and smiled.

JW Kiefer

Jared's heart leapt at her smile and his face flushed. At least it felt like it did. Could someone who wasn't technically alive actually blush? Suppressing his emotions, he quickly forced his face back into a mask of apathy. He couldn't allow himself to be distracted by his conflicting emotions for her.

Scowling, Vlad closed his eyes and massaged the bridge of his nose. "Fuyuko, of all of the foolish things you have done out of anger, this is by far the worst."

Jared sighed and stood a little straighter as the intense pressure evaporated. Trembling, Lady Fuyuko got to her feet. She swayed slightly as she turned to face Vlad.

"I did not bring her here," she replied, her voice shaky. "She followed you on her own. I came to retrieve her, when I saw..." Her eyes blazed to life again and her voice hardened as she swung around and pointed an accusing finger at Jared. "The kiainahito."

Jared noticed frost forming on Tzedakah as the temperature instantly dropped. It was so cold that even the warmth from the angel's fire seemed to weaken. Wisps of condensation formed miniature clouds around each of the vampires' mouths as the temperature in the little clearing plummeted to near freezing.

"Jared," Sanctuary said, scanning the field. "Has your link with Tzedakah improved since last we met?"

Jared shook his head and watched as the warmth from the angel's eternal fire intensified, causing the frost on Tzedakah to instantly evaporate.

"I feared that would be so," he sighed. "If teleporting out of here is not an option, then fighting our way free is our only course of action."

Famine

Sanctuary glanced at the confrontation happening between the two vampires. "I am unsure of what is occurring here, but it seems that there is dissention in their ranks. We may be able to utilize this to our advantage."

"How so?" Jared queried, unintentionally glancing over at Jasmine.

Frowning, Sanctuary followed his gaze.

"What is the matter? Is she a threat? I do not sense any great power from her, but I admit your connection to Tzedakah gives you insight I do not possess."

Jared shook his head and faced the angel, looking away from Jasmine. He couldn't let on that he knew her and was unsure of his feelings for her. If the angel found out, he might consider him compromised.

"No," he replied. "Just keeping tabs on where all of the enemies are."

Sanctuary nodded and turned his eyes back to the other vampires. "Vlad is by far the most dangerous foe on the field, but do not underestimate the White Lady; she is fearsome in her own right. The others are merely pawns, but dangerous in large numbers."

Jared glanced at each enemy in turn, his eyes once again lingering on Jasmine. Thankfully Sanctuary was too distracted to notice this time, but she had. She winked at him, and he pretended to clear his throat and turned away quickly.

"If we can use their conflict as a distraction," he continued, "we should be able break through the lesser vampires on one side. Making our escape before Vlad or the White Lady have time to react."

Jared nodded, ignoring Jasmine's gaze which he knew was still on him. Gritting his teeth against the sudden surge of intense sexual desire, he forced himself to focus on what Sanctuary was saying.

Damn it, her vampire seduction mojo is ridiculously distracting. I can't focus. All I want to do is run to her and tear her clothes off.

"No matter what else happens here, we must kill her," Tzedakah asserted suddenly, simultaneously dampening the intensity of Jasmine's influence like he had done at the hospital.

Sanctuary was too preoccupied by his planning to notice Jared's expression darken.

Shaking his head, he glanced at Jasmine again. "Why?"

Tzedakah didn't respond.

Jared's frown deepened and he narrowed his eyes. "Oh, right," he scoffed. "I forgot she's nothing more than a monster needing to be put down."

"Have you forgotten that she tried to murder Dana?" the sword retorted.

Jared blinked a few times before dragging his gaze away from Jasmine. She was still swaying slightly from the psychic pressure and the fall. He hadn't forgotten, but he still didn't want to kill her if it could be avoided.

"Jared," the sword pressed. "You need to trust me. She is more dangerous than even the Ancient One."

Jared screwed up his face and glanced at the two arguing vampires. "The what?"

"Vlad," he replied. "But it is not important. What is important is that you trust me. Allow me in and I will do what needs to be done."

Jared gritted his teeth. "No."

Furrowing his brow, Sanctuary looked down at him. "Is everything all right?"

Jared nodded, ignoring the sudden rush of emotions Tzedakah shot into his mind. "Yeah, everything's peachy."

Pursing his lips, the angel stared at him for a few seconds before turning back to the vampires.

"If you insist," he said skeptically. "But if I were you, I would take what Tzedakah says seriously."

"Of course you would," Jared groaned. "Both of you are the same. You ask for unconditional trust, but give no explanation other than, *it's for the greater good*, or *if you don't do what I say something terrible is going to happen*. Did it ever occur to either of you that just being straight with me might get better results?"

Sanctuary sighed. "I guess it is our nature to be cryptic. As immortals, we perceive things differently from you humans and we fear that trying to explain things from our perspective would only confuse you and cause unnecessary delays in vital actions."

"Really," Jared scoffed. "You're going with that excuse? If you hadn't noticed, thanks to this hunk of metal I am no longer mortal, so that line doesn't track."

"Fuyuko, take Jasmine back to the farm and leave this to me," Vlad ordered, interrupting their argument and reminding them of the current danger they were in. His tone left no room for debate.

JW Kiefer

Nodding, they both turned their attention back to the unfolding conflict. They could continue this argument later. Well, if there was a later. They had to get themselves out of this mess first.

The sound of bone and sinew cracking erupted from the White Lady and Jared's mouth dropped open in transfixed horror as he watched her neck elongate. White scales rippled and undulated as her porcelain skin changed from human to reptilian.

She bared her teeth, which extended into wicked-looking ivory daggers. Flicking her now- forked tongue rapidly like a serpent, her once beautiful, almond-shaped. azure eyes slowly transformed until they were yellow and reptilian. Coiling like a viper ready to strike, her head swayed back and forth on her unnaturally elongated neck like a cobra. Ignoring Vlad, the angel, and everyone else in the clearing, her glare was completely fixated on him.

"No, I think not," she hissed. "This time my vengeance will not be denied."

"Fuyuko!" Vlad shouted as the temperature suddenly plummeted.

Before he could finish his sentence, a blast of cold air exploded outward from the White Lady in a devastating wave. The sounds of screaming and the clatter of metal rang out as the frigid wind slammed into the surrounding crowd.

Snarling, Vlad lifted his hands in front of his face. His feet dug into the ground, churning up dirt as gust continued to swirl and buffet him, threatening to force him backward. Gritting his teeth, his eyes narrowed in anger, he stood his ground.

347

Famine

The other combatants didn't fare as well. Unable to keep their footing, the lesser vampires were violently tossed about by the icy gale. Their screams and the sickening sounds of tearing flesh and clashing steel echoed in the swirling tempest.

It was taking every ounce of strength he had just to keep his own footing, and Jared desperately searched for Sanctuary in the chaos. He exhaled in relief as the unwavering light emanating off Sanctuary let him know the angel was still in the fight.

His heart threatened to beat out of his chest as he realized he had lost sight of Jasmine in the turmoil. Straining to see through the churning storm of debris, he was unable to make out anything. He had to get to her. Had to protect her if he could.

He growled and gritted his teeth as Tzedakah mentally reproached him for his concern. He didn't care. Vampire or not, she had once been his lover. And not only was he not going to kill her, but he was going to help her if he could.

He hadn't the foggiest idea how he was going to do that. Was it even possible to help her? Could vampirism be reversed? Shaking off his thoughts, he turned his focus back to the problem at hand. First he had to find her in this mess before he could even think about helping her.

"Jared, look out!" Tzedakah warned.

Too late. Pain erupted in his abdomen and his stomach lurched as he felt himself being propelled upward. The world spun around him, and vertigo set in as his brain was unable to process which direction was up or down. Tzedakah's voice echoed hollowly in his mind like distant thunder from a coming storm, but he couldn't focus on what he was saying.

His arms were suddenly pinned to his sides as something grabbed hold of him and started wrapping itself around his body. Whatever it was slowly constricted, forcing a groan of pain from him as the pressure on his body increased.

Unable to move and unable to see in the churning storm, he struggled in vain to free himself from the vise-like grip. A shadow moved by his feet, and he watched as the monstrous face of Lady Fuyuko materialized out of the darkness.

"I may not be able to destroy Tzedakah," she hissed, her forked tongue brushing his cheek, "but I will settle for killing you instead."

He couldn't hear the sound of his bones cracking over the howling of the tempest, but he was certain from the pressure Lady Fuyuko was exerting that they must be. Sanctuary was nowhere in sight, and his perception of Tzedakah made the sword feel like it was a world away.

For all of its power, the blade sure seemed to be inconveniently unavailable whenever he needed it. He was sure it was most likely his fault, but he didn't care. Tzedakah had infuriated him. Especially with what he had done at the farmhouse. Or, rather, made him do.

In the past, Tzedakah had simply overridden his will and taken control. In those instances, he felt like a passenger in his own skin, like he was watching himself from somewhere else. What the sentient sword had done the other night, however, was something entirely different and absolutely unforgivable.

The world lurched suddenly, and he felt himself rapidly plunging downward. Gritting his teeth, he braced himself for the inevitable impact.

Stars exploded behind his eyes, and he blacked out for a second as his body hit the ground. When he came to, the earth was once again rushing towards him. This time he managed to stay conscious when his body slammed into it.

"Murderer! Murderer! Murderer!" Lady Fukuyo shrieked in a furious mantra as she continued to smash him repeatedly into the ground.

Jared felt the unexpected sensation of weightlessness before finding himself staring up at the night sky. It moved across his field of vision too quickly to make out any details before he found himself looking back at the ground. The earth flew past just as rapidly, and then he was once again looking back up into the night sky.

The world continued to rotate around him in an indistinguishable blur, until the spinning was abruptly stopped by the unyielding trunk of an ancient oak tree. It cracked and shook violently, throwing shards of bark in all directions as his body crashed into it.

A few leaves gently meandered past him, one softly landing on his right knee which he noticed was facing the wrong direction. Slowly blinking away the fog, it took him a moment to realize he was sitting upside down with his back to the ground and his legs in the air.

The world was bathed in a soft hue of sapphire blue, which let Jared know he still had hold of Tzedakah. Thank the Lord for small mercies. As long as he still had it in his possession, there was a chance he would make it out of this alive. Well, as alive as he was anyway. Of course this was all Tzedakah's fault, though. What had he done to inspire such hatred from the vampire?

The swirling gale abated, and the wind abruptly ceased as he braced himself for another attack. It didn't come, and he righted himself as debris and earth fell to the ground around him. Bodies and armor were strewn everywhere. Some were even hanging from trees, many of them bent in unnatural ways.

Why had she stopped? Unable to connect with Tzedakah in any meaningful way during the attack, he had been unable to defend himself. It made no sense. She had him dead to rights, so why had she stopped?

Groans and moans from the scattered vampires warned Jared the battle was not over, just temporarily on hold. Realizing he only had a few precious seconds to act before they regrouped, he scanned the scene for the White Lady.

He located the big angel first, who was still standing in the same place he had been when it all started. Their eyes met, sharing the same look of relief. A shriek of pain and rage shattered the calm and they turned defensively in the direction of the noise.

Their eyes went wide and their mouths dropped open in shock when they located the source of the scream.

"What the hell?!" Jared exclaimed.

Vlad had Lady Fuyuko by the throat, who had returned to normal human proportions, and was holding her suspended off the ground. Red tears were streaming down her face, leaving bloody streaks on her cheeks as she futilely kicked and thrashed in his grip.

"Let me go!" she wailed between sobs. "Aiko! Daisuke! Kenji!"

She continued to shout the same words over and over again, her voice never wavering in its intensity. Shockingly to Jared, he didn't find the vampire lord filled with rage or anger; instead, his eyes were sad and his expression sorrowful and gentle.

He glanced at Sanctuary and noticed that he, too, wore a sullen expression and stood with his shoulders slightly slumped. What in the world was going on? Why wasn't anyone doing anything? It was like some unseen force had reached down and simply paused the fight like in a video game.

In confusion he glanced from Sanctuary to the two vampires, and then it hit him. She was shouting names. A lump formed in his throat as Fuyuko finally broke and her cries devolved into incoherent sobs. They were obviously the names of people who meant a great deal to her, but who?

A twinge of emotion from Tzedakah invaded his thoughts. Was it sorrow he was sensing? No, not sorrow. Regret possibly? Raising the sword until it was eye level, he stared at it as he tried to make sense of the conflicting emotions the sword was radiating.

An idea formed in his mind, and he narrowed his eyes. He was unsure if it was born from his own contradictory feelings for the sword or from Tzedakah's own emotions, but the more he thought about it the more certain of its truth he became. The pain Fuyuko was expressing could only be the pain of a mother who has lost a child.

Jared's expression hardened and he pressed his lips into a thin line.

"What did you do?" he accused softly.

Tzedakah was silent, but due to the strong emotions it was exhibiting their connection had intensified and it couldn't hide its thoughts from him. What he was sensing was subtle, more like an echo of a past occurrence rather than something current. It confirmed to Jared that his deduction was correct.

"Was she even a vampire when you murdered her children?"

Silence.

"Answer me," he demanded coldly.

Nothing. The sword remained quiet, but the emotions grew in intensity with every passing moment. Rage and anger. Wrath and a need for justice. An overwhelming and desperate need to balance the scales. Jared knew that feeling well, having experienced it himself.

Now, loathing and regret. No, not loathing exactly, but self-loathing? Something about the emotions were off, as if they weren't Tzedakah's but someone else's. A past bearer perhaps?

A face flashed in his consciousness. Long black hair pulled up in a ponytail, tied with a red sash. Sad, almond-shaped eyes rimmed with pain. The same nightmare black as his own. A strong, noble jaw and a frowning mouth set in determination.

The name of the man came easily to his lips. Yoshida. But he knew that wasn't his real name. His real name had been lost to the sword long ago. Or was it recently? He was unsure, as the sword didn't experience time linearly. It didn't matter. Others referred to him as the Shogun, and that was how she remembered him.

Snowcapped mountains suddenly sprang up around him, invading the little clearing. A homey cottage made of timber and mud materialized, wisps of smoke drifting from its stone chimney. He could smell the burning fire from the hearth. Creaking and clacking against the front of the home, a door hung off kilter swaying in the winter wind.

Wrinkling his nose at the overwhelming scent of iron, he was not surprised by the blood pooling in the doorway. Knowing what he would find should he enter, he turned away.

A man dressed all in black, his pants held up by a red sash, stood facing away from him and looking downward. A katana the color of iron hung at his side, glowing brightly, the azure light from the blade making the snow appear blue.

Jared knew the man instantly. The Shogun. There was something lying in the snow at his feet. Straining to see what it was, he sucked in a breath as the Shogun turned to look at him, revealing the prostrate form of a boy.

A stain of dark red appearing black in the sword's light gradually pooled beneath his head. The boy's eyes, fixed and lifeless, stared up at the heavens; his expression frightened, exposing the terror of his last moments.

"He was luring nearby children to his mother," the Shogun explained, his voice devoid of passion.

Glancing at the house, he sighed, his shoulders stooping slightly. "They all were."

A wail of agony split the air, and just as quickly as the vision appeared reality reasserted itself and it was gone. Blinking away the disorientation he found himself staring at the White Lady, who was still struggling against Vlad's grip and again shouting the names of her loved ones.

Had the scream been in the past or the present, or both? Uncertain, he had a gut feeling it was the latter. What he had just experienced was most certainly a memory. The memory of when Tzedakah had murdered Fuyuko's family.

"They were luring innocents to their deaths," Tzedakah stated, mirroring the Shogun.

"He was just a kid," he retorted.

"Yes, but no less a monster than his mother."

Gritting his teeth so hard it was audible, he growled, "Everyone is a monster as far as you're concerned. Except you, of course."

Going silent once again, the only response the sword gave was the continuing flow of confusing emotions. Pain, anger, regret, certainty, and then uncertainty.

How could a child be evil? Tzedakah had to see that, had to understand that. Vampire mother or not, it was a child. Sure, he had known children who had experienced true horrors in their young lives and some of them had done terrible things in response. But they were victims, not monsters. Weren't they?

Uncertainty threatened to shatter his carefully crafted world view. Had the Shogun been right in what he had done? Was it justice? His parents and society had drilled into his head that killing someone was always wrong, no matter the reason. Sure, he did believe in the death penalty in extreme cases but, overall, killing someone should only be a last resort. Especially if it was a child. Shouldn't it?

He felt the soothing warmth from the angel before his hand rested on Jared's shoulder. Supernatural peace washed over him, calming the raging storm in his mind.

Thankful for the gesture, he unconsciously placed his own hand atop it. Sanctuary always seemed to know when he needed reassurance. The holy peace even stilled the raging emotions coming from the sword, doing what neither of them had been unable to do, bringing clarity to both of them and bringing them back into harmony.

"Perhaps," Vlad said, breaking the stalemate, "we should continue this another day."

Quietly sobbing, Fuyuko hung limply in Vlad's arms. Jared couldn't see her face through the mess of black hair covering it, but he could still feel her eyes boring into him. Though her anger was temporarily spent, it was not gone. It would never be. Sooner or later, this situation would have to be dealt with.

Nodding, Sanctuary scanned the field. The vampires were regrouping, and if they didn't withdraw immediately it would soon be impossible to. If Vlad was willing to end the hostilities, then they would take him up on his offer.

His heart suddenly pounding, Jared stiffened and whipped his head back and forth, searching the field. Where was Jasmine? In all of the confusion, he had forgotten about her.

Famine

He sighed in relief when he saw her stumbling out of the trees. Her long blonde hair hung wildly about her head and her white gown was even more dirty, but she seemed none the worse for wear. Reaching up, she pulled out a small twig that had lodged in one of her curls.

The smile she gave him quickly turned to a frown when she saw Vlad and Fuyuko. The big vampire's expression brightened when he saw her, though.

"Jasmine, my dear," he said, obvious relief in his voice. "Come and help me with Fuyuko, please."

Jasmine shot Jared a quick glance before turning to walk towards the two vampires. Her shoulders erect and her head held high, she made her way next to Vlad.

Bending slightly, she put one arm under Lady Fuyuko's and took her from Vlad. Turning, she started away, Fuyuko's shoulders still occasionally shaking with sobs.

She hadn't gotten far before Vlad's cold voice stopped her in her tracks. "We will discuss your disobedience when we return to the compound. I fear I have been too lax with how much freedom I have allowed you to have. I think a stricter set of boundaries may be in order."

She gnashed her teeth and narrowed her eyes. Not turning to face him, she nodded in acknowledgment before resuming her march. Vlad's eyes never left them as they marched slowly towards the tree line.

"Do not let her leave this place," Tzedakah commanded, so forcefully that Jared doubled over and nearly fell. Groaning and grasping his head with one hand, he swayed unsteadily.

Reaching out to him with one massive arm, Sanctuary attempted to stabilize him.

"Are you all right? What has happened?"

The commotion drew Vlad's attention and he snapped his head around, his eyes blazing.

Sensing the tension from their master, the vampires who had managed to regroup all snapped instantly into action. Like a well-oiled machine the warriors surrounded them again, leveling their weapons determinedly.

In response to the threat, like a star readying itself to explode, the light from Tzedakah unexpectedly burst forth in pulsing waves so bright that it lit up the clearing as if it were midday. Those that still held shields took refuge behind them as Vlad, clenching his fists and turning his face away, once again stood his ground.

Realizing that something was wrong, Jasmine swung her head around just as the light hit her. Screaming, her eyes watering, she threw up her arm to block the intense light, nearly dropping Lady Fuyuko. Somehow, she managed to hold on to the limp vampire, who was still sobbing softly.

"Jared!" Sanctuary shouted, unaffected by the light. Just like when his connection with Tzedakah was tenuous, Sanctuary's voice seemed to be distorted and distant.

"I'm sorry," Tzedakah said, his voice soft and almost apologetic. "But I cannot let her leave here alive."

It was the last thing Jared heard before the world went dark.

Unable to sleep, Dana sat staring out the window of her bedroom. Her mind raced with thoughts of her cousin, her family, the strange compound they had found, the deputy sheriffs who had accosted them, and of course Jared. No matter how hard she tried to push those thoughts out, she always returned to them.

It was quiet except for Jeremy's loud, rhythmic snoring from downstairs. Oppressively quiet. It was a starless night, and the little bit of ambient light was being taxed as it attempted to hold back the encroaching darkness. Not looking at anything in particular, she couldn't help but notice the dark shadows surrounding her house. They seemed to inch closer each time she glanced away from them.

Shuddering at the deep sense of foreboding accompanying those shadows, Dana shifted in her seat. Pulling her knees up and hugging them to herself, she felt like a little girl again, scared of the bogeyman or some other such childhood nightmare.

Stiffening and jolting upward, her eyes darted back and forth, searching the shadows. Something had just moved near her bed. She was sure of it. Heart beating so loudly it drowned out Jeremy's snoring, her breath quickening, she peered into the darkness, waiting for whatever it was to move again.

After a few seconds she slowly exhaled, releasing the breath she hadn't realized she was holding. Nothing was there, just the usual clutter in her room. Intentionally taking another steadying breath, she released it gradually, calming herself down. Her heart returned to its normal rhythm as she relaxed.

"You're starting to lose it, girl." The sound of her own voice brought her back to reality, though the tension and feelings of being watched didn't completely subside.

Could anyone blame her? Who wouldn't feel the same way after experiencing what she had? In the last few days she had seen her best friend murdered by his brother, had nearly been murdered herself, been dragged into some weird federal conspiracy, and to top it all off, no one seemed to have any memory of it but her. Now her cousin had gone missing, throwing the rest of her world into chaos.

The only good thing that had come out of the whole situation was Jeremy, and he was an infuriating nuisance she couldn't seem to get rid of. One corner of her mouth quirked up as she thought of him. Irritating though he may be, she was glad he was here. If it wasn't for his odd appearance at the hospital and insistence on accompanying her, she would be facing this completely alone.

Feeling her eyes getting heavy, she stretched and yawned. Maybe she was tired enough to finally go to sleep. Everything would be clearer in the morning after a good night's rest. Taking one last glance out of the window before turning in, she jumped and blinked a few times as a burst of bright light lit up the night sky.

"What in the world?"

Squinting into the darkness, the light continued to pulse methodically, illuminating the horizon in a soft shade of blue. Could it be lightning striking off in the distance? No, no clap of thunder followed. If it wasn't lightning, what was it?

Another burst brighter than the others drove away the shadows, revealing dark clouds and giving the distant hills an ominous look. Just like when she was a kid, her heart beat faster as fear threatened to overwhelm her. Her imagination went wild as thoughts about the end of the world swirled through her mind. Even when she was a kid, the stories of the Rapture and the Apocalypse gave her nightmares.

Shaking her head she set her jaw, driving away the fearful thoughts. No, there had to be a logical explanation. If not lightning, then something else. A blown transformer perhaps. Something like that would certainly account for the glow.

"That's weird. What do you think is causing it?"

She jumped and spun around, her hands flying up defensively.

"Whoa," Jeremy protested, his own hands held up placatingly. "It's just me. Calm down already."

Scowling, her heart beating so hard she could literally feel it physically, she picked up a nearby pillow and hurled it at him.

"What the hell are you doing in my room?"

Deftly deflecting the fluffy missile, he smirked, his eyes drifting down to her pink unicorn sleep shorts that were more like panties than shorts and barely covered her.

One eyebrow shot up.

"Unicorns?"

Turning various shades of red she tore at her blankets, pulling them close in an attempt at covering herself. They twisted from the sudden movement, and she kicked and contorted, trying to unravel them. Failing spectacularly, and only managing to cover one leg and, thankfully, her unicorn shorts, she gave up the fight.

Her chest heaving from exertion, she glared up at him icily. Face turning an even darker shade of red when she noticed him staring at her cleavage. Attempting to pull the tangled blankets up higher to cover her torso, all she managed to accomplish was to twist the blankets up further and expose more of her legs and waist to Jeremy.

"If you don't come up with a very good explanation for why you're in my room," she intoned, her voice low with barely contained anger, "I'm going to shoot you."

Snorting, Jeremy straightened. He sucked on his teeth, his eyes bright with mirth. Eventually he turned away, but not before stealing one last appreciative look.

His expression hardened as he squinted out the window. Each pulse from the peculiar light illuminated his features and made his skin appear blue.

"I woke up and saw the flashes and thought maybe there was a storm," he replied. "I heard you moving around up here and thought I would check on you and see what you made of it."

Angry and embarrassed, she didn't move her body but followed his gaze with her eyes. There was an unnatural thrumming of electricity in the air that intensified with each pulse of light. Her skin broke out in goose bumps with each wave.

"It's steady," he said, pointedly not looking at her. "Too consistent to be lightning or a blown transformer."

Still dressed in the same clothes as earlier, he ran one hand through his unkempt brown hair. He exhaled heavily, a barely perceptible shiver running through him.

"Can you feel it?" he asked, his voice low barely a whisper—as if he was afraid of disturbing some unknown entity. "Power and...something else. There's a spiritual battle going on there."

Surprised by the earnestness in his voice, she turned to look at him. Sure enough, there was nothing but sincerity on his face. The lack of his usual sarcasm meant he really believed what he was saying, no matter how crazy it sounded to her.

Suppressing the illogical thoughts threatening to overtake her logical mind, she huffed. Of course he would say something like that. To him everything was supernatural, but she had lived too long and seen too much to buy into that. There was always a rational explanation, even if she couldn't explain why every instinct inside her was screaming that he was right.

"I suppose you're going to tell me it's vampires again, or maybe witches this time," she scoffed, banishing her misgivings to her subconscious. She would deal with her questions later. Right now, she needed sleep.

Grunting, he glanced at her. "Something like that. Maybe Bigfoot. I'm not sure. Sasquatches like to have big parties every so often just to throw everyone off. Haven't you read about it in the tabloids? It's some big government conspiracy. Every time they throw a shindig, the powers that be say it's 'swamp gas' or some such thing."

Dana snorted back a laugh. There was the sarcastic jerk she knew. Jeremy's joking made the atmosphere seem lighter and less heavy somehow. Her fear evaporating, she couldn't help smiling.

"All right," she said with a yawn. "I forgive you for invading my privacy, but we have another long day tomorrow and we both need to get some sleep."

Suppressing yet another yawn, she got to her feet and shuffled over to the door. She held it open and waved her hand in invitation for him to leave. Realizing her unicorn shorts were again visible—as were her legs—she glanced up, her expression stern, expecting to see him staring at her again. He wasn't and her face flushed, this time not with embarrassment but annoyance.

Why wasn't he noticing her? He hadn't been able to keep his eyes off her earlier, so why wasn't he even glancing her way now? Self-consciously she pulled at her shirt, trying to make it longer so it covered more of her waist.

Whatever, it didn't matter. She didn't care what he thought anyway. He was just an annoying jerk who had followed her home, and as soon as they found her cousin she would be rid of him.

Clearing her throat loudly to get his attention, she beckoned exaggeratingly at the door again. When he didn't respond she ground her teeth and clenched her fists.

She stood straighter and her eyebrows shot up when she saw what he was doing. He was squinting and peering out the window, his hands pressed to the glass. The blue glow was softer than before, but still there, and it cast shadows over him.

"What is it?" she asked. "You see something?"

He didn't respond, just moved his face closer until it was nearly pressed against the window. Curious now, she started moving towards him.

"What do you see?"

"Shh!" he hissed, waving a hand for her to be quiet.

"How many times do I have to tell you not to do that," she scolded, moving to stand next to him and pressing herself gently up against his side.

Stiffening slightly, he didn't pull away but continued staring out into the night. He was warm and still smelled of spearmint. Shivering, she pressed herself closer, allowing his body heat to warm her.

Following his gaze she squinted, trying to see what he was looking at. There was nothing new there, just the same scenery as before. The light wasn't as bright, but nothing appeared out of the ordinary.

She gasped and gripped his arm hard as the light pulsed bright again, illuminating the sky.

"No way," she breathed, her voice trailing off. "It can't be."

In the sky, glowing a bright orange as if on fire, was the silhouette of a winged humanoid creature. The light flared again, dissipated, then flared again. This time, whatever it was had disappeared.

They both stood speechless, their gaze fixed on the spot where the angel—that's the only thing it could be—had been. A shiver ran up her spine and the goosebumps returned as her mind raced to try and make sense of what she had just seen.

They continued their vigil, neither speaking until the light dimmed and eventually faded out. They didn't move for a long time, afraid to, lest they shatter the moment.

"Well," Jeremy said, breaking the silence, his voice soft and contemplative. "I'm tired and, like you said earlier, we have a lot to do tomorrow."

He turned away, moving towards the open door. She held on to his arm, not wanting to let him go. She needed to be reassured. Needed to know that everything would be okay, that the world she knew was not being irrevocably shattered. There had to be a rational explanation for what they had seen. There had to be.

Turning to glance at her hand, he frowned. He didn't pull away, though, and she tightened her grip. Sighing, he looked up at her, his eyes anxious.

Famine

"Tell me that wasn't what it looked like," she asked, her eyes pleading.

He shook his head. "I can't."

Gently breaking her grip, he turned and slowly shuffled towards the door. His shoulders were slumped and he sighed heavily, seemingly worried about what was happening but powerless to do anything about it.

Unsettled and feeling very much like a child again, she wanted him to stay with her. There was a strength and kindness to him hidden behind his gruff, uncaring exterior, and she needed that.

"Wait," she began to say before stopping short. Angry at herself for what she was feeling, she pushed them away. No, she just needed sleep. Everything would be clearer in the morning and life would be back to normal.

He turned to look at her, his face questioning.

"Never mind," she said, waving her hand dismissively. "Get some rest and I'll see you in the morning."

He nodded and grunted, turning away. Then he shuffled out of the room, closing the door behind him.

Everything will be okay in the morning, you'll see, she thought as she got into bed and drew the covers up. Turning on her side, she closed her eyes and tried to calm her racing mind.

It couldn't have been an angel, could it? Was the last thought to flit through her mind before sleep took over.

It was like watching the world through the eyes of a first-person video game. Tzedakah had taken control of him, but not as completely as at the farmhouse. Thankfully, he hadn't sent him back to the void. This time was more like before. He wasn't completely in control of his actions, but he did have a limited ability to affect what was happening. Seething with anger, all he could do was watch helplessly as his body suddenly surged towards Jasmine. As if on cue and following his lead Sanctuary burst into flames and rocketed skyward, at least ten vampires right on his heels.

He barely had time to think before Jasmine's terror-filled eyes filled his vision. His arm lifting on its own in spite of his attempts at halting it, the iron blade cast her pretty face in azure light that made her blue eyes even deeper.

"No!" he managed to shout, willing his hand to the right.

Famine

Holding his breath as the blade surged forward, he pit all of his will against the sentient sword. His heart beating wildly in his chest as he came so close to Jasmine, he could smell the acrid metallic scent of blood on her breath.

Oh, God. Oh, God. I've killed her.

His stomach dropped as he looked into her eyes. He was on the verge of tears, anger and sadness threatening to overwhelm him.

What had he done? No, what had Tzedakah done? Fury welled up from deep within him, setting his world ablaze and driving away the sorrow. The sentient sword was a monster. So certain of its own moral rightness, it couldn't see any other point of view. None of the nuances of humanity made any sense to it. There was only black and white, good and evil.

Searching her eyes for the fear and pain he expected to see there, his heart leapt when she smiled instead. Turning her head slowly to one side, she revealed a long red line on her cheek. Drops of crimson trickling from the wound meandered down her pale face.

Unsteadily she reached one hand up and placed it gently on his face. "I knew you couldn't do it."

Continuing to defy Tzedakah, his own hand shook wildly as he reached up and placed it over hers. The smile never faded as she searched his face.

"There you are my love. My Jared," she breathed, her eyes brightening.

Pain erupted in his head and Jasmine's face blurred as Tzedakah's voice thundered in his mind. "You will obey me."

Staggering backward he clutched his head, gritting his teeth.

"Jared, you don't understand," the voice continued, each word a smashing hammer blow. "She is dangerous. She must be destroyed."

Shaking his head and falling to one knee, he tried to drive away the onslaught of thoughts and emotions. So consumed was he by his internal turmoil, the commotion from the greater battle raging around them was nothing more than white noise.

He was aware of Sanctuary high above, his flaming sword burning a swath of destruction through the leaping vampires, but he didn't care. The only thing that mattered to him was Jasmine, and the sword.

"Why?" he managed through gritted teeth. "Why is she so dangerous?"

"You must trust me. She is."

"You still haven't answered my question."

The world slowed around him and then came to a stop. An eerie silence fell over the scene, and he became acutely aware that he was unable to move. His eyes still saw and his ears still heard, but it was as if someone had reached down and simply paused the earth.

He moved his eyes back and forth and noticed Vlad only a few meters away, arms stretched out towards him, his face a mask of rage and fear. The big angel was now somewhere to his left, about five vampires attempting to dogpile him to the ground.

"I have been patient," the sword said, its voice no longer a pounding force but still loud in the unnatural quiet.

"But my patience is finally at an end. This constant battling against me needs to stop."

"Or what?" Jared spat back. "Will you send me to the void permanently?"

No audible response, but Jared could feel the sword's anger and frustration.

"I will not," it replied haltingly, its words lacking conviction.

Jared grimaced. "I see. Well, if that's how it's going to be, then do it already."

More frustration and uncertainty?

"I do not wish to," it answered after a second's hesitation. "I..."

Sudden realization dawned on Jared as Tzedakah's conflicting emotions continued to flood into his mind. "You can't, can you?"

More silence, but this time Jared sensed recognition in the sword. He had hit the nail right on the head. For all its bluster, the sword needed him.

So, their relationship was more symbiotic than the sword had let on. He wasn't just a tool for it to use as it wanted, but something more akin to a partnership of sorts. All of the times previously where his connection to the sword had failed now made sense.

"There are rules to how this all works, aren't there? Guidelines and limitations you haven't told me about or rather have been keeping from me."

No response.

"Nothing to say?"

"We were created for a purpose," the sword answered. "It is more than simply being an *executioner for the universe*, as you put it. Just as a tree is created for a reason, so were we. Every other attribute we possess is either focused on the task we were made for or is inconsequential. Our own feelings and thoughts on it do not matter. There is only the role and nothing else. You need to trust that I know what our part in this universe is. So when I tell you to act, you need to respond unquestioningly."

Jared ground his teeth. "Okay. I can accept that you know more than me, but the world is not so black and white, and every living being's actions are not so simple. Reasons and experiences must be considered when passing out judgement. Can't you see that?"

More conflicting emotions came from the blade and then a sudden flash of another person. A memory like before. This one was of a woman standing over a man on his knees, Tzedakah glowing brightly in her hands. He was looking up at her, his eyes hard. A young girl, her clothes tattered and filthy, was pressed up against his back with one arm holding her protectively.

The stench of blood was everywhere and splashes of red stained the floor and the walls. A different man, this one overweight and arrayed in fine clothing, lay between them, his head removed.

"I cannot," she says. "I will not. He was only defending his child."

A sense of understanding or sympathy flashes through the sword. It is alien and the blade is uncertain of how to respond.

373

Famine

The woman's arm dropped as the glow from the blade dimmed. Her eyes were filled with sadness as she examined the man.

"Go," she said in the same ethereal voice that Jared possesses and then turned to walk away. "Take your child and go."

The entire scene faded but the emotions from it lingered.

Jared felt the same sense of uncertainty from Tzedakah the women did. As if this feeling of sympathy was foreign to him and he was questioning its validity. No, rather questioning his reality. If what she was saying was in fact truth, then everything the sword understood about the universe and its place in it was brought into question.

"No," it said finally, certainty quelching the conflicting emotions. "There is only the just and the unjust. Guilty or innocent, there is no in-between. I am sorry, Jared, but the woman must die."

Jared's eyes narrowed and he braced himself for what he knew was coming, but it never did. Before the world had time to snap back into motion, an arm wrapped around his shoulder. Hot breath washed over his cheek and he wrinkled his nose at the sudden strong scent of wine.

"Trouble in paradise?" a French-accented voice asked softly, the speaker's mouth only inches from his right ear. "Tzedakah is such a, how you say, ah yes, uptight fellow. That is the correct use of that phrase, no?"

Rage, revulsion, hatred, and fear—so many emotions and feelings slammed into Jared all at once. Before he had time to process them all the sudden sensation of pressure in his abdomen drew his attention. Blinking, he stared perplexedly at the long slender piece of metal jutting from his stomach. It glowed brightly, casting a violet sheen over his face.

"What," he manages to say before a pain more intense than any he had ever known exploded in his gut. He screamed. Not the simple scream of a man in pain, but something far more visceral and primal.

The world snapped back into motion, bombarding Jared with a cacophony of sounds and sensations. People were shouting and the clash of battle echoed loudly from all directions. He couldn't focus on anything but the pain. It was all-consuming, and it felt as if his very soul was burning.

He searched his thoughts for any sign of the sentient sword, when he felt himself being lifted off the ground. Nothing at first. The same disconnect as usual, but somehow more complete as if the blade in his stomach has utterly severed his connection to Tzedakah. Then, as if mirroring his own shouts, the sword shrieked.

Jared's appendages hung useless as he was hauled upward. He tried to struggle, but was devoid of strength and only managed to impale himself further. Tzedakah continued screaming, his shouts and the constant pain drowning out everything else.

Dana's face suddenly appeared before him, her beautiful brown eyes bright and full of life. Smiling, she reached up and brushed a stray lock of hair from her face. Jared unsteadily lifted one hand, attempting to caress her cheek.

Famine

Was this the end or a dream? If it was the end, it was certainly different from the last time. Of course, last time the peace of death had been stolen from him by the sword, and he couldn't remember anything before the void. If Dana's face had been a comfort for him then, those memories were lost.

"Well, *mon ami*, I am truly sorry it has to end this way. I wish our dance could have been longer, but alas it must now come to an end. Do not fret, Tzedakah will find another bearer before your corpse has time to cool. It is his way. We are nothing more than tools to them."

"No," Tzedakah's interjected, his voice calm and commanding. It pierced through the pain and confusion, clearing Jared's mind. Dana's face vanished, and with it the peace it brought.

The pain remained, but was overcome by a rising rage welling up; not only from the sword, but Jared as well. Feeling his strength returning, he lifted Tzedakah and thrust the glowing blade viciously back and downward at the Frenchman's head.

"*Putain*," the Musketeer cursed as he dodged to the side, Tzedakah missing his head but clipping his wide-brimmed hat.

Growling, and continuing to spew a stream of curses in both French and English, the Musketeer grabbed the hilt of his sword with both hands and twisted.

Relief surged over Jared as the pain instantly ceased when the Musketeer's rapier was wrenched free of his body. That relief was only temporary, however, when he realized he was once again tumbling helplessly through the air.

"Crap."

This time, however, Tzedakah and he were in perfect unison. Before he reached the rapidly approaching forest, he tucked his legs and rolled in midair, so his entire body was facing back towards the Musketeer with his legs facing the onrushing trees.

As soon as he felt his feet connect with the trunk of a tree, he collapsed his legs and sprang off it. Using the large trunk as an anchoring point, he launched himself back at the Musketeer like a heat-seeking missile.

Tzedakah leading the way Jared streaked across the field, a trail of azure light in his wake. Finally managing to reseat his hat the Musketeer noticed him just in time to bring his own blade up, deflecting Jared's attack.

Sparks of blue and violet exploded from the two blades as they met. Using the force of the clash to increase his inertia, Jared surged upward into another roll directly above the Musketeer.

Completely focused and in perfect unison with Tzedakah, his movements were instinctual, and the sword reacted to him as if it were an extension of himself. With the speed of subconscious thought everything became possible. Even the laws of physics seemed to bow to their will.

His feet struck solid matter, even though there was nothing but open sky around him. Subconsciously, he knew that what was happening shouldn't be possible, but it was happening nonetheless. Once again using his legs as springs he rocketed back downward, aiming for the Musketeer.

No normal being would have been able to evade the attack, but the Musketeer was no ordinary creature. Like

Famine

Tzedakah he was a being of immense power and will, and his smile was from ear to ear as he planted his own feet and launched upward.

They met somewhere in the middle; a shockwave being created from the clash of their blades. As if the open sky itself were solid ground they jumped back and forth, springing at each other repeatedly, sparks of power and waves of energy exploding around them each time they collided.

Gone was his uncertainty and lack of trust for the sword. It was replaced by an all-consuming rage that created a clarity of purpose that unified Tzedakah with its wielder. Jared Cadrett had vanished, replaced by a being that was something else entirely.

The Musketeer's smug grin filled his vision and then it flickered and winked out, and Jared was suddenly staring at his back. Without thinking, he spun and hit the Musketeer with a wicked two-handed sideways strike. Tzedakah flashed azure and left a streak of color in the darkness that lingered for a few seconds before fading.

Realizing his danger, the Musketeer reacted quickly enough to deflect the force of the blow with his own blade. The energy of the strike sent him spinning across the clearing instead of cleaving him in two.

The entire scene was a cacophony of battle sounds, but Jared barely noticed. He was fixated on the Musketeer. Even Jasmine had become nothing more than an afterthought. All that mattered was the Musketeer and his vile blade.

Somewhere in the back of his mind he knew something was wrong. Why was Jasmine so important? Was he supposed to kill her, or save her? Maybe the angel would know. Where was the angel anyway?

A vampire warrior came into view, a large pike in his hands. Jared swatted him away as if he were nothing more than a gnat. Two more appeared and he cut them down just as effortlessly. He continued onward, his eyes fixed on the Musketeer.

A scream to his left drew his attention. Turning his head in the direction of the noise, he noticed Jasmine and Vlad. The large vampire had a limp Lady Fuyuko draped over one shoulder and was attempting to drag Jasmine into the safety of the forest.

Narrowing his black eyes and setting his jaw, he turned towards them. Now he remembered the monster must be destroyed. All of them must be destroyed. They preyed on the weak and their existence could not and would not be tolerated. They were creatures of injustice, and he was justice itself.

Vlad's eyes widened and his movements became more frantic when he noticed Jared's slow approach.

"Jasmine," he commanded. "We must leave this place now."

Continuing to try and pull away but unable to break Vlad's grip, she looked around frantically for Jared. Her face lit up when she saw him coming towards them, but quickly darkened when she noticed the stern look on his face.

"You see?" Vlad pleaded. "Your former lover is not here to rescue you, but to kill you. I know you do not completely trust me, but all I have ever desired is your good. To protect you and help you fulfill your destiny, but I cannot do that if you keep fighting me."

Her eyes searched the face of the creature stalking towards them for any sign of the man she knew. They then widened in shock when she gazed into the bottomless darkness of his eyes and saw nothing but certain death there.

She stopped struggling and slumped her shoulders. All her hopes dashed, she didn't look at Vlad but nodded slightly and allowed herself to be guided away. He sighed audibly, his shoulders relaxing, and repositioned his grip on the unconscious White Lady while placing himself between Jasmine and the oncoming Jared.

"Renauld?" he called as he backed away, his eyes never leaving Jared. "I trust our deal is still valid?"

The Musketeer instantly materialized between Jared and the retreating vampires, his arms stretched wide, grinning like a lunatic.

"Of course," he replied, his sword in front of him in a salute directed at Jared.

Jared growled as the darkness in his eyes writhed and reached out angrily toward the Frenchman. Tzedakah's glow intensified as Jared lifted the blade into a two-handed offensive position.

"Finally!" the Musketeer shouted in elation. "You decide it is time to get serious. Come then, *mon ami*, and make this worth my time."

anctuary cut down a vampire, which exploded into flames and turned to dust. Calmly he scanned the battlefield, looking for Jared. More vampires came at him from his left and he dispatched them quickly, his flaming sword cutting through them with ease, leaving nothing more than ashes blowing in the wind.

"God's grace, how many of them are there?" he murmured as five more stepped up to engage him. "For every one I destroy, two more rise to replace it."

Finally spotting Jared, he moved towards him but stopped when he saw the Musketeer. The Frenchman stood between Jared and him.

"No," he growled, incinerating two more vampire warriors. "He is not ready for this battle."

A sense of urgency drove him, and his flaming blades whirled a deadly swath of destruction through the vampires in his way. Five more died screaming at his feet but were replaced instantly. No matter, he would destroy them all. How dare they oppose the Living God? Their very existence was an abomination, and they would not hinder him from reaching Jared.

Setting his jaw and narrowing his eyes in determination, he plowed forward. He shouted no battle cry nor bellowed his defiance, but simply charged forward, his big frame a fiery comet of destruction that slammed into the amassed vampires. The force of his charge scattered them and sent them flying in all directions, each one screaming as the holy fire that engulfed him incinerated them before they hit the ground.

Free of the vampire warriors, he charged towards the Musketeer. This time he would end his wretched existence. Jared was not ready to face him, so he needed to stop the duel before it truly began. Sensing Tzedakah's power growing, he wondered if maybe he made a mistake. Perhaps Jared finally merged with the sword enough to at least stand a chance against the Musketeer. Either way, if the Frenchman chose now to appear then he had his reasons, and his reasons were never good.

Vlad noticed him approaching and his eyes narrowed. He passed Fuyuko to Jasmine, who hurriedly threw her over one shoulder.

"Take Fuyuko and go. I will be right behind you."

She looked hesitant and couldn't hide her glance at Jared, then nodded and quickly disappeared into the shadows. Jared moved to stop the retreating vampires but was instantly countered by the Musketeer, his face a mask of fury.

Setting his jaw, his lips pressed into a tight line, Vlad moved to intercept the angel. His eyes glowed a steady red as he stepped between Sanctuary and Jared.

Raising one arm with his palm up, he declared, "I'm sorry, but I cannot allow you to interfere."

The big angel slowed, his eyes blazing. "Vlad, I agreed to allow you to withdraw, and I will still honor my word, but only if you leave now. But if you stand against me, I will destroy you."

He shook his head, a look of resignation on his face and determination.

"No, my old adversary, I am afraid that a truce is no longer possible. I know Renault is not capable of destroying Tzedakah, but he can kill the current wielder. It will take time to regroup and find another. That is time I sorely need. We are too close to the end to allow it to intervene now."

"Then so be it," the angel declared, leaping into the air, his flaming swords leading the way.

Bracing himself for the attack, Vlad bared his fangs, his hands rising reflexively into a defensive stance, his talon-like claws reflecting the light from the angel's fire. The Musketeer's voice suddenly cut through the tension, drawing everyone's attention.

"Are you sure this is the battle you wish to fight?"

The question was directed at Sanctuary, who halted in midflight and then slowly dropped back to the ground. Uncertainty on his face, he directed his attention towards the Frenchman. Vlad, too, glanced over at the Musketeer in uncertainty but never truly took his eyes off the angel.

Famine

Now we come to it. Despite all of his promises, the Musketeer couldn't care less about the vampire's agenda. To him, the machinations of all of the races were nothing more than games. Every wielder of Avlah was, at their heart, evil, but Renault was a creature of pure chaos. Intelligent and scheming in ways that only made sense to him, his plans were nuanced and filled with layer upon layer of malice. There was no telling what he would do, but you could be assured it wouldn't be pleasant.

Smiling, the Musketeer looked around exaggeratingly. Tapping one index finger on his lips, he crossed his arms in thought.

"Something seems to be missing, no? What can it be?"

His smile turned mischievous, and Sanctuary could almost see a faint twinkle in the blackness of his eyes.

"Shall I tell you? No, I think not. I would not wish to spoil the game."

Grinning, he turned back to Jared and winked.

"Do you wish to wager a guess? I am sure Tzedakah knows, but I am positive he will not admit it. No, that would be too...inconvenient for him. I think that is the word, no?"

Jared growled low and guttural but seemed uncertain. He glanced around, searching for clues, but his gaze never completely left the Musketeer. It lingered on the place where Jasmine fled before turning back to Renault.

Keeping Vlad in his periphery, Sanctuary also searched for anything out of the ordinary. The remaining vampire warriors had fled, and the little clearing was quiet, save for the standoff. Nothing seemed out of the ordinary, nor could he pinpoint anything that was missing.

The Musketeer tapped his wrist as if he were touching a watch.

"The clock is ticking, and time is running out." He turned to Jared. "You can still catch the vampire woman if you go now. I will not stop you."

"Renault," Vlad protested, his scarlet eyes flashing. "We had an agreement. You gave me your word."

The Musketeer waved his hand dismissively. "Be quiet, Vlad, the adults are talking."

Fuming, his face turning a dark shade of red, the vampire lord moved towards the Musketeer. With a minute gesture of his gloved hand, Vlad froze in place. The veins in his neck bulged as the vampire strained to move, but to no avail.

What was he up to? Clearly, he didn't care about the vampires, but why bother to hinder them? In truth, not getting in their way would cause more chaos for the world. It made no sense.

"So, what will you choose, *mon ami*? Do Tzedakah's bidding and kill the woman you once loved, or perhaps stop another from dying this night?"

"No," Sanctuary breathed as the missing piece finally dawned on him. "Jared, we must go."

"No." Jared's response was cold, his voice ethereal and distant. "The abomination must die tonight. She cannot be allowed to live."

It was obvious that Tzedakah was the personality currently in control. Sanctuary could sense Jared still there, but their shared connection was stronger now, and Tzedakah's influence and will were too powerful.

Famine

"Jared," Sanctuary said, his voice pleading. "Think. What is missing, or rather who is missing? Who has been in the company of the Musketeer as of late?"

There was a slight spark of recognition on his face and the angel recognized it. Blinking slowly, he deliberately turned to look at Sanctuary.

"Steve," he declared haltingly, as if waking from a dream. "Where is my brother?"

His eyes widened at the realization, and he grasped the big angel's shoulder tightly.

"Dana."

The cadence in the voice was now more akin to Jared's, but there was still much of Tzedakah in it. It was almost as if the sword shared Jared's fear, or rather the two were more connected than the last time Sanctuary had seen them.

Leaving any questions he had for later, he nodded and grimly turned to face the still- grinning Musketeer. Raising one arm, his burning blade pointing directly at the smiling man, he said nothing. He didn't have to; the Musketeer's broad sneer was all the confirmation he needed that his silent threat was understood.

If any harm had come to Dana, the Angel would be back to finish what was started.

Renault bowed slightly, tipping his hat with one gloved hand in acknowledgment. No, their battle was not over. Not by a long shot.

Turning to go, the angel placed a reassuring hand on Jared's shoulder.

"I assume you know where she lives?"

Never taking his anger-filled eyes off the Musketeer, he nodded.

"Will Tzedakah take us there? It would be faster than flying while carrying you."

"I will," replied the voice, the same strange mixture of Tzedakah and Jared.

Turning to face the angel, he placed on hand on his shoulder.

"Brace yourself," Jared intoned, and before the angel had time to reply there was a flash of blue light and then they were gone.

The Musketeer's shoulders shook as he chuckled. Continuing to stare at the place where Jared and Sanctuary had been standing before teleporting away, he waved one hand in a dismissive gesture.

Vlad gasped and nearly fell over as the petrification that was placed on him dissipated. He straightened, cricking his head back and forth slowly, his neck making loud popping noises.

"You had better have a good explanation for why you did that," he intoned nonchalantly.

The Musketeer snorted. "Or what? Think before you reply, Vlad. If I were you, *ami*, I would be very careful of making idle threats you do not have the power to perform."

Biting back a retort and gritting his teeth, his face a mask of anger, Vlad said nothing in reply.

Glancing sideways at him, one side of his mouth turning upward slightly, the Musketeer nodded.

"A wise choice, *pote*."

Famine

Clearing his throat and flexing one arm, Vlad looked back in the direction Jasmine fled with Lady Fuyuko.

"Did Lord Azrael truly go to kill this Dana they mentioned?" he asked.

The Musketeer shrugged.

"Perhaps. But that is none of your concern."

Turning to face the large vampire, his nightmare eyes dangerous, he reached towards the vampire. Vlad stiffened reflexively and grimaced.

"I assume you did not trust me and that is why you went after Tzedakah on your own," he stated with a casualness that not reflected in his eyes.

Narrowing his own eyes, Vlad was silent.

Sighing heavily, the Musketeer rubbed the bridge of his nose. After a few seconds he glanced at the obviously tense vampire, whose lips were now set into a firm line, his large ivory fangs exposed.

"I am going to make one thing clear, Vlad." His tone was icy, the usual cheerful demeanor gone. "If you try to murder Tzedakah's bearer again, I will destroy you. That kill is mine and mine alone. Is that understood, *mon ami*?"

Vlad opened his mouth to speak, but whatever he was about to say stuck in his throat at the upraised hand of the Musketeer.

"Think well before you answer, *fourmi*. You know full well my threats are not idle."

All color draining from his already-pale face, Vlad nodded in affirmation.

"Good," the Musketeer said, the smile returning to his lips. "Now that all of the unpleasantries have been addressed, we can resume our little game."

"You know what is at stake here, Renault," Vlad stated, again finding his voice and his courage. "It is more than just my coven. Hell, if she is who I believe her to be, the ramifications extend not just to vampire kind but to all of those like me."

"I am well aware of your legends. In fact..." He lifted the glowing sword to his face, the soft amethyst light throwing shadows over his features which are distant, as if he was reliving long lost memories. "We were there when your fathers came to this realm and before they rebelled. Oh, my dear Vlad, we know indeed what is at stake for your kind. We were there when the first of your kind came out screaming from your mothers' wombs to infest this world."

He turned to look at Vlad, who was watching him, his expression solemn. "We were also there when your kind ruled this world, subjugating humanity and setting yourselves up as gods. We were there when the Almighty smote you in His wrath and drove you into the shadows, no longer able to procreate naturally. Do you really believe she will be able to change that fate?"

"Yes," Vlad replied solemnly. "If she is who I believe her to be."

Nodding dismissively the Musketeer turned away, heading towards the trees and the welcoming shadows the forest provides. A section in the darkness suddenly began to warp and grow even more black, forming a portal of sorts.

Famine

Just as he was about to step into the void, he turned and looked back at Vlad.

"I will keep my word and make sure that Tzedakah is a game-piece that stays off the board. But I would not place my hopes in legends and fairytales, *mon ami*, even those as old as yours."

His final words a warning that hung heavily in the air, he dipped his head and tapped his hat with one gloved hand in a salute before turning and vanishing into the waiting darkness.

Dana woke with a start. She was instantly alert, no trace of sleep lingering. Her heart was beating hard and fast, and all of her senses were hyper-focused on one specific point in the darkness.

There was something there, she was sure of it. Something that meant her harm. Something menacing and malicious, but no matter how hard she tried she couldn't move her head or look away. She was transfixed.

Even her body refused to obey, though the part of her brain that controlled fight or flight was fully activated and screaming at her to move. All she could do was stare impotently into the darkness.

Fear was something everyone experienced, but terror was something entirely different. Most people didn't ever experience true terror. That awful sensation that doom was imminent and there was no escape from it. The kind of fear that both drove one to hysteria and complete focus at the same time, making every moment seem like an infinity. It was the kind of horror that serial killer victims or plane crash victims must experience, she supposed.

Come on, girl, she thought to herself. *You're not a child; there has to be a rational explanation. It's just sleep paralysis or some such thing. There is nothing there in the shadows. Calm down.*

Taking deep breaths, she managed to force her eyes shut but was still unable to turn her head. Not being able to see only intensified the feelings of dread, but she wasn't going to give in to it. She was too old to believe in monsters under her bed, no matter how loud her brain was shouting at her.

Not even when she was young did she experience anything like this. It was a new experience for her, but one she could rationalize. She still wasn't completely awake, and when her body finally woke fully it would all go away. She would open her eyes, and nothing dangerous or malicious would be in her room. All she would find would be the normal accoutrements that were supposed to be there.

Taking a deep breath and exhaling slowly, she finally opened her eyes and stared into the darkness. Though not as intense as before, the feelings were still there. The darkness did seem to be deeper where her senses were telling her the danger was, but she couldn't find anything out of the ordinary.

She tried to move but her body was still in revolt. She gasped and her eyes went wide and felt like they were going to pop out of her head. Something moved in the shadows. It was slight and barely perceptible, but there was movement.

Her heart was beating so fast that it felt like it would burst out of her chest and the rhythm so loud it drowned out all sound. *This can't be real. It can't be. It's just a trick of the light. Isn't it?*

A silhouette appeared in the shadows, rising out of the blackness. It shuffled forward, the dim light from the window illuminating a figure with dead eyes and a twisted smile. The shape looked almost human, but not quite. Its features were misshapen and its body and arms too long.

"Dana," it whispered in a raspy, deep, inhuman voice that turned her blood to ice.

"Move, damn it!" she screamed in her mind. "Move!"

Her body refused to listen even though every instinct in her told her to run, to flee. All she could do was stare wide-eyed and helpless at the shadowy form as it inched ever closer to her.

It raised one hand, its fingers spread. She watched as they elongated, becoming wicked- looking talons made of solid shadows. Somewhere deep in her subconscious, she recognized those sinister claws. Panic took hold of her and phantom pain erupted in her stomach as she recalled the sharp cut of those nails. The same ones Steve had nearly gutted her with.

"No," she tried to scream, but all she managed was a very tiny whisper. Not even her voice would obey her; she was completely imprisoned in her own body. Completely trapped in this waking nightmare.

Steve, if that was what this thing was, inched closer and the shadowy claws extended until they touched her exposed foot. He slowly raked them along her big toe, leaving a thin line of red and searing pain where it touched.

Wake up, Dana. You have to wake up. This is just a dream. It's not real.

Feeling her sanity wavering on a thin line, she frantically tried to move, tried to wake herself up. Nothing worked, and she screamed in her head as he sliced another one of her toes.

A few tears meandered down her cheek and dropped to her sheets. The Steve monster cocked its head and reached down to wipe one away. His breath was hot on her face and smelled of sulfur.

He retreated to his original place and rubbed his fingers together, observing the wetness before licking his finger.

"I never understood why tears are salty," he said absently. "I guess it has to do with lubrication, or some such thing."

He shrugged and turned his attention back to her. If her heart beat any faster she was sure it would explode, ending this nightmare and her life.

No, this was just a dream. It was an extremely horrific one, but a dream, nonetheless. She would wake up from it, she had to keep reminding herself of that. Steve was only in it because she hadn't had time to process what he had done to her, and this is her subconscious's way of making her deal with the trauma. Besides, he was dead. She had made sure of that herself. Wasn't he?

He turned and smiled at her, his mouth unnaturally elongated and crooked. His exposed teeth were long and sharp, and layered almost like a shark's. They popped and ground noisily as he flexed his jaw, his head cocking thoughtfully.

"The mind does find ways of bringing suppressed things to the surface," he said as if in answer to her thoughts. "But really, were you actually that traumatized by what happened? I did kill the love of your life, but you seemed to bounce back pretty quickly, in my opinion."

Now she knew it was a dream. The only way this thing could know what she was thinking was if it was. It had to be, and if it was it couldn't truly hurt her and she could wake herself up.

Steve's rasping laughter brought her attention back to him, but this time anger drove away the fear. How dare he invade her dreams? This was her mind. Subconscious or not, she wasn't going to sit still and allow him to defile it. Her eyes flashing and her neck straining, she struggled to move. Struggled to get at him.

"Well, if this is nothing more than a dream then you would be right about waking up," he chuckled. "But I am afraid, my dear Dana, that you are very much mistaken in your assumption that I can't hurt you here."

Pain erupted in yet another toe and she was forced to blink away the tears burning her eyes. Trying in vain to scream, the only noise to escape her lips was a barely audible whimper.

No. No. No. This isn't really happening. You have to snap out of it.

If she didn't soon, her mind would crack. The impotence mixed with pain and helplessness was threatening to shatter her psyche. Every second felt like an eternity, and she knew she wouldn't be able to hold out for much longer.

Oh God, please help me. I know You're there, Jesus, so please do something.

The howl of rage that escaped Steve's mouth shocked her back to clarity. He was doubled over, holding his head in both hands and gritting his teeth, his face a mask of agony.

"Don't you dare," he roared, his voice deep and animalistic, "say that Name. Don't you dare."

Jesus? Was that what had gotten to him?

"Stop it!" he bellowed in response.

But the voice. The voice was not Steve's. At least not the Steve she knew. It was someone or something else's entirely. Every inch of her body seemed to crawl at the sound, as if her very being rejected it. It felt dirty and wrong. Unnatural, as if it didn't belong in this reality.

Jesus. Jesus. Jesus. Jesus, she continued in an unending mantra. Each time she thought the Name, the creature shuddered and stumbled as if struck by some unseen hand.

"Enough!!" The creature's shout of defiance sent a psychic shock wave smashing into her that drove her deeper into her mattress and sent her thoughts reeling.

Her life-giving mantra interrupted, all she could do was watch helplessly as Steve slowly straightened, regaining his composure. This time, there was no smile on his face as he leaned forward and hovered over her.

"You will pay for that, little human. I can assure you."

The creature's icy cold voice sent shivers up her spine. Still unable to make any audible noises, her mouth hung open in a silent scream as the creature forced images of horrors beyond any human imagination into her mind.

"Please," she managed to whimper when the pictures finally ceased.

"I admit," it stated casually, "I thought this a fool's errand. I care little for Tzedakah or his wielder and would not have helped the Dark One if Steve had not desired it. I now see why he hates you so; no mortal has angered me in such a way in an especially long time. I will very much enjoy breaking you."

Paralyzed but unable to look away, she watched in horror as moved forward and placed his hand on her head. Darkness slowly enveloped her until all that remained were his glowing red eyes.

A scream fractured the silence, and she wondered at it until she realized it was her voice she was hearing.

"No!" she wailed the moment she regained her voice. "No!"

Her eyes rolled back in her head, drool formed on her lips, and her voice cracked as she continued to wail. There was no sense of time as the horrors consumed every part her. Every second felt like a thousand years, and she knew her mind was unraveling.

Her last thought was another desperate plea to God. It was feeble and there was barely any force behind it, but it was there. A small flicker of hope shining in the overwhelming darkness. The dark pressed in around it, attempting to snuff it out. Steve's unwavering will against that tiny spark.

Just before her last bastion of will was overcome, there was a flash of blinding blue light. It burned her eyes, making them water, but before she was forced to look away she was sure she saw the silhouette of a person wrestling with Steve. Her mind was unable to process what was happening and with a suddenness that caused her muscles to spasm and her body to violently jerk, it consumed the darkness, shattering the nightmare.

Her stomach lurched as she felt herself being propelled upward by this immense power which surged through her body like lightning. All the horrors the creature had been inflicting upon her ceased, and peace washed over her mind until all that remained of the nightmare was an echo.

The creaking sound from her bed frame as she dropped heavily back onto it brought her back to awareness. Cautiously she forced her eyes open, expecting to see the monster still at the foot of her bed. Her eyelids heavy with exhaustion, it took every bit of strength she had to keep them open as she scanned the room.

Her heart still racing and her breath coming in ragged gasps, she braced herself for another attack. It never came. To her great relief, Steve was gone. He had completely vanished.

It was a long few moments before she finally allowed herself to completely relax, and for her heart and breathing to return to some semblance of a normal rhythm.

"It's over," was all she managed to utter as weariness and sleep overcame her. "Thank God it's over."

Dana slowly crept her way back to consciousness. With crust covering her eyes, it took quite a bit of effort for her to pry her eyelids open. Gritting her teeth when waves of pain shot through her arms and legs she groaned, throwing one arm over her face to block out the invading sunlight that had the audacity to stream in through her window.

"Why does everything hurt?" she whined.

Fragmented memories of a man *was it Steve Cadrette?*, raced through her mind. Vague impressions of someone having been in her room accompanied by a very strong recollection of pain and terror gnawed at the back of her consciousness, setting her heart racing.

Sighing, she shook her head, clearing the cobwebs in her brain, the beating of her heart decreasing as she forced herself to relax. That had been one doozy of a nightmare.

Famine

She couldn't recall the last time a dream had disturbed her to this extent.

The scent of fresh coffee forced its way into her thoughts, making her mouth water. The loud gurgling of her stomach reminded her that she had eaten very little yesterday and needed food. The smell that came next sent her stomach into an eruption of protesting noises.

"Is that bacon?"

"Yeah," replied a man's voice, sending her leaping out of bed. Her blankets were still wrapped weirdly around her body, and she nearly fell over in her struggle to free herself.

When she was finally able to find some semblance of composure, though not completely extricate herself from the blankets, she glowered daggers at the man who had spoken.

He stood in the doorway, his broad shoulders propped against the door frame. The same shirt he had been wearing the night before was wrinkled and half tucked into his pants, clinging to his average but muscled frame. He lifted a white mug with Binghamton PD in bold blue letters to his mouth and took a sip.

Raising one eyebrow, Jeremy let his gaze drift over her. His brown eyes bright and his mouth quirking up in amusement as he appraised her, he thrust his arm towards her, a large mug in his outstretched hand.

Her face flushed as she tried in vain to use the tangled blankets to cover herself better. Giving up, she pressed her lips together and, kicking her way free, reached out and took the mug.

She closed her eyes and sighed deeply as she lifted the cup to her nose, breathing in the sweet nutty aroma of coffee. The hot liquid nipped at her lips and tongue as she gingerly took a sip.

"Now that is exactly what the doctor ordered," she murmured contentedly, her eyes still closed.

The fact she was in her night shirt and panties and completely exposed forgotten, she took another long, glorious sip. Feeling Jeremy's eyes still on her, she glanced sideways at him.

"You're lucky you brought a peace offering," she said before taking another sip. Her face was still slightly flushed as she positioned her arms in a way that blocked the view of her chest.

He chuckled while taking a drink of his own coffee, his dark eyes sparkling.

"I'm guessing it wouldn't have gone well for me if I hadn't?"

She shook her head, feeling her mouth quirk upward slightly.

"Wrath of God kind of pain."

"Good thing I did, then."

Taking one last quick sip before setting the cup on her dresser, she waved at Jeremy dismissively.

"Offering excepted. Now get out of my room, peasant, before I have you flogged."

"Okay," he replied, turning to go, his eyes lingering an extra second longer, a faint hint of red on his ruddy cheeks. "I made breakfast. Your plate is on the table when you're ready. I'm gonna take a shower if that's all right?"

Famine

Not waiting for a response he closed the door, leaving her alone again. She rolled her eyes, but let her own gaze linger before she pulled open the top drawer of her dresser to retrieve fresh underwear and socks.

God, he was annoying. He was like a stray dog you couldn't get rid of because you fed it too much. Hopefully, when they found her cousin, he would go back to where he had wandered in from.

Of course, the lingering effects of the nightmare had vanished as soon as she heard his voice. Had he somehow driven them away?

Snorting, she shook her head, dismissing the thought. No, the lingering effects of dreams sometimes lasted a long time after waking, but they always faded in time. That's all it was.

Pulling on the pair of jeans she had left on the floor the previous night; she examined herself in the mirror. Dark circles rimmed her brown eyes and the ponytail she had neglected to take out was gnarled and tangled. Her olive skin was still a bit pale, and her lips were chapped.

"You look awful, girl," she grumbled.

Stripping off her shirt, she had a new bra and T-shirt on before the sound of the shower reached her. There was a lot that they needed to do today, so she quickly returned to the mirror to examine herself appraisingly.

Even though she was still technically on hiatus, she wanted to get to the station and talk to the Captain. If anyone could help find her cousin, it was him. Well, there was another who could help even more, but Hell hadn't frozen over yet, so she certainly wasn't going to ask *him*. But was Jermey right, and she was wrong not to reach out to him?

Shaking away her doubts, she returned to the task of getting ready. No, even if he was inclined to help, she didn't trust him. Frowning glumly, she poked at her puffy cheeks, squinting to see if that made them look any better.

Nope. Still look like I haven't slept in a month.

Straightening with a frustrated groan, she roughly pulled the rubber band out of her ponytail and began fixing her rebellious hair.

What did it matter anyway? She had no one to impress. Who cared what she looked like? She had to find her cousin, and the state of her hair wasn't going to help with that.

She quickly finished getting ready but couldn't help glancing in the direction of the bathroom. The grumbling in her stomach reminding her that she was famished she went back to the task at hand, plopping down on her bed and bending down to put on her socks.

Her stomach dropped and her breathing quickened when she saw her right foot. Three thin red lines stared angrily up at her. Three scratches that looked strikingly like the ones the demon Steve had given her in her nightmare.

It couldn't be, could it? No, it had to have been a nightmare. Wasn't it? She had to have been dreaming. There was no way it could have been real. Could it have?

An icy chill ran up her spine and she shivered. Gritting her teeth, she dismissed her misgivings. No, she must have scratched her foot in her sleep or something. It happened all the time.

Famine

Yeah, that was the explanation. Maybe her mind had contrived the whole nightmare in response to her scratching herself while she slept. That made sense. It was rational. Far more rational than Steven actually being in her room last night.

Shrugging away her doubts she pulled on her socks, wincing when the fabric touched the deep scratches. She really had gotten herself good. She didn't have time to dress them, so she pulled on her socks and headed downstairs. The scratches were superficial and would be okay till later.

She had just taken her first glorious bite of bacon when Jeremy finally joined her in the kitchen. Her eyes were closed, and she was slowly chewing, savoring the perfectly cooked morsel.

"Oh God," she purred. "This is so good."

"Glad you..." She cut him off with a raised hand.

"Don't talk. Your irritating voice will ruin the moment."

Jeremy snorted. Rolling his eyes he pushed past her, bumping her arm slightly as he did. Smirking, she swallowed and then set on the rest of her breakfast like a starving animal.

He poured himself another cup of coffee and leaned against the counter, his brow furrowed. His hair was still a little damp and clung to his face like wet noodles. Squinting and scowling, he looked like a stray dog that had just been forced to suffer through its first bath in ages.

"When I'm done here, I'm going to head down to the station."

Jeremy took another long sip of his coffee and continued to stare off into space. Sighing deeply, he didn't respond. She turned to look at him.

"Did you hear me?"

He smacked his lips and took another sip from his mug but didn't show any signs he had heard.

Frowning, she waved a hand at him in agitation.

"Hey, Earth to Jeremy. You still with me here?"

He blinked a few times before glancing at her.

"What?" he snapped, annoyed.

Her face a mask of confusion at his sudden outburst, she turned and looked up at him. What had gotten under his skin? His demeanor had completely changed. Of course, taciturn seemed to be normal for him, but he had seemed almost sweet earlier.

"What crawled up your skirt?"

"This whole situation crawled up my skirt," he said, his voice thick with agitation. "If I hadn't met you or Jare..." He stopped himself, his face flushing slightly. Before he could say anything else he took another swig of coffee.

Had he just been about to say Jared? Had he known Jared? Is that why he had been so insistent on going with her? Had he been hiding that from her? If so, why? What in the world was going on? Everyone seemed to know more than she did, and it was beginning to infuriate her.

She felt her face flushing. "I said," she replied, every word slow and deliberate and masking her thoughts and her rising anger. "I will be going into the station as soon as I am done with breakfast."

Jeremy furrowed his brow again.

Famine

"So, you're still not going to call your FBI friend?"

She stiffened. "I'm not having this discussion again."

He rolled his eyes.

"Of course we're not. That would just be the most logical course of action. Oh yeah, I forgot, you're a woman and logic doesn't factor into your decisions."

"Careful," she replied through gritted teeth. "Your misogyny aside, I have my reasons."

Scoffing, Jeremy rolled his eyes.

"Oh yeah, I remember your reasons." He applied air quotes to 'reasons'. "You just don't trust him. Of course you have no reason not to trust him, you just simply don't. So logical."

Her knuckles white from the death grip she had on her fork, she squinted her eyes and set her jaw. How could she explain without ripping open the still unhealed wound that was Jared's murder? Her current thoughts aside, she was beginning to trust Jeremy but she wasn't ready to let him in that far. She had been too vulnerable with him already and she was pretty sure he was hiding his true intentions from her.

Shaking away her thoughts, she steeled herself. *I don't have time for this. Every second we waste talking is a second Sophia loses.* Biting back any further retorts, she dropped her fork noisily onto her plate and quickly stood. Making her way to the sink, she haphazardly dropped it in with a clatter.

Turning and walking out of the room, she called over her shoulder, "The train's leaving in five. Be ready if you're going with me."

Steve stumbled into the throne room, the acrid smell of burning flesh and singed hair following in his wake. Holy fire really sucked. He understood why Jared was there, but an angel? What business did it have with him? Maybe it was Dana's guardian angel.

Either way, they had interrupted his fun. He had no plans of killing her, just torturing her for a while. If the demon hadn't intervened, they both would have been toast. Wow, Jared had been pissed. He would have actually killed him this time if he'd had the chance.

Wait, was he still on fire?

Swiveling his head back and forth and lifting his arms, he did a quick check just to be safe. Nothing. His clothes were still smoking slightly, but no flames.

Sighing with relief he stumbled over to a large velvet couch, oblivious of his surroundings. Plopping heavily down upon it, he closed his eyes and exhaled. It made a sound like air being slowly let out of a balloon as he sank down till his knees were almost eye level.

Groaning, he rubbed his forehead with one hand. "Well, that sucked."

"Oh, you look like you need a massage," a feminine voice purred into his ear. "Here, let me help you."

He was gently but forcefully turned so his back was facing the mysterious voice. Strong fingers slowly explored his back and shoulders. Not opening his eyes, he let out a contented sigh as what he could only assume was a goddess rubbed and prodded him. It didn't take long before the heavenly fingers found a deep knot in one shoulder and the pressure there increased.

He gasped as pain took his breath away. It wasn't a sharp pain, but a good pain that let him know the woman had found a spot of tension that needed to be attended to.

"Oh, honey," he groaned. "That's the place. Right there."

"Hard day?" the woman asked, her voice alternating from concentrated to husky.

"You have no idea."

"Tell me about it," she purred, her voice sending shivers over his entire body.

Suddenly aroused, he tried to turn and look at her. She pressed hard on the spot again and he contorted and turned back forward.

"Now, now," scolded the women playfully. "Don't move; I am not finished yet."

Before she was even done speaking her soft lips pressed against his neck, sending lightning through his entire body. He moaned loudly as the lips made their way up to one of his ears and then back down again.

It was taking every bit of control to not turn and throw himself onto the woman, who smelled of lilacs. He could feel her ample breasts pressed against his back and couldn't stop his imagination from running wild.

The entire world fell away and all he knew was that he wanted her. Wanted her more than he had ever wanted anything. Nothing mattered but her. He would kill for her. He would even die for her.

"That's right," she purred. "I want that, too. So desperately."

Like someone had flipped a switch, all of the sexual tension evaporated. The scent of lilac was replaced by the acrid, metallic smell of blood and death. He felt the woman tense as she noticed the sudden change in his demeanor.

In the time it took her to move her hands, he had a tendril of shadow tightly wrapped around her throat. Standing slowly, he lifted her so she was suspended four feet off the ground.

She croaked and clawed at the shadow, her feet kicking futilely. She was pale and beautiful, with long auburn hair that curled to the middle of her back. Bright red eyes bulged from her delicate angular face, unfocused and glassy. Blood trickled from where her ivory fangs had bitten into her lips as she struggled.

Smiling, Steve crafted another tendril of shadow, its point sharp as a razor. It sped towards her, stopping only centimeters from the center of her bosom.

Famine

"Nice try," he chuckled. "But sadly, the thing inside me isn't interested in being fed on. Pity, I was just starting to have fun."

"Please put Esmerelda down," a deep voice commanded. It wasn't angry, but it held authority.

Steve was suddenly aware that he was not alone. The entire room was filled with people. Well, if you could describe vampires as people. The entire room was filled with former people. Men, women, and even a few children all glowered back at him. Some had weapons, but most were dressed in formal wear.

Were they having a party?

His eyes went to the ornate iron throne resting on a dais at the front of the massive room. Sitting on it, his fingers laced and his chin resting on his hands, was Vlad. Leaning on the throne next to him, his usual smile plastered on his face, was the Musketeer.

With a deep sigh he retracted his tendrils. Esmerelda dropped heavily to the ground, her red gown crumpling around her. Coughing and wheezing, she massaged her injured neck. She glowered up at him, her red eyes burning with hatred and, if he was not mistaken, fear.

He winked at her and she hissed, baring her fangs. Her face drained of all color when he raised one hand and pointed it at her, dark shadows coalescing at his fingertips. She scurried away on all fours like a rat, fleeing to the safety of her kin.

"Must you accost my guests?" Vlad asked with a sigh.

One side of Steve's mouth quirked up slightly. He straightened and brushed himself off and turned to face the throne.

"I'm pretty sure I was the one who was accosted."

"Even so," Vlad said, not masking his annoyance.

A soft whimper drew his attention and he turned to see what it was that had made the noise. A large cage hung from the ceiling to his left, swaying slightly. It creaked and groaned as what was held captive in it struggled.

"What's in the cage?" he asked, curiosity getting the better of him.

"We were just about to have dinner," Vlad replied gravely. "My guests have traveled far and are famished."

He looked from the cage to Vlad and then back at the cage. Dinner? Examining the cage, he finally noticed the numerous pairs of eyes looking down at him. Some were wide with fear, while others pleaded with him to save them. All of them, he realized with a start, were children.

Vlad was a monster, but torturing children? There were just some lines one shouldn't cross. Sudden displeasure from the thing inside him washed over his mind. It apparently had no qualms with murdering children. Of course, from what he could gather, it pretty much wanted to murder everyone.

"You don't approve," Vlad observed, a hint of amusement in his voice.

Steve shrugged, hiding his apparent discomfort. If he was honest with himself, he felt more apathetic than disturbed. At least more than he usually felt for others.

Famine

Children had always been a soft spot for him, but now even strong feelings seemed distant as if he was experiencing his life as a spectator instead of a participant. He had, after all, murdered an infant when taunting Jared. Of course, he couldn't be entirely sure if it had been him or Azrael who had done the deed.

I suppose I have you to thank for that, he thought.

No response. What did he expect from the grim demon? He had no false assumptions that it actually cared about him. No, he was a tool for it to use. Sure, it gave him immense power, but what toll it took for those powers had yet to be determined. Every second it dwelled in him he felt his true self slipping away more and more. Cell by cell, he was slowly being transformed into something else.

He became aware that the hall was silent. Coming back from his internal contemplation, he was surprised to notice that every eye was upon him. Some were bright with reverence. Others displayed unveiled terror.

All except Vlad and the Musketeer. Vlad still held his hands steepled under his chin and was leaning forward slightly, watching him. His expression was subdued, the former mirth gone. Renault, of course, was grinning, his eyes sparkling with mischief.

Examining the room, he wondered what had happened. He shuffled in place and his right foot bumped up against something at his feet. His eyebrows shot up as he took in what was lying there. It was the headless corpse of a women dressed in a red gown.

A crimson pool of congealing blood ran from the hole in the creature's neck, slowly flowing in all directions.

Suddenly, aware he was holding something in his left hand, he lifted it to examine it.

The severed head of Esmerelda, her eyes wide and fixed her mouth open in a silent scream, greeted him. Blood trickled from it, splattering his pants and the ground at his feet.

"Huh," was all he managed.

Lowering his arm but not dropping the head, he smiled and shrugged again. Whatever had happened, he had no recollection of it. The head and the body erupted into flames, and in a matter of seconds were nothing but ashes.

"I'm guessing my demonic companion didn't take kindly to being seduced."

Silence from the crowd. Well except the Musketeer, who chuckled softly. He really did seem to enjoy anything chaotic.

Sighing heavily, Vlad sat back in his chair and massaged the bridge of his nose with one hand.

"I assume your wrath is sated, Lord Azrael, and that we may proceed. The dawn is quickly approaching, and the Council of Elders has much to discuss tonight. Current events have led to an urgency and a need to act sooner than planned."

It is and they may, the demon thought into his mind.

Steve nodded stiffly; his lips pressed into a thin line. He really hated it when Azreal took him over. Especially when he couldn't remember the fun. If he was honest with himself, he was afraid that one of these times he wouldn't return at all. Would he even know it had happened or, just like now, would he simply disappear?

Famine

Vlad visibly relaxed and waved his hand dismissively.

"Now, Renault, if you would not mind, please take Lord Azreal's vessel and leave us. You may stay if you wish, but it can be...unpleasant for humans. I would recommend you retire to your rooms for the rest of the evening."

The Musketeer seemed disappointed, but he and Steve decided to take their leave. As soon as they were out of sight, the sounds of revelry resumed.

They continued in silence past armored sentries, who all bowed in deference to them. A couple, both dressed in black formal wear, writhed in one corner. Their moans of pleasure followed the two as they passed. They eventually made their way to the apartment they both shared.

It was a large suite with a living area and two bedrooms, each with their own full bathrooms. Like everything else in the compound, it was utilitarian with very few frills. Of course, that didn't apply to the throne room— and he was sure Vlad's personal chambers as well.

Steve plopped down on one of the two black leather couches in the room. It made squeaking noises as he settled in, planting his feet on the oak table that separated the two pieces of furniture. Stretching both his arms outward he closed his eyes and leaned back against the cool leather.

He could sense the Musketeer watching him. Shifting in an attempt to get more comfortable he tried his best to ignore the man, if that was indeed what he was.

He was exhausted and wanted to just rest or, if possible, take a quick nap. It wasn't like they were going to be doing anything else tonight with dawn quickly approaching.

414

The Musketeer cleared his throat loudly and Steve groaned.

"Can't I just get a few minutes of down time?"

That annoying chuckle was his only response.

He cracked one eye open. The Musketeer was sitting on the couch across from him, legs crossed arms folded, and that damn grin plastered on his face.

Sighing heavily, he opened his eyes and fixed them on Renault.

"The answer you are looking for is no."

"I have already, how you say, *deduit*? No, deduced. Yes, that is the word. I have already deduced that."

Steve rolled his eyes.

The Musketeer fixed his nightmare-black eyes on him, sending shivers up his spine. Gritting his teeth he narrowed his eyes, attempting to deflect the penetrating stare.

It felt to Steve like every bit of skin, muscle, and sinew were being stripped away, exposing what was beneath. No matter how hard he struggled, he couldn't escape the dark gaze. Not even his deepest thoughts could be hidden from the Musketeer.

The Musketeer's smile vanished, and he growled. He let out a stream of what Steve could only assume were curses in French.

Jumping to his feet, he started pacing back and forth.

"Damn that interfering *le facheux*."

Deciding it was better not to speak, Steve followed him as he continued his pacing. Eventually slowing and coming to a stop, his expression became contemplative.

Famine

"Well, I should have known that Sanctuary would have gone with him. I had hoped his history with Vlad would prompt him to return to the clearing. I miscalculated his attachment to Jared, or rather his hatred for Azrael. All in all, despite your poor performance, what I desired was accomplished."

Accomplished? That angel had nearly turned him into a piece of fried chicken. Also, he had barely even got started with Dana before the two of them showed up and interrupted his fun.

The Musketeer crossed his arms and turned his head slightly, looking sideways at him.

"Yes, yes. I never expected you to get very far with the woman. She was meant only as a distraction for Jared. I assumed that fool of a vampire Vlad would try to deal with him on his own. Can you believe it? If I hadn't intervened Tzedakah would have made mincemeat out of him, ending his grand plans. Of course I had, however, expected Sanctuary to leave Jared and return to the clearing. He truly hates Vlad. Even more than me I suspect, and he desperately hates me."

He trailed off, mumbling to himself.

Steve slowly rose to his feet.

"You used me as bait," he growled.

Power coursed through his body as his growing anger stirred the dormant monster inside him.

Slowly turning to face Steve, whose hands were now alive with congealing shadows, the Musketeer grinned. Instantly his blood seemed to freeze in his veins. Even the demon, so powerful and obviously not an ordinary creature, seemed uncertain.

"I would very much like for you to try that, *mon ami*," he replied, his eyes twinkling but his voice flat and menacing. "As much fun as it would be, now is not the time for such revelries."

Steve relaxed but didn't lower his hands. He didn't trust the Musketeer any more than he trusted Azrael, but he was tangled up with them both and doubted he would be able to disentangle himself from either of them even if he wanted to.

"To answer your question, yes. Your only purpose there was to rattle Tzedakah's bearer and make him concentrate his focus even more heavily on her. If he thinks she is in danger, there is nothing that will stop him from going to her. Not even, I would wager, Tzedakah."

Steve blinked and lowered his hands. So, it was a two-fold plan. To save Vlad's sorry butt and to distract and cause more conflict between Jared and Tzedakah. He had to admit it was genius, even though he was still furious.

The Musketeer turned and made his way towards his room. Steve didn't think the man needed sleep, but he did like to spend a lot of time alone. Well, not exactly alone since he suspected the sword he carried was actually alive.

The Musketeer turned slightly before entering his room.

"Do not feel too bad about your failure. In the end it works in our favor. Now the angel will also think she is the center of our attention. It may not stop them from completely interfering, but it will, if nothing else, distract them for a while."

Having nothing more to say he closed the door, ending the conversation. Steve continued to stare at the closed door, his thoughts racing. Azrael was silent, but his presence was always lurking inside him.

He turned and made his way to his own room. Shrugging to himself, he realized he wasn't really angry anymore about being used. All in all, he had been able to torment Dana even though his fun was interrupted, and that always brightened his day.

They arrived at the precinct after shift change, thankfully avoiding the usual morning chaos. Most of the cruisers were leaving, the lot almost empty. Only high-ranking officials had parking spaces near the precinct, so once the patrols left for the day the lot was usually barren.

Binghamton was not a large city, but there were usually people milling about. Even during the night, you could usually find someone walking the streets. Unlike the metropolises of New York or Chicago, Binghamton was more of a big town than a true city.

Mrs. Rodriguez was in her usual perch by the door, her graying brown hair up in a bun. Her wrinkled but strong hands were shaking slightly as she adjusted a tattered and faded poster that hung by the door on the community corkboard.

Smiling, Dana walked up to her. Mrs. Rodriguez was a fixture here and had been since she started. It was good to know that in the chaos of life some things were constant. She needed that consistency today more than ever. At least here in this place, in small-town America, she always knew what to expect. Here the world made sense, and she desperately needed something to make sense.

Squinting, she examined the poster. It was the picture of a Hispanic girl of about twelve. The gap-toothed smiling face staring back at her was faded and gray from exposure to the elements and gave the child a ghost-like appearance. The wording had long ago faded to the point of illegibility, but she could still make out the date the girl went missing.

January 12, 1990. Wow, that was over thirty years ago. Shocked at how well maintained the poster was, she gingerly reached out and pressed down a wayward corner. The tape holding the paper had come loose. It was still sticky, so that meant someone regularly came out here and reapplied it.

Mrs. Rodriguez gently rested her fingers on the face, as if by touching the picture she could somehow touch the missing child.

"Thank you for your help," she whispered softly, her voice rough. "I long ago stopped printing these, but I can't let this one go."

Dana was silent, not wanting to interrupt the elderly woman. Jeremy huffed and shifted awkwardly, but she ignored him. God, he was impatient. For someone who talked to God and was obviously a good person, he sure seemed annoyed constantly by the world and the plight of its inhabitants.

Inching closer, attempting to read the name on the poster, Dana asked, "Who is she?"

"My daughter."

Dana nodded slightly. "Did you ever find out what..." She broke off and cleared her throat before continuing. "I mean, did you ever find her?"

The old women didn't turn to look at her but pressed her thin lips together and let out a deep sigh. The corners of her mouth turned up slightly, and she glanced at Dana out of the corner of her eye. Her deep brown eyes were still bright and alive and had the appearance of a younger woman's.

"It's okay, dear. You don't have to tiptoe around the issue. Not anymore, anyway. To answer your question, no. We never found her."

Dana suddenly sensed, or rather smelled, Jeremy's face directly next to hers. The distinct odor of spearmint giving him away.

"I'm sorry."

Mrs. Rodriguez smiled and patted Dana on the cheek.

"No need to apologize. You police did everything you could to find her. I know she's most likely dead, and I should let go, and I have mostly. All that's left is this one poster. I just can't bring myself to take it down, because if I do it's like she truly is gone forever."

"I completely get that," Jeremy chimed in, his eyes serious but warm. He reached up and fixed the same rebellious corner Dana had. "I would feel the same way."

Famine

Mrs. Rodriguez's eyes were wet as she patted him on his face as well and turned back to rest her free hand on the picture once more.

"Thank you both so much for your kindness. I've been coming here as often as I could since she went missing, and you are the first people in years to ask me about my little Rosa."

Sniffing slightly the old women cleared her throat, straightened, and then with a smile gave them both one more pat on the cheek.

"Well, I must be going. One of my greatgrandchildren is waiting for her abuela to take her to the park."

With that said, she turned and slowly made her way down the now-busy street.

Dana and Jeremy watched her go, both quiet and contemplative and neither wanting to be the first to break the silence. How many people like Mrs. Rodriguez were there in the world? People who had no idea what had happened to their loved ones. People who would never truly get closure.

Sighing, she turned and glanced up at Jeremy. He was staring into space where the older women had gone, lost in his own thoughts. His eyes seemed haunted, and his ruggedly handsome face was sad.

It dawned on her as she studied his features that it was his job to find people like Mrs. Rodrigez's daughter. How many had he failed to find? How many mothers, fathers, brothers, sisters, aunts, and uncles had he had to tell that their loved ones were never coming home? How many times had he watched hope fail? What kind of damage did such things do to a person's soul?

As a police officer, especially a homicide detective, she understood a bit. How many families had she notified that their loved ones were dead? What Jeremy did, however, was on an entirely different level.

She couldn't imagine being the one to tell a family that she had no idea where their loved one was or what had happened to them. The uncertainty and helplessness must be torture. A torture that you carried with you till the day you died. How much pain, loss, and futility did he hold in his soul?

He noticed her looking at him and frowned.

"What?" he grumbled. "Do I have something on my face?"

And there he was. The same old curmudgeon she had become familiar with. Maddeningly frustrating, boorish, self-centered, and difficult, and yet she was starting to warm to him. Underneath that hard shell was a good man. A good man who actually cared, even though he did everything in his power to try and hide it.

Most of the time she wanted to throttle him, but she had to admit to herself she really was grateful for him. Her already weak faith may have been shaken by Jared's death, but she couldn't deny that Jeremy being exactly where she needed him to be at exactly the right time was eerily coincidental. Almost like divine appointment, if she actually believed in such things.

"Nothing," she replied, turning towards the door. "Come on, let's go inside and see what help we can drum up.

At least maybe the captain can make a few calls and get things moving better."

"You know what I think," he said gloomily.

Sighing, she pushed open the door and they walked inside. Grumbling under his breath, though not too much, she noticed, Jeremy followed after her. His hands were in his pockets and his shoulders slumped, as if he had resigned himself to some unpleasant fate. He was so ridiculous.

After having confirmed with the officer at the front desk that the captain was indeed in his office, she had Jeremy sign in and made their way toward the captain's office.

The familiar scents and sounds brought out a feeling of security in her and she sighed deeply, letting out the tension that had built up over the last few days. It was good to be back here. Back in the place she considered her true home.

Sure, her house was where she lived, but if she was honest with herself the station was where she truly felt at home. Where she truly felt safe, especially after her dream last night. Shaking off the feelings of helplessness that came with the memories, she continued on.

They passed the desks of other officers, some busily working, others pretending to. How many times had she been both? Smiling, she nodded politely at her colleagues, moving quickly to avoid getting entangled in any conversations that might distract her.

She would catch up with them all later when she could properly process all that had happened. Properly deal with Jared's death. The emotions that flooded through her when she thought of him were still nearly debilitating, but she forced them back into the dark recesses of her subconscious and continued towards her objective.

She felt Jeremy's eyes on her but ignored him. God, for such a self-centered man he sure was empathic. He had noticed her expression change and was now looking at her with concern. Of course she wasn't all right, but they didn't have time for a pow-wow to discuss her feelings. Her cousin didn't have time for it.

Frowning, she steeled herself against his inquiring gaze and quickened her pace, putting a few steps between them. The captain's office was just around the corner, and she was impatient to talk to him. She desperately needed his help, and she was hopeful he would. He always had in the past.

Turning the corner, the familiar face of Officer Tucker came into view. He was a pudgy middle-aged man with unkempt sandy brown hair and round, but not unattractive, features. Over six feet tall, with broad shoulders and muscular legs, he was the kind of man you knew could be a knockout if he could just get his diet under control.

He looked up from the documents he was examining, his intelligent dark blue eyes instantly scanning them and trying to place them. They brightened upon seeing Dana but narrowed slightly when they took in Jeremy. He didn't know him, and anyone he didn't know was a potential problem.

"Hey, Tuck," she said with a tired smile. "I need to talk to the captain. It's pretty urgent, so if you don't mind, I'll show myself in."

Famine

He stood quickly and blocked her way, his eyes moving from her to Jeremy and back again.

"Sorry, Detective," he apologized. "But the Captain is currently in a meeting and gave orders not to be disturbed."

His narrowed eyes kept glancing at Jeremy. He must be suspicious of him. She would be if she were in his place.

"It's okay, Tuck," she replied with a warm and reassuring smile. "He's with me. Helping me with my cousin's disappearance. That's why we're here. I need the captain's help with something."

He turned to look back at her, his expression was still hard but sympathetic. He shook his head slightly.

"Sorry, Dana, but he said no interruptions. I would let you in if I could, given the circumstances, but his orders were explicit. He is not to be bothered or interrupted till he's done."

Grimacing, she turned to see who the captain was meeting with. The blinds were drawn but one was slightly askew. There was just enough of a gap for her to see inside. She saw two men sitting in front of the captain's large mahogany desk. All she could make out from this angle were the backs of their heads.

The captain's hands were steepled and his posture rigid as he listened patiently to the one on the right, who was waving his hands animatedly as he spoke. Neither of them looked very happy.

Who were these guys? Sure, the Captain had to meet with lots of people and put out lots of fires, but you could cut the tension in that office with a knife. One of the men turned slightly, revealing his face, and she gasped.

Growling, she attempted to push past Tucker.

"Hey," he grunted, grabbing her by the arm and attempting to restrain her. "Detective Campbell, please stop."

Dana noticed Jeremy starting to move in her direction but hesitating as two more officers rounded the corner in response to the commotion.

"Aw, hell," he growled, uncertainty in his eyes. She could see his brain working. Should he help her and risk getting arrested or see how this all played out? She knew he would eventually act, since that was who he was, and she couldn't allow him to get involved.

"Detective, please calm down and just hold on a second," Tucker pleaded. "I'm sure he will be more than happy to see you when he's done."

"Sorry, Tuck," she apologized as she turned and drove her right fist into the side of his head.

There was a loud crack and Tucker instantly dropped to the floor, dazed. Pushing past him, she could hear the shouts of the approaching officers and the loud cursing of Jeremy.

Anger giving her tunnel vision, she barely registered the commotion around her. Reaching out with trembling hands, she slowly turned the knob and stepped into the captain's office.

She could hear Jeremy intercepting the pursuing officers, their shouts echoing somewhere in the back of her mind, but she didn't care. She was furious. The captain looked up and his expression darkened as he dropped his hands.

Famine

The two remaining men turned to look at the person who was causing all the commotion. One was Deputy Jenkins and the other, who she had seen through the blinds, was Captain Fox. The son of a bitch had a broad, condescending smile plastered on his face.

"Nice to see you again, Detective," he drawled. "How's the search for your cousin going?"

W hat's he doing here?" she fumed, pointing a shaking finger at Captain Fox.

Captain Jackson, an African American man of average height and build, his dark close-cropped hair streaked with gray hinting at an age older than his face exhibited, narrowed his chocolate brown eyes and pursed his broad lips. Crossing his arms, he let out a disappointed sigh.

His uniform was pristine, and his perfectly polished badge reflected the ambient light like a search beacon. His glare was no different, and it seemed to reach directly into her soul. As angry as she was, his fatherly stare brought the gravity of what she had, and was currently doing, crashing down on her.

Steeling herself against the emotions rising in her, she met his gaze with an unyielding one of her own. As much as she respected him, there was too much at stake to back down now. She couldn't, however, shake the feeling of dread that was slowly creeping into her subconscious from seeing that punk Captain Fox here in his office.

"Discussing you, actually," he stated, his eyes flicking to the commotion behind Dana.

Folding his arms over his chest he stared up at her, his eyes narrowed slightly. He glanced at the commotion in the hallway, noticing Jeremy for the first time, his arms skyward in response to the two officers leveling tasers at him. He was shaking his head and shouting something that was indistinguishable through the glass window of the office.

"Maybe you should attend to your friend first," he suggested, sitting back slightly.

"He'll be fine," she replied with a dismissive wave. "Answer my question. Why is he here?"

She nodded at Captain Fox, who now had a look of innocence and confusion plastered on his stupid face. It was an obvious performance, and no one was buying it.

Sighing, the Captain motioned to an empty chair in the corner.

"Close the door and take a seat, Detective."

"I'd rather stand."

"Dana, that wasn't a request," he stated. There was ice in his voice, and his tone suggested he would tolerate no arguments.

"Fine," she spit, slamming the door and turning to grab the chair. She thumped it down a few feet from the desk and dropped dramatically onto it. Slumping slightly and hunching her shoulders like a petulant child, she glared daggers at the two sheriffs.

"I'm waiting," she said, her voice thick with irritation.

The muffled sounds of Jeremy being restrained made her grimace, but she didn't turn to acknowledge what was going on out in the hall. He'd be okay. She'd clear it up when she was done with the Captain. The responding officers most likely assumed Jeremy was the one who hit Tuck, but she'd sort it out later. A quick stint in the lock-up would probably do him good anyway.

She winced at the memory of what she just did and the look of surprise on Tuck's face when she hit him. He was a friend, only doing his job, and didn't deserve that. Her temper had gotten the better of her and she had acted without thinking. The weight of just how much trouble she was probably in slammed into her, making her grimace. Feeling terrible, she glanced towards the door, but her attention was instantly brought back by Captain Fox clearing his throat loudly.

"Like I was saying, Captain," he continued, his tone grave but sympathetic. "I spoke to the ambassador and, given the disappearance of her cousin and what she has been through over the last few weeks, he is willing to overlook the trespassing. Given, of course, that Detective Campbell promises not to go near his property again."

Ambassador? Wait, so that bizarre complex concealed in the woods was some kind of home for a diplomat? That couldn't be right. What diplomat in their right mind would build a compound so far from any actual federal facilities? Plus, there was no way what she had seen could possibly be a personal dwelling. No, she was certain it was some kind of compound. She had no idea what it was used for, but it wasn't for living in.

"So, wait," she interrupted. "That strange facility is the residence of an ambassador or something? No way. Pardon my French, but that's bullshit. My gut is telling me that something bad is going on in that place, and I would wager an entire year's pay that it has something to do with my cousin's disappearance."

Captain Jackson slammed his fist onto the desk, cutting her off and knocking over a picture of his wife and two children. It clattered loudly to the floor, silencing the entire room. He was actually shaking with fury, his eyes blazing.

"Detective Campbell, I advise you to be quiet. You're in enough trouble as is. "

Her eyes were wide with shock at the outburst. The Captain had never in her entire career spoken to her that way. In truth, he had actually been pretty easy on her if she was being honest. In fact, if the other officers hadn't taken a liking to her, she would most likely have had to deal with a lot of animosity about it. She had always looked at him as a mentor or even father figure, but now she feared she may have gone too far.

He glared at her a few seconds longer, allowing the moment to sink in before turning back to the sheriffs and motioning for them to continue. It worked, and Dana slouched uncomfortably in her chair.

Fox cleared his throat and tried in vain to hide a satisfied smile.

"As I said, Ambassador Durgala is willing to forgive the trespass. He likes his solitude and that is why," he turned to look at Dana, putting emphasis on his words and directing them at her, "he chose to place his personal estate here in Western New York. He lives in the deep woods of his country, preferring the quiet and privacy it gives him, and Chenango County affords him those same comforts."

Looking as glum as she felt, she crossed her arms over her chest and turned away from him, refusing to meet his eyes. She could feel the satisfied smile and that made her even more angry. Oh, if she weren't already in a whole world of hurt, she'd knock that stupid grin right off his face. Better judgment winning over, she chose to sit quietly instead. She would reason with the Captain after they left. He would hear her side of the story and then he would understand. Wouldn't he? He had to. She had no one else to turn to.

Jeremy's words about calling Johansson for help nagged at her subconscious. No. Absolutely not. She did not trust Johansson, and she would only play that card if the actual stinking apocalypse was upon them. She recognized the doubt in her resolve, however, but shook her head, driving it away. She would cross that bridge when she came to it. She wasn't there yet, but her cousin's time was quickly ticking away.

Captain Jackson, his expression returning to that of a professional, nodded. "I'm sure Detective Campbell understands the grace she has been given and will act accordingly. Please extend my apologies to the ambassador." He stood and extended his hand towards the door. "Now, if you don't have anything else to discuss, please show yourselves out. Give my regards to Sheriff Taylor and let him know I will be contacting him personally when I get a chance."

Captain Fox nodded, and both men rose and turned to walk toward the door. Dana stayed seated, refusing to show the two sheriffs even the slightest hint of difference. Jenkins reached it first and opened it. She expected to hear more commotion, but all that fluttered in were the usual sounds of a busy police station. Jeremy was either already in lock-up or had managed to talk his way out of trouble. She hoped it was the latter, but it wouldn't make her sad if he had been detained. He needed a good kick to his ego, though she bet it wouldn't be his first time in jail.

Before closing the door, Captain Fox turned and gave her a nod.

"Detective, always a pleasure," he said as he closed the door.

"Go jump off a cliff," she growled back.

As soon as the door closed, Captain Jackson dropped heavily into his chair. It unleashed a symphony of creaks and groans as he sat back, closed his eyes, and massaged his temples.

"Can you believe that jerk?" she asked.

His only response was a deep sigh. She inched forward in her chair and thrust an arm towards the door.

"I can't believe he came here and tattled on me like I was a two-year-old or something. I mean, really? What happened to interdepartmental courtesy? Not only was he a complete jerk when I was searching for my cousin, but now he comes here and tries to get me in trouble. Captain, I know that there is something fishy going on out there and he and that neanderthal Jenkins railroaded me when I was investigating. I have good reason to believe my cousin was in the woods near there."

Captain Jackson's expression darkened, and he sat up and leaned towards her, steepling his hands. Anything else she was about to say stuck in her throat and she quickly sat back, her hands in her lap.

"Dana," he said, his tone serious. "Do you have any idea what you've just done? The hornets' nest you just kicked?"

Her brow furrowed, she queried, "What do you mean?"

"Let me tell you," he continued, ignoring her statement. "Before these two gentlemen came to my office, I got a call from the governor. Yes," he said, raising a hand and cutting her off before she could speak. "That governor. And after that, the mayor. You know what they said? Let me tell you. They said that in no way are we to look into or bother Mr. Durgala again, and if they even so much as hear a whisper that we did it will mean both our jobs or worse."

He let the last statement hang in the air, his expression hard and unyielding. If she wasn't mistaken, there was also fear in his eyes. Veiled, but she knew him well enough to recognize it. What in the holy hell was going on here? The governor and the mayor? What kind of man was this Durgala that he would scare someone like the captain?

"Dana," he said, bringing her back to the moment. "I will do everything I can to help you find your cousin, you know that, but Mr. Durgala and that compound are off limits. Do you understand me? No exceptions."

Famine

Staring dumbfounded, she said nothing. There were so many protests in her mind. So many arguments, but they all died as she looked into his eyes. They were the pleading eyes of a man scared not only for himself, but for her. There was genuine fear and hopelessness in them, as well as sternness. This man who was a bastion of strength and justice in her life was powerless, and with that realization her hope shattered. If he couldn't help her then no one could.

Jeremy's words resurfaced in her mind, bringing not only anger but a spark of hope. There was one person who may be able to do something. A person who was in a place of power higher than the captain. Yes, she had said she would only go to him if she had no other options, but now she was out of options. If Jared were still here, he would back her up, but he was gone and she couldn't rely on him anymore. The thought of him reopened the wound in her heart, but she suppressed the tears that threatened to come, turning them into determination instead.

"Dana," he repeated, bringing her attention to him again. His eyes were still pleading. Pleading for her to understand.

She nodded and stood. Straightening, she crossed her arms and pursed her lips. He was still seated and, even though she was almost a foot shorter, she seemed to tower over him. Her eyes blazed with fire as she looked down on the man she had once respected more than any other in her life, save her father.

She understood why he couldn't help her. Understood what he would be giving up if he did, but it still hurt. In this terrible moment all of the trust she had for him, for the police and for the whole damn justice system, dissipated. If the institutions she had believed in no longer fulfilled their purpose, then she would go above them. And if that didn't work, she would go around them and do it herself. Her cousin may already be dead, and if she was, heaven help those responsible. If the system wouldn't bring them justice, she would.

Turning, she moved to the door and opened it. The captain's voice followed after her.

"Dana, let this go. I am begging you. Let this go."

She closed the door behind her, shutting out his pleas. There was no way in Hell she was going to let it go, even if it meant her job. Hell, even if it cost her life. She stormed off down the hall, leaving the captain and possibly her entire career behind.

Sophia huddled in the corner of her cell, her knees pulled up to her chest, her eyes shut and her hands covering her ears. Dust particles lazily danced in the beam of light drifting from the small window, seemingly at odds with the chaotic screaming she was failing to drown out. It felt like the shrieking had been going on for hours, but in truth it had probably only been a few minutes. The brightening glow from the window told her dawn was near, and that meant an end to the night's horrors.

Thank God. She couldn't take much more. It was obvious that the victims were children by the octaves of their screams. Children. How could they do that? They were all monsters, that's how. If she wasn't in this cell...

If you weren't in this cell, what?

For all her false bravado, there was absolutely nothing she could do. She was powerless. She hadn't even been able to save herself, so what made her think she could save them?

Tears flowing now, she lowered her hands and hugged her knees closer. Thankfully the noises of death had finally ceased, her soft sobs replacing them in the void. The children's wide, terrified eyes haunted her every thought. Her imagination ran wild with dreadful images of what was happening to them. All faces she knew and had come to love. All pleading to her for help. Begging for her to end the horror.

She was the oldest of the captives in her pen, so the others looked to her for comfort and strength. It broke her heart to leave them when she had attempted to escape, but she had convinced herself that it had been necessary. They needed help. Help she couldn't provide on her own. Of course, even if she had gotten away, who would believe her anyway? If she had managed to find help, they most likely would have tossed her in the looney bin and thrown away the key.

No, her cousin would believe her. No matter how outlandish her claims were, Dana would believe them. They were more like sisters than cousins, being only a few years apart in age. A deep bond had formed between them in their early years in spite of how much of a brat she had been. If she had managed to get free and make it to her cousin, she would have received the help she needed. Dana had always been one of the fiercest people she knew. Competitive to a fault, she always had to be the best at everything. She hated losing and would have found a way to save not only her but all the captives.

Famine

Jumping to her feet she started pacing, renewed hope burning in her heart. Like the sky, her expression suddenly brightened. Dana was probably out there right now, searching for her. In fact, she almost certainly was. Maybe their situation wasn't as hopeless as it seemed. Dana was like a bulldog, and when she had a scent no one was able to stop her from pursuing it. All she had to do was stay alive until she came for her, and she was absolutely certain Dana would. She had to.

What if Dana never came? What if no one came? Was she going to die here, just like those children in the other room? She had no idea where she even was or how far from civilization her captors had taken her. Sure, in her escape she had stumbled onto a farmhouse, but who knew how far out in the wilderness it had actually been?

She stopped her frantic pacing and leaned heavily against the bars. Sighing, she ran a hand through her matted hair. One broken nail caught in the mess of tangles, and it pulled painfully as she tried to extricate it. Frowning, she decided to flail her hand around wildly as if that would actually help. It didn't but only made it worse. Now not only was her finger entangled, but her scalp hurt too.

Her lip started quivering as a few stray tears slowly dripped onto her dirty cheek. She wiped at them with her free hand, smearing the filth around. She hissed and blinked furiously as some of it got in her eye. Forgetting that her nail was still tangled in her hair, she pulled the offending tuft out painfully as she attempted to rub her ailing eye.

"Holy Hell," she shouted, digging her fists hard into her thighs. "God, fricking..."

She caught herself before taking the Lord's name in vain and chose a different stream of curses. Given where she was, not angering the one being in the universe Who could help her was definitely a smart decision. Mama's girl knew how to swear, though, and every expletive her mind could conjure spewed forth in a loud stream of filthy language.

Her tirade over, she slumped to the floor with a thud, the back of her head resting against the bars. Blind in one eye, her scalp burning, grimy, tear-streaked, and probably smelling worse than a dumpster, she sat on the cement floor, shoulders slumped, eyes shut and face in her hands. She shook every few seconds from quiet sobbing as hopelessness seized her heart like a vise.

"Are you alright?"

Jumping at the sound, her head snapping towards it, she scuttled reflexively away from whoever had just spoken. Her eyes wide and her chest heaving, she scanned the room for the source of the voice. The light from the window was now streaming more intensely, bringing greater clarity but deepening the shadows. Two glowing red eyes peered at her from deep within the withdrawing shadows.

"Kat?" she asked tentatively.

The little vampire appeared, gliding forward until her face was barely visible in the expanding light. Silent as a ghost, she seemed almost spectral. More shadow and spirit than flesh and blood. Those unblinking and expressionless eyes never left her, causing her to shudder involuntarily. Blood trickled from one side of her mouth, reminding

441

Sophia in no uncertain terms that Kat was not necessarily her friend but a dangerous predator. Had she taken part in the earlier festivities?

Kat retreated back into the shadows, her glinting eyes the only thing remaining visible. Sophia noticed the increasing brightness as the sun rose higher in the sky, solidifying that daytime was finally upon them. The little vampire continued to stare but said nothing. She was apparently awaiting a response to her earlier question.

"Not really," Sophia sniffed.

"They didn't harm you, did they?" Kat asked, her voice flat and emotionless.

Sophia couldn't tell if she hid her emotions or simply didn't feel them anymore. Either way, the almost robotic tone to her voice was unsettling. It made her seem less human. It kind of reminded her of the interviews she had seen with serial killers. The tone of voice displaying their complete lack of empathy. To normal people it was instantly noticeable and unnerving, even if you didn't completely understand why.

"No," she replied, her head turning to face Kat, her irritated eye squinting still. "Not this time."

Either Kat was playing off having taken part in the earlier massacre, or she hadn't been involved. It didn't matter anyway. She was still one of them and had certainly participated in such *merriments* in the past. Kat's almost childlike interest in her didn't change that. In fact, she still wasn't sure if Kat's curiosity with her was some remnant of humanity slipping through or the concern one shows a pet.

"Why are you crying, then?"

442

Sophia huffed. "Oh, let me think. Maybe it's because I was kidnapped, held against my will, terrorized, surrounded by death, deprived of food and water, and waiting to be murdered as a food source. Oh yeah, and vampires are real. You pick which one that best suits you."

Turning away, she closed her eyes and tapped her head against the bars.

"I really thought I could escape. I was sure of it. And when I did, I knew I could get help. Real help, not just some people concerned, but genuine, honest to God help."

"Against vampires?" Kat replied, the skepticism was obvious in her voice. "Against..." Her voice cracked a bit. "Him?"

"Yeah," she answered, her voice strong with confidence. "My cousin is a cop. A detective, actually, and she would have found a way."

Now it was Kat's turn to scoff. "The police can't help. Some have tried over the years. All of them were stopped by him."

She turned back to look at Kat, her expression serious. The vampire was more visible now in the growing daylight. Kat shifted under her gaze and rubbed at one of her wrists. Why was she doing that? It seemed to be an anxious tick, as if she was hiding something. Wait a minute.

She shot up, eyes narrowing. Turning to face Kat, she placed her hands on the bars. "Where's the bracelet I gave you?"

Kat avoided her eyes and shifted nervously. "I dropped it."

Panick seized her heart. "Dropped it where?"

Famine

"In the forest," she replied, still avoiding her gaze.

She let out the breath she had been holding.

"That's good. I'm not sure how they would react if they found some random bracelet lying around. I bet they could tell it was mine from my smell or something. That would be bad. They would probably think I had escaped again and..." She shivered. "Well, I'm sure it wouldn't be pleasant."

Smiling slightly, she glanced at Kat and frowned. She still looked like a little girl caught with her hand in the cookie jar. What was going on with her? Was there more to the missing bracelet than she was saying? Determined to find out what it was she was hiding, she beckoned for her to come closer. This made her shy away even more, as if the shrinking shadows could protect her from Sophia's questions.

"Kat, come here. We need to talk."

Kat shook her head and continued to rub her wrist.

"Yes," she reprimanded gently.

"No, I will burn in the light," she countered.

Sophia let out a deep sigh. "All right. But I know you aren't telling me something. Something that has to do with where you lost the bracelet."

Kat was silent for a second before finally responding. "You promise you won't be mad at me if I tell you?"

She shook her head and crossed a hand over her chest. "I promise. Cross my heart and everything."

Something resembling determination settled on the vampire's delicate features as she made up her mind.

"Okay," she said, nodding her head slightly. "I often leave the grounds to...hunt."

Sophia grimaced and swallowed back a bit of bile as she thought about what *hunting* meant.

"Don't worry," she continued. "I never hunt humans. Well, not anymore anyway. While I was out, I wandered over to the farmhouse where the White Lady found you the day you tried to escape."

Sophia grimaced and scrunched up her forehead at the memory. The sting of it was still fresh and she had to suppress the sadness and feelings of guilt threatening to bring the water works again. Sniffing back tears, she drove the memory away and focused on Kat's story.

"There were a lot of people there. All of them moving about like ants. There was blood everywhere and it was making me very hungry, so I got close to them. I promise I wasn't going to kill them or anything like that. I was just curious."

She looked up at Sophia for affirmation that she believed she hadn't been planning on murdering her family. She nodded and gestured for her to continue. It was so surreal comforting a kid-sized vampire, or any vampire at all for that matter.

"Like I said I was curious, so I got real close. All vampires can become nearly invisible to humans if we want to, so no one saw me."

"Wait a minute," she interrupted. "You went out in the daytime? I thought the light hurt you."

"It does," she affirmed. "But if you stay to the shadows, you can avoid getting burned. It was nearly sunset anyway, so I wasn't really in any danger."

Famine

Well, that explained how the White Lady had managed to track her even though it had been daylight. Of course, that smelly monster always following her around didn't seem to be bothered by sunlight, so I guess he could have tracked her.

"Anyway, there was this pretty woman and some scruffy-looking guy. I'm pretty sure he knew I was there, because he kept glancing at exactly where I was hiding."

"Were they cops?" she interrupted, her heart beating a little faster. "Maybe detectives?"

Kat shrugged. "There were a lot of people there, so maybe."

A pretty woman who could be a detective. If that was Dana, then maybe her situation wasn't completely hopeless after all.

"What did she look like?"

"Who?" Kat asked.

"The pretty woman," she responded impatiently.

"Well," Kat said, looking to the left slightly, her eyes unfocused. "Kind of like you. Same nose for sure, but brown hair instead of yellow."

Sophia slammed a hand into the bars and grinned. "I knew it. I knew she would be looking for me. Did she say anything about me? Anything at all?"

Kat nodded and her expression turned to one of relief. "Yeah, she was part of a large group of people who were looking for someone. They mentioned your name, so I figured they were looking for you. That was one of the reasons I wanted to get close to them."

Too excited to completely listen, she started pacing again. Dana was close if she had made it to the farmhouse. There was no way she would have thought it was a coincidence that a family was massacred in the same area she was most likely suspected of having been in. The place they were keeping her was a good distance from there and deep in the forest, but she had hope now. Hope that Dana would find her way here and rescue her.

"That's where I dropped the bracelet," she heard Kat say.

"You did what?" she asked, the mention of the bracelet bringing her attention back to the conversation. In her excitement she had forgotten about the bracelet.

"I dropped it where the pretty lady and the scruffy guy could find it," she responded, uncertainty in her voice. "Was that okay?"

"Did they find it?" Her heart was racing so fast she thought she would pass out.

Kat nodded, the corners of her mouth turning upward.

"I dropped it right at the mouth of the trail you used when you tried to escape. It leads directly here."

She nearly jumped for joy as she pumped a fist in the air. Moving quickly to the bars she peered at Kat, her eyes bright with renewed hope.

"You beautiful little vampire," she praised. "Did they get the hint and follow the trail here?"

Kat nodded again. "They were followed by two nasty familiars. I was scared they were going to kill them, but they didn't harm them, only made them leave. I was hungry, so I didn't follow them, but the pretty lady seemed like she was going to come back."

Bobbing her head up and down vigorously, she pushed herself off the bars and placed her hands on her hips. Dana had found her. Even though she had been driven off, she had found where they were holding her and that changed everything.

The sound of someone coming drew her attention to the door. When she turned back to warn Kat, the vampire had vanished. No matter, Dana knew where she was. And it was only a matter of time before she came for her. All she had to do was survive till then, and she would.

"Hello, child." The voice that spoke to her out of the darkness of the doorway turned her blood to ice and silenced the renewed hope that was steadily growing in her heart.

It hadn't taken long to get Jeremy out of lockup. Tuck, as soon as he had come to, had vouched for him and all charges had been dropped. Her situation, on the other hand, was a little more complicated. She had caused quite a scene and had even assaulted a fellow police officer. To his credit Tuck had forgiven her pretty quickly, citing all of the loss she had faced recently as the reason. Not wanting an internal investigation, it really hadn't taken much convincing for the captain to drop the matter. She was, of course, now on medical leave until she had been cleared by a psychologist.

That was just so great. She hated head shrinks. Pretty much all cops did.

The sun shone brightly on them as they walked out of the station. Jeremy stood a few paces away, his arms crossed, refusing to look at her. He was so angry that she swore she could see an actual storm cloud hovering over his head. She really didn't blame him. If Jared had done that to her, she wouldn't have talked to him for a week.

Scrunching up her brow, she absentmindedly twirled a stray lock of hair. Why had she compared him to Jared? Jeremy wasn't her partner like Jared had been. Was she subconsciously starting to look at him that way? Sure, she had developed a certain level of affection for him, but nowhere near the kind of feelings one had for a partner. The two of them had been through a lot over the past few days and she had come to rely on him, but a partner? No way. Not like Jared.

As usual, thoughts of Jared threatened her barely controlled composure and unshed tears rimmed her eyes. Sniffing, she turned away from Jeremy and quickly composed herself. There was no time for grief and no time to unpack her confusing feelings towards Jeremy. Sophia was counting on her and, judging by the extreme reaction from pretty much everyone in the State of New York with any kind of political power, she had pulled the right string.

"Come on," she commanded, starting off in the direction where she had parked her car. "We've got work to do."

He pretended not to hear her and continued to glower at everything and everyone but refused to follow. She had made it clear across the busy street before realizing he wasn't behind her. Her face turning red and her lips pressed so tight that they were invisible, she turned and waved her arms back and forth.

"You coming or not?"

"Not," he retorted, still refusing to look at her.

God, he was such a child.

"Whatever," she countered, turning away and continuing in the direction of her car. "Do what you want."

"I will," he yelled back.

"I'm sure you will. You always do," she shot back.

"What's that supposed to mean?" he replied, his voice thick with anger.

She turned back to look at him and noticed him jogging across the street, weaving through the rush hour traffic. She stopped and waited as horns blared and drivers cursed at him. Shooting angry gestures and shouting back, he eventually made it across to where she stood waiting. Wheezing and slightly out of breath from the exertion he frowned down at her, his hands on his hips and his eyes blazing.

"Say that again," he dared. The fact he was slightly out of breath lessened the weight of his words, but there was no doubt he was furious.

"What? That you always do what's best for yourself regardless of what anyone else thinks or needs? The fact you're just a selfish, boorish, crotchety, self-absorbed human being? Is that what you wanted me to repeat?"

The grinding of his teeth was audible, and she imagined she could actually see lightning and hear thunder developing in the cloud over his head.

"Really?" he asked, his voice thick with indignation. "How the hell do you know? You've only known me for a few days, and in that time, I have fought vampires for you, trudged all around hick central looking for your cousin, and put up with your constant mood swings. I can assure you, honey, that was not what I wanted to do. Not at all."

His words stung, and her face fell as tears welled up in her eyes again. Even so, she refused to back down. She was tired, angry, sad, and confused. All at the same time. Uncertain of what to do yet certain she had to do something. Everyone who had any power had refused to help her, and she felt completely and utterly alone. Everyone but Jeremy, who for reasons she didn't understand, was still around even though she was treating him like crap. Absolute crap. She really shouldn't be acting this way, but she couldn't stop herself.

"And furthermore," he continued, his voice rising. "What about you? Who just punched a fellow servant of the law, leaving me to take the fall for it? Selfish, my butt. You're the selfish one. So bound up in your own problems you're willing to plow through everything and anyone who gets in your way, consequences be damned."

He paused, gasping for breath, still wheezing from his jog across the street. People were staring uncomfortably at them now, and a few even looked concerned. The wall holding back her emotions finally shattered and tears flowed unchecked as she sputtered incoherently, her brain searching for a proper comeback.

He rolled his eyes. "Seriously?"

Rubbing her cheeks, she glared up at him. "What's the matter? Too emotional for you? Can't handle my girly outburst? Why don't you just leave? I don't need you anyway. Everyone leaves in the end and you're no different. My mom, Jared, that liar Johansson; they all left me, and

I've managed quite well without them. I will find my cousin on my own. I don't need any of your help."

Brow furrowed, he rested his hands on his hips. "What in the hell are you talking about? And who's Johansson? Besides, Jared's not..."

He bit his lip before he could say anymore. Noticing the sudden cut-off she narrowed her eyes, her tears temporarily forgotten. The sounds of downtown flowing around them she glared at Jeremy, who looked like someone who had just been caught with his hand in the cookie jar.

"Go ahead," she said, the fire in her eyes belying the calm tone in her voice. "Finish what you were about to say."

"I asked you who Johansson was," he retorted, deflecting her probe. "Is he the mysterious FBI guy you refuse to ask for help? Did you two have a falling out or something? You labeled him a liar; is that why you won't call him?"

"Don't change the subject," she retorted. "Finish your sentence."

Her cheeks stung from crying and her face felt flushed, but she was absolutely focused now. He knew something he wasn't telling her. Just like Johansson, he was holding things back from her. What he said and did now would determine if she would ever trust him again. If he lied to her like Johansson, then she was done with him. If not, then she might be able to truly trust him.

Her emotions a torrent raging in her heart, she stared deeply into his eyes. Subconsciously she ran a hand through her unkempt hair. Her heart was beating so fast she could almost hear it audibly. Somewhere deep in her core she desperately hoped he would tell her the truth. Why did she care so much if he did? Why did she want him to tell her the truth? No, need him to?

Unsure of what was happening in her feelings, and unable to unpack it all, she waited for him to respond. He met her gaze, his eyes boring into her as if he could sense every one of her secret thoughts. They stood like that, measuring each other for what seemed to Dana to be an eternity before he finally sighed and ran a hand through his hair. Rubbing his neck and groaning softly, he cocked his head to one side and looked at her.

"All right," he said, resignation in his voice. "I knew Jared. He's actually why I was in the hospital."

Blinking rapidly, she shook her head slightly.

"What?"

"I knew Jared. We were...friends. Sort of."

"Let me get this straight," she replied, her voice way too calm. "You knew Jared."

"Yes."

She gestured with one hand.

"Go on."

Throwing his hands up in mock submission, he rolled his eyes.

"That's it. I knew him. Nothing more to the story."

Crossing her arms over her chest, she shook her head. "You said he was the reason you were in the hospital."

Narrowing his eyes and placing his hands defiantly on his hips, he intoned, "Drop it. It's not important."

One of Dana's eyebrows shot up. "Well, you better make it so and quick or this partnership, or whatever the hell it is, is over."

Growling, Jeremy threw his hands up in frustration, his face skyward.

"Why do You always get me into such frustrating situations? I mean, can't you just send me somewhere easy for a change? Is that too much to ask? Maye some old cat lady who needs one of her missing cats found. That would be a real nice change of pace."

Dana watched his rant patiently, having grown used to his tantrums. For a grown man he seemed to often act like a toddler. Some women might find it charming, but she just found it annoying. Of course, Jared had been prone to overreactions as well, just not as bad or as often. Maybe that was why she had warmed up to Jeremy so quickly. Did he remind her of Jared?

Shaking her head, she brought her attention back to the conversation at hand. There was no time to unpack all of the raging emotions and feelings she was experiencing. There would be time for that later. He knew something he wasn't telling her; she was certain of it. At the very least he claimed to know Jared, but he had never mentioned Jeremy to her. As his partner she knew things about him no one else did, not even Jasmine, so it was strange he had never spoken of him.

"You done?" she asked, barely able to keep the growing frustration out of her voice.

Sighing, he turned and looked at her.

Famine

"No, this conversation is far from over," he said loudly, his voice once again directed skyward. "As far as what you want to know, I can't tell you any more than I already have. I knew him, and when I noticed you at the hospital, I decided he would want me to tag along and watch out for you. That, and God ordered me to."

"Can't or won't?"

"Really?" he growled, his eyes flashing. "Even if I told you everything, you wouldn't believe me. I told you vampires were real, and even with all of the evidence you saw with your own two eyes you still refuse to believe in them. So, if I told you something even more crazy, you would just say I'm lying and push me away all the same."

"How do you know that?" she shouted back, tears rimming her eyes. "You don't know how I would react."

"Really? Isn't that what you did to Johansson?"

"This isn't the same thing," she stammered. "He lied to me."

"How so?" Jeremy asked, his voice softening a bit.

"He just—" She couldn't hold the tears back anymore and they rolled down her face unchecked. "He knew more about what's going on and refused to tell me. Jared died in my arms, and I know Steve killed him, but no one else seems to remember that. To the rest of the world, it's like it never happened. That bastard knows, but he refuses to let me in. Do you have any idea how that makes me feel?"

Jeremy shook his head but stayed silent.

"It makes me feel completely and utterly alone. Like I'm crazy. Everyone I even think of telling looks at me like I'm just dealing with grief and being hysterical. I know what

I saw the day I shot Steve, and I can't tell anyone for fear of being accused of PTSD or, worse, being sent to the looney bin."

"What did you see?" he asked softly.

Forcefully wiping the tears from her cheeks, she sniffed. People were beginning to avoid the two of them, some even moving across the street before reaching them. Raising her head she looked into his eyes, her own showing a desperation she'd had no idea she felt. Would he believe her, or would he think she was crazy?

Drawing closer, he lifted a hand and gently wiped a stray tear from her cheek.

"Tell me."

She searched his eyes for any signs of deception, but all she found was genuine sincerity. More tears welled up in her eyes as hope forced its way into her heart. Maybe, just maybe, she didn't have to be alone anymore. Maybe here was someone who would believe her.

"I," she stammered. "I saw Jared. I saw him right before I passed out after shooting Steve. I know it sounds crazy, and I probably wouldn't believe me if I were you, but I'm certain it was him. I feel like I'm losing my mind, and the world keeps falling apart around me, preventing me from catching my breath."

As soon as the words left her mouth, the crippling loneliness shattered. Light flooded her world and the darkness that had gripped her heart dissipated. Before she knew what was happening, he drew her into his arms and held her close, her head resting on his broad chest.

Famine

"I believe you," he whispered softly, the spearmint on his breath inducing familiar feelings of childhood safety and security.

They stood there together as the world passed. Neither caring about the looks people were giving them. Her back rose and fell with each sob as he held her. Pressing herself harder into his embrace, she allowed his warmth and strength to envelop her. No matter what happened from here on out, one thing was certain: She was no longer alone, and that changed everything.

Sniffing and wiping her cheeks as she pulled away from him, she searched his face and found only sincerity in his eyes. He really did believe her. Of course, there was still the matter of him hiding the fact that he knew Jared, but she was done trying to take on the world alone. If she could trust Jeremy even though he was hiding things from her, then maybe it was time she forgave Johansson.

Gritting her teeth at the anger she still felt for the agent, she nodded as she came to a decision. One she should have made sooner. Reaching into her jacket, she pulled out her cell phone and dialed. Looking into Jeremy's eyes as she put the phone up to her ear, she knew from his slight nod that he understood.

Maybe the hidden compound and its mysterious owner had nothing to do with her cousin's disappearance. The way the local law enforcement had acted in response to their presence and consequential reactions from pretty much anyone in a position of authority made her think otherwise. All that didn't matter. She was finally ready to call in the big guns, and no one was going to stop her from seeing if her cousin was there. Not even the president himself.

Rolling her eyes at the satisfied smile on Jeremy's face, she couldn't help her own smile as the call was picked up on the other end.

"Tom," she said, already starting off toward where they had left the car. "I need your help."

Jared watched Dana and Jeremy from the shadows of a nearby parking complex. Tzedakah had cloaked them and had assured him that not even the most sophisticated technology could reveal them. Grimacing at how out in the open they were, he wished that Tzedakah had taken them somewhere less conspicuous. He did believe the sword, of course. He had seen too much not to. If he had to guess, Tzedakah's cloaking was something more like dimensional phasing. They could see the world around them but were just out of sync enough that the rest of the world couldn't see them.

I wonder if that's how Steve managed to use the shadows to teleport himself during our fights. Perhaps he was accessing a dimension of shadows that's close to our own. Wasn't that in fact what the spirit world was? A dimension that coexisted alongside the physical realm, unseen but merged somehow? His thoughts returned to his two friends.

When he saw Jeremy pull Dana into a close hug, his body went rigid. An anger so hot he thought it he might actually catch fire rose unchecked at the sight of them embracing. Even Tzedakah seemed to be affected by the sudden surge of emotions, the sword's feelings mirroring his own. As if on cue the nightmare-black shadows in his eyes began writhing and reaching out towards the two, as if they would seize them and drag them into the void they had become.

Before he realized what was happening, the world twisted around him. Not a gentle phasing as he had experienced in past transitions, but a warping, stomach-churning whirlwind; as if the entire universe had just been flushed down a drain. His eyes remained fixed on the two friends who stayed constant as the rest of his world descended into absolute chaos. Everything swirled and bent around that one fixed point, blurring into an indistinguishable mass of images and colors.

He knew he was screaming, but was unsure if it was from rage, pain, or both. The sudden awareness of another voice in the chaos took him by surprise. It, too, was shrieking unintelligibly, and it didn't take him long to realize it was Tzedakah. What in God's name was happening to them? A sudden clarifying rage surged up, driving out the uncertainty and fear. He narrowed his eyes, completely focused on his two friends. It didn't matter what was happening. All that mattered was the betrayal before him. How could she do this to them? How could they both? She

461

was theirs, and no one was going to take her away from them. Especially not him.

His hand tightening around Tzedakah he forced himself forward, defying the raging chaos that now seemed to set itself against them. It buffeted him relentlessly, attempting to keep him in place, but a sudden burst of sheer power exploded forth from Tzedakah, driving it back. The pressure seemed to lessen, and with each steady step he drew closer to Dana and Jeremy.

They would pay for this treachery. They would pay for this injustice.

"Son," spoke a soft but firm voice in the churning madness. It was clear and filled with authority and unquestioning power.

He stopped. Blinking slowly, his mind clearing, he slowly returned to himself. The turmoil around him continued, but all of the anger and hatred that had so completely consumed him instantly evaporated at the sound of that single word. Even Tzedakah returned to a gentle glow rather than the angry searing inferno it had been just moments ago.

"What was I about to do?" he mumbled to himself, as if trying to remember a dream he had just awoken from.

Raising the sentient sword, he examined it. The blue-black of its aura was steady, but peaceful. Breathing in a deep, steadying breath, he allowed his own emotions to calm. When he finally looked back up the world had returned to normal. It was, however, now nighttime. No trace of the chaos remained. It was as if some unseen hand had simply reached down and erased it from existence. The subtle sounds of a city getting ready to sleep were all that remained. Its familiarity was a comforting rock in the fading echo of the madness he had just experienced.

"We almost..." he stammered.

"We did," Tzedakah responded, his usually harsh demeanor subdued.

Was it experiencing the same shame he was feeling? Could it even feel such emotions? For some strange reason he was sure that the sword had become attached to Dana, and was genuinely upset that they had wanted to hurt her. It was almost as if it too had a sincere affection for her. Was it possible that his own feelings were influencing Tzedakah?? He knew he was losing himself more and more each day, becoming the thing Tzedakah wanted him to be, but was the sword changing as well?

Looking around, he wondered aloud, "Whose voice was it I heard?"

"The One above all," Tzedakah replied reverently.

Jared scrunched up his forehead. "The One above all?"

"Yes," it replied.

"You don't mean—" he asked incredulously, his eyes widening with awe.

"Yes," Tzedakah answered before he could finish his sentence.

"Dear God," he whispered.

"Indeed."

Shaking his head, he pursed his lips. "But why? I mean, as far as my experience has gone, He very rarely interferes so...openly."

Famine

"The angel might be a better person to ask such questions."

Jared rested his head in one of his hands and sighed.

"I," he stammered. "I don't understand why I was so upset. I mean, sure, seeing her hugging Jeremy made me angry. I'm still angry, but what in the actual hell just happened to us?"

The sword was silent. He sensed apprehension and even a subtle fear from it. Was this a new experience for it? There was so much he didn't know about the blade. So many things he still didn't understand. One thing he knew for certain: if God, or whatever it was, hadn't intervened they would have killed Jeremy.

He grimaced at the thought of his friend. He might not want to kill him anymore, but he was still furious with him. How could he take advantage of her like that? She was hurting and going through hell, and he was making a move on her. Who did that? Besides, he knew how Jared felt about her. He shook his head, driving away the dark thoughts and intense feelings threatening to rise up again.

No, Jeremy was his friend; he wouldn't do that to him. It was more than likely just an innocent gesture meant to comfort a hurting friend. Plus, he thought, his heart dropping slightly in his chest, could he even be with her anymore? He was, after all, dead. Or, rather, undead, if you could call it that. He really had no idea what he was, but one thing Tzedakah had made abundantly clear was that there was no returning to his old life. Was it possible for Dana to be a part of this new existence?

Intense emotions suddenly bombarded him, and he staggered on his feet. Bracing himself against the wall of the building, he shook his head, attempting to stem the tide of sensations. Pain, sadness, rage, love, the flow of feelings was jumbled and muddled, as if whoever was experiencing them was just as confused as he was. As before, the world swirled around him, threatening to swallow his already-fragile psyche.

Tzedakah, glowing a brilliant blue, was a shining beacon in the raging tempest. Focusing his attention on the pulsing light, he allowed it to stabilize his mind. As quickly as it started the storm ceased, leaving him breathing heavy and barely standing.

"How many more times is that going to happen?" he croaked.

Sensing the same psychic pain from the sword, he brought it up till it was eye level. Squinting, one eye slightly more shut than the other, his lips pressed into a thin line, he glared at the sword. Over the last few days a theory had been ruminating deep in his mind, and now he felt it had been confirmed. Just as he was losing himself to the sword, it was possible that the sword was likewise being influenced by him.

"That was you, wasn't it?" he inquired. "For all of your coldness you actually have feelings, don't you?"

As usual, no response. Grinding his teeth, he shook the sword in frustration.

"Really?" he growled. "The silent treatment again? Well, you can be as tight-lipped as you want, but I'm beginning to figure some things out. Your feelings may be buried deep, but they're there."

"Or..." he continued, his brow furrowing slightly and his tone becoming more thoughtful. "Maybe you don't actually have emotions of your own, but as a side effect of our symbiotic relationship you're experiencing mine."

Anger and more confusion from the sword. No, not confusion necessarily, but uncertainty. Like a teenager who is experiencing love for the first time. Excitement and apprehension, hope, and the fear of rejection all jumbled together in one big mass of confusing emotions. And Tzedakah had no idea how to handle them. As completely ridiculous as it seemed, this creature that had existed for countless millennia was completely and utterly lost?

The sword still refused to speak, but the sensations it was radiating confirmed much. It didn't matter whose emotions they were. If they couldn't deal with them, then one thing was abundantly clear: some monster like that Musketeer guy would swiftly and painfully put an end to their association. That might be just a hiccup in the long life of the sentient sword, but for Jared it meant the end of this life. Regardless, if Heaven was in fact real and paradise was in his future, he still wasn't ready to let go. There were still too many things left undone.

Plus, Dana needed him. Steve was still out there, and he had made it clear he was coming for her. She knew too much and there was no way he was going to allow her to live. Also, his brother knew she would never let him get away with what he had done to him or, if she believed him still alive, allow him to hurt anyone else.

Moreover, there was this new, and quite frankly absurd, threat of Jasmine and her vampire friends. He was still having difficulty wrapping his head around that. Vampires were actually real. It really shouldn't have come as a surprise, given his recent experiences. I mean, why not? He was brought back to life by a talking sword and Steve was a demon-powered serial killer. Of course, vampires were real.

No, he couldn't fall apart now. He needed to stay the course for at least as long as it took him to stop Steve and make sure Dana was safe. They just had to hold it together until then. After that, they could stop and take all the time they needed to figure out their relationship.

Sensing Tzedakah's agreement, with renewed determination he turned his attention to their next move. Steve and the mysterious Musketeer character were the most serious threat, but for some reason Tzedakah couldn't track them. Certain they would show their faces again; he decided that Jasmine and the vampires were a more viable target. Besides, maybe it was possible for him to actually save her.

Sensing Tzedakah's agitation and obvious dislike of Jasmine, he realized attempting to save her may be more difficult than simply overcoming vampirism... even if that were somehow possible. The sword would most certainly push him to kill her, and he wasn't sure he had the strength to defy a determined Tzedakah. Either way, confronting the vampires was something he could do now. He needed to move. Needed to act.

Famine

Setting his jaw and nodding, he twirled Tzedakah in his hand. With a snarl of determination, he slashed downward, cutting a hole in the fabric of time and space. Stepping inside and vanishing, his last words echoed in the night: "Let's go slay some vampires!"

* * * *

A man watched from the shadows as Jared vanished. Of average height and dressed all in black, the man scanned the area where he had just been. After a few more seconds of nothing happening he ran one hand over his head, the buzzed black hair prickling his fingers. Squinting his hawklike brown eyes, he continued to scan the area as he reached into the interior pocket of his leather jacket and pulled out a cell phone, hit a few buttons, and then held it to one ear.

"They just left," he said in a gruff voice that indicated a pack-of-cigarettes-a-day habit. "Yeah, both of them. I'm guessing it was you she called? Oh, and be advised, the sword might also be on the way. I stuck around like you ordered just in case, looking for anything unusual, and I saw—no, felt—a shifting energy signature near where they were, but it disappeared a few hours after your girlfriend and the idiot left."

Chuckling at the response of the person on the other end of the line, he pulled out a fresh pack of cigarettes. Holding the phone with his shoulder and one cheek he began to tap the pack vigorously against one scarred and gnarled hand. Opening the pack and popping one into his

468

mouth, he pulled out a silver zippo lighter and flicked it open.

"You can screw whoever you want, I don't care," he replied, lighting the cigarette. "Whatever you say, boss. I can see why you like her. She's got a rocking body. Curvy yet athletic."

Snorting out a laugh that sent tendrils of smoke pouring from his nostrils, he continued. "In all seriousness, though, are we going to engage the vampires? We usually stay out of their way unless they get in ours."

Thrusting both hands into his pockets, the cigarette dangling from his lips, he turned and started walking, the phone still propped precariously between his shoulder and neck.

"You know how I feel about it," he continued. "I hate the bastards. If it were up to me, we'd have wiped them all out by now."

Moving his chin, he allowed the phone to drop into one waiting palm as he flicked the cigarette away with the other. Returning the phone to his ear and retrieving a kunai throwing knife from one of his many jacket pockets, he began flipping it casually as he walked.

"Aye, Aye, Cap'n," he said, moving into the shadows. "I will rendezvous with the others and meet you at the compound. I hope you know what you're doing. Either way, it should be fun."

ophia's eyes were wide as she focused on the hulking form in the doorway. Shadows swirled around him, making it hard for her to distinguish any fine details. That really didn't matter since his red eyes were visible through the darkness and they drew—no, demanded—her attention. Glowing the color of blood, she was hypnotized by them and was unable to rip her gaze away as he entered the small chamber.

The shadows enveloping him billowed outward like a cloak blown in the wind, covering the small window and blotting out what little light the blossoming day was providing. If she was able to take her eyes off of the man she would find the darkness oppressive, and her cell filled with ominous shadows. She could not, of course. No mortal could. She remained slack-jawed, gawking in paralyzed terror as he approached.

The very air became overwhelming, and she slouched, as if bearing some heavy weight. Her knees shaking and her mouth suddenly as dry as a desert, she fidgeted under his piercing gaze. Though her head felt as if it would explode from the intense pressure of those eyes, she still could not bring herself to look away. In truth, she doubted she could do anything more than fall to the ground and whimper pathetically while begging for her worthless life. She was beneath him, nothing more than food. Like a pig or chicken was to humanity.

Sniffing the air, he smiled.

"I see my daughter favors you. It has been a while since she has had someone to...play with."

Was he referring to Kat? No one other than the White Lady had been in to visit her, so it stood to reason he was speaking of her. How did he know she had been here? Did he know about the bracelet? Oh God, please don't let him have found out about that.

Smiling and waving his hand dismissively, she suddenly found herself sitting back on the ground next to the far wall. Blinking rapidly, she slowly shook her head in an attempt at driving away the cobwebs in her mind. How in the world did she get all the way over here?

"What?" she stammered. "When did I move?"

"There is no need to fear," he purred, as if in answer to her earlier thoughts. "I am not here to harm you. I merely wish to talk."

Talk? What could she possibly have to talk about with him? Of course, if he knew about the bracelet. Couldn't he simply pull that out of her mind, though? Why initiate a discussion when he could just read her thoughts. Maybe he couldn't? He certainly had the ability to sense her fear, but did he have the ability to read her mind?

She thought of driving a stake through his heart and watching him die. Making the images as visceral and real as she could in her mind, she watched his expression. His grin widened, displaying wicked ivory canines. His red eyes twinkled with what seemed like mirth, but other than that he gave nothing away.

"I find it strange that my daughter has taken an interest in you. In all the years she has been in this place, never before has she befriended anyone. If I am to be honest, I feared she was too broken by what happened when she changed."

Sophia said nothing but continued to watch him warily, the defiance in her eyes hiding the terror she actually felt. Absentmindedly he picked at one of his nails, deep in thought, before sighing and returning his attention back to her.

"I would have killed her, you know. When she was first born."

Sophia narrowed her eyes but continued to stay silent.

"You think me a monster, I am sure. Regardless of your harsh judgments of me, it would have been a mercy. As you see, we do not age but stay exactly as we were when we were created. If one is a child, then they stay as one for eternity. Anyone can see how that would be a problem for beings such as us."

He waited for her to respond, and when she didn't, he sighed and continued.

"In truth, if it had not been for Fuyuko's intervention I would have. You see, she has an affinity for children. I suspect that if she were to have her way, we would not keep them here. Being what we are, she understands the need to keep feed stock, but she always goes out of her way to provide extra comforts for them."

Sophia snorted.

"I understand your doubt, but it is true," he said, smiling to himself. "An extra blanket for the cold, a fire that never dies, extra food or medicine when sick. You have not been here long, but if you had been you would know of what I speak. It truly is remarkable. I, of course, do not share her sentimentality, but I do understand it. It is the compassion of a parent, and, as I too am a parent, I understand her. It is why I allow it."

Her expression thoughtful, she turned to look where Kat had vanished. The little vampire who had been through so much. The little vampire who had become a friend to her in this hell she had found herself in. Perhaps not all of them were as heartless as Vlad. After all, they had once been human and maybe echoes of that humanity still remained in some.

Noticing her expression, Vlad nodded.

"To you we appear as monsters, but we are not so. We are merely what we are. A race different from yours. A race that was nearly driven to extinction for simply existing. Once, long ago, we coexisted, working together to dominate this planet. We are not so different. We love, we have children, we eat, we drink and be merry. All of the same desires run through us that you experience."

473

"Except you eat us for food," she said, her voice cracking slightly, belying the confidence she was trying to project.

He chuckled. "Well, there is that, yes. But it does not have to be so...horrific. You yourselves keep feed animals, and their lives are good. Some even better than those that are wild. Some even become beloved pets that are treated like family."

"This place speaks otherwise," she replied icily. "Besides, most humans would reject being pets."

"I would wager so would most dogs and cats."

She had no retort to that and chose not to respond. He did have a point, she admitted. Wait. How could she be taking his side even remotely? He was a blood-sucking abomination, and nothing like her. Wasn't he? Doubt began to creep slowly into her mind. Were the vampires monsters? Maybe she was wrong about them. Kat certainly was different, and if she believed his words then on some small level so was the White Lady. Perhaps things were not as simple as she supposed them to be.

A warning rose somewhere deep in the back of her subconscious. It was soft at first but continued to grow, until it was so loud it drowned out everything else. Shaking her head and blinking, she forced the crushing influence out of her mind. It was then she realized what had been happening. He had been projecting his will upon her and something deep inside her recognized it and rejected it.

His eyes turned a darker shade of red, and the smile he now gave her was no longer welcoming but fierce.

"Well done, little one. My deduction was right about you. You are strong. Fuyuko sensed it when she invaded your mind, and Kat's gravitation to you was another indication that you are more than you appear. Perhaps I made a mistake in choosing Jasmine. Or rather," he reasoned, his eyes glinting excitedly, "I have been blessed with more than one potential candidate this generation."

Reaching inside his shirt, he pulled out a long gold chain with a small vial attached to it. Reverently he held it up for her to get a better look at. Amber in color, fashioned of gold and adorned with glittering rubies, it gave off a soft red incandescent glow like plankton sometimes did when churned up in the ocean by ship's propellors.

Instantly captivated by the beautiful ampule, she couldn't stop herself from reaching for it. Smiling, Vlad didn't stop her as she inched closer, one hand outstretched, her eyes fixed on the vessel. It called to her somehow. A siren song that stirred her heart with longing. She had no idea what was inside the tiny container, but whatever it was its pull on her was virtually overwhelming.

He closed his fingers around the flask, severing the connection, cutting off the beautiful song. She immediately returned to herself, shocked to find her hand stretching through the bars only inches from Vlad's closed fist. Her eyes wide, her breathing quick and shallow, her instinct was to draw back. But she hesitated. The music was still there, calling to her. It was faint and distant, nothing more than a small echo on the wind, gentle and enticing. No longer a deafeningly persistent tone, but a soft and beguiling whisper.

Famine

"What—" was all she could muster.

Vlad's smile was genuine as he replaced the locket to its hiding place under his shirt.

"You hear it, don't you? Her call."

Swallowing, she nodded slightly; her gaze still transfixed on the place where the vial had been.

"Only a few can. Only those who are chosen by her can hear her melody."

Shaking, she drew back a step, but her eyes remained vacant and staring as if she was experiencing something only she could see. Her heartbeat wildly in her chest and she shook slightly, like an addict suffering from withdrawal.

"Whose call is it?" she asked, her voice shaking and nothing more than a whisper.

"Mother's," he replied reverently.

Screwing up her face in confusion, she continued to back away. The farther she moved from the vial the less the song, if that indeed was what it was, affected her.

"Whose mother?" she asked.

"Why, our mother," he replied, standing to his feet, his face alight with reverence. "The mother of all my kind."

The farther she got from whatever or whoever it was that called to her, the more she felt like herself. All of the fear and anxiety returned in force, however, but so did her determination to survive and the hope that her cousin was coming.

"Amazing," he whispered, his voice awash with awe. "Though many call me a fool, I cannot help but hope. No, have faith that after several millennia and countless failures our mother would return to us. The Council of Elders in

476

their despair no longer believe it possible, but I still do. Though only a tiny portion of her essence remains, the appearance of two possible receptacles for her glory is an irrefutable sign that not even they can reject. A clear indicator that now is the time of her return."

Her mind racing with too many thoughts and emotions to process, she backed even farther away from the ranting male. What was he talking about? Who were the elders and this mother he spoke of? She didn't understand what was going on, but she had a sinking feeling growing in her stomach. Whatever he was talking about, she was pretty sure it wasn't anything good. At least not for her, the children being held here, or even mankind as a whole.

She had to find a way to free herself and the others, and she had to do it soon. Whatever it was the vampires were planning was quickly coming to a head, and she needed to get everyone out of there and fast. If she didn't, then she was certain they would all die. Given the last few days' festivities, she doubted many remained alive. With the appearance of so many more vampires, it was a good possibility that half or more of them had already been murdered.

How many children were still alive? Each one of their little faces moved quickly through her mind and she sniffed, fighting back tears. Horrible images of the terror they must have felt as they were being murdered threatened to overcome her. Gritting her teeth, she instead allowed those thoughts to fuel her resolve. They would not get away with this, she would make certain of it. Even if it was the last thing she did.

Famine

Lifting her head, she forced down her own terror and, straightening her shoulders, glared at Vlad with a defiant resolve she didn't know was in her. Hesitantly she took a step closer and pointed a finger at him.

"Mark my words," she intoned, her voice shaking from both rage and fear. "I will make you and all your kind pay for what you did to those children."

He raised an eyebrow and chuckled, his eyes bright with mirth.

"Oh really? Many have made similar proclamations, and all have failed to fulfill them. What makes you different?"

Having no retort, she said nothing but continued to stare daggers at him. She really didn't know what she could do against such powerful enemies, but somewhere deep down she knew she would. Somehow, she would repay him, at least for all the pain and loss he had caused.

Sensing her resolve, his smile widened and his eyes glinted.

"Perhaps you will, little one," he answered with a slight nod of his head. "I would greatly like to see you try. Now, however, we must see what the fates have in store for us. If you survive what is to come then perhaps you will have the power to destroy me, though you may find the desire lacking. Either way, it is time for you and Jasmine to be presented to the Council."

He lifted one arm and gestured, and her world went black.

The sudden invasion of light hurt Sophia's eyes and she squinted as they adjusted to the sudden brightness. The hard, cold of the surface beneath her indicated she was probably lying on the floor. The surface was smooth, not rough and unforgiving like her cell had been, so she definitely was no longer there. For one, the light, though very subdued, was far brighter than the luminosity of the chamber they had held her in. Then where was she?

Turning over, she suddenly gagged as the intense, sickly sweet, metallic scent of blood and death assaulted her senses. Having been starved and deprived of only the basic amount of water, she retched. But nothing came up. Becoming acutely aware she was not alone, she jumped or rather stumbled to her feet. Whipping her head back and forth and still squinting slightly, she instantly dropped into a fighting crouch. Having trained in sports and martial arts since she was young, her instinct was to fight.

Famine

Her heart beating a million miles an hour from the adrenaline coursing through her body, she blinked rapidly to try to bring the blurry room into focus. When she was finally able to see clearly, she wished she had stayed on the floor. Every single person in the room, if that is what they were (and she sincerely doubted they were), was completely focused on her.

There were so many of them. At least a hundred if she had to guess. All of them were dressed in elegant formal wear, as if they were attending some kind of royal ball. Men and women of every race and creed were represented. Some wore medieval-style armor and brandished weapons that made them look like extras in a fantasy movie. One was even dressed like a sixteenth-century musketeer, complete with rapier and all.

Lady Yuriko was in attendance as well, her shimmering ice blue gown pristine and cold. Just like her eyes. Thankfully, the emaciated monster that was always accompanying her was nowhere to be seen. She thanked God for small favors, though she was sure he was lurking nearby just out of sight. Shivering at the thought of the horrible creature, she hugged herself reflexively.

She continued scanning the room and her jaw dropped as she took in the size and opulence of the chamber. Gold chandeliers encrusted with what looked like precious stones hung from the ceiling, glinting with candlelight. Elaborate tapestries covered the walls, depicting events from ages past, each one appearing ancient and hand woven. They must be hundreds of years old and priceless. If not, they were certainly excellent reproductions. Statues and busts of all shapes and sizes were on display as well, making the entire place feel like the throne room of some kind of royalty.

A soft chuckle drew her attention, and she slowly turned in that direction. Her foot caught on something as she moved stumbling slightly. Stupefied, all she could do was stare at the scarlet cloth her foot had snagged on. Her head bobbing back and forth like some deranged bird, she realized in horror that she, too, wore a ball gown. Brilliant scarlet in color, low cut and tapered in at the waist, it ballooned slightly, cascading down till it touched the tops of her feet. Realizing her unkempt hair no longer hung around her face, she gingerly reached up and touched her head to find her hair washed and combed and held up by a slender crown. The metal felt cool to the touch, and she felt stones embedded in it as her fingers brushed against it.

Had they bathed and dressed her when she was unconscious? She ground her teeth, and her face flushed bright crimson. What else had they done to her without her knowledge? Her eyes suddenly became the size of saucers, and one hand shot to her neck, groping frantically at her skin. After a few seconds of panic, she let out a slow steadying breath.

No bite marks. At least none she could feel any way. That was good. She couldn't help but feel violated, but at least they hadn't bitten her.

"Do you like the dress?" a deep, masculine voice asked.

Snapping her head in the direction of the speaker, she finally noticed the massive throne that was only a few feet in front of her. Vald sat imperially atop it, his head resting on one hand, his legs crossed. His red eyes were alight with pleasure and she blushed in spite of herself at his appraising gaze. Tall and exceptionally handsome, he was adorned in a well-tailored black suit and white shirt, the blood red cape he always wore peeking out from the sides of his throne.

As impressive as he was, he was not what drew her gaze. Hanging from his neck was the mysterious vial. Eyes going wide she reflexively lifted one arm, reaching for the beautiful ampule, and as if in a trance took a step towards Vlad. The haunting song called to her, and it was growing in intensity with each passing second.

"Not yet," he said, freezing her in her tracks. His voice was gentle but thick with authority.

No matter how beguiling or intense the song of the vial, she could not defy the immense pressure of his will. Both were forces of nature pressing against her. One calling to her, the other keeping her at bay. The strength of both were overwhelming to her mortal psyche and she felt as if she would be torn apart.

Just when she feared she was going to break, the song abruptly ceased. She slumped wearily to her knees, her chest heaving as she gasped for air. Her head swam and black spots danced in her vision as oxygen flooded into her lungs. The tension from both powers had literally stolen the breath from her, and she coughed and sputtered as she gulped in the precious life-giving air. It was like being trapped in the gravity well of two enormous stars, both exerting equal force in opposite directions.

"Do you see?" he asked the throng, standing to his feet and raising his arms in triumph. "It is as I said. Fate has blessed us. Our mother has heard our cries and responded in our time of need."

The room was absolutely silent, and Vlad's words boomed through the quiet like a gun shot. It even made it through the ringing in her ears, which thankfully was beginning to subside. She had no idea what he was talking about, though it was a good bet she had something to do with it. The growing dread in her subconscious was a warning that she had to find a way to escape. There was literally no time to waste.

Where was Dana? She was positive that she was the lady Kat had encountered. If she knew her cousin as well as she thought she did, then she would be on her way. But if she didn't get here soon it probably wouldn't matter. Shaking her head and gritting her teeth, she drove away her despairing thoughts. No, Dana was going to make it in time. She had to. Her cousin was literally her only hope, and she was betting all her chips on her.

Her eyes subconsciously drifted towards Vlad and the vial. Even with its song muted she could still feel it calling to her. She wanted to know what or who it was that sang to her. The voice was almost that of a long-lost forgotten friend. One she loved dearly, and it broke her heart to lose. Deep longing engulfed her. A desire so great it made her heartbeat fast and her breathing quick. Did she even want to be rescued?

Another voice interjected, drawing her attention, temporarily severing the song's enchantment.

Famine

"With all due respect, we have heard this all before. You have been making the same declaration for nearly a millennia, and each time you were wrong."

The speaker was tall, well over six feet, but nowhere near as imposing as Vlad. His blond hair which was pulled back into a ponytail swung slightly from his obvious agitation. Somewhat overweight, his stomach pushed a little against his slate-colored vest which was overlaid by a black tuxedo coat with tails. Like most of them his skin was pale and faintly ashen-colored, making it impossible to distinguish his race from its hue. The long face, strong jawline, high cheek bones and hawklike nose hinted at a Germanic origin. Of course, his thick accent was a dead giveaway that he was German, or rather some ancient predecessor.

"Lord Vlad, as you well know, the Council of Elders has declared that it is time for us to leave behind such fairytales. It has been several millennia since our mother was murdered and all of our attempts at resurrecting her have failed. And, as you well know, each attempt we make depletes a portion of her precious essence, till all that remains is but a pittance. You have, at best, one more attempt before she will be lost to us forever."

Murmuring broke out among the gathered vampires, most in concurrence with Lord Dietmar. It was obvious that the vampire nobles did not necessarily agree with Vlad's beliefs, but only Lord Dietmar appeared to have the courage to express their collective misgivings.

"Lord Dietmar, your objections are well known to everyone, since you never cease to repeat them," Vlad replied, his voice thick with annoyance.

"And I shall continue to repeat them until you hear them," he retorted. "Vlad, you have to see reason. This time will be the same as all the others. Each time we put our hopes in the ritual of resurrection we are disappointed, you most of all." He lifted his hands in a gesture of futility and his tone softened. "Vlad, my friend, we all wish to see the return of our mother, but it is time we accept that just simply is not possible. No matter how much you or I wish it to be so."

Vlad sat back in his throne and steepled his fingers, his gaze fixed on Lord Dieter. The fire in his narrowed eyes betraying his outward tranquil expression. Despite Lord Dietmar's seeming friendliness, there was an undercurrent of tension between the two of them that signified a long-standing quarrel.

Vlad was silent for a long while, his eyes never leaving Lord Dietmar. The vampire lord met his gaze with equal determination, neither of them willing to give in to the other. After what seemed to Sophia to be a painfully long time, Vlad finally replied.

He did not break eye contact with Lord Dietmar as he raised his voice, addressing the entire gathering. "What would you say if I could prove that this time was different?"

The change in the atmosphere was instantaneous as the curiosity of the crowd was piqued. They again started to murmur excitedly. Lord Dietmar's expression darkened as his domination over the narrative began to unravel.

Famine

"Vlad," he interjected, raising his voice in attempt at reasserting his control. "You made such claims before, and every time you were mistaken. We can no longer afford to waste our time and energy on your childish fantasies. Mother is lost to us, and it is time you accept this and move on."

There was a collective gasp of shock from the vampire nobles and every one of them fell silent, their attention riveted on the two lords. All of them knew it was very dangerous to insult Vlad the way Dietmar just had. Even Sophia found herself holding her breath, her anxiety temporarily forgotten.

One corner of Vlad's mouth lifted slightly and his eyes glinted triumphantly. Despite Lord Dieter's arguments, he had managed to grab everyone's attention.

"Maybe we should ask the Council what they think on the matter," he replied confidently.

Lord Dietmar fidgeted, his eyes slowly moving left and right as many voiced their agreement with Vlad's proposal. The others simply nodded their heads or stayed silent, their expressions curious.

Lord Deiter suddenly whirled on Sophia, thrusting his hands in her direction. She flinched in response and reflexively lifted her own arms defensively.

"You have made a serious mistake in judgment if you think this piece of meat you dressed up and paraded before us will change our minds," he spat. "We all grow weary of your endless declarations of providence and fate. Every hundred years or so you bring some urchin before us and declare her the savior of all, and each and every time you are proven wrong. This one will be no different."

Again, the atmosphere of the crowd changed, the majority seeming to have been swayed by Lord Dieter's statements. He straightened his posture and lifted his chin in triumph, his mouth turning up into a smug smile.

Vlad's own smile didn't fade as he beckoned to someone at the back of the hall. Everyone turned in unison to see who it was he was gesturing to, including Sophia. They were all silent as Jasmine, dressed in a radiant gown of pure white, entered the chamber, escorted by Steven.

Famine

Jamine's blonde hair practically glowed in the candlelight as she glided into the room. Just like Sophia, she wore a thin crown fashioned of almost translucent gold. Hers, however, contained one massive red ruby directly in its center. The gem reflected the ambient light, making her golden hair seem like it was flowing with thin strands of blood. Her white gown, which sparkled and shimmered as if it were made entirely of moonlight, only came to the middle of her shoulders and accentuated her ample breasts and shapely curves. It somehow defied physics by staying perfectly in place as she lifted one arm to Steven, who took it.

The crowd parted and no one spoke as they slowly walked through the gathering. As they passed, each man stared with unrestrained lust and the women with undisguised jealousy. Her beauty was staggering, and so captivating that even Sophia found herself gawking. Steven, who was likewise dressed for the occasion and a genuinely handsome man, was dwarfed by her loveliness even with his hair styled and well-fitting black suit with violet shirt. He walked beside her, his usual disarming smile on his face. The smile that had drawn many women to their deaths.

Lord Dietmar was forced to move out of the way as the two took their places next to Sophia. Steve nodded and winked at her before withdrawing. Still gawking, Sophia subconsciously ran a hand through her hair and fixed her gown. Younger and more athletic in build and lacking Jamine's curves, she did not even come close to matching the older woman in physical attraction. Compared to her she looked more like a teenage boy. If it were possible to pick someone to be a vampire goddess, then Jasmine would be at the top of the list.

Lord Dietmar pushed them aside to stand between them and Vlad. The expression on his face was one of contempt, and he threw his hands at the three of them in agitation.

"What do you expect to accomplish with this display? We have seen this pageantry countless times before and, as I have already pointed out, each time it failed. Vlad, you have yet to show us anything that would convince us this time it will be different."

"The fact that there are two candidates this time instead of one does not at least pique your interest?" he asked calmly.

Lord Dietmar closed his eyes and rubbed the bridge of his nose, and when he finally spoke his tone was slow and deliberate, as if he were speaking to a petulant child.

Famine

"Lord Vladmir, even if we had enough essence to evaluate them both, and I doubt we do, the result would still be the same. Only this time, any remaining vestige of our mother would be lost to us. Unless you have something else to add, it is time we finally move on from this dogmatic hope we have been holding on to. To put it bluntly, all our forebearers are gone and none of them are coming back."

"Are you sure of that?" Vlad challenged.

Lord Dietmar shook his head and sighed. "We are all tired of this, Vlad. It has gone on long enough. Nothing you can say or do will change our minds."

Vlad's eyes twinkled as he stood and motioned toward Steven.

"Lord Azreal, come forward."

The crowd gasped and Lord Dietmar's face went even paler as Steven stepped forward. His gate was twitchy, and tendrils of darkness leaked from every pore in his body, gradually consuming him with each step he took. By the time he reached the front of the room and stood facing the gathering, he had been completely consumed by shadows. Two enormous crimson eyes opened in the darkness, glowing brightly with malice. He glared imperiously at the gathered crowd as massive dragon-like wings formed out of the flowing darkness, stretching outward and skyward.

In unison everyone in the room fell to one knee, their faces bowed. Everyone, except Lord Dietmar and Sophia. The vampire lord's eyes were wide as saucers and his mouth hung open, jaw moving up and down as if he were attempting to speak, but nothing came out. Sophia shrank back from the nightmare, too terrified to move. Her legs shook uncontrollably and every hair on her body stood on end at the unnatural aura emanating from the creature.

The demon swept its gaze over the entire room, its eyes boring into each one in turn as if it was contemplating annihilating the lot of them. It finally came to rest on Lord Dietmar, who squirmed in his place, his mouth still hanging open and still silent. Lord Azreal the Ancient flicked one hand and a wave of pressure so intense it felt like the earth's gravity had increased two-fold flowed from him. Those that were already kneeling were pressed down even farther by the powerful force but unharmed. Those who remained standing, however, were violently thrown to the ground.

"I wonder where a pathetic weakling such as yourself finds the audacity to make proclamations about powers far beyond your feeble comprehension," Azreal intoned. "If, as you say, your forebearers are never returning, then how is it I stand before you now?"

All Lord Dietmar could muster in response was a muffled groan.

"I should destroy you for your insolence," Azreal said. "But in my mercy, I will not. However, if you ever speak such blasphemy in my presence again, you will beg for death before I am through with you. Is that understood?"

Azreal flicked his wrist again and the immense pressure immediately dispersed. Many gasped quietly, taking in gulps of air, while others exhaled, letting out the breaths they had been holding. Sophia stirred and got shakily to her knees. Her head throbbed and she felt a little nauseated but was otherwise unharmed. Lord Dietmar remained prostrate before the hulking demon, occasionally letting out soft whimpers of either fear or pain.

The demon scanned the crowd one last time before moving back in the direction of Jasmine. As he walked the shadows evaporated, transforming the thing back into Steven. By the time he reached Jasmine's side he had returned to his original form. He stumbled slightly as if he were in pain but caught himself before falling. His lips were pressed into a thin line and the corners of his eyes were narrowed slightly. He took a second to compose himself before bending and offering his hand to Jasmine.

She took it and he gently helped her to her feet. The rest of the crowd stood as well, their excited voices echoing through the hall. The implications of what they had just witnessed changed everything. For the first time in millennia one of the Grigori had returned, and if Lord Azreal had found a way, then maybe this time would be different for them as well.

Vlad lifted his fists in triumph.

"Hear me, brothers and sisters. Not only has providence sent us two worthy candidates to be the vessel for our dear mother, but the return of Lord Azreal is a sign that the balance of power in this world is about to shift!" he declared. "The hour we have waited countless millennia for is finally upon us. Make no mistake, all these omens have affirmed that tonight is the night everything changes."

The roar of the crowd was deafening. Vlad beamed with satisfaction as he reveled in the adulation. There was electricity in the air, and even Sophia could not help but be swept up by it. His energy was infectious, like a good preacher who has mastered his craft. It drew you in and made you feel that, just maybe, what he believed was possible. Steven, however, stood stoic, his smile gone and a slight grimace on his face. Vlad had just confirmed his theory of what the demon was doing to him.

Vlad reached into his shirt and pulled out the vial, displaying it before the congregation. He waited for the enthusiasm to settle before speaking.

"Before you, contained in this vessel, are the last drops of our mother's essence. Lord Dietmar and his supporters would have you believe that we should lock it away in reverence, because all previous attempts at using it to restore our mother have failed."

His gaze swept over the gathering, appearing to stop on each individual as if he were addressing them personally.

"I, however," he continued, "have faith. Faith in the signs we have been given, faith in the wisdom of our forebearers who, at great peril to themselves, defied the creator and saved a small amount of her blood. My brothers and sisters, now is the time for us to have hope. The presence of two worthy candidates, the return of Lord Azreal, and the many signs we have witnessed in the spiritual realm all declare that today is the day our faithfulness will be rewarded."

Even Sophia found her heart leaping at his words. Vlad's eyes glowed a brilliant scarlet, with both power and enthusiasm. He lifted the vial higher and radiant light exploded outward, bathing the crowd in crimson as if the blood in the vial were stretching out to embrace them all. It pulsed gently with the rhythm of a beating heart, and all were enchanted by it, powerless to tear their gaze away.

Sophia's heartbeat so hard she thought it must be audible. Goosebumps exploded on her skin as the siren song from the ampule intensified a hundred-fold. It pulled at her very soul, and before she knew what she was doing she found herself reaching for it. The smile on Vlad's face was wide and exulted as she and Jasmine both instinctively came to stand before his throne. Both stared at the vial, glassy eyed as if in a trance.

Vlad stepped down and stood before the two women. He presented the locket before them, its soft illumination soaking them in crimson. Eyes wide, hands shaking, they reached out for the vial. Vlad did not stop them, allowing them both to touch it reverently. Neither attempted to grab it or wrest it from his grip, but simply rested their fingers gently on the smooth surface.

The anticipation was palpable as Vlad reverently opened the vial. As soon as he did an overwhelming presence exploded from it, filling the room with its energy. What little remained of the vampire progenitor was magnificent and dreadful, with the terrifying force of a god of old. It was nothing more than an echo of her lost power, but it still completely overwhelmed the vampires. Some fell to their knees, openly weeping, while others simply stood in awe, mouths agape and speechless.

Vlad motioned with one hand and both women knelt. Moving to stand before Jasmine first he lifted the vial and turned, releasing a single drop of crimson liquid. Tilting her head back and opening her mouth, she accepted the offering. Her eyes were bright with anticipation and bore into Vlad with an undisguised malice he did not seem to notice. All pretense of civility was gone. She would become the vampire queen and finally have the power to free herself from him.

Next, he moved to stand before Sophia. His smile was genuine and warm as he held the vial over her head. Everything in her told her to flee, but she could not. It felt like bugs were running rampant underneath her skin and warnings were exploding in her subconscious like nuclear bombs, and even when her very soul begged for her to run, she didn't. The song was just too beguiling. It promised esoteric knowledge and ancient mysteries to be revealed. It—no, she—promised power and a metamorphosis that no mortal before her had been offered.

With her spirit and soul screaming in protest, she bent her head and opened her mouth. A single tear broke free and trickled down her cheek as the drop hit her tongue. The blood was warm and tasted like copper, bringing with it memories of sucking on cut fingers as a child. The screaming in her subconscious abruptly ceased and was replaced with an intense feeling of sadness. That, too, dissipated, leaving her feeling hollow.

For what seemed like an eternity, nothing happened. Both women fidgeted uncomfortably and the anticipation in the gathering began to change into apprehension. Sophia's expression was one of relief, though her eyes seemed filled with disappointment. Jasmine, however, was gritting her teeth in frustration and clenching her fists at her sides. No one spoke as they waited for something to happen.

Famine

Vlad took a step back, the corners of his eyes tightening slightly though his expression remained expectant. He was just about to speak, when Sophia suddenly gasped. Everyone's attention instantly snapped to the young woman who was now writhing on the ground, clutching at her stomach in pain. Her eyes were so wide they threatened to pop out of their sockets, and her mouth was open in a silent scream.

Vlad's triumphant expression returned as he swept his hand over the prostrate girl. His voice was nearly hysterical with glee as he shouted.

"Behold our mother's return!"

Before he could finish his proclamation, the room erupted into chaos as an explosion tore the doors at the rear of the room apart, showering the entire hall with splinters of wood and fire.

Dana and Johanson's main strike force poured through the broken door, weapons firing. The vampires nearest to the door were turned into piles of ash and flame in a matter of seconds. A vampire dressed in some kind of metal armor and brandishing a cross bow popped out from behind a corner and fired. The bolt missed her head by inches, the wind from it rustling the hair of one ear.

"Holy crap!" she shouted, falling backward. "Was that an arrow?"

"Fortress, Edge, and Sidewinder, engage the nobles but make sure to be mindful of any possible hostages," Johanson ordered, lifting her with one arm while firing a succession of quick bursts with the other. "Make sure you avoid civilian casualties at all costs, but make sure none of the nobles escape. Understood?"

He looked like a comic book hero, his long, black leather duster fluttering as he moved. Black high-tech armor covered his massive frame as his dual pistols barked loudly, taking out three vampire guardsmen. A fourth vaulted over the three he had just killed, thrusting a long spear directly at the big man.

"Look out!" Dana shouted, bringing her own pistol up to fire.

The vampire was too fast and there was no way she would be able to fire in time. To her amazement it hit some kind of energy shield, sending up sparks as it was deflected harmlessly to the side. The vampire bared its fangs and roared, redoubling its efforts, thrusting viciously at Johanson, each time receiving the same result. He lifted one arm and casually blew its head off, the creature bursting into flames and incinerating.

He turned and nodded his appreciation to Jeremy, whose hand was still outstretched in his direction, a faint glow emanating from his fingers. Jeremy frowned and grumbled something under his breath, but nodded in response before turning his attention back to the fighting.

Dana fired helplessly into the fray, each time missing her intended target. The attackers were just too fast. Impossibly fast. Grimacing, she realized that Jeremy had been right all along and that she owed him an apology. Vampires were indeed real and were trying to kill her. Her world had drastically changed over the last few days, and she could never go back to her normal life.

Even though he had not been truthful with her, she now realized that Johanson was trying to protect her in his own way. After that realization, she'd broken down and called him. She really had no idea what to expect when she did. Maybe some advice or tech help. Maybe even a call or two to some of his contacts, but a full-on assault of the compound was not even on her radar. His response to her had been almost immediate, as if he had been waiting for her to reach out. Within hours he and a strike team of heavily armed federal agents—if that was indeed what they were—had rendezvoused with them.

As usual, that bothered her. He was always two steps ahead, knew more than he would say and could not truly be trusted, but she was willing to let go of her misgivings if it meant helping her cousin. Jeremy had been right about that as well, and that irritated her to no end.

She lifted her Glock 22 duty pistol and fired, comforted by the familiarity of it in her hands. She knew the weapon like she knew herself, having trained with it since her days in the academy. Jeremy, of course, was not carrying anything but still managed to hold his own even though he did not have a weapon.

The vampires dodged her shots, moving so fast that Dana had trouble tracking them. Before she even knew what was happening there was at least a dozen more of them attacking from all directions. Every one of the assailants was dressed in the same black metal armor and brandishing some kind of medieval melee weapon. One of them even had a large shield.

They dodged and weaved with supernatural speed, but the strike team kept pace with them, their own responses just as fast. They made quick work of the attackers, fanning out into a defensive position. Each member of the ten-man strike team wore nondescript black body armor and bore high-tech weapons. All but one of them was well over six feet tall and massive, like giants in a fairy tale.

The one who wasn't was as muscular as he was wide, and looked almost like a Tolkien dwarf with a long red beard, compact frame, and barrel chest. His black tactical armor was bristling with pockets, extra magazines, and what looked like a spiked mace hung from his hip. His black helmet, which covered most of his head and was held on by a chin strap, made him almost look like a turtle. His call sign was Fortress, and he was one of the three Johanson had sent after the nobles.

Another bolt whizzed past her head, and she instinctively dropped to one knee and fired in the direction of the missile. She hit the shooter center mass and he toppled backward, bursting into flames. Continuing to fire, she steadily moved forward with the rest of the team, searching the chaos for any sign of her cousin.

On their right, the man known as Edge, who looked like some kind of biker, cut down two vampires in formal wear and killed two more with throwing knives. A young Mediterranean-looking soldier, whose call sign was Sidewinder, zipped around in a blur on their left, leaving piles of ash and flame in his wake. He wore a strange-looking exoskeleton over his black body armor and moved impossibly fast. The dwarf, Fortress, tore through the enemy at the front of the line, sending vampires flying in all directions with his spiked mace. They cut down the enemy in droves and still more came on. For every vampire they killed, two stepped up to take their place.

Suddenly a wave of darkness swept through the force, knocking them in all directions. Edge flipped twice before slamming hard into a wall. He slid to the floor and lay still, his sword clanking from his hand. Sidewinder sped over to his fallen comrade, fending off the swarm of vampires that looked to take advantage of the unconscious man. Fortress, who had been at the front of the line, disappeared into the shadowy cloud. The clashing of weapons and his loud roar radiated from within the darkness.

"Get back!" Johanson shouted, pushing Dana behind him. He leveled his gun on the cloud of writhing darkness, unable to fire for fear of hitting his man.

Jeremy stepped forward, threw out his hands, and screamed, "Jesus!"

A burst of blinding light shot forth from his fingertips, cutting a deep trench in the blackness and revealing two men in combat before they were swallowed up again by the darkness. Growling, he opened his mouth to shout again when he suddenly doubled over, the white aura surrounding him dissipating. He coughed and blood spattered the floor at his feet. Confused, he looked down to find a thin glowing blade sticking out of his stomach, a dark red stain slowly moving outward from the injury turning his shirt crimson.

"Now, now, now," said the Musketeer, his tone stern like a teacher scolding a disobedient student. "We cannot have you doing that, now, can we, *mon ami*?"

"No!" Dana yelled, turning her pistol on the man, her hand shaking as tears formed at the corners of her eyes.

He moved, putting Jermey between them and denying her a clean shot. Jeremy grit his teeth in pain, his hands hanging limply at his sides.

"Go to hell," Jeremy gurgled, spitting blood with the words.

"All in due time," the Musketeer chuckled. "Today, however, I have other things attend to. You, on the other hand, are probably not going to make it."

"Renault," Johanson said calmly, leveling his two pistols at the man. "Let him go."

The Musketeer narrowed his eyes, the corner of his lips turning up into a sneer. "Traitre, do not pretend you care about the prophet. We both know he is nothing more than a, how you say *outil*? A tool, that is it. He is nothing more than a tool to you. One that you will use and discard when it is no longer useful."

Dana grit her teeth in impotent fury as she fought to get a clear shot. Not again. How could it be happening again? First Jared, then her cousin, and now Jeremy. Just as before, she was powerless to stop someone she cared about from getting hurt.

No, not this time. This time she would find a way. She had to. Her heart couldn't handle having another person she loved murdered in front of her. Pushing aside her rising despair she focused down the sight of her weapon, taking aim at the Musketeer's head. All she needed was a clear shot.

"I would not do that if I were you," the Musketeer said, twisting his blade for emphasis. Jeremy screamed, his body contorting with pain.

"Stop!" she shouted, tears now staining her cheeks. "Please."

He laughed a merry laugh, the kind one makes when they are thoroughly enjoying themselves, and then twisted the blade again. Jeremy groaned, convulsed and then spat more blood, his eyes rolling back in his head.

Johanson let out a low growl, tightening his grip on his pistols, but he too had no shot. The conflict escalated around them, vampires and humans dying in droves, neither side gaining the advantage. The seemingly endless barrage of vampire warriors, however, gave them a clear advantage the longer the fight continued.

Johanson narrowed his eyes and dropped his hands.

"All right, Renault," he said. "Go ahead. Kill him."

Dana's eyebrows shot up and she glared at him incredulously, but did not lower her own weapon.

"What the hell are you doing??" she demanded.

"You're right, I don't care about him," he continued, ignoring Dana. "Go on and kill him. The moment you do, however, I will kill you."

"My dear Shamsiel, do you really think you can?"

"Kill him and we will find out."

"Are you insane?!" Dana shouted, her hands shaking and her eyes blurring with tears. "What's the matter with you?"

Johanson said nothing but continued his game of chicken with the Musketeer. Desperation and fear threatening to overcome her, she glanced at Johanson but never fully took her eyes off the Musketeer. She was barley holding it together and now the man had decided to go off the rails.

"What will it be, Renault?" he asked, one of his hands twitching slightly.

"I think..." he replied, his free hand suddenly snapping up and plucking something out of the air. With a wink, he displayed the .305 Winchester bullet he had just caught before discarding it. He wagged a finger at him and made a clucking sound with his tongue. "That you insult me with such obvious tactics."

Johanson suddenly grabbed Dana and twisted to the side as a large projectile flew past, missing them by mere inches. Whatever it was smashed into the wall with a crash. In a blind panic she fought against him, trying desperately to see what was happening to Jeremy, but he held her fast. He whipped his head in the direction of the sound and grimaced.

About six feet from the floor, Fortress' feet dangled limply out of a man-sized hole. A fine cloud of dust gently drifted around the depression as large cracks spiderwebbed outward from the opening. A few pieces of broken drywall fell to the ground, scattering dirt and debris in all directions.

"Damn," he snarled.

Dana turned in the direction Fortress had been catapulted from, and her mouth dropped open in horror. Walking calmly toward them, wreathed in writhing shadows, was Steven. Not the Steven she had grown up with, nor Steven the rock star, but Steven the monster. The one everyone assured her must have been a figment of her imagination. The same Steven who had somehow impaled her from across a field without a gun and murdered his brother, the man she loved.

uyuko, take the girl and withdraw," Vlad said calmly. "I will be along after I have dealt with our uninvited guests."

"You take care of her yourself," she hissed. "I do not care for your precious new lover. Besides, if she is indeed who you say she is, could she not simply dispose of them herself?"

He whirled on her, grabbing her by the throat and lifting her off the ground. She thrashed and clawed at him, attempting to free herself from his grasp. With icy contempt he tightened his grip till she stopped struggling, though the glare of hatred in her eyes let him know she was far from done.

"I am not talking about Jasmine, but the other girl," he said impatiently. "The transformation is not yet complete and must not be interrupted until it is fully finished. Everything depends on this."

Fuyuko glanced at Sophia, who was clutching her stomach as she writhed on the ground. The girl's eyes were shut tight from pain and her teeth were chattering as if she were freezing. She was covered in sweat and her skin was pallid and grayish in hue, with dark red veins spiderwebbing over her features. They pulsated and writhed under her skin like some kind of parasitic worm.

Upon seeing the state of the young girl, Fuyuko stopped her struggling and nodded. She hated Jasmine and never truly trusted her, but this girl had done nothing wrong. In fact, she realized now that the child was not much younger than she had been when her family was murdered. Her eyes softening, she nodded.

"What?!" Jasmine protested as Vlad let go of Fuyuko.

She thrust her hands at Sophia angrily. "Her? You're going to save her? So, everything you said to me was a lie? You promised me power and god-hood, and now you choose her instead of me?"

He leveled his gaze on her, his eyes flashing dangerously.

"Careful, little one."

"You are just like every other man who has come into my life," she continued, her voice rising, and pointed a finger at him accusingly. "You use me to get what you want and then throw me away when you're done."

"Who is using whom?" he inquired.

She went stiff and her eyes narrowed.

"What did you just say?"

"Oh yes, I know of your scheming and your plans to murder me," he continued, crossing his arms and sneering down at her. "You thought to use my devotion to Mother and your potential match to her against me, and perhaps if you were selected you would have succeeded. But our mother, in her great wisdom, rejected you and chose another. You are nothing more than an arrogant whore who sought to prostitute herself for power and failed."

With a growl, she flung herself at Vlad. He casually swatted her aside with one hand like a bug. She landed hard at Fuyuko's feet, a bruise already forming on her cheek. Her head spinning, she tried to rise, but the White Lady kicked, sending her sprawling. Tears in her eyes, she crawled toward Vlad and grabbed his leg.

"Please," she begged, her face now streaked with tears and makeup. "I'm sorry. I will do anything you want, just don't cast me away."

His eyes softened, but his voice remained harsh. "Do not let it be said I am unmerciful, and you are, after all, one of us. I will forgive your trespasses this time, but know this: any favor you once had is gone. If I sense even a hint of deception from you, I will not think twice before ending you. Is that understood?"

She nodded and he helped her to her feet. Fuyuko rolled her eyes in contempt as Jasmine fixed her dress, straightened, and then walked over to stand next to her.

"Now, both of you take the girl somewhere safe," he said, turning away. He began rolling up his sleeves and then turned back to look at the two women. "And if even one hair on her head is harmed, I will hold you both responsible."

The look in his eyes was all the confirmation they needed his threat was genuine. If anything should happen to Sophia, he would make sure they begged for death before he was done with them.

Both women hated Vlad in their own way but neither had the power to defy him, so they bent down to retrieve Sophia, who had stopped struggling and was now moaning softly and mumbling deliriously. Fuyuko swatted Jasmine's hand away with a snarl and she recoiled in anger.

"Why'd you do that?" she protested, massaging her hand.

"I do not need your help," Fuyuko bit back, lifting Sophia with ease. "Lord Vlad may be fool enough to still trust you, but I do not."

Without another word she turned and took off towards the rear exit. Jasmine glared hatefully at the ice vampire before skulking after, her mind racing. She was furious, but not completely out of options. There was still Jared, but he had tried to murder her. And there was the French guy, who Vlad called Renault. The vampire lord seemed genuinely wary of him, maybe even frightened, and that gave him potential. If she could somehow seduce him, then perhaps she might still be able to salvage the situation.

Before she made it to the doorway the air in front of the opening started to shimmer, forming a tear in space. Fuyuko made it through just as something started materializing out of the rift, but Jasmine didn't. She barely managed to put on the brakes before crashing headlong into it. Wildly dodging to the side, she instinctively dropped into a defensive crouch. Her jaw dropped as Jared stepped out of the fissure, his glowing sword in both hands, a look of absolute fury on his face.

Famine

He slowly scanned the room before fixing his eyes on her. Those black holes tore into her soul just as they had before and she gasped, staggering slightly from their weight. Why was he here? Had he come all this way to kill her? Not seeming to recognize her he turned away, taking in the battle. When his gaze returned to her, his expression softened and recognition dawned in his eyes. To her astonishment, instead of killing her he bent down and offered her a hand.

"You okay?" he asked in that ethereal voice of his.

She nodded, allowing him to help her up. He continued holding her hand even after she had got to her feet, and her heart fluttered a bit. After her transformation all she had cared about was power, but upon seeing him now, something inside her stirred. Was it possible the woman she had been was still alive in her somewhere? She had desired to use him against Vlad, but looking into his eyes now, seeing his smile, made her feel the same way she had when she finally realized she loved him.

"What are you doing here?" she stuttered.

His eyes turned even blacker, and his expression darkened at her question.

"We have come..." He grimaced and clenched his fists, cutting himself off. When he had finally composed himself he continued. "I'm here to save you if I can."

Her brow furrowed in confusion, and she searched his face.

"So, you're not here for Dana?" she asked, and then instantly regretted it.

"What?" he exclaimed, his head snapping around frantically. "Dana's here?"

Most of the room was obscured by a massive cloud of darkness and he squinted, trying to peer through it. Her heart sank as he pulled his hand out of hers. He didn't seem to notice as she took a step back, her expression downcast.

Why had she mentioned that stupid woman's name? Even now she was still getting in the way.

"As touching as this reunion is," Vlad said, drawing their attention, "I cannot allow you to interfere. I knew I could not trust that bastard Renault, but I had hoped to avoid this confrontation. No matter, I will deal with you myself."

With blinding speed he lunged forward, but stopped abruptly as Jared stepped in front of Jasmine, placing himself between her and Vlad. Her eyes went wide in surprise as he put his arm on her protectively.

Vlad's brows shot up and his expression became curious. "Now, this is interesting. A Justice protecting a vampire. Has she actually succeeded in seducing you? Given all I know of Tzedakah I doubt it, but today is, after all, a day for miracles, so anything is possible."

Jared narrowed his eyes, tightening his grip on the sword, but stayed silent. Resting her hand lightly on his shoulder, Jasmine stepped out and stood next to him. She slid her hand down till it rested on his. He stiffened, his sword hand trembling slightly, but didn't shy away. Instead, he gently squeezed it reassuringly before lifting his sword in a two-handed defensive stance. She matched his posture, lifting her own fists, her eyes intense with resolve.

Famine

"Perhaps I misjudged you, little one," Vlad mused, shaking his head. "It seems you have found the ally you hoped for after all, but you may find that this sword cuts both ways. No matter, I will kill you both and then deal with the rest of the invaders."

Before he finished his last word he suddenly surged forward, launching a series of rapid punches. He was impossibly quick, and his hands alternated between each of them, driving them both back. Jared and Jasmine were just as quick and they blocked each strike, managing to launch a few counters in response. Tzedakah flashed and cut and Jasmine clawed and punched, each time missing or being deflected. They continued this deadly dance, moving about the throne in a blur, neither side gaining a clear advantage over the other.

Suddenly turning into mist, Jasmine surged forward and then materialized close to Vlad, landing a succession of quick jabs to his midsection, while Jared simultaneously launched a wicked one-handed swing at his head. Vlad took the punches, allowing their force to propel him backward, causing Jared's attack to miss, cutting nothing but a single lock of his hair.

Vlad countered with a quick punch to Jared's face, sending him reeling. He then twitched a finger and Jasmine suddenly gasped and fell to the ground, gritting her teeth so hard her fangs bit into her lip, drawing blood. She lay at his feet, contorting and writhing as if a thousand volts of electricity were surging through her.

Jared recovered quickly and in a rage, he charged, swinging Tzedakah in a wild downward slash. Vlad easily evaded the blow and landed a right hook to the side of his head. Jared grunted but took the blow, allowing its momentum to carry him into a spinning kick which connected with Vlad's midsection, doubling him over. He then followed up with a wicked knee to the jaw that snapped his head upward and back. The vampire stumbled away, only making it a few feet before finally coming to a halt.

Jasmine gasped and coughed violently as Vlad's spell was interrupted. Grimacing in pain, she turned over and pushed herself to her feet, blood dripping from her lips staining her gown crimson. It felt like she had been struck by lightning, and she was struggling to get to her feet. Jared came over and helped her, his gaze never leaving Vlad.

His eyes were narrowed, and he was gritting his teeth. Once again there was the slightest tremor in the arm holding his sword, as if it was fighting him somehow. Vlad noted this as well, and the corners of his mouth turned up slightly.

"I see. The sword does not quite approve of your feelings for her, does it? How do you expect to defeat me while fighting it at the same time?"

Jared grimaced but said nothing. He tightened his grip on the blade and its aura intensified, as if in defiance of Vlad's words. The smile never left the vampire's face, though his eyes narrowed, and he visibly tensed.

"I am through talking," Jasmine snarled, tendrils of frost forming on her fingertips.

The temperature around her plummeted and ice formed on the ground under her feet. She lifted her hands, a blast of ice exploding from her fingers. Before the particles struck him Vlad made a sign in the air with one finger and a shield of fire burst into existence, intercepting her attack. Steam erupted where the two elements met, obscuring their view of him.

They had no time to react as Vlad burst through the mist, striking Jasmine with a vicious uppercut while simultaneously knocking Jared aside with a back hand. Her entire body exploded upward, but Vlad snatched her out of the air with one arm before she had time to register what was happening. Dazed, her vision blurring, she feebly clawed at the hand closed around her throat. In desperation she scratched at his face and sent waves of cold surging into him, but he knocked all her attacks aside with ease.

Pulling her close, his breath smelling of death and blood, he hissed, "I have had enough of you, little one. I should have listened to Fuyuko and ended your insignificant life the first time you disobeyed me, but once again my kindness proves a weakness. I will now rectify that mistake."

Unexpectedly Jared appeared next to Vlad, the air around him sparking and shimmering with blue-black energy. Vlad spun just as he thrust Tzedakah forward, but was too late. The blade slid hungrily into the vampire's flesh, its satisfaction at bringing justice to the vampire paralleled in Jared's own emotions. They locked eyes and Jared smiled victoriously.

His grin faltered, however, when Vlad's lips curled into a triumphant smile.

"What—" he stuttered, looking down in confusion.

He had felt Tzedakah bite into his flesh, why was he not dead? It made no sense. When he looked back up, all he saw were Jasmine's beautiful blue eyes staring back at him and his heart plummeted.

"Jared," Jasmine whimpered, lifting one hand and gently resting it on his cheek. "I...I'm sorry..."

Darkness engulfed everyone and everything as Steven slowly strolled toward them. Even the sounds of the battle itself were swallowed by his passing, fading to nothing more than background noise. The Musketeer, cackling like a jackal and still holding a now-limp Jeremy, moved aside for him. Dana tried to push Johanson away but he held her fast with one arm, his other pointing his weapon at Steven.

Steven looked like some kind of demonic monster from a nightmare. Half his face was dark gray with one large red eye glaring hatefully at them, while the other remained human. Large fangs protruded from his grinning mouth and a snake-like tongue flicked, snapping at the air around his lips. Flexing his hands as long talons burst from his fingertips, he hunched forward, allowing the massive batlike wings on his back to unfurl.

"Shamsiel," he said, his voice Steven's and yet not. "I figured it was only a matter of time before you intervened."

The human side of Steven's face grimaced and the corner of his eye narrowed and twitched as he let out a low growl. As monstrous and powerful as they were, neither of them had total control over the other. Steven stubbornly refused to allow Azrael to completely overtake him, even though the pressure of the demon's will constantly threatened to overwhelm him.

He feared what would happen if he did, knowing deep in his heart that eventually the creature would destroy him altogether and he would cease to be. All that he had been, all he was, and all he would ever be would eventually be consumed and replaced by the demon. For now, however, they agreed on this one thing: they were going to kill Dana and every other creature that stood in their way.

Johanson nodded, but didn't lower his weapon. He relaxed his hold on Dana and she pushed away from him, training her own weapon on Steven. As terrified of him as she was, her attention was more focused on Jeremy. She glanced in his direction, her heart racing with anxiety. She breathed a sigh of relief when he stirred, his eyes flicking open and slightly looking back at her. The corners of his mouth lifted, and he winked.

"It's good to see you again, Dana," Steven said, drawing her attention back to him. This time his voice sounded more human than when he had addressed Johanson. "I must admit, I was disappointed when we were interrupted the other night."

Famine

All of the terror and pain of what she thought had been a nightmare flooded back into her consciousness, but rather than overwhelm her it fueled her resolve. She gripped her pistol with both hands and took a step toward him, eyes blazing.

"I seem to remember turning your chest into Swiss cheese the last time we fought."

His smile broadened, baring his teeth. "Yes, you did, right after I spilled your guts all over that field. How are you healing, by the way? Still in a lot of pain?"

"Good enough to take you on."

"Oh really?" he snickered. "I'm pretty sure I got the better end of that trade."

He turned to look at Jeremy and raised an eyebrow. "Friend of yours?"

She glanced at Jeremy, her anxious expression betraying her bravado. His head swiveled between them and his eyes brightened with mischief.

"Oh, I see. More than a friend. Didn't wait long to move on, did you? What will Jared say when he finds out?"

"Shut up," she snapped, her hand shaking in rage, tears brimming in her eyes. "Don't you dare speak his name."

Sneering, he beckoned for her to come at him. "What are you going to do about it?"

Her world went red and she took a step toward him, but was intercepted by Johanson. Once again she fought against him, but this time he shook her violently until she stopped trying to get around him.

"Think of your cousin!" he snapped. "She's still alive here somewhere and needs your help. Plus, if we charge in blindly, the Musketeer will most likely finish off Jeremy in response. We have to be smart here or none of us is coming out of this alive. Trust me. You worry about your cousin, and I'll take care of Jeremy."

How could she have forgotten about Sophia? Her cousin was the reason she had come here in the first place. Jeremy had even placed his own life on the line to help save her. Glancing at him, she realized she had to keep it together. Not just for her cousin but for Jeremy. Her expression hardening with resolve, she nodded.

With a nod of his own he turned and addressed Steven, his gaze hardening.

"Azrael, you are a fool," he said, a wolfish grin spreading across his face. "You don't give a rat's ass about the vampires or their patron, yet here you are exposing yourself on their behalf. I don't care if it's the influence of the human you possess or just that you're too stupid to see that Renault is using you. Either way, it was a very big mistake to reveal yourself to me."

"Dana!" he shouted, pushing her aside and lifting his pistols. "Go find your cousin."

Both guns roared as, instead of bullets, blasts of white-hot plasma burst from their barrels, tearing through Steven's defenses and setting the darkness surrounding him a blaze. Stumbling, Dana gawked as Johanson moved like lightning, continuing to fire and keeping Steven occupied and buying her time to escape.

Her heart threatening to beat out of her chest she ran, not looking back though she was worried about Jeremy. She still didn't completely trust Johanson, but she had no choice if she wanted to rescue her cousin. It was impossible for her to succeed on her own, and if Jeremy had taught her one thing it was that she wasn't alone anymore.

Cackling with glee, the Musketeer put his mouth to Jeremy's ear and said, "Well, I guess this time I do actually get to kill you. Any last words?"

"Yeah," he slurred, throwing his head back savagely and smashing it directly into his face. "I'm not through yet."

Renault's head snapped back forcefully, sending him stumbling backward and pulling his sword out of Jeremy's torso as he did. No longer being held up by the blade, Jeremy started to fall, but was saved right before he slammed headlong into the floor by the speedy Sidewinder. With a satisfied smile, Jeremy flipped the Musketeer a double bird as the duo sped away to safety.

Fuming, but honestly impressed Jeremy had got the better of him twice, he chose not to kill him. At least not today anyway. He instead lifted his sword in a salute, presenting Jeremy with an honor he reserved for only a few. As soon as his human shield was gone the sniper from before unloaded on him, sadly not giving him the time to ponder just what he would do to Jeremy the next time they met.

Moving so fast he seemed to be standing still, the Musketeer evaded the deadly missiles which peppered the floor around him harmlessly. Yawning with boredom, he casually scanned for the shooter as he moved, almost missing Edge who was lunging at him from the left, attempting to disembowel him. Clucking his tongue and waving an index finger disapprovingly while simultaneously dodging, he grabbed his wrist and twisted, sending him careening in the opposite direction.

Having gotten Jeremy to safety, Sidewinder attacked from the right, trying to capitalize on the distraction. Without missing a beat, the Musketeer threw one leg out, tripping Sidewinder and sending the soldier spinning. He slammed into the floor multiple times, pieces of his high-tech armor soaring off him before finally sliding to a stop and lying motionless.

Bullets continued flying around him, none of them hitting their mark as he renewed his search for the sniper. Johanson was still trading blows with Steven, his plasma blasters lighting fires all around the demonic monster and keeping it at bay. He figured he should help, when he noticed Dana running towards the edge of the shadowy darkness. In a flash he was in front of her, blocking her way.

Eyes wide, she skidded to a halt, nearly plowing into him before quickly backtracking while lifting her pistol and firing.

"I cannot have you leaving so soon," he said, shaking his head disapprovingly. "How you say? Oh yes, the party is just getting started."

Instead of fear, all Dana felt was fury as she faced down the man who had tried to murder Jeremy. Her cousin temporarily forgotten she unloaded on him, continuing to pull the trigger even after the slide had locked open, signifying it was empty. Breathing heavily, she stared dumbfounded at the man who stood unharmed, his plumed hat cradled lovingly in his hands, one finger poking out of a small hole in its brim.

Famine

"You monster!" he exclaimed dramatically. "You savage. How could you do such a horrible thing? What has this hat done to you that you would treat it so?"

While he was preoccupied with his hat she quickly retrieved a replacement magazine, snapped it into place and released the slide, chambering a fresh round. He was on her in flash, wrenching her hand painfully. The weapon clattered to the floor and skidded away, getting lost in the writhing darkness.

He smelled of roses and pomanders as he leaned in, his expression grave. "I honestly had nothing against you and was only using you to distract Jared, but you have injured my hat and I am afraid I cannot overlook that."

Swallowing hard, she tried to pull away, but his grip was like iron. She had seen how fast this man moved and knew she couldn't escape him if she tried. Her mind racing, she searched her brain for solutions but came up with none. There had to be a way. Johanson was still occupied with Steven, Jeremy was most likely dead, and the rest of the strike team was either engaged or incapacitated.

Almost on cue, as if he was reading her mind, he said, "Time's up."

Violet-black light bathed her features as the Musketeer placed the edge of his rapier against her neck. Eyes wide, her lips pressed tight, she tried to shy away but found that her body wouldn't respond. It drew a thin line of red, sending small droplets of blood meandering down her neck. Frantic now, she tried to scream, but even her voice refused to obey her.

A sudden blast of fire and heat exploded around them, staggering him and making his sword slip from her skin. It also shattered his paralyzing hold on her and she gasped, stumbling away from him. Smoke obscured her view as the wall of shadows dividing the room burst into flames. Coughing, she searched for a way around the inferno. Then it suddenly died, taking with it the barrier of darkness.

As the smoke cleared, the entire battlefield came into view. Johanson was standing over a smoking Steven, both pistols aimed at his head. Sidewinder and Edge sill lay unmoving where they had fallen as skirmishes between vampires and soldiers continued throughout the room. Piles of smoking ash mingled with blood, making the floor slick, while the pungent smell of burnt flesh and gore hung thick in the air.

Dana noticed Jeremy, his eyes closed, resting with his back against the far wall. Her heart leapt. A giant of a man, built like a Mack truck, with dark brown eyes and a thick beard, fussed over, him binding his wounds. He wore the same high-tech armor as the other soldiers, but the red cross on his helmet indicated he was a medic.

Johanson had kept his promise, and Jeremy was safe for the moment. Temporarily forgetting about her cousin, she moved toward him before the drama unfolding by the throne drew her attention. Jared cradled the limp form of Jasmine in his arms, her hand resting gently on his cheek as Vlad stood over them, arms crossed, grinning triumphantly.

Mouth dropping open, she slowed and came to a stop, blinking in confusion. Her world spun as she stared wide-eyed at the man she loved and the girl who had broken his heart. But it couldn't be him. She had held him as he died, had attended his funeral, had comforted his parents as they lowered him into the ground, and yet there was no mistaking him.

She shook her head in denial as recollections of both Steven and the Musketeer having mentioned Jared's name flashed in her head. Their words hadn't registered in the heat of battle, but now they came crashing back with perfect clarity. Plus, when she had first met Jeremy he had said that he *was* a friend of Jared's, not that *he had been* a friend of his. It was beginning to make sense now.

Her anger rising, a vague memory suddenly jogged loose from somewhere deep in the back of her mind. It gradually surfaced, blurry at first then, with a jolt, became clear. Jared hunching over her, his face close, his eyes blacker than the deep void of space. Her hand reaching for him as she declared her love right before her world went black. She had reasoned it to be nothing more than a fever dream while unconscious. But now, given everything else, she knew it to be a memory.

Strong arms wrapped around her, shocking her out of her trance. She stiffened as the Musketeer put his lips to one of her ears. His breath was hot on her skin, and it sent shivers up and down her spine.

"I suppose you feel like a fool," he chided. "I would if I had been lied to by everyone close to me, including the man I loved. I was going to kill you, but now I have found a more entertaining use for you. How do you think he would react if he saw you in pain?"

Gritting her teeth, she struggled against him. But his grip was too strong.

"Oh no, you are going to watch every agonizing moment as I use you to turn the man you love into a monster."

Fuyuko ran. Ran as fast as her immortal legs would carry her. Turning into mist would be faster, but she couldn't while holding the girl. With a whistle she summoned Nayati, who appeared out of thin air, running up beside her as they weaved through the dark hallways. The sounds of battle were everywhere, not just in the throne room. Johanson had been thorough as usual and had brought enough troops to invade a small country.

Skidding to a halt, she peered around a corner. A group of enemies was slowly making its way down the hallway that led to the holding pens. They moved in single file, their attention in all directions, their weapons at the high ready position. These men were too well armed and trained to be the local law enforcement they controlled, and she hissed in frustration. They were, of course, no match for her or the wendigo, but she couldn't engage them without risking harm to Sophia.

She may not necessarily buy into Vlad's fanatical belief in the return of the vampire matriarch, but she couldn't deny that something peculiar was happening to the girl. Contrary to most legends, only people with the right latent DNA in their blood could actually be turned into vampires. The rest simply died. She had smelled the markers in Sophia, but in all her long years she had never seen anything like what was happening to the girl.

"Nayati," she whispered, motioning to the soldiers who were now only a few feet from the bend in the hall.

With a snarl the wendigo leapt around the corner and barreled into the unsuspecting troopers, their shouts of shock quickly turning into shrieks of pain. Weapons barked futilely and men screamed as the wendigo tore them apart. She waited till the gunfire died before moving into the hallway.

Crimson fluid spattered the walls like some kind of surrealist painting, and the stench of gunpowder and blood hung thick in the air. Dismembered bodies and discarded weapons lay strewn throughout the hallway, their faces frozen in expressions of agony. There was even a severed hand still clutching a pistol, which she casually stepped over as she made her way toward the door to the pens where they housed human livestock.

The soldier lying nearest the doorway was still struggling, his feet kicking as the wendigo bent over him, tearing large pieces of flesh from his neck and shoulders. He gurgled and sputtered before going still, which only accentuated the loud gulping noises Nyati was making as he

Famine

consumed the man's flesh. He stood as she approached, his face covered with blood and gore hanging from his mouth.

As always, his beady black eyes were wild with ravenous hunger. It didn't matter how much the creature ate. He would never be satiated. The pain from the hunger was unbearable and eventually drove all of his kind mad. Not unlike her own never-ending thirst, which could only be contained but never satisfied. Such was the curse of those who were born from the blood of the fallen angel known to the ancients as Famine. The very creature Vlad believed Sophia was becoming.

Fuyuko motioned toward the door and the wendigo cracked it open and peered into the darkness. Not seeing any danger, he pushed it open the rest of the way before stepping inside. She followed, her eyes instantly adjusting to the darkness, the stench of filth and human waste causing her nose to involuntarily crinkle.

Light trickled in from the few small windows in the large barn-like chamber, casting dark shadows. Out of those shadows, eyes stared back at them. Some wide with fright, some filled with tears, others dull and distant. Children of all shapes and sizes huddled together in the shadows. They shied away from the wendigo, who gazed at them—salivating like a starving man seeing a buffet.

"Nayati," she snapped. "Go check the courtyard to see if it is clear."

He whimpered like a begging dog before reluctantly turning and speeding off toward the large door at the other side of the room.

A soon as he left, a few of the children cautiously crept closer; their faces covered in dirt and grime, their clothes tattered. They looked up at her, eyes pleading, and her heart went out to them. Sure, she fed on humans. But never children. They always reminded her of her own babies who had been taken from her long ago.

A small girl no more than eight grabbed the hem of her dress and stared up at her, eyes wide. "Lady, I miss my mommy and I'm scared. Can I please go home now?"

Swallowing, Fuyuko fought the tears that threatened to come as she met the girl's gaze. Oh, how she wished she could help her. Help them all, but if Vlad was right then Sophia was more important. Besides, the compound was compromised. And even if their forces managed to kill all the invaders, more would eventually come, and the children would be found and freed.

Smiling reassuringly, she reached down and gently mussed her hair.

"Do not be afraid, little one. You will be going home soon, I promise."

Others came forward, slowly at first and then gaining confidence. Those that still had the strength to move huddled around her, eyes bright with hope. Excited conversations broke out among them and some hugged each other and wept. The White Lady who had always been so kind to them said they were going home, and with the absolute faith only children possessed they believed her.

"Quiet down now, children," she scolded, her voice rising slightly. "The men who will be taking you home will be arriving soon, so go gather your things and wait for them."

Nodding eagerly and thanking her they scattered in all directions, too excited to stand still. All except the little girl who still held tight to her leg. She refused to let go. Fuyuko frowned down at her but was not angry. If she could bring her along, she would. But the girl didn't have the marker in her, and she would just be killed by the others if she did. Plus, children who were turned were doomed to stay children for the remainder of their existence, and that was a worse curse than dying.

"What is your name, child?" she asked, gently running her fingers through the girl's gnarled dark hair.

"Mable," she replied sheepishly.

"Well Mable, I promise you it will be all right. The men will come as I said, and they will return you to your family. You have my word."

"Your word is worthless," said a voice from the shadows.

Snarling, Fuyuko turned, placing herself protectively between the child and the speaker. The little girl clung to her, one eye peeking out from behind her leg. The others went instantly quiet, trained by experience to make themselves as invisible as possible at even the hint of danger.

"I remember you saying something similar to me once."

Kat stepped out of the shadows, her eyes glowing red with anger. She was dressed in a dark gray T-shirt and jeans, and her normally unruly hair was held up in a neat ponytail.

Her demeanor and bearing were that of a much older girl compared to her diminutive stature.

"Do you remember that, Mother?" She emphasized the word "Mother" in a way that made it sound like a curse. "Everything will be all right, child, you said. There is no reason to fear, you said. We both know what happened after, don't we?"

"I had no part in what happened to you," she snapped back.

"Of course you didn't," she scoffed. "You are never responsible for what happens. Not Miss Fuyuko. She loves the children and takes care of them as best she can, except when it actually matters. That is what you tell yourself, isn't it? How you justify looking the other way as we are murdered and tortured."

"You do not know what you are talking about," she countered, her voice lacking conviction.

Kat raised an eyebrow. "I don't? How many children have you failed to protect? I mean, besides me and my brother. Do you remember them all, or have you forgotten them like you forgot your own children?"

The temperature instantly plummeted and Fuyuko nearly dropped Sophia as she tightened her grip on the little girl, who grunted and squirmed uncomfortably.

"Shut your foul mouth," she warned icily.

Kat glanced at the little girl and casually said, "Do you know you're hurting her?"

Fuyuko snapped her gaze downward and quickly let go of the little girl. She scurried away, her eyes wide and filled with tears. Fuyuko's expression was one of horrified guilt, and she retreated into the shadows.

"I prove my point. You may have convinced yourself you are their mother, but you aren't. You took them from their real parents."

Gritting her teeth, Fuyuko composed herself before turning to face Kat. She repositioned Sophia on one shoulder and lifted her chin defiantly.

"I have done many things I regret," she said. "This is just one in a million I will learn to live with."

That said, she turned her back to Kat and started off toward the exit.

With a snarl Kat jumped in front of her, blocking her way. Dropping into a defensive crouch, she pointed at Sophia.

"You aren't going anywhere with her."

"Move out of my way before I kill you," she said coldly. "I do not have time to waste on you."

A loud explosion followed by gunfire drew their attention, and Fuyuko cursed in Japanese. There was no time for this kind of delay. Whatever was happening throughout the compound was quickly escalating, and she needed to get the girl to a safe place where the transformation could be completed without interruption.

Sophia groaned, and Kat tensed and took a reflexive step closer.

"Drop her," she demanded, her voice thick with anxiety. "Drop her now."

"You leave me no choice," Fuyuko said before whistling. "I warned you."

Before she had finished speaking, Nyati lunged at Kat from behind. The little vampire was quicker and had smelled the wendigo sneaking up on her. With feline speed she flipped onto his back as his claws raked the air where she had been standing. In the span of a few seconds, she had torn out one of his eyes and turned his back into mincemeat.

He howled in agony and thrashed wildly, attempting to buck the little vampire off, but she stubbornly held on. Fuyuko tried to get around them but was unable as they spun and whirled in front of her, Kat continuing to tear at the beast as he tried in vain to dislodge her. By sheer fortunate chance the wendigo finally managed to grab hold of one of her legs, and with a snarl he wrenched her from his back and slammed her hard to the ground.

Unfazed, she clawed and bit his arm, tearing more chunks of flesh from him. He countered by slamming her into the ground two more times before hurling her into a nearby wall. She smashed into it with a sickening thud and then dropped to the floor, dazed.

He stalked toward her, his remaining eye narrowed in rage, blood pouring from the countless wounds she had inflicted. Blinking away the fog in her head, she tried to rise but fell painfully back to the floor. She lay helplessly on her side, glaring defiantly at him. Her eyes flicked to Sophia, and she realized that she had to get up or her friend would be lost. Ignoring the screams of her injured body, she pushed herself to her feet and once again blocked their way.

"You're not going anywhere with her," she stuttered, swaying on her feet. "Now put her down or I will make you."

Famine

Fuyuko shook her head. "I do not understand why you are fighting us. I do not mean to harm the girl, but help her. I know you developed a friendship with her, so why not stop this nonsense and simply come with us?"

She extended a hand to Kat, who stared dumbfounded at it.

"You have my word that I mean the girl no harm."

Kat's narrowed her eyes, set her jaw, and planted her feet.

"Yeah, like I said before, I know what helping her means. I will not let you do that to her. Drop her and go or I will kill both of you."

Lady Fuyuko didn't laugh or grow angry at the threat, but instead her eyes became sorrowful.

"Child, you are already too late to prevent that."

Shaking her head in disbelief, Kat pointed a finger at Fuyuko accusingly.

"You're lying."

She shook her head sadly and turned so Kat could get a better look at Sophia. Upon seeing the red veins and the grayish hue of her skin the little vampire dropped to her knees, her hands limp in her lap, tears flowing from her eyes. Kat wiped at them with one palm while still shaking her head in denial.

"No. it's not true. I'm not too late," she said, her voice cracking. "I have to protect her. I can't fail her the way I failed to Mike."

"I am truly sorry, child," Fuyuko said, nodding to Nyati, who grabbed Kat by the throat and lifted her off the ground. "Your friend will die and there is nothing you can do to change that. But be comforted. She will rise again, reborn as a god."

This time she didn't fight back as he squeezed. Tears staining her cheeks, she fixed her gaze on her friend as the edges of her vision started going black. She had failed her and now they both were going to die.

"I'm sorry," she managed weakly, never taking her eyes off her friend.

Just as her world went black, Sophia's eyes snapped open and she screamed.

Jasmine's hand went limp, and he caught it in his own as it fell from his face. Instead of bursting into flames her body simply disintegrated, her ashes falling from his arms like sand through an hourglass. The last part of her to collapse was her gaze, which stayed fixed on him till the end. The part of his heart that had remained human broke as he watched the light leave them.

He said nothing as the embers that had been her hand filtered through his fingers. Even Tzedakah was uncharacteristically quiet. He had expected the sword to make some statement about her being a monster and that she'd needed to die. Mercifully he seemed to understand just how much this was affecting Jared and stayed silent.

"I am sorry she had to die," Vlad interjected. "I truly am. If it is any consolation, you will soon be joining her."

His words barely registered as Jared continued to stare at the pile of ashes. He had failed to save her, just as he had failed her as a lover. No matter how much he lied to himself about it, his feelings for Dana had always got in the way of his love for Jasmine. He had thought that if he could save her, in some small way it would make up for hurting her. Now she was gone, and he had lost his chance at redemption.

His face grave, Vlad lifted an arm and his fingers extended into sharp talons. Before he could strike, however, a woman's scream split through the air, drawing his interest. It was loud, as if it were being amplified somehow, and those that were not already out of the fight turned their attention towards the shout.

Dana hung a few feet of the ground, the Musketeer's glowing blade sticking out of one shoulder. Her face contorting in agony, she screamed again as he lifted her higher, displaying her to Jared. Blood dripped liberally from the tip of the blade, staining the floor red.

Jeremy, who had regained consciousness, tried to stand but couldn't. He tried to rise again, his face a mask of rage and pain. But his injuries were too severe, and he didn't have the strength. When he tried for a third time, the medic, whose callsign was Flatline, pushed him forcefully back down and held him in place. Gritting his teeth in frustration, all he could do was watch as the he tortured her.

The Musketeer twisted his blade just a bit and Dana's eyes flew open. She shrieked again, but this time with less force. Her eyes rolled around in her head as her struggling became less frantic. She was fading fast and her gaze fixed on Jared, who still seemed to be in a trance.

Famine

"Jared," she murmured, starting to lose consciousness. "I..."

The Musketeer's grin was so wide his face looked like it might split in half as Jared's head snapped in his direction. The fool had finally noticed, and those black pools of writhing darkness fixed on her before turning to the Musketeer, reaching out for him in fury. A heavy dread fell on the room and every person in it halted in their tracks and stared uncomfortably at Jared.

Realizing his chance to attack was quickly passing, Vlad forced back the sudden crippling fear filling his mind and struck. Without taking his eyes off the Frenchman, Jared caught his wrist midflight. Tzedakah's light grew in intensity and pulses of power poured from the blade as he stood and turned to face Vlad. The muscles in the vampire's jaw bulged and his eyes were wide with panic as he frantically strained against his grip.

"I am going to kill you for what you've done," Jared promised.

His voice was ethereal and terrible, and sent shivers down the spines of all who heard it. Johanson turned his pistols on him, slowly backing away and urgently shouting orders into his radio. Steven slowly got to his feet and fell into a defensive crouch, his red eyes glowing, the ancient demon inside him uneasy. Everyone else in the room—vampires and humans alike—also took instinctive steps away from him, their conflicts forgotten.

"I will not allow you..." Before Vlad had time to finish his sentence, Jared drove Tzedakah into his chest and the vampire exploded. Unlike the others, he didn't burn or turn to ash. He just simply disappeared, his body completely vanishing.

Without missing a beat, Jared turned to face the crowd of terrified onlookers. Just as before, the world was swirling around him, his vision tunneling to a singular point. His gaze was fixed on Dana, who hung limp on the Musketeer's sword. Anger so hot he felt it would burn him alive gripped both him and the sword. The Musketeer would pay for what he had done to their love; they all would. None of them were just. All were guilty, and he would bring each and every one of them to Justice.

For the first time since he had been resurrected, he and Tzedakah were in complete alignment. Both ceased to exist as separate entities and became one. Gone was the internal conflict that had made them weak. They were the all-powerful living embodiment of Justice, and they were angry.

A fierce wind suddenly began to blow around the chamber, growing in intensity until it was a howling gale. Statues, chairs, people, and anything else that wasn't securely tied down were thrown about violently as the storm grew in intensity. Surges of blue-black lightning cracked loudly as the wind howled throughout the room. One bolt struck Vlad's throne, splitting it in two as if spitting on the vampire's memory.

The Musketeer was laughing so hard he nearly dropped Dana as screams of terror and pain rose above the clamor of the wind. He of course was barely affected by the storm and stood easy in the whirlwind. The entire throne room was in complete chaos, and it was glorious. Finally, after all his careful planning, he had gotten what he wanted. He had broken Jared's spirit, driving him to finally allow Tzedakah in completely. Well, as completely as he could at this stage of the game, but the trauma and pain absolutely made him much more entertaining. Not necessarily powerful enough yet to kill, but absolutely more fun to play with.

It was a pity that fool Vlad had to die. But the girl who had responded to the ancient blood had escaped, so it had worked out in the end. The apocalypse grew ever closer with restoration of each ancient god, and that meant chaos. And that was exactly what he wanted. More shrieks echoed in the turmoil as Jared killed them. He wondered how many of them were human and how many vampires. Could he even tell the difference anymore, or were they all simply monsters to him now?

Ash and blood mixed with the rest of the debris, staining the whirlwind red and gray as vampires and humans alike died. A flash of blue-black light and another scream. An explosion of fire and a howl of rage. In a panic, a vampire dressed in a tattered tuxedo fell into the eye of the storm. His eyes wide, he clawed at the ground as something unseen dragged him shrieking back into the storm. A soldier stumbled out of the torrent, turning and firing as he fled. He only made it a few feet before there was a flash of movement and he collapsed to the floor, his head rolling away in a trail of blood.

Enhanced with demonic strength, Steven stood with his hands in front of his face, shielding his body from the swirling debris. Somewhere deep in himself, he felt bad for

Jared. Terrified of him, but sad nonetheless. He obviously couldn't empathize with him since he was a true psychopath, but there was a small spark of something akin to regret that was directed at his older brother. The demon, on the other hand, was terrified and wanted nothing more than to flee.

The Musketeer popped into existence next to him, making him start. He carried Dana over one shoulder, the blood from her wound soaking his uniform. It was splattered all over the silver skull on his pauldron, making it look even more unsettling.

His grin widening, he pointed to the swirling storm. "You feel like playing with your older brother?"

Steven could feel Azrael's apprehension, and that made his decision for him. He hated the demon even though it had given him power. It was obvious Azrael was altering him, and that eventually he would no longer be himself. He had contemplated ending his life, but just wasn't the kind of person who did such things. Plus, he was sure the demon would intervene if he tried. Jared, on the other hand, had the power to kill both of them. Either Jared killed them, or he killed Jared. It was a win for him either way.

Nodding, he flung himself into the cyclone; the animated shadows he emitted mixing with the wind, turning it black.

Nyati jerked at the shout and turned, dropping Kat. She fell to the ground, landing face down on her hands and knees coughing violently. She looked up, her eyes clouded with tears, to see the blurry shape of someone standing directly next to the wendigo. There was a flash of movement, a gurgling cry, and blood suddenly spattered across her face, causing her to jerk and fall backward. Shocked and frightened, she scurried away from the attack on all fours like a crab as the wendigo was literally torn in two.

She skuttled a few feet before stopping and wiping at her eyes, attempting to clear her vision. The blood mixed with her tears, making it even harder to see, and she gasped as the person who had murdered Nyati suddenly stood over her. They bent down and she threw her arms up defensively and shied away, slapping at the hands reaching for her.

"Kat, calm down. It's me," said a familiar voice.

She stopped struggling and slowly lowered her arms. She stared up at the speaker, blinking rapidly in an attempt at clearing the moisture out of her eyes.

"Sophia?" she asked tentatively, still squinting.

"Yeah," she replied, extending her hand again.

Kat took it and she helped her to her feet.

"You okay? I woke up just as that monster was hurting you."

Before she had time to finish her sentence Kat threw herself at her, burying her face in her dress.

"Hey, it's all right," she said, holding her tight and running her hands gently through her hair.

"I thought I lost you," Kat cried, her voice muffled by the fabric of Sophia's dress.

"You didn't. I'm okay. Honest."

She looked around dazedly as if she was unsure of where she was. How had she gotten here? Lifting her hands, she stared dumbfounded at the blood on them. What had happened and why were her hands covered in blood? The last thing she remembered was Vlad forcing her and that other woman to drink something. It had tasted like metal and burned her throat. After that she had passed out.

Wait, was she in the pen? How had she gotten here?

Still bewildered, she scanned the room. Remarkably she could see everything clearly, even though there wasn't much light. And the smell. She could literally smell everything. The sweat and, was that fear, from the children hiding in the shadows. Since when could she smell fear? She could even smell the decaying leaves outside and a chipmunk or squirrel that was somewhere nearby. Not only

543

could she smell the critter, but she could hear it as clearly as if she were standing directly next to it.

"What is happening to me?" she asked, her eyes distant and her brow furrowed.

"You are changing," said Fuyuko, drawing her attention.

Narrowing her eyes, she let out a guttural snarl and placed herself defensively between Kat and the vampire.

"Don't you touch her," she warned.

As disoriented as she was, she still recognized the White Lady. With frightening speed she charged Fuyuko, grabbing her by the throat and lifting her off the ground with one arm. The White Lady futilely clutched at her arms before lifting her own hands in a gesture of surrender.

"I would not think of harming the girl," she croaked.

"I don't believe you," she snarled, unexpectedly gripping the woman's head with both hands.

Just as she was about to tear the foul vampire's head off, the sweet scent of something delicious drew her attention and she sniffed at the air like an animal. Whatever it was seemed to be coming from the direction of where the children were huddling. Her stomach constricted and growled, and she suddenly felt famished as if she hadn't eaten in days. The cramping in her stomach became so intense that she doubled over, dropping Fuyuko, her face screwing up with pain.

This time it was Kat's turn to help her, and she did her best to keep the swooning woman steady. Sophia leaned heavily on the little vampire, who strained under the larger girl's weight.

"What is happening to me?" she groaned.

"You have been chosen," replied Fuyuko, massaging her throat.

"I have been what?" she slurred.

"Chosen by Mother to be her vessel. It is a great honor. At least so Vlad believes. I am not so sure yet. Though I will admit you are already stronger than you should be at this point in the change."

Was she talking about the voice from the locket? Is that who had been calling to her? She vaguely recalled Vlad mentioning that what remained of their mother's essence had been in the locket. Something about only having enough for one more attempt. It was all very fuzzy, but some of it was starting to come back to her.

A voice called to her from deep within her mind. It was muffled at first and indistinguishable, but it slowly grew in strength until it rang clear in her consciousness. It was the voice from the locket, and it was singing to her. Her own heart instantly responded to the enchanting melody by nearly beating out of her chest. Blinking and stiffening, she looked around for the singer.

"Hello?" she called, looking around the room. "Where are you? I hear you singing, but I don't know what you're saying."

Kat stared at her, worried. The little vampire followed her gaze but saw nothing out of the ordinary. There were no strange scents in the air, nor did she hear anything unusual.

"Who are you talking to?" she asked, her brow scrunched in confusion.

Famine

Fuyuko suddenly stepped close and grabbed Sophia's face, turning her head so they were face to face. Sophia did not pull away but allowed her to peer deeply into her eyes. Fuyuko watched Sophia's dark green irises began to bleed red until both her eyes—sclera and all—were the color of blood. She gasped, flinching as the pupils also shifted from normal to something more akin to a cat's.

"Shinjirarenai," she breathed, one hand covering her mouth reflexively.

Kat's gaze flipped back and forth between the two, completely baffled. What had she seen that had startled her so completely, and who was singing?

"Hai, kodomo, soreha watashidesu," Sophia responded instinctively, shaking her head in confusion.

The crippling pain in her abdomen was beginning to subside, and she was starting to feel more like herself. The smell from the children, however, still pulled at her senses, making her stomach growl. She did her best to ignore it, but it took all her will not to go looking for the source of the scent.

Fuyuko's ice blue eyes grew to the size of saucers, her mouth agape, before dropping to her knees and pressing her face to the floor, arms outstretched toward Sophia.

"Did I just speak Japanese?" she asked, bewildered. "And why is she bowing to me now?"

Kat shook her head, shrugged, and then turned to look at Sophia. The moment their eyes met, she gasped and took an involuntary step backward.

"What's the matter?" Sophia asked, stepping toward her and reaching out to her.

"Don't touch me!" she exclaimed, shying back even farther and glaring warily at the outstretched hand like it was a viper that might bite her at any moment.

"She is afraid of us, though she has no reason to be," replied a female voice.

This time she actually spun in place, searching for the speaker. Kat backed away even farther as her eyes darted angrily around the room.

"Who are you?" she demanded.

"I am Kadejah," it replied.

"Kadejah?"

At the mention of that name, Fuyuko let out an excited stream of what sounded like exultated praises in Japanese. Kat continued to look puzzled, and Sophia couldn't blame her. She was just as confused as the little vampire.

"Are you who was calling to me from the locket?" she asked out loud.

"I am."

The sounds of explosions and shouting drew her attention, and she turned towards the door that led outside. Amazingly she could hear men coming, their voices as clear as if they were in the room with her. She also smelled them, and again her stomach growled and cramped hungrily.

Fuyuko rose to her feet and reverently approached Sophia. Her expression was grave, and she glanced nervously in the direction of the door.

"We need to leave before they discover us."

Kat also seemed nervous, and she let out a little growl and slowly backed away from the entryway. She understood why they were worried, since she could hear the soldiers moving around directly outside the door. Even though Kat was different from the other vampires, she highly doubted the soldiers would care.

"Do not worry, daughter, I will deal with them," spoke Kasdeja in her mind, the danger in her voice sending shivers up her spine.

She had a feeling that protecting her meant using her body the same way she had when Sophia had killed the wendigo. The sensation that flooded into her mind was one of affirmation.

Great, she can read my mind as well as use my body.

"Get behind me," she said to Kat, who hurried to her.

She quickly moved the girl behind her, one arm shielding her protectively. The White Lady came and stood next to her, fingertips glowing and ice forming at her feet. She had no idea why she felt the way she did, but something inside her told her the men coming were enemies. Not just to her, but to her children as well.

That thought made her pause. She didn't have any children. Was she sensing what Kasdeja was feeling? The fierce maternal instinct to protect both vampires was overwhelming. It was an entirely foreign sensation to her, and yet somehow completely natural, as if she had always been a mother.

With a crash the door exploded inward, throwing shards of metal and debris flying in all directions. The children screamed and her ears rang as smoke filled the room. Guns firing, the soldiers stormed into the chamber, the light from their helmets reflecting off the smoke and obscuring their exact locations.

Her hearing temporarily stunned from the noise of the explosion, the sound of her own screaming was muted as if she were submerged in water. She had no memory of lifting her hands, but they were outstretched in front of her a brilliant shield of shimmering transparent light extending from them, intercepting any bullet that flew near the three of them.

The gunfire ceased as the men moved swiftly into the room, their rifles swinging in all directions, hunting for threats. There were about ten of them and they gradually became visible through the dissipating smoke, drawing closer by the second. The lead man gestured with one arm and the group fanned out from the doorway in two staggered rows.

They didn't move far before they spotted them and the lead man yelled, "Contact!"

Kat stepped quickly out from behind her, waving her hands at the soldiers and attempting to warn them of the children in the room. Even the White Lady seemed to be genuinely concerned for their safety and dashed forward, her own hands up in surrender, shouting for them to stop. The soldiers trained their rifles on the two of them and Sophia's heart sank as she realized that both of them and possibly the children were going to die, and there was nothing she could do to stop it.

"Yes," purred the voice in her head. "But I can. All you need do is take my hand."

Something deep inside her screamed in protest. It was a primal instinctual warning that rose up from her very soul. Her human soul that she now realized was on the verge of death. Deep down she understood that if she accepted the creature's offer she would be forfeiting her humanity. But if she didn't, Kat and the children would die.

Gnashing her teeth in frustration, she watched helplessly as the soldiers took aim and fired. Intense feelings of anxiety and urgency flooded her mind as the thing inside her cried out for her children. They were all going to die if she didn't do something.

It frantically begged and pleaded with her, and with tears streaming down her face she heard herself shout, "No!"

Power like nothing she had ever experienced flowed through her body and the world slowed to a crawl. Ancient and otherworldly, it felt wrong and yet right at the same time, burning so hot within her she was sure she would spontaneously combust. The floor at her feet melted and cracked as visible tongues of fire erupted about her.

Raising one arm she stretched out her fingers and energy burst from them, disintegrating the bullets in midflight. It continued forward, slamming into the soldiers, tearing a swath of destruction through the center of their ranks, incinerating all it touched. They screamed and died, and she laughed.

Time snapped back into rhythm, and she moved forward, her hand still outstretched, her eyes burning as hot as the ground at her feet. Insects. How dare they threaten her children? Their fear smelled delicious and so did their blood. Sadly, she had burned some of them and their plasma would be useless to her. No matter, unlike the lesser of her children she could simply consume their life force directly. It was, after all, a more elegant way to feed and a lot less messy.

Her mouth watering and a wild, feral grin stretching across her face, she suddenly closed her fist, turned her hand, and pulled it backward as if she was tugging an invisible thread. The pathetic creatures didn't scream or thrash about but simply dropped to the ground as she tore out their life energy.

Eyes wide she shuddered with pleasure as it flowed into her, filling her like some kind of twisted battery. The pain in her stomach instantly ceased, as did the insistent overwhelming hunger. She flexed her hands, feeling the strength flowing into them, and she knew she could tear a grown man apart if she chose to. This was the raw unadulterated power of human life. The power that only a god could wield, and it was now hers.

Throwing her head back, she laughed a deep hearty laugh and then turned to survey her handiwork. The dead soldiers lay in twisted heaps where they had fallen, their weapons scattered about them. Their skin was gray, emaciated, and hanging of their bones like corpses that have been out in the sun for too long. Even their eyes had withered, shrinking until they nearly disappeared into their sockets.

"Sophia, are you okay?" Kat asked pulling on her arm, her eyes filled with concern.

Was she Sophia anymore?

Blinking, she lifted her hands and examined them. She had murdered those soldiers with only a gesture. The old her couldn't do things like that.

Famine

"You are no longer human, but you are still you," said Kadejah in her mind, in answer to her unspoken questions.

Hearing another person's voice in her head was disconcerting to say the least, and she grimaced. Nodding, she turned and forced a smile.

"I'm fine. Are you or the other children hurt?"

Kat furrowed her brow and looked at her with an expression that clearly said she didn't believe her. She nodded and then looked at the dead soldiers, and Sophia was surprised to find that the little vampire was neither horrified nor shocked by the carnage. If anything, her expression was one of indifference. In truth, Sophia felt the same. Where she should be revolted by her actions, she felt nothing.

"Why should she care about them?" asked Kasdeja. "They would have murdered her, Fuyuko, and even the children without a second thought. You were right to do what you did."

"Was I?"

Somewhere in her mind her conscience objected, but the feelings that usually accompanied it were nothing more than echoes of a human soul that was rapidly fading.

"Do you think yourself a monster for what you did? Do we not have just as much right to defend ourselves as these humans? They chose aggression even after we tried to warn them of the children. So, who is the monster here? We who acted in defense of ourselves and the innocent, or those men who chose malicious violence."

It made sense, and she found herself nodding reflexively. These men, no matter their intentions, would have murdered them all if she hadn't acted. Maybe she wasn't a monster, but she certainly wasn't human any longer. As soon as she had embraced Kasdeja her humanity died, and she had become something else. She could blame the thing inside her for her actions, but deep down she knew the truth. She alone had chosen to kill those men.

Turning to look at her two children, she smiled comfortingly. Kat had been more than a friend to her and, even though there was still a part of her that hated Fuyuko, she understood her now. Plus, what mother could hate her own child?

"I think it is time we leave," she said, stepping through the corpses scattered in front of them. "Don't worry about the children, they will be okay."

All three of them walked to the door and out into the darkness. Being the last to exit, she paused and turned ever so slightly, looking back. Her heart ached inside for her old life. For her cousin who she was sure was in there somewhere, attempting to rescue her, but she was already too late. Her cousin Sophia was dead and wouldn't be coming home again.

Her face set and a strange feeling of excitement in her heart, she turned and followed the others into the shadows, leaving everything she had ever known behind.

Dana came to just as Steven flew past, black smoke leaking from his wounds instead of blood. His shadow tendrils lashed at Jared as he burst into view and were intercepted by a fiercely glowing Tzedakah. Like an octopus he jammed two tendrils into the ground, bracing himself while simultaneously launching a flurry of strikes with the others. They whipped about, snapping at Jared from all sides, searching for a way through his defenses. Even though he countered each one, the constant barrage managed to hold him at bay, driving him back slightly.

Both men attacked and defended with supernatural speed and Dana couldn't follow their movements. The wind was slowing as Jared pushed more and more of his concentration into battling his brother, who managed to hold his own even landing a few near hits. Everything caught in the storm began to crash around them like meteors as the wind finally dissipated entirely.

Something fell only a few feet from her and she jerked instinctually, sending pain shooting through her body. Heart pounding, her eyes blurry with tears, she saw it was the body of a soldier, his eyes wide and fixed, mouth open in a silent scream. He lay unmoving, his death stare seemingly focused on her. She stared in horror at the man, unable to tear her gaze away as the sounds of debris and bodies hitting the floor echoed throughout the room.

When she was finally able to pull her eyes away from the corpse, she searched the carnage for any signs of life. She breathed a sigh of relief when she spotted Jeremy, still sitting with his back against the wall, the medic still by his side. Both seemed worse for wear but alive. Johanson was nowhere in sight but his entire strike force littered the room, either groaning in pain or unmoving, and she doubted he was far. A few vampires still lived, but they didn't dare move from their hiding places for fear of being discovered by the nightmare slaughtering their kin.

The Musketeer's attention was completely focused on the fight, so he didn't seem to notice her as she slowly began dragging herself toward Jeremy. The pain was unbearable, and she nearly lost consciousness a few times as she inched toward him. Her eyes kept drifting to Jared. How had he survived, and why hadn't he contacted her to let her know he was still alive?

Certainly, her hazy memory of him standing over her had been true and not a dream. His very real presence here was proof of that, but why had he stayed away? After all they had been through, how could he simply abandon her like that? How could he allow her to believe he was dead? Did he have any idea what that had done to her? Did he even care?

Suddenly one of Steven's shadow tendrils smacked the floor next to her, forcing her into a sideways roll. Narrowly avoiding being struck, she was forced to evade two more times before she finally made it safely out of range of the battling titans. Grimacing in agony, her vision blurring, she willed herself forward. She was only a few feet from where Jeremy sat when the medic noticed her. He instantly jumped into action, rushing to her side and dragging her the rest of the way.

Breathing heavily, her eyes pressed tight with pain, the man gently rested her next to Jeremy. She knew it was him by the subtle scent of spearmint, and she couldn't help but smile. Her head dropped to rest on his shoulder as the medic gingerly examined her wound. She relaxed as she felt his arm settling around her. For better or worse, they were in this together. Jared may have abandoned her, but Jeremy hadn't, and that meant something to her. Even though he had kept the fact he knew Jared was alive from her.

"Ow," he groaned. "If I had known Renault was going to try and disembowel me again, I would have left you on that hospital floor."

She rubbed her head against his shoulder. Even his constant grumbling was endearing and comforting for some reason. She winced as Flatline pressed something tender, and Jeremy tightened his hold slightly.

"Hey, butter fingers, be careful," he scolded. "Can't you see she has a bowling ball size hole in her gut? Did you learn medicine from a cereal box or something?"

Flatline grunted but ignored him and continued dressing her wound.

The battle still raged in front of them, neither monster able to get the upper hand. If the Musketeer had noticed her escape, he didn't let on. From what she had seen of the man, she was sure he had simply let her go. He had gotten what he wanted and had no more use for her.

"Wait," she said suddenly, her eyes never leaving the battle. "Again?"

"Why do you think I was in the hospital? I certainly wasn't there for my health. That bastard broke, like, fifty of my ribs."

"You only have twenty-four," she chided.

"Yeah, and he broke most of them. Stupid Angel, stupid Justice, and stupid woman. I should have just stayed in the city."

She chuckled at that and instantly regretted it. His expression changed from grumpy to one of concern as she tensed in pain.

"You all right?"

Grimacing, she nodded.

"I'll live...hopefully."

"You will," chimed in Flatline. "His cut wasn't meant to be lethal. It looks like he intentionally focused on causing pain instead of killing. I've stopped the bleeding, so you're out of the woods for now, though I need to get you to a hospital ASAP."

"Like I said before, he's a bastard. A pretty much unkillable one, but a definite bastard."

Famine

What did he mean when he said angel, what was a Justice, and how could the Frenchman be unkillable? No one was unkillable, though she had to admit that her reality was currently being shaken and maybe unkillable wasn't such a far-fetched concept anymore. Just look at Jared. He had absolutely died in her arms and yet here he was very much alive. Even what she knew about death was being turned on its head.

"Look out!" Jeremy shouted.

Her insides felt like they were going to become her outsides as she was suddenly pulled to the side, Jeremy rolling on top of her. Something hit the wall directly where she had been sitting. It took her a minute to free herself from under Jermey and she stared in horror at the unconscious form of Steven, who lay unmoving below a dent in the wall. One of his arms was bent unnaturally, faint wisps of black smoke hovering in the air around him.

"Well done," the Musketeer cackled, applauding and drawing Jared's attention.

Jared turned his dark eyes towards him, his face a mask of calm. He raised Tzedakah and pointed it threateningly at him. It flared brightly, and the Musketeer's own sword flared in response. He drew the glowing weapon from its scabbard and dropped into a one-handed defensive stance, the other hand up and the tip of his blade pointing at Jared. The room was once again filled with palpable dread as the two blades reacted to each other. They were like fire and ice, or two magnets with reverse polarities.

"I told you I would kill you," Jared said, his voice low and menacing.

"Did you now," replied the Musketeer, showing his teeth. "Now that you mention it, I do seem to recall you saying something like that. To be honest, I only pay attention to things that are important and, *mon ami*, your pathetic threats are not."

"You are a murderer and a monster, and your time has come," Jared replied evenly, not seeming to be affected at all by the Frenchman's jab.

One of the Musketeer's eyebrows shot up.

"*I* am a monster? Look around you, *mon ami*. Did I kill all of these men? Men who were only guilty of coming here to rescue children. Tell me, did they deserve to be slaughtered so mercilessly?"

Jared glanced around, his calm expression cracking slightly. Had he murdered these men? Shaking his head he grit his teeth, his sword arm dropping slightly. Was he a monster? Tzedakah flared brightly, drawing his attention. The consciousness of the sentient sword flooded into his mind, calming him and bringing with it clarity. They were Justice itself, and all of their actions were just. They were not monsters; everyone and everything else was.

"No," he replied confidently, his eyes returning to the Musketeer. "These men deserved to die. They were all unjust and guilty. Maybe not as guilty as you, but guilty nevertheless."

"Truly? Guilty of angering you perhaps, but nothing more. Look, even your beloved Dana thinks you are a monster," he observed, pointing toward her and Jeremy. "She is so terrified of you that she has run into the arms of another man just to get away from you."

Famine

He slowly turned his head, his black eyes writhing, his dark gaze seeing all. It fell on them both, Jeremy still lying protectively atop Dana—his feelings for her burning brightly, evident to the dark gaze. It revealed all. Nothing could hide from it, not even the potential feelings Dana likewise had for Jeremy. They glowed softly in her heart, a budding flame just beginning to burn, still uncertain.

Anger so hot it felt like it would incinerate the entire world welled up from within him and just like before the world dissolved around him. His entire universe collapsed into a singular point as both his and Tzedakah's hearts shattered at the revelation. Gone was any semblance of reason. Even Tzedakah, a creature made to be cold and fair, was being enveloped in the swirling mass of emotions.

How could they do this to them? How could they both betray them like this? They loved her and she was in the arms of another man. Not just a man, but a friend. A friend they had trusted. It was unthinkable. It was unjust. Tzedakah had little experience with such strong emotions. And his inability to cope with them affected Jared, whose own strong feelings mixed with the sentient sword's, overwhelming them both.

The very universe seemed to be cracking around him as he slowly started walking towards them. Forgotten were the Musketeer and Steven. Forgotten were the vampires and their machinations. None of them mattered. All that mattered was the crippling pain. All that mattered was their betrayal, and they were going to make them all pay for what they had done to them.

JW Kiefer

Flatline attempted to intercept them, but was sent flying with a wave of their hand. The crack from the big man hitting the far wall resounded ominously as Jared continued his approach undaunted. They had not intended to kill the man, but he was in the way and had to be removed. No matter, his life was insignificant.

Jeremy slowly pushed himself up and stood unsteadily, putting himself between Dana and the oncoming Jared. His mouth moved as he attempted to reason with him, but Jared couldn't hear him. He was too lost, and nothing Jeremy could say was going to bring him back from the depth of his despair. He raised Tzedakah and the sword flew toward Jeremy, who closed his eyes and winced but stood his ground.

The darkness of the void was absolute. Curled into a fetal position, he seemed to spin aimlessly through the blackness. There was no light, no life, and no hope. Everything that ever was and ever would be had simply ceased to exist. Everything but the void, which closed in around him like a vise, smothering any remaining vestiges of self. Even the sentient sword was gone, his ever-present consciousness stripped from him.

No, not everything. The pain of loss and the anger remained. It continued burning in his chest unchecked, like a forest fire. A raging inferno that charred and consumed his heart. What had he done to deserve such heartbreak and pain? Had he not tried to be a good person? Had he not chosen a profession that served his fellow man? So why had this happened to him?

He didn't deserve it. Didn't deserve to die like he had, didn't deserve to lose the love of his life just when he had found her, and he certainly didn't deserve to be brought back by Tzedakah to be used as a tool for his crusade. It was unfair. It was unjust.

The darkness, seeming to sense his despair, closed even tighter about him. This was the void. This was the outer darkness, and it existed to destroy such emotions. All who came here ceased to be. This was the place between. The place of nonexistence. No love, no hate, no pain, no feelings at all, just the nothingness of the void. Even the seemingly empty vast space between galaxies had substance, but not the void. It clung to him, eating away at his soul, threatening to consume everything until nothing of who he was or would be remained.

Closing his eyes, he gave into it. It was simpler this way. Why had he fought against it so frantically? Why had it terrified him? He was, after all, already dead. Isn't this what he had wanted? The gentle sleep of death and the sweet serenity that came with the end of his mortal life. He could let go of the pain, let go of the rage, let go of the life he was desperately clinging to. Let Tzedakah use his body as an instrument of Justice. He no longer cared.

He felt the satisfaction in the void as he welcomed its embrace, accepting its promised oblivion. But before he could close his eyes forever, a light so bright it threatened to sear itself into his retinas burst into the void. Holding one arm up to shield his face from the dazzling illumination, he squinted into it and gasped.

A man, burning with the intensity of the sun, slowly walked toward him. All that was visible through the brightness was a silhouette, but somehow, he knew it was a

Famine

man. As he advanced Jared realized with a start that the light didn't emanate from him, but it was him. He *was* light, and all of the visible light in the physical universe was merely an echo of him. Nothing but an imitation of the real thing.

It was beautiful and warm, and stirred in him every good and pleasant emotion he had ever experienced. Memories of his parents, his childhood, his brother, his sister, the first time he had hit a homerun, the first time he had fallen in love, the first time he had felt the presence of God— all of those feelings were but echoes of the joy he now felt, and the intensity from it brought tears to his eyes.

The void shrank away as the being approached. No, not shrank away but bowed in submission, as if this man was its master. Jared could feel the disappointment of it, its tendrils reaching out for him like a child testing its limits.

"No," commanded the man, and his word was law.

Not like the unstable rules of man, but the voice of one who defined the very fundamental guidelines that made up the universe. It was melodic and lovely, yet thunderous and terrible at the same time. It was absolute power, unquestioned authority, and yet tender and filled with love and mercy. And when this man breathed but a word all creation obeyed, even the void.

The man turned his gaze to Jared, kindling in him a mixture of both hope and terror. Here was a being so far beyond him that the word 'fear' could not describe what he could do if he chose, and yet he knew he was not here to hurt him.

"Son," said the man, and he instantly knew it to be the same voice that had brought him back from the brink of despair before. "Let go. All will be well. I promise."

With those words a dam broke in his soul, and his personality came flooding back. Not just the Jared he had been, but the person he was becoming. There was still pain, but it no longer consumed him. Somehow the man's words had snuffed it out like water smothering a flame. Even his very spirit could not defy this man's words. It was not a matter of whether he believed him or not, his words were simply truth.

Reaching out, he touched Jared's shoulder. And the physical world instantly exploded around him, replacing the void. It all transpired in the span of a heartbeat and before he knew what had happened, he found himself staring into the wide eyes of Jeremy.

His friend shut his eyes, screwed up his features, and turned his head away in anticipation of the blow he knew was coming. The tip of his sword was only an inch from his friend's throat, the blue-black glow from Tzedakah reflecting brightly off his olive skin. Everything seemed to be moving in slow motion, and it felt as if he was watching himself from somewhere outside his body.

"No," ordered the voice from the void and he immediately froze in place the momentum of his thrust aborted.

"That was disappointing," the Frenchman grumbled, not aware of the being that had intervened. "I guess I will just have to kill them myself. Maybe then you will finally shatter the bonds that bind you. Either way it will be more fun for me in the end."

Drawing his rapier, he lunged forward, but before his blade could contact Jeremy a brilliant light exploded directly in his path throwing him backward. He flipped in midair and landed on his feet like a cat his rapier up in a defensive position. As the light waned enough for him to see it revealed standing next to Jared the translucent silhouette of a man. His arm was stretched outward palm up as if it were shielding them.

With a wave of his hand the entity literally stopped time, and the world simply froze in place. Nothing moved save the Musketeer and the entity of light. It had removed him from time and space separating him from the others so it could deal with him unhindered.

"You," he growled a slight tremor in his voice. "You have no right to interfere."

At his accusation power erupted from the being in the form of immense pressure. Unable to withstand it the Musketeer fell to one knee gritting his teeth as he attempted to defy the being. He threw every bit of his will at the unyielding strength and nearly got back to his feet before his legs buckled and he was forcefully driven face first to the ground.

Completely immobilized, he glared hatefully up at the Lord of Light. Just like Tzedakah, the blade he bore was more than just a weapon. It was a living representation of a force of nature and there were only a few powers in the universe that could oppose it and this being was the most powerful of them all.

JW Kiefer

Knowing he could not defeat him he gave up struggling and chose a different approach.

"I know you will not destroy me." He stated. "Your own rules will not allow it."

The pressure increased in response, but the Musketeer's conviction didn't waver. The rules were clear and no matter how intense the threat, the Lord of Light would not go against the rules.

"But I wonder," he continued though his voice cracked from the force being exerted on him. "How long it will be before he realizes exactly what it is you have done to him. Before he realizes just how great the price is you are asking him to pay. How do you think he will respond when he finds out?"

No response, though the Musketeer thought he could sense the slightest hint of uncertainty from him. Showing his teeth, he sneered.

"One thing I do know for certain, is that when that time comes, I will be waiting."

"Begone," was all the Lord of Light said in response and both the Musketeer and Steven simply disappeared.

Like someone snapping their fingers, time reasserted itself and the sounds of groaning men and the wails of the dying once again echoed throughout the room. To everyone else in the universe it felt like a mere blip in the matrix. A slight moment of disorientation and then all was normal again. No one would ever know what had happened to both Steven and the Musketeer, their memories would forever be clouded on the issue.

Famine

Disoriented from being thrust back into this reality Jared was confused and the events that had just unfolded were cloudy and vague. Everything was hazy and surreal as if he were waking from a dream. He knew he had done terrible things but couldn't completely recall them. It was like trying to remember a memory from childhood that had faded and was now nothing more than an echo.

When the expected pain didn't come, Jeremy tentatively opened one eye, all color draining from his face as he saw how close the tip was to his flesh. One more millimeter and he would have been toast. He let out a slow steady breath releasing the built-up tension, but didn't dare move for fear it might set Jared off again. He had no idea what had stopped him, but he didn't want to jinx it.

"Jared," asked Dana, her voice quivering slightly.

He blinked at the sound of her voice, his eyes searching for her. Her arms limp at her side she sat with her back against the wall. Stepping away from a visibly relieved Jeremy he lowered Tzedakah and took a step towards her, but stopped as she flinched, her eyes widening in fear.

Shame hit him hard in the gut as he realized what he had almost done. How could he have even thought of hurting her. If the powerful entity from the void had not chosen to intervene, he very likely would have at least killed Jeremy. Even the sentient sword was unusually subdued and penitent as if it too shared his sentiments.

"Dana," he stuttered, but the words died in his mouth.

What could he say that would make it all better. How could he even begin to explain what had and was happening to him. He didn't understand it himself. He certainly

JW Kiefer

couldn't justify the carnage he had just wrought or what he had almost done to her. Looking into her earnest but fearful eyes he realized at that moment that his presence was hurting her.

She had watched him die and somehow, he was here in front of her, but not the man she had loved; something else. A frightening monster from the shadows that she could never love. He searched her eyes and saw hope there and yet uncertainty and he knew he had to let her go. It would break her heart all over again and he hated himself for it, but being with him would only prolong the inevitable. This realization severed the one remaining strand keeping him tied to his old life, and it broke something deep within him. Stiffening, he slowly turned and started deliberately walking away.

Tears flowing from her eyes she reached a hand towards him.

"Jared wait," she called her voice pleading. "Please."

Ignoring her, he fixed his gaze. It took every ounce of strength both he and Tzedakah had to not turn back but he knew they had to let her go. No matter how much it hurt, they had to. Even if it left a scar on her heart that might never heal.

Unsure of what the future held and with a sense of finality, he lifted the sentient sword, it flared brightly and then they were gone.

Epilogue

Dana watched placidly as the children were attended to. Her body felt like it had been through a grinder, and she was exhausted. Jeremy had already been taken to a hospital and as she waited for her turn she watched the emergency medical teams move from child-to-child checking for injuries while social workers took down names and information. Hopefully they will be able to locate the families and have these children back home soon. Of course, none of them would ever be the same. It was impossible for anyone to go through what they had and come away unscathed.

Thankfully, none of them were injured to badly. Most suffering from varying levels of malnutrition and dehydration, only a few needing more intensive medical treatment due to injuries. All in all, it was a good day for the authorities. If her search for her cousin hadn't led her here, then who knows if these children would have survived.

Hugging herself, she shook away the dark thoughts turning to look at the five small black bundles laying across from where she sat. Sadly, she hadn't been in time to save all of them. According to the coroner these children had died sometime in the last day or so. All being killed by exsanguination. It was a small mercy that she hadn't been the one to find the bodies, but she doubted she would ever forgive herself for not getting here in time.

Grimacing, her thoughts drifting to her cousin. Where was she? All of the evidence led here. and yet they hadn't found her. She must have been here. Tears forming at the corners of her eyes she clenched her fist. What if theses monsters had killed her or worse.

"Damn. Damin it to all fucking hell."

The tears came freely now, and she drew her knees up to her chest and hugged them ignoring the pain. Not only had she been too late to save some of the children, but she had failed her cousin. Suddenly overwhelmed she rocked back and forth occasionally wiping away the tears staining her cheeks. The realization that Jared was alive, her suspension from the force, her strange uncertain feelings for Jeremy, not to mention the fact vampires were real and now this. She would have to tell her family that she failed to find Sophia. As soon as she had finally stopped moving, it had all come crashing down on her like an anvil.

Could she ever go back to her old life? Did she even want to? Everything that had happened over the last few days had shaken her faith in everything she held dear. All of the institutions she had trusted in had failed her. Even her own captain and police department had let her down. Everyone, that is but Johanson. Well and Jeremy but that was a whole other can of worms needing to be unpacked.

"Hey," said a deep male voice drawing her attention.

Famine

Wiping away the tears and sniffing she looked up to see Johanson walking toward her.

"You, ok?"

Nodding she couldn't help but glance at the tiny body bags again. His own gaze straying to them his lips pressing into a thin line.

"Even though we rescued a lot of children today," she said her eyes never leaving the bodies. "It still somehow seems hollow."

He grimaced and nodded.

"Makes you angry, doesn't it?"

Her brow furrowing, she turned to look up at him.

Yeah, she was angry. Furious in fact.

Not only had the system failed her cousin, but it had failed these children and their families as well. In fact, not only had they failed them, but she was pretty certain they had been directly involved somehow. If not through their own actions, through their inactions.

What was the saying? All it took for evil to prevail was for good man to do nothing. She was never one to buy into the conspiracy theories having dedicated her life to law enforcement, but now everything had changed. Not only had the institutions failed, but they actively got in the way.

All of the events of the last few days flashed through her mind. So much death. So much hurt. It seemed to her like all of the light in the world was quickly being swallowed up by the darkness and no one was able to stop it. It enraged her. If it were up to her, she would kill every single monster in this world. Bring every one of these bastards to justice.

"It does," she said turning to look up at him.

JW Kiefer

The corners of his mouth rising slightly, he bent down and looked her directly in her eyes.

"You want to do something about it?"

Famine

JW Kiefer

Excerpt from The Complete Compendium of Supernatural Entities, Their History and How to Combat Them

By Professor Serafim Athanasiou

Concerning Vampires

To talk about vampires, we must first mention that they are in fact a class of Nephilim. As you know, all paranormal entities and supernatural creatures can be traced back to the spiritual realm or spiritual dimension.

To call it a dimension is a misnomer, since it is not a separate reality from our own, but rather a joined universe that interweaves with ours. It is not visible to the physical eyes, but it can interact and affect it. Likewise, the physical can interact with the spiritual and was designed to do so.

There are laws that govern this interaction, and they have been created and instilled by YHWY. Only He can change them or supersede them, though He seldom does. Nephilim are a result of the unnatural interaction of both the spiritual and the physical since they are the children of both humans and angel. These beings were destroyed and hunted to near extinction after the flood, but their spirits still wander the earth as demons or other supernatural entities.

As I mentioned earlier, inside most humans are traces of this Nephilim DNA. Science has mistakenly designated it neanderthal or caveman DNA, but the learned know that

575

Famine

it is the taint of Mount Herman. If enough of this DNA is present in a human host, it can be activated by dark powers causing the human to literally change at the cellular level into something that is no longer human. As far as we understand, vampires like other such creatures are created in this manner.

"After having dispatched the mother who had slain and fed on her entire family, little ones and all, we waited and observed the bodies anticipating their unholy resurrection. Alas, none of them reanimated but remained very much dead."

Monsignor David Falkirk, 1654 Exter England

Who can become a vampire?

This is something that is not completely understood by the learned, but the accepted belief is that, if a vampire bites a person and that human has enough Nephilim DNA in their blood, then it will start the rewriting process causing the human to literally die to its old self and become something new.

We do not completely understand all of the mechanics that are involved in the change, but one thing we do know is that not all humans transform when bitten. Unlike the portrayals of modern pop culture, a vampire cannot chose who to bestow the dark gift upon. It is completely determined by how much latent DNA resides in the victim. From all of our gathered information we can deduce that vampires do however have the ability to sense those who are prone to the change.

When bitten, a type of venom is injected into the victim causing euphoria, pain, or terror depending on the type. This toxin appears to provide the necessary material to start the altering process being a sort of catalyst for vampirization. It seems a person who is bitten with either no unnatural DNA or not enough, will not turn. They will not necessarily die, but in some cases will be killed by the venom. Usually, however, they simply become a food source for the vampire being kept alive until their bodies give out and they pass away.

One question that has arisen and been debated at nauseum, is whether or not prolonged exposure to Nephelium or watcher spirits can activate the change or if a bite is required. Since we still do not completely understand what facilitates the change in humans, it is still uncertain, but it is reasonable to assume that like other monsters in their class, they too can be created in this fashion.

"While following the blood trail of a deer I had wounded, I came across a naked woman of exceptional beauty. I was dismayed to find such a vision of loveliness so far out in the forest, and I surmised she must be one of the Fae. Before I knew what I was doing, I found myself in her arms. I could not help myself even though I was married, and we made love among the trees of the forest. The euphoria I experienced was beyond any mortal sexual encounter, and after what seemed like hours she vanished leaving me alone once again. Drained of all vitality I somehow stumbled back to my home only to be met with exclamations of alarm as I appeared to have aged ten years in those few hours."

Stanislav Maersluft, 1572 Holy Roman Empire Germania

Famine
Do all Vampires Drink Blood?

No. Some syphon life force in other ways. Some feed through touch or sexual contact, while others feed on the human soul, attempting to break it through trauma or sexual immorality. They then feed on the shards and find sustenance from the brokenness.

All vampires, however, require some form of lifeforce to live and maintain their power. The more life force they consume, the more powerful they become. A hunger that is overwhelming and never satisfied is a defining trait of all vampires which are a class of Nephilim attributed to the Watcher Kasdeja or "Famine".

Are Vampires Undead?

No. Though some live on as specters and are still very dangerous even after their physical body is destroyed.

Which Watcher is the father of Vampires?

Kasdeja is the mother of vampires. Yes, unlike the other Watchers she is a female spirit. Since all angels are in a sense neither male or female as other mortal beings are, she appears as a female and tends to mate with men.

Kasdeja's body was destroyed in the last battle between men and Nephilim, and her spirit is imprisoned and is waiting for her children to release her. They have a vial of her blood and all that is needed is one drop introduced into a worthy offering in order to draw her spirit to it. Since she is a spirit, she requires a human body to inhabit in order to return. The person must have the right type and amount of DNA for this to work. She will rewrite the persons DNA taking over their being eventually destroying them in the process and remaking them into an exact replica of her original self.

The vampires and the other children of Kasdeja have been looking for a suitable offering for thousands of years but all attempts at reviving her have failed. Their supply of blood is growing thin causing them to be more careful in their attempts. This has meant that a lot of them have given up on bringing her back, while others continue their hope that she will return. We should all pray that they continue to fail, for if they succeed much death and misery will follow.

Types of Vampires

Strigoi: These are the classical vampires from European lore and the kind most people think of when they mention Vampires. They look like humans and have long fangs that they use to bite their victims injecting their venom and draining their blood.

Like most Nephilim they have enhanced strength, senses, durability, healing abilities and have thermal vision. They will burn in sunlight and can be hurt or weakened by objects of faith. Essentially immortal, they will live as long as they have blood to drink and never age, though they become more corpse like the longer they go without blood and can die of starvation.

These are the most common form of vampire encountered. They are also susceptible to fire and extreme heat, but make no mistake, they do not die easily.

Revenant: Similar to the strigoi revenants retain their human features. More giant like, they tend to be between 7 to 8 feet tall but can be larger. Their muscles and bones are denser, and they have greater strength and durability than the lesser strigoi.

They have the same abilities as their lessor kin while also having the ability to hypnotize, turn into shadow or mist, fly, enhanced speed, use magic, use psychic attacks, control lesser minds and syphon life force through touch.

They cannot be burned by sunlight, though it does weaken them and most tend to avoid the day preferring to be active at night. Like all vampire species, they can be debilitated or driven away by holy relics, though the person's will and faith must be greater than the vampire they are facing.

The legendary myth of Dracula is about a revenant, though it is unknown if he actually existed. Immortal and nearly impossible to kill, they tend to be the rulers of the vampire world. The older they become, the more powerful they grow. Thankfully, there are very few Revenants recorded and generally only one or two are known to be created every few generations. They are immune to all elements and cannot be harmed by fire or cold.

Rokurokubi: These are vampires that are generally found in Asia because they settled in that region after the flood. It is unknown if living isolated from the European vampires caused their different evolution, but they have slightly different powers from their European counterparts.

Like their European cousins they also appear human, but they have the ability to extend their necks like a snake. When they do they transform reptilian and can use their long necks to crush, strangle or assault their prey like a python. Likewise, they also have enhanced strength, senses, durability, speed, reflexes, can hypnotize, use psychic attacks, control lesser minds, and have the ability to heal and regenerate wounds.

Like most vampires they drink blood but can syphon energy through their elongated necks and drain prey in their grip of their life force. Like the revenant, they can go out in the sun but are even more debilitated by its light than their cousins. Holy objects and faith repel and weaken them, and they tend to avoid churches.

A select few can also control cold and minor weather creating gales of frigid wind and freezing temperatures. They are immune to cold but are very susceptible to fire and extreme heat.

Draugar: Generally found in Scandinavia, these vampires are different from their European and Asian cousins. Giants that generally stand over seven feet tall, they are strong and durable. Monstrous and massive, their skin is either pale white or ash black. Unlike the others, they don't just drink blood but will eat the flesh of their victims.

People who transform into a draugar appear to die while undergoing the metamorphosis and are usually buried only to rise up a few days later. Constantly smelling of death and decay they tend to return to their graves to sleep during the day. This gave rise to the legend of warriors returning from their grave to become undead fiends that terrorize humanity.

Having enhanced strength, durability, healing abilities, eyesight, and speed, they are generally warriors and enforcers for others of their kind. More giant than human, they cannot blend into normal society and generally hide in caves or forests only encountering humans when hunting. This gave way to many of the ancient myths of trolls and other such cave dwelling monsters.

They hate the sun which will weaken and burn them and because of this they only hunt at night. Being very durable they are extremely hard to kill or injure, though they can be harmed by any weapon that can penetrate their stone like skin. They are impervious to cold but are susceptible to fire and will usually avoid places where large fires have been built. Like all of their kind they are repelled and weakened by objects of faith.

Famine

Other Children of Famine

<u>Wendigo:</u> The wendigo is similar to the vampire in that it has a hunger that is never satisfied. More like the Draugar, it craves human flesh for its sustenance. Unlike the vampire, the older these creatures become, the less human they appear. Like their Norse cousins, they smell of death and decay and it is impossible for them to mask their stench. Not only do they give off an aura of malice and wrongness, but the strong stink of a wendigo also precedes it making it hard for them to hide.

Possessing enhanced strength, speed, senses, and durability, they are dangerous foes. Like their cousins they have the ability to heal and can even regenerate their entire body if their head is still intact. This extreme regenerative ability leads to their constant need for protein and animal fats giving them a continuous insatiable hunger. The more they consume, the stronger they become, but likewise, the more they consume, the more monstrous and less human they become.

The term wendigo is derived from the native American peoples, but it is also known by other names. Trolls are the most common name attributed to them in the European countries and they are considered a type of Djinn in Arabia. In Asia they were often called **Krasue** which is a term that can still be found in modern Asian pop culture and legend.

Very susceptible to fire, which gave rise to the European legends that you must burn a troll to kill it, burning them is one of the most common means of combatting them.

In some cultures, trolls can be turned to stone by the sun, this is a misnomer and a legend that was born out of their sensitivity to light and their inability to blend into normal human society.

Wendigo's can be harmed the same way normal humans can, but due to their regenerative abilities, they are near impossible to kill, fire being the only known way to decisively destroy them.

Like most children of famine, wendigo's are weaker in sunlight and their eyes which have evolved to see at night become almost useless the brighter the light. Usually gaunt and long limbed with large black bulbous eyes, they seem more like an emaciated corpse than a human.

Generally, they walk or move on all fours like an animal but will walk upright and move like normal humans when blending in. They are known for long dagger-like teeth and claw-like fingers that grow into something akin to the talons of a raptor, which they use to tear and rip the flesh of their prey.

Ghoul: In the Arabic world there is a type of monster that is known as the Ghoul. This term is given to any class of creature that consumes human flesh or drinks blood for sustenance.

Similar to the North American Wendigo and Norse Draugar the Ghoul can be classified as a child of Famine. Unlike their vampire cousins, the ghoul generally appears corpse like and inhuman. Having a strong aversion to sunlight, they are always seen at night and tend to wander the desert preying on wayward travelers.

Like the wendigo, they have long dagger-like teeth and talon like claws protruding from their fingertips. Similar to a mole their eyes are small and upon a quick glance can appear nonexistent. Especially in ration with their unnaturally large mouths which stretch from ear to ear giving them a perpetual and unsettling grin.

They have excellent night vision and an exceptional sense of smell that can track prey from up to a mile away. Humanoid in shape when clothed they can pass as humans in the dark or in large crowds, but the smell of death usually makes it hard for them to blend in. Like most Nephilim they possess enhanced strength, durability, and speed.

In similar fashion to their cousins, ghouls are weakened in sunlight and should always be fought during the day if possible. They have an aversion to holy objects and are weakened or repelled by strong faith.

Having no real regenerative properties, ghouls can be injured and destroyed by most natural means. They tend to travel in packs like hyenas where you encounter one there will always be more.

Even though they are somewhat weaker than their cousins their pack-like mentality makes them very dangerous, and they should never be underestimated. When you find one, always assume there are more.

Succubus and Incubus: These creatures are more akin to demons than vampires. Nephilim spirits that are consumed with sexual perversion, they can possess humans and cause their DNA to morph into a version of themselves. They consume life force through sexual exchanges and cause their prey to experience an intense sense of euphoria. This euphoria is so powerful that it has an extremely strong addictive effect on all that encounter them.

They also possess the ability to exude an overwhelming attraction and lust that entices people to them. They tend to use this ability to not only ensnare victims but keep them entranced and addicted to them. In this way they can gain power and position in society or influence over others. These creatures can hide in plain sight and unless they become overzealous in their feeding, usually go unnoticed by society.

Not only do they possess the ability to create extreme lust and attraction in humans and lesser beings, but they also have the ability to heal, enhanced speed, enhanced durability, enhanced strength, minor hypnotic and mental control abilities, the ability to use magic, and the ability to sense the weakness of lust in others. Succubae and Incubi become more physically attractive the more life force they consume. The longer a person is in contact with one of these creatures the greater their influence over them will become.

Appearing as unnaturally attractive humanoids, they gravitate towards areas where beauty is important often being found in the entertainment industry. They can be harmed the same way normal people can, though the stronger they are, the more durable they become, some even said to have been bullet proof. Generally, what will kill a human will kill them.

Famine

One distinction between them and other vampire type creatures is that when their body is destroyed their spirit lives on and wanders the earth looking for a new host to corrupt. In this spirit form, they continue to attack humans using sexual pleasure and desire to drain their victims life force in order to continue existing. This is why succubae, and incubi can be both a physical and a spiritual entity.

Other Variants: Generally, it is believed that any creature that suffers from a need or hunger that can never be satiated are attributed to the fallen angel Kasdeja. One exception to this rule is the zombie or undead, which are creations of Azrael the Watcher of Death.

All of Kasdeja's children have a constant need to consume lifeforce in order to sustain their existence or power. The less they consume, the weaker they become and the less threatening they are. Most are creatures of the night and are either harmed by or dislike the sun, though some have the ability to move in the daylight unhindered.

As I have said often, be prepared for anything since it is very possible that there are still many variants we have yet to encounter.

Authors Note

I hope you enjoyed Famine: Book 2 in the Justice Cycle. Like all authors, I would appreciate it if you would leave a review. Every review helps.
SERIOUSLY! Leave a review! You can't tell, but I am waving my hand in front of your face and using a Jedi mind trick on you.

"You will leave a review. And these are not the droids you're looking for."
After you leave a review if you would like to peruse the wonders my imagination conjures, you can find me at JWKIEFER.COM and Medium.

Drop me a line, leave a comment, or sign up for my email list. I am always looking to connect with other people who share my nerdiness.
Thanks again.

Jay

About the Author

J W Kiefer is a father, minister, novelist, script writer, actor and blogger who hails from the Southern Tier of Western New York State. He has a degree in Theology and Church management as well as a degree in liberal arts. He is also a reserve Green Lantern; and when duty calls, can be found assisting the rest of the core in interstellar matters. An avid vocalist and worship leader, he loves to belt out Disney tunes, especially when it is most awkward and embarrassing for his children. His other pursuits include cosplay, gaming with his kids, watching paint peel, and observing the occasional pot hoping to see it boil.

If you are interested in more information about J W Kiefer he can be found at: JWKIEFER.COM

www.ingramcontent.com/pod-product-compliance
Lightning Source LLC
Chambersburg PA
CBHW032252020726
47495CB00001B/80